ALL MY LOVING

BUTLER, VERMONT SERIES, BOOK 5

MARIE FORCE

All My Loving
Butler, Vermont Series, Book 5
By: Marie Force

Published by HTJB, Inc.
Copyright 2020. HTJB, Inc.
Cover Design by Kristina Brinton
Print Layout: E-book Formatting Fairies
ISBN: 978-1950654970

Reading Order for Green Mountain/Butler, Vermont Series

CHAPTER ONE

*"Tell me, what is it you plan to do with your
one wild and precious life?"*
—Mary Oliver

*D*ays after the fire at the inn, the smell of smoke clung
to Amanda's hair and skin, the stench pervasive
despite multiple showers and shampooing her hair so many
times, her scalp had begun to hurt. As she sat in front of the
woodstove in Landon Abbott's cozy cabin, Amanda noted the
irony of needing the fire to stay warm when fire was the thing
she was now most afraid of.

While a late-May Nor'easter raged outside, she had nothing
but time to think and relive the horror of her near-death
experience.

It'd been a week since the Admiral Butler Inn had burned,
trapping her with a badly sprained ankle until Landon's identical twin brother, Lucas, had come to her rescue. They'd been
on the way out of the room when the ceiling had come down on
top of them, trapping them.

She shuddered every time she thought of that explosive
moment and how Lucas dove on top of her. He'd been the more

badly injured one, suffering a broken arm that had required surgery to repair, as well as smoke inhalation.

Amanda had been briefly hospitalized to receive oxygen and IV fluids as well as treatment for her ankle. When she was released, Landon had brought her home to his place to recover, as the next closest lodging was two towns away.

Since most of her possessions had been lost in the fire, Landon had bought her new jeans, sweaters, pajamas, socks and underwear at his family's Green Mountain Country Store, probably in consultation with one or all of his three sisters. They would've been able to accurately guess her sizes. He'd even gotten her a new coat and boots to navigate the lingering mud season, and his family had delivered enough food to feed ten people.

Her own mother had been in a panic after hearing about the fire. Once Amanda finally succeeded in assuring her that she was fine, her mother, who was also her boss, had sent a new cell phone and laptop. They were already configured to the company's servers, so she could get back to work whenever she felt up to it.

She had everything she needed to resume her life already in progress, if only her hands would quit trembling. If only she didn't see and hear and smell the fire every time she closed her eyes. If only she could shed the bone-deep fear that followed such an incredibly close call. She'd relived it a thousand times, from waking up to find the room engulfed in fire, to jumping out of bed and landing wrong on her ankle, to Lucas storming in to rescue her and shielding her from the falling ceiling with his own body.

There'd been just enough time before Lucas showed up for Amanda to contemplate the very real possibility that she might die from the flames and toxic smoke that filled the room so quickly, she barely had time to process what was happening, let alone react, before it became too late to do anything.

Prior to the fire, she'd been on autopilot, traveling through life with no attachments, no responsibilities other than work, no emotions and a stubborn refusal to reexamine her painful past. After the fire, she could think of little else but what she might've missed if she'd died that night.

For one thing, she'd never been truly in love. She'd been in lust that she'd mistaken for love, but that didn't count. In the seconds before Lucas arrived to save the day, it had occurred to Amanda that she could actually die before experiencing true love. She'd never skied or zip-lined or bungee-jumped or traveled to Europe or been on a cruise or gone swimming in the Pacific Ocean. Even though she'd been to Los Angeles for work at least six times, she'd never once bothered to swim in the ocean. She'd always assumed she'd have plenty of time to do those things. There was always more time to be had in the future.

Now she knew better.

After being reminded that time was finite and how quickly the future could be stolen from her, Amanda had begun a list of the things she'd never done. She wanted to take piano lessons, climb a mountain, learn to drive a stick, have an orgasm *with a man*. Amanda underlined those three words multiple times. She'd had plenty of the solo kind, as well as a few from trying out her company's product line, but never once with an actual man.

Her body shook with sobs that came over her with alarming frequency every time she thought about how much she would've missed, how close she came to losing *everything*, of dying before she ever got around to actually *living*.

In addition to making a list of all the things she hadn't done, she was also listing her mistakes.

1. Dropping out of college before finishing my degree.
2. Never actually choosing a career, but falling into a job that paid the bills.

3. Getting a second credit card. The first one had been more than enough.
4. Dating both Landon *and* his twin, Lucas—huge mistake.

She'd caused trouble between Landon and his brother, who was also his closest friend. Amanda deeply regretted that. When they'd asked her out—at the same time—she'd panicked and said yes to both of them, not thinking it through or weighing the many ways it could turn into a catastrophe. Mostly, she'd wanted to avoid hurting any feelings since her company had just landed a major account with their family's business.

In truth, she figured they'd asked her out because they were fascinated by a woman who spoke about sex toys the way other women discussed shoes or jewelry. She'd grown numb to the salacious nature of the products she represented, but Lucas and Landon had been seriously intrigued.

It hadn't taken long for Amanda to realize she would've been far better off kindly saying no to both of them. The situation had gone from innocent fun to messy in the course of two days. After a delightful evening with Lucas, she'd truly connected with Landon, which was baffling. How could she have such different reactions to identical twins? It hadn't made any sense to her, but the fact remained—she was attracted to Landon but not to Lucas. He was a great guy—fun and funny and entertaining.

But there was just something about Landon…

He was everything his brother was and somehow more. When she looked at his golden-brown eyes and dirty-blond hair and sweet, sexy lips, she wanted things with him that she hadn't wanted with anyone.

Not that it mattered now. She'd made a hot mess of things by dating him and his brother, and even though Lucas had since met and fallen for Dani and her baby daughter, Savannah, things had been awkward with Landon before the fire and were even more so now.

No wonder she'd never been in love. Clearly, she sucked at dating. And now she was holed up in Landon's house, recovering from her fire-related injuries and contending with an emotional tsunami that would freak out any man, let alone one she'd kinda sorta dated before things got weird. She ought to get the hell out of Butler and go home to her mother in St. Louis. Her mom had called daily on Landon's house phone to check on her since the frightening night of the fire.

"I'll send a ticket," her mother had said. "Come home. Let me take care of you."

Amanda loved her mother, but feared if she went home, she might hunker down, pull the covers over her head and never leave again. That was not an option. The plan was to stay with Landon until her ankle healed enough that she could get around better, and then she'd get back to work and figure out what was next. She'd given up her apartment some time ago, rather than pay rent while she traveled nonstop for work.

Before the fire, she'd decided to stay in Butler for a while longer to work on the rewrite of the product catalog and had been halfway through the project before her laptop went up in the flames. Thankfully, she'd saved a backup copy to an external server, so she didn't have to start over. But she had no desire to work, not to mention her concentration was nonexistent.

Outside, the wind howled as driving rain fell in quantities she'd never seen before she arrived in the mountains of Vermont's Northeast Kingdom. Landon was out there somewhere, working with the search-and-rescue team to find some missing kids.

He'd been gone for hours, giving Amanda way too much time to think and add to her lists. Another mistake had been to nurse a crush on Landon after causing so much trouble for him—and not just with his brother. They were sharing close quarters in his small cabin. He'd given her his bed and was bunking on an air mattress in the living room. He said he didn't mind, but of course, he probably did. He was too nice to say otherwise.

5

As soon as she could walk without hobbling, she'd get out of his house. She'd decide where she wanted to make a home base, get an apartment and figure out her shit. Once she did that, maybe she could start working on that list of things she'd never done.

A knock on the front door startled Amanda out of her thoughts, giving her a welcome respite from her own hyperactive brain.

Landon's mother, Molly, stuck her head in. "Just me with dinner. Don't get up."

"Come in. Please tell me you didn't come out in this storm just to bring me dinner."

"Oh, this is nothing. There's an old Vermont saying that if you don't go out in bad weather, you'll never go out."

"Still. It's very nice of you."

"I thought of you home alone while Landon is out with the search-and-rescue team and thought you might like some company."

To her dismay, Molly's kindness had Amanda crying *again*. "I'm sorry. I can't believe I have any tears left. I've done nothing but cry since the fire. I cry at commercials on TV."

"That's totally understandable." With her usual efficiency, Molly removed her boots and coat and carried in a tote bag. "You had a terrible scare, and it's only natural you'd be upset afterward."

It was so much more than the fire, not that Amanda could tell Molly that.

"I'll put your dinner in the oven on warm, and you can have it when you're ready. It's pot roast."

"Thank you so much. It smells delicious." She choked on a sob and pulled yet another tissue from the box Landon had gotten for her. "I'm so sorry about the waterworks. Landon says I'm like a hot spring."

Molly smiled and came to sit next to her. As always, Molly's long gray hair was braided, and her pretty, youthful face belied the fact that she'd raised ten children. "You look like you could use a hug from a professional mom. Would that help?"

Wanting that more than anything, Amanda nodded and went willingly into the arms of Landon's mother.

"My poor, sweet girl. It's only natural you'd be emotional after what you've been through."

"The fire was so frightening, but it's not just that."

"If you need to talk to someone, I'm more than happy to listen." Molly pulled back and straightened Amanda's hair. "And I promise whatever we talk about stays between us."

Amanda desperately needed to talk to someone, and she'd already cried all over Landon for days. "I'd like to talk about it." Maybe if she did, she might be able to stop crying every five minutes. After another pause, she forced herself to say the words. "I had something happen, twelve years ago. It was a very big something that I don't ever talk about."

Molly only listened, which Amanda appreciated.

"After that, it was like I shut down. I threw myself into school and then work." She wiped away new tears with yet another tissue. "I did really well in my job, became my company's top salesperson. I traveled almost nonstop from one trade show to another, from one product install to another, kept my head down and just powered through. And then the fire happened, and since then... It's like everything I refused to feel for all those years is trying to get out all at once, and I think that's why I can't seem to stop crying."

"That's a lot to process on top of the fire."

"It is, and Landon has been an absolute saint about it. I'm sure he's regretting asking me to stay with him after days of histrionics."

"I doubt that. He's enjoying having you here."

"He is? How do you know that?"

"Because he told me so when I helped him pick out clothes for you at the store."

"Thank you for doing that." Amanda wiped yet another flood of tears. "Everyone has been so kind. Your family is amazing."

"That's nice to hear. I'm glad you think so."

"Everyone thinks so."

"I'm proud of them."

"It helps to talk to someone. Thank you. I haven't wanted to unload on my own mom or my friends because they aren't here, and it would upset them, and Landon has done enough for me."

"I'm happy to listen, sweetheart, and you're right. It would upset them. There's nothing worse than knowing one of your babies is hurting and there's nothing you can do about it."

Nodding, Amanda wiped tears from eyes that felt raw and achy. "I want you to know, this isn't me at all. I'm not a basket case, I swear. I'm a planner. I plan every minute of every day so I know exactly what I'm doing. I follow strategic and marketing plans at work."

"The fire upset your plans and forced you to live without one for the time being."

"Yes, exactly, and I feel like I'm adrift at sea or something."

"You will for a while, and then you'll start to figure out a new plan. I also had something happen to me when I was a senior in high school. I lost someone very close to me. Took me years to move past that, and it wasn't until I met Linc and fell for him that I truly confronted the loss, so I understand better than you might think."

"I'm sorry that happened to you."

"Thank you."

"So you don't think I'm a total loon because I can't stop crying?"

Molly smiled. "Not at all. I've known some real loons in my time. What you're feeling is totally normal. The fire was a big wake-up call, a reminder that nothing is guaranteed."

"It really was. Just when I think I'm getting better, Landon does something nice for me, and I dissolve into tears all over again. The poor guy can't catch a break with me."

"I'm sure he's just fine. He understands you're emotional after the fire."

"There's emotional, and then there's me. I've been taking it to a whole other level lately. I wouldn't blame him if he sent me packing."

"He's not going to do that. You weren't there, so you don't know how he jumped right in to volunteer when we discussed that you'd need somewhere to go after you were released from the hospital. He wouldn't hear of any other plan but you coming home with him."

"I... I didn't know that."

"You're here because he very much wanted you to be. People tend to underestimate him and Lucas. They think the two of them are nothing more than silly clowns—and they can definitely be that. But there's a lot of substance beneath their tomfoolery."

"I've seen that since the fire. He's been incredible. He hasn't left my side, except to go to work, since I got here."

"That sounds like him. He's true blue, but you don't need me singing his praises. You've seen it with your own eyes."

"I have."

"Don't worry about being emotional around him. He can handle it."

"I'm not sure that I can."

Molly laughed. "I bet you're stronger than you think. In the time we've known you, all I've seen is a strong, capable, competent, intelligent woman."

The kind words from someone she greatly respected had her weeping again. "You see? All it takes is someone being nice to me, and I'm a disaster."

Molly hugged her again. "I promise you'll get through this strange phase, and you'll start to get used to feeling all the things again. Maybe it'll turn out to be a blessing that this happened. It's not healthy to stuff your feelings into a box for years on end. That's not sustainable long-term."

"Is that what happened to you?"

Molly nodded. "I was numb for five years. I met Linc right after I graduated from college, and when I started to feel all the things for him, I had a similar reaction. I finally grieved the boyfriend I'd lost. It was like a delayed reaction. I knew Linc was the one for me when he never blinked an eye at me crying over another man."

"I've cried more about the thing from high school in the last week than I have in all the years since it happened."

"Because the fire opened the door to all those old emotions. I'm so sorry you're hurting that way. I wish there was something I could do to help."

"This has helped. More than you know. Thank you for listening and for understanding."

"I do understand, and I feel for you. Emotional overload after years of numbness is tough to take."

"It is, and it helps to hear it might be normal, despite how it feels."

"It's completely normal." Molly handed her yet another tissue. "I promise you're going to survive this, and perhaps be better off once you figure out how to process everything you're feeling."

"I'll have to take your word on that."

"You have my number if you ever need to talk. I'm always available to you."

"Thank you so much, Molly. For dinner and for listening."

"Any time. Hang in there. Like the storm raging outside, the one raging inside you will pass, too, and I promise you'll be just fine."

Amanda hugged her. "I hope you're right."

"I usually am. Just ask my children."

Laughing, Amanda said, "How do you stand knowing your sons are out in this awful storm?"

"They're very well trained, and they love what they do.

Besides, all Vermonters are used to bad weather. It doesn't faze us."

"You're made of hardy stock, as my mother would say."

"We have to be. Reach out if you need anything at all. You're not alone with the Abbott family in your corner."

Amanda got up and hobbled to the door to see Molly out. "Thanks again."

"Take care of yourself, Amanda."

"I will."

Amanda waved from the door as Molly drove off, and then she locked up since she had no way to know when Landon might make it home. She decided to retrieve her dinner from the oven and enjoyed every savory bite of the meal Molly had brought. It was so nice of her to do that, and to listen to Amanda's troubles, too.

Molly had given her a new perspective by telling her there would be sunshine after the rain and that the emotions battering her since the fire were actually healthy despite how dreadful she felt at the moment.

That was the best news she'd had in days.

CHAPTER TWO

"A goal without a plan is just a wish."
—Antoine de Saint-Exupéry

*L*andon trudged through wind, driving rain and ankle-deep mud that slowed him down. A spotlight attached to his helmet provided limited help in seeing through rain that hadn't let up in hours. Mother Nature was being a serious bitch this year, with the rainiest May on record extending mud season weeks longer than usual. After this latest downpour, they'd be in for more mud when they should've been settling into summer.

His voice had gone hoarse from screaming the names of the three teens who'd gone missing almost four hours ago. They were tourists from southern Connecticut who'd had no idea they'd entered a whole other world in the Vermont mountains. They'd thought it would be fun to leave their hotel for a late-afternoon hike.

During a Nor'easter.

Now Landon, four of his six brothers, their cousins Grayson and Noah, and ten others from the Butler Mountain search-

and-rescue service were trying to find them. Good times. In the meantime, the rain fell and accumulated at an alarming rate as the temperature continued to drop. The very real fear of flooding hung over the effort. A few years ago, a spring storm just like this one had caused the creeks to overflow into the town.

No one knew what the kids had been wearing when they left the hotel, but the searchers were operating under the assumption that they were in no way prepared to be out in weather like this for hours.

Landon was connected to the rest of the team by satellite radios that conveyed the coordinates of each searcher. The radios made it possible to split up and cover more ground rather than rely on the buddy system, like they had before satellite technology made it safe to work alone.

He welcomed the time to himself to ponder the confounding situation with his sexy roommate. Having Amanda living in his cabin was wonderful—and torturous. The house was so small that her distinctive sexy scent invaded every corner of the place. He had to move her toothbrush to get to his own, had to step over her pile of folded clothes to get to his closet. She was everywhere he looked, and he liked looking at her—a little too much, if he was being honest.

He'd tried to keep his distance, to give her room to recover and cope with the emotional overload that came from surviving a fire, but it was hard to keep your distance from someone when you were living practically on top of each other.

Not that he'd mind being on top of her.

"Cut it out," he muttered as he stopped moving to take a breather. The mud was getting so deep, it was becoming harder to get through it, not to mention the cold was seeping through his foul-weather gear into his bones. He reached into his pocket for a protein bar and downed it in three big bites, chasing it with Gatorade.

Amanda was in no condition for him to be thinking of her that way. The poor girl hadn't stopped crying since the fire, and the last thing she needed was him panting after her. But what did it say about him that he thought she was the prettiest girl he'd ever seen, even when her face and eyes were red and puffy from crying? What did it say about him that he wanted to wrap his arms around her and make everything that was hurting her better? He didn't dare do it, but oh, how he wanted to.

The radio came to life with a query from his brother Wade. "How long are we going to look?"

His brother Will said, "I was just at the firehouse. The parents are hysterical. All they could talk about was how they're good kids—on the honor roll, varsity athletes. We gotta keep going."

Landon had known someone was going to say it. They never gave up before they found the people they were looking for. Most of the time, they were alive, if half frozen and suffering from exposure. It'd been a few years since they lost someone on the mountain. He'd like to keep that record intact and knew his brothers, cousins and friends felt the same way.

The kids they were looking for were someone's sons, grand-sons, brothers, friends. Whenever they looked for missing people, Landon tried to imagine it was one of his siblings or cousins, and he tried to give strangers the same effort he'd give his own family.

He continued on, powering through the wet, heavy mud as he blazed a trail in the direction where the teens were last seen. No one knew how far they could've gotten before the storm intensified, so they were basically looking for needles in the proverbial haystack.

"Connor! Jeremy! Michael!"

He'd called for them so many times by now, his voice was nearly shot. But he kept going, kept yelling out the names every few feet, while trying not to think about the situation at home.

Easier said than done. He liked thinking about her, loved having her living in his cabin, even though he hated the reason she needed shelter, and was upset to see her so undone for days now. Landon wouldn't wish getting caught in a fire on anyone. It was terrifying, even when you were wearing fire-retardant equipment and equipped with oxygen.

He wouldn't soon forget realizing the roof had fallen in on the room where Lucas had gone to rescue Amanda. Knowing two people he cared about were in mortal danger had been one of the most frightening experiences of Landon's life.

His identical twin was his best friend. The thought of even a day without Lucas was unfathomable. A week after the fire, Landon still felt sick when he considered the magnitude of what he'd nearly lost that night, especially since things between him and Lucas had been tense after they both went out with Amanda.

She'd tried to be nice to them when they'd asked her out at the same time, but had ended up in a bad situation when both brothers had a great time with her.

Lucas had been so upset about the situation with Amanda, he'd left town to get away from it all. On that trip, he'd rescued Dani and her baby girl, Savannah, and had fallen for both of them.

With Lucas now out of the Amanda picture, Landon had been trying to figure out his next move, while also trying to get a read on her and whether she wanted to hang out again as more than just platonic roommates.

Before the fire, Amanda had stayed in Butler to work on a rewrite of her company's catalog. Lucas had pointed out that she could've done that anywhere and had made the choice to stay in Butler, probably because of Landon.

Landon had been skeptical about that and had planned to talk to her about what, if anything, was going on between them, but then the fire had happened, and they'd had far bigger things to worry about ever since. So he still had no clue what she was thinking where he was concerned, but she was staying in his cabin, so that gave him an advantage he hadn't had before.

For all the good that'd done him. In between her bouts of weeping, they'd barely exchanged more than ten sentences per day as they discussed what they wanted to heat up for dinner from the ton of food his family had made for them.

With her feeling so fragile, this was no time to push her in any direction. However, he was miserable from wanting something more substantial with a woman for the first time in his adult life and having no earthly idea how to make it happen.

He was jolted out of his thoughts by a noise that had him stopping to listen more closely. When he didn't hear anything, he called out again for the boys.

The weak sound of "help" came from his right.

Landon set off in that direction while keying his radio to report in. "I might have something." He pushed hard through the mud, mindful of staying on the path so he wouldn't fall down the side of an embankment. Their team knew this mountain so well they rarely had to worry about falling. However, situational awareness was critical so they didn't end up needing to be rescued themselves.

"Are you out there? Let me hear you!"

"Help! Over here!"

"I've got them," Landon reported.

The team would use his coordinates to send in backup.

One of the boys was standing, waving to him as he battled his way through brush to reach them. "Are all three of you here?" Landon asked.

"Yeah, but Michael... He stopped talking an hour ago."

Landon pulled his backpack off and moved quickly to withdraw thermal blankets for each of them. "Help me get him wrapped up."

The boys had created a bunker of sorts under a grove of trees, and from the indentations in the mud, he could tell they'd been huddled together to share body heat, a smart move that had kept them warmer than they would've been on their own. "Which one of you is Connor?"

"Me." They wore sweatshirts and jeans that were completely soaked through. Even in late spring, hypothermia was a real concern in the mountains, especially under these conditions.

"That means you're Jeremy?"

"Yeah."

Landon gave them protein bars and bottles of Gatorade to start getting them rehydrated and then reported in. "All three are alive. Michael is unresponsive, possibly hypothermic. We need to get him out of here."

"On the way," Landon's eldest brother, Hunter, replied. "Five minutes out."

"Can you two still walk?" Landon asked the other boys.

"I can," Connor said.

Jeremy's teeth chattered so hard he could barely speak. "I-I th-think s-so."

With Hunter's help, Landon could carry Michael out.

"We've got a two-mile hike to get out of here. We're going to have to move fast for Michael."

"We can do that," Connor said, glancing at Jeremy.

Jeremy nodded.

"We're really sorry," Connor said, sounding tearful. "We never should've left the hotel. We didn't mean to go so far."

"Let's not worry about that right now. Let's stay focused on getting you guys warmed up."

"N-never b-be w-warm a-again," Jeremy said, shivering.

"Yes, you will. I promise."

Hunter arrived on the scene, and between the two of them, they hoisted Michael up and headed for the trail, following it for two long miles before they reached a clearing where a fire department SUV waited to transport the boys. They loaded Michael into the back, while the other two boys got into the back seat.

"Let's go with him," Landon said.

Hunter got into the front seat with one of the other searchers driving, and Landon crawled into the back with Michael. On the way to the hospital, he removed Michael's soaking-wet sweatshirt and used the supplies in his pack to start an IV to pump some fluid into the boy. He was grateful to feel a regular, though shallow, pulse.

"Is he going to be all right?" Connor asked, looking over the seat, his face muddy.

Landon noticed a cut under Connor's left eye that would need attention at the ER.

"I think so." Landon didn't tell him that he'd probably found them with very little time left to spare for Michael.

Jeremy sobbed as he shook violently.

The boys had learned a tough lesson about mountain life, and it was one they weren't apt to forget any time soon.

THE DOGS WERE IN THE YARD WHEN MOLLY RETURNED HOME TO the barn she'd shared with her husband, Lincoln, for close to forty years now. It never failed to stir her to see their home lit up at night and to think about how the place had looked the first time they saw it. Linc had bought a wreck, sight unseen, and they'd created a home where they'd raised ten children. And now, as their children settled into marriages and long-term relationships, their family continued to grow.

"There you are," Linc said when he met her at the door. "I was just starting to wonder if you'd forgotten the way home."

"Never." She kissed him and let him help her out of her coat. "We're going to need to towel off those pups. They were rolling in the mud."

"They do love them some mud season."

"Indeed."

He grabbed the old towels they used for the dogs and handed one to her. "Ready?"

"Let's do it."

He let in George and Ringo, both of them female yellow Labs named for members of Lincoln's favorite band. They were the third George and Ringo they'd had, along with three Johns and four Pauls over the years, each of them beloved members of the family.

Molly dried Ringo while Linc wrestled with George. Both dogs thought they were playing, which made for a challenging and funny few minutes.

"Why do they always think that's a game?" Linc asked after the dogs had run in to warm up by the hearth in the family room.

"Every one of them is the same that way."

"How was your visit with Amanda? Is she any better?"

"Physically, she seems to be getting around much better, but emotionally, she's dealing with a lot after the fire."

"Which is completely understandable."

"Yes. Any word from the boys?"

"Nothing yet."

"I sure hope they find those kids."

"They will. They always do." He put his arm around her and guided her to the sofa in the family room, where they spent most of their time.

"What's Max up to?"

"Not sure. He went up to give Caden a bath and put him to bed. Haven't seen him since."

"Is he bummed about missing out on a search party?"

"I don't think so. He didn't want to leave Caden when he was fussy and teething. That boy has got his priorities straight."

"Yes, he does," Molly said. "I'm worried about Landon in this situation with Amanda. She's dealing with an awful lot in addition to the fire, and I just hope he's not going to end up disappointed."

"Your dad and I were talking about that today. Amanda is a lovely woman and very good at her job."

"But?"

"I was telling Elmer she's been here awhile now, but I don't feel like we know her much better than we did when she first arrived."

"I suspect that's about to change."

"Is that right?"

"Uh-huh." She'd seen a side of Amanda tonight that gave her all-new perspective on the woman who had Landon's head turned all around.

"So you feel like it's going to be okay between the two of them?" Linc asked.

"I'm not completely sure yet, but we should know fairly soon if they're going to make a go of it."

"I sure hope they are. I've never seen him this way over a woman."

"He was once. Remember Naomi?"

"The girl who died when they were in high school?"

"Yes."

"I knew he was terribly upset about that."

"We all were. But Landon was devastated. I think he had real feelings for her that he was only beginning to understand when he lost her."

"Huh, I don't remember that."

She patted his leg. "That's okay. I was on it, and I got him through it. Took some time, though, and if I had to guess, she's the reason he's never given his heart to anyone else. He discovered a long time ago that love can be so very painful."

"Why can't I remember this?"

"We had a lot going on in those days. I'm sure there're things I don't remember."

"I doubt that. You're always one step ahead of me. Been like that from the beginning."

"I have to keep you guessing, or you might lose interest."

His low chuckle made her smile. "No chance of that, as you

well know. In fact, why don't we turn in early tonight? I'm feeling particularly *tired* tonight."

Tired had been their code word for *meet me in bed* when they'd still had a barn full of kids. "I'm rather exhausted myself tonight."

Linc shut off the television, banked the fire and closed the glass doors to the fireplace. Then he held out his arm to her.

Molly tucked her hand into his arm and followed him to bed while saying a silent prayer for her sons who were battling the elements looking for the missing kids, and a special request for wisdom for Landon as he navigated the situation with Amanda. Molly liked her for him and thought they'd make a wonderful couple.

But the two of them were a long way from happily ever after.

AS HE ROCKED HIS BABY SON, MAX ABBOTT HEARD HIS PARENTS come up the stairs, go into their room and shut the door. He didn't want to think about why they might be going to bed so early. With the wind howling and the rain beating against the windows, he thought of his brothers out in the storm looking for the missing kids and wished he was with them.

He loved his son more than he'd ever loved anything, but sometimes he missed his old life. In the seven months since Caden had arrived, everything about his existence had changed to accommodate his son. That was how it should be, but still... At times like this, with a long, boring evening stretched out before him, he yearned for what used to be.

Thank God for his parents, a thought he had at least once every day. But even having them by his side through this first year with his son couldn't fill the gaping loneliness he felt at times like this. Everyone else was out living their lives, and he was at home with a baby son who was his sole responsibility.

Sometimes he even missed Chloe, Caden's mother, who'd

disappointed him so profoundly. He'd heard from a college friend that Chloe was still in Burlington and dating someone new. Good for her. Did she ever wonder about him or their son or how the baby was doing or how he was handling being a single parent?

Probably not. He'd worried about her after the night of Hunter's wedding last Christmas when she'd come to the house and signed the papers his cousin Grayson had drawn up, surrendering her rights to Caden. Max had been concerned about postpartum depression and whether there was more he could've done to support her. But after checking in with numerous mutual friends who'd reported that she didn't seem depressed at all, he'd let it go. Clearly, she'd moved on with her life, and he needed to do the same.

Except, how could he do that with a seven-month-old infant who relied on him for everything? He didn't often indulge in this level of morose thinking, because, really, what good did it do? He loved his son, didn't regret for one minute having custody of him and would do anything for him. But being a single father at twenty-three was a tough spot to be in. No question about it.

Max was inordinately blessed to have his big, loving family all around to help him any time he needed it. His mom was amazing about watching Caden while Max was at work, and both his parents were willing to take him so Max could occasionally go out with friends or his siblings.

But at the end of the day, the responsibility for the tiny bundle in his arms was all his, and at times, the weight of that responsibility threatened to crush him.

Not all the time, but far too often to ignore.

Sometimes he wondered if he was the one with postpartum depression.

He stood and carefully transferred Caden to his crib in the tiny room that adjoined Max's. He and his dad had knocked down a wall to make the room for Caden in what used to be a closet. Max stared down at his sleeping son for a long moment, wondering what would become of the two of them.

Would they always be alone, or would he meet someone who could be a partner to him and a mother to Caden? And did he even want that? He was only twenty-three. What were the odds he'd meet anyone in the next few years who interested him enough to lock himself in for life?

He probably needed to accept that he was going to be alone with his son for the foreseeable future and make peace with that.

The other day, his brother Colton had told him he needed to get laid, as if that would fix everything. However, Max had to acknowledge that since Colton had mentioned it, that was all he could seem to think about.

Remember sex? Yeah, it'd been a while…

For a time, he'd feared Chloe had ruined that for him, too, but since Colton had brought it up, Max had found out otherwise. Not that there was any chance of it happening any time soon.

Ugh, he hated being in such a funk, especially since he loved every second he got to spend with his son. It was almost painful to leave him for the seven or eight hours he spent at work five days a week. Every afternoon, he rushed home to be with him, to play with him, to feed and bathe and rock him. But after the baby went to bed, the nights were long and boring.

And lonely.

Growing up the youngest of ten kids, Max had never experienced true loneliness before he had Caden. It had gotten so bad lately, he'd actually gone so far as to set up a Tinder account that he'd yet to make live because he wasn't sure he wanted to go that route either. With cell service nonexistent in Butler, he could access it through the Wi-Fi at home or at work on the mountain, the one place in the area that had good cell coverage.

However, something was keeping him from pulling the trigger. Perhaps because he was a father now, and the thought of dating didn't appeal the way it used to.

With Caden down for the night—at least for now—Max went into the bathroom to shower.

As he stood under the hot water, one thing he knew for certain was that he was sick of his own thoughts—and his own company. Something needed to change, but he'd be damned if he knew what.

CHAPTER THREE

*"In preparing for battle, I have always found that plans are
useless, but planning is essential."*
—Dwight D. Eisenhower

*L*andon got home after midnight, cold to the bone after
spending hours in the storm. Even with the best gear
money could buy, he was half frozen and exhausted
from fighting the elements. All he wanted was a hot shower, a
bowl of soup and to sleep in front of the woodstove. That was
the only thing that could truly warm him up after a night like
this.

But when he walked into his cabin, he found Amanda asleep
on the air mattress, in the spot he wanted.

Oh well, he thought, *she's going to have to share.* He was too
cold to sleep anywhere but right next to the fire.

He took the hottest shower he could stand, changed into
sweats and a long-sleeved T-shirt, heated some hearty beef-and-
potato soup from a container his mom had sent over and took it
to sit on the sofa, which was close to the fire but not close
enough.

As he ate his soup, he noticed a notebook on the floor next to

Amanda and picked it up to see what it was. Before he realized he was seeing something he probably shouldn't, he'd read her list of mistakes, and then, intrigued by the insight into a woman who was somewhat of a mystery to him, he flipped back one page to read her list of things she still needed to do. The last one caught his eye. Have an orgasm *with a man.* Underlined three times.

Landon nearly choked on his soup and quickly put the notebook back where he'd found it, feeling guilty for having looked at something that was none of his business.

But damn… She'd never had an orgasm with a man. Did that mean…

No. Stop. It's none of your business. Except there was more than one item on her list he could help with, in addition to the one that had stood out like a beacon. He'd be more than happy to help her with that.

Stop.

Do. Not. Go. There.

She's your guest, recovering from a traumatic experience and a painful injury. You've got no business thinking of her as anything other than that. Landon knew his conscience was right even if it was a pain in his ass.

He had no idea what was going on with her or with them or if they even were a *them* or which end was up. He probably ought to figure out the which-end-was-up stuff before he further contemplated being the first guy to give her an orgasm.

Disgusted with himself and the direction his thoughts had taken, Landon put his bowl in the sink, went to the mudroom closet and grabbed the sleeping bag he used for cold-weather camping. He spread it on the floor next to where Amanda was curled up on her side under a down blanket, put more wood in the stove and got into the bag, zipping it to the top and making sure that no part of him was touching any part of her.

This was just about proximity to heat, pure and simple.

But damn, she'd never had an orgasm with a guy…

Landon really wished he hadn't looked at her notebook, as he wasn't likely to forget that little nugget any time soon. He was as tired as he could recall being in a long time, but sleep proved elusive as he stared up at the ceiling and thought about the many ways he might give sexy, puzzling, elusive Amanda an orgasm she'd never forget.

AMANDA HAD NEVER BEEN SO WARM, SO COMFORTABLE, SO...
When her foot connected with something hard and solid next to her, her eyes opened and blinked Landon's sleeping form into focus. Oh. So he was back. That was good. He'd told her he would probably be gone for hours and that she shouldn't worry if he didn't come back that night.

But she was glad to see him anyway.

For a second, she wondered why he was sleeping on the floor and then realized he must've been frozen after being out in the storm and had wanted to sleep close to the fire—and she'd taken his usual spot. She ought to get up and move to the bedroom, but she was so warm and comfortable that she stayed put and took advantage of the opportunity to observe Landon asleep with the embers from the woodstove casting a warm glow on his handsome face.

Unlike Lucas, who had a beard, Landon was clean-shaven, a look Amanda preferred to the beards so many Vermont men sported. In Amanda's opinion, it would be a crying shame to cover a face like Landon's with hair. She would never forget the first time she'd seen him, sitting next to his equally handsome twin, the two of them bombing into her product line presentation at their family's store. They'd come in still wearing gear after having worked a fire scene.

Both had been covered with soot that hadn't done a thing to dim their sexy appeal—or their humor.

Amanda had done tons of presentations by then, but they'd helped to make the one with the Abbotts that much more memorable. And when they'd both asked her out afterward, she'd been caught unprepared to handle a double dose of hot male firefighter. Which was how she'd ended up saying yes to both of them, setting off a chain of events that had caused considerable trouble for all of them.

Although for Lucas, the trouble had led to true love. From what she'd been told, he'd been upset about her accepting Landon's late-March invite to their joint birthday party at the barn where they and their eight siblings had been raised. Looking to clear his mind and steer clear of her and Landon, Lucas had headed out of town for a few days. He'd met single mom Dani and her baby daughter, Savannah, when he rescued them after Dani's car slid off the road in the snow.

Landon's sister Hannah had told Amanda that Dani hadn't left Lucas's side since the fire at the inn and was nursing him through his recovery from a broken arm and smoke inhalation.

Amanda was happy things had worked out for him and Dani, who had lost the baby's father in a tragic accident while she was pregnant.

Even after tragedy, some people got lucky a second time. Things worked out for them. Amanda had begun to think she wasn't one of the lucky ones, because nothing ever seemed to work out for her. Sure, she had a nice job that she enjoyed, and it paid her well enough, but it was really just that—a job, not a passion. She'd studied marketing before she dropped out of college and had fallen into the job with the company her mother worked for, selling intimate products, mostly targeted toward older people who were looking to spice things up in the bedroom.

She'd taken endless amounts of teasing and abuse from her friends when she first took the job, but they'd gotten over that after the first six months when they ran out of jokes about things that go buzz.

Landon let out a quiet little snore and startled awake to find her watching him sleep, like a creeper. "Hey," he said, his voice gruff. "Are you all right?"

He asked her that ten times a day since the fire. "I'm okay."

"Can't sleep?"

"The wind woke me a while ago."

"Sorry to crowd you, but I needed the heat after being out in the storm."

"I'm not crowded. It's fine. Did you find the kids?"

"We did."

"Oh, thank goodness. Are they all right?"

"Two of them are. The other was in rough shape, but he should be fine once they get him warmed up."

"That's a relief. Their parents must've been beside themselves."

"There were a lot of happy tears in the ER."

"It's so incredible the way you and your brothers and the others risk your own lives to save people you've never met."

"We like doing it—and we get paid for it, so there is that."

"Still, you'd probably do it for free if you had to."

"I have done it for free," he said with an endearing grin. "And I'd do it again. We know this mountain as well as we know our own backyard at home, and we love battling the elements to rescue someone who didn't know what they were getting into up here. People think because they've seen crazy weather elsewhere they understand it. There's our kind of crazy, and then there's all other kinds."

"Your mother must be on some really good meds with the way her sons are constantly risking their lives."

Landon laughed. "You'd think so, but she's super chill."

"She was here earlier. She brought me dinner, and we had a nice visit."

"That's nice of her. She'd tell you that having ten kids means you can't sweat the small stuff, because all you'd do is sweat."

"Having her sons out in a raging storm isn't small stuff."

"To her, it's just another day. We've been doing it for years.

Hunter and Will have been on search-and-rescue teams since they were in high school. The rest of us followed as we got old enough."

"You're a bunch of studs."

He rolled his eyes at her. "If you say so."

"I say so. Most sane people want a woodstove, a blanket, a good book and some hot chocolate during a Nor'easter. You guys want to trek through the woods looking for lost people."

He laughed again. "We don't *want* to do it. Unfortunately, we're *required* to do it several times each winter when someone gets lost. And we get called out in the spring and summer, too, when hikers fail to return on time."

"It's very cool to someone who's a total wimp when it comes to the cold and bad weather."

Landon turned onto his side to face her.

This was starting to feel an awful lot like pillow talk, not that she minded pillow-talking with him. From the first night they'd gone out, she'd found him easy to talk to. Their conversation had flowed effortlessly as he'd entertained her with stories about growing up with nine siblings. She'd also enjoyed hearing him talk about being a volunteer-turned-paid firefighter with the Butler Volunteer Fire Department and the travails of overseeing the family's Christmas tree farm.

But what she'd really liked best about him was the way he'd listened to her when she responded to a question about her life. He'd seemed genuinely interested in everything she had to say. That's not to say that Lucas hadn't been every bit as lovely a dinner companion. It was just that, for whatever reason, she'd connected on a deeper level with Landon.

"How's your ankle?"

"A little better, but it's still so swollen."

"Sprains are the worst. They take forever to heal."

"I'm sorry it's taking so long. I should get out of your way and go home to my mom. She's calling me every day and asking me to come home."

"You're not in my way, and you're welcome to stay as long as you want. I like having you here."

"You do?"

"Yeah, it's fun."

She gave him a skeptical look. "You think it's fun to have a roommate who steals your bed, stinks like smoke and never stops crying?"

Landon's grin did wondrous things for his already exceptionally handsome face. "Yes, I think it's fun to have you here."

"You're not right in the head."

"Believe it or not, I've been told that before."

Amanda laughed.

"And you don't stink like smoke."

"Yes, I do. It's all I can smell."

To her great surprise, he leaned in close to her, picked up a chunk of her hair, brought it to his face and took a deep breath. "Nope. You smell like honey and something else. Something sweet…"

"Oatmeal." His closeness and the intense way he looked at her made her feel breathless. "It's the shampoo."

"You don't smell like smoke." He let her hair slide through his fingers while she watched, her every nerve ending attuned to him. "And I really do like having you here, so stop worrying about things that don't matter, okay?"

"Only if you'll tell me when I start to smell like old fish." She laughed at the face he made. "My grandmother used to say that, after three days, guests start to smell like old fish. And I've already been here longer than three days."

"And you smell like oatmeal and honey and nothing at all like old fish—thank goodness."

"If that changes, you have to tell me to get out. I really can go home to my mom, even if she'd drive me crazy with the hovering."

He further surprised her when he took hold of her hand and

brought it to his lips, setting off goose bumps and other curious reactions when he kissed her knuckles. "Don't go yet."

She swallowed a huge lump that had taken up residence in her throat. "Why?"

"Because I like having you here. I like you. I want the chance to get to know you better. I wanted that before the fire, and I only want it more so now."

It was the most either of them had said about their "situation," such as it was, since the fire had upended everything.

"Please stay."

"If you're sure it's no bother."

"I'm very sure it's no bother."

"Okay, then."

"Okay, then." He dropped back to his pillow but held on to her hand.

When she woke up in the morning, he was still holding her hand.

CHAPTER FOUR

*"We climb to heaven most often on the ruins of our cherished
plans, finding our failures were successes."*
—Amos Bronson Alcott

*T*wo days later, Landon was no closer to figuring out
how to take the next step with Amanda than he'd
been before their middle-of-the-night chat, and he was beginning to feel a bit desperate. Before much longer, she'd be recovered enough to leave his home and resume her life elsewhere.

If he didn't do something—soon—he was going to miss his
chance with her. Yesterday, as he'd dabbed antibiotic ointment
on the healing wounds on her back, he'd wanted to spin her
around and kiss her so she'd know exactly how much he wanted
her. But he couldn't take advantage of the fact that she'd trusted
him enough to recover at his home or cross lines she might not
appreciate. He wasn't even entirely sure she liked him the way
he liked her, which was making him crazy.

Women had never been much of a mystery to him, not like
this, anyway. He was having the worst time reading her. One
minute, like when they'd held hands and talked deep into the

night, he'd felt fairly confident they were on the same page. But since then? Nothing.

Desperation had brought him to his sister Hannah's home at the end of an overnight shift at the firehouse. He stopped to say hi to Dexter, the baby moose Hannah had taken in, and was rewarded with a cold moose nose to the palm of his hand. "You're getting big, pal. What's Hannah gonna do with you when you're full-grown?"

"I'm going to continue to love him and be his mother," Hannah said from the doorway, where she stood with her daughter Callie in her arms and their dog, Homer Junior, at her feet. His eldest sister had long brown hair, which was twisted into a messy bun, and the dark eyes she shared with her twin, Hunter. "What brings you by so early?"

"I'm in need of some sisterly advice."

"And as you know, I have plenty of that."

"Which is why I'm here."

"Come in."

As Landon followed her inside the house, he removed his boots and left them on a rubber mat. The rain from the other night had begun to dry up, but the mud was back for a second visit this spring.

She handed Callie over to him. "Coffee or hot chocolate?"

He sat at the table with the sturdy baby on his lap while Homer rested on the floor nearby. "Whichever is easiest."

"I just made hot chocolate for myself."

Callie lunged for a spoon on the table and had nearly popped her own eye out before Landon caught up to her.

"Damn, she's quick!"

"Nolan says she has the fastest hands in Butler."

Hannah poured a mug of steaming hot chocolate for him and topped it with whipped cream out of the can.

"Remember me and Luc getting in trouble for eating all the whipped cream right out of the can?"

"More than once, as I recall."

34

"Mom learned to hide it from us."

"That, all cookies, all chips and anything else that wasn't nailed down. But you didn't come here to relive old times. What's going on?"

"Amanda."

"Ah," Hannah said. "I wondered what was happening there."

"Nothing is happening! Not one thing, other than a middle-of-the-night conversation that felt promising, but then nothing came of it."

"And you're frustrated by that?"

Landon gave her a withering look. "Yes, I'm frustrated. I like her. I think she likes me. She's living in my house, which is, like, five hundred square feet, but it may as well be separate countries. I feel like I have this amazing opportunity with her, and I'm somehow managing to blow it without even trying."

Hannah tipped her head as she studied him with that intense big-sister way of hers, as if she could see right through him. Which, of course, she could. That had always been the case. She was ten years older than him and Luc and had been like a second mother to them. "Are you even trying?"

He stared at her in shock. "What do you mean?"

"What, specifically, are you doing to indicate your interest in her?"

"Other than inviting her to stay with me while she recovers?"

"Yes, other than that." While Landon's mind raced to keep up with her, Hannah continued. "You had the night out at the inn. You brought her to your birthday dinner. You saw her here and there over a few weeks. And then the fire happened."

"Right."

"So since the fire, what have you done to re-spark the romantic portion of the program? Pardon the fire pun. And giving her a place to stay is only part of it. That was nice of you. I'm sure she appreciates it, but does she know you did that because you want your friendship with her to be more than friendship?"

35

"I, um... Well, I sort of assumed she'd figure that out when I offered to let her stay with me."

Hannah cracked up laughing. "How can you be so cute and so stupid at the same time?"

Landon frowned at her. "Mommy is being mean to me, Callie."

The baby responded by whacking him in the head with the spoon.

"That's right, Cal," Hannah said. "Hit him upside the head. He needs it."

"Is this supposed to be helping?" Landon asked.

"You have to do *something* to make her realize you're interested in her as more than just a platonic roommate."

"Like what?"

"Take her out again, to start with. When was the last time she was out of the house?"

"She hasn't been out since she left the hospital. I figured with the crap weather we've been having, she was safer at home while still on crutches. And besides, you guys made so much food for us, we can live off that for two more weeks."

"And isn't that romantic! Leftovers for days and days. Take her *out*, Landon. Take her somewhere nice and romantic and spend some money on her and make her feel special. While you have her attention, mention you want to be more than friends with her. The poor girl probably can't figure out whether you're putting her up out of pity or if you genuinely like her."

"She knows I like her."

Hannah propped her chin on her upturned hand. "You're sure of that, rock star? Or have you finally met a woman who isn't doing gymnastics to get your attention, and as a result, you have no idea how to get hers?"

Landon scowled at her. "That's not what this is."

"Oh, no? You don't think so? I think that's exactly what this is. You're so used to women falling all over themselves to get close to you that you have no earthly clue how to deal with one who doesn't do that."

"If she doesn't do that, maybe she's not into me." And why did that possibility make him so sad? Probably because he really liked her, and he didn't want to blow his chance with her.

"I've seen her with you. That's not the problem."

"What do you mean?"

"She likes you."

"How could you tell?"

"She pays attention to everything you do and say, and she stays close to you the whole time you're together."

"And you don't think that has anything to do with being intimidated by our massive family?"

"Amanda doesn't strike me as an easily intimidated sort of woman. Look at what she does for a living."

"I can't even think about that," he muttered.

Hannah giggled behind her hand. "You've found the female version of you—someone who could have any guy she wants—and you have no idea how to win her over because you've never had to *try* before. The same thing happened to Luc with Dani. I talked to Gramps about it. He said he told Lucas that when it really matters, you have to *try*. Same goes for you, sport."

"You seem to be enjoying this a little too much."

Her laughter made Callie chuckle, too. "Are you kidding? I love it! I've waited all your life for this moment. From the time you and your equally adorable brother were born, people have gravitated to the two of you. After you became teenagers, it was mostly female people. Neither of you has ever had to *work* for it before."

"That's not true."

"Yes, it is. Female attention has come too easily, which is why nothing ever stuck for either of you until Lucas found someone who mattered enough to bother. Why do you think Dani and Savannah are with him now? It's not because he casually said, 'Hey, babe, you want to come home with me?'" Her impression of Lucas was shockingly good. "It was because he made the *effort* to have a *real* relationship with her. *That's* the secret sauce, Landon. It's called *effort*."

"Effort. I can do that."

"Can you?" Hannah asked warily. "It means you have to actu- ally *do* something other than sit back and wait for her to come to you."

"Yes, you've made your point on that."

"Am I wrong?"

"Not entirely…"

Hannah lost it again, laughing so hard she had tears in her eyes as she reached for Callie.

Equal parts annoyed and amused, Landon handed the baby over to her mother.

"So what's your plan?"

"I'm going to ask her if she'd like to go out to dinner."

"That's it?"

"That's not enough?"

"No, Landon," she said, sounding exasperated. "That's not enough. You have to make it clear to her that you're asking her out on a *date*. Not just to consume a meal outside your own four walls. Please tell me you see the difference."

"I do," he said, laughing at the way she spoke to him as if he were five rather than twenty-seven. "I get it. I hear you, and I'll make sure she knows it's a date."

"How're you going to do that?"

Landon had to think about that for a second. "What if I tell her I really enjoyed the last time we went out together, and I've been waiting for her to feel up to doing it again? And would she like to pick up where we left off before the fire by going out to dinner tonight."

"That's pretty good."

"Only pretty good?"

She gave him a calculating look that made him feel a tiny bit sorry for his brother-in-law, Nolan, who didn't stand a chance against Hannah. Case in point: the baby moose living on their property. If Hannah had her way, Dexter would be sleeping between her and Nolan. He'd drawn the line at allowing the moose inside the house. "Stop at the grocery store and get flowers to take home to her. Tell her you were thinking of her while you were out and were hoping you could talk her into an actual out-of-the-house date tonight."

"That's a good idea."

"Do you need me to write that down for you?"

He shot her a withering look. "I'm good. Thanks."

"If you really care about her, Landon, *show* her. Show her in everything you do and say. Make it obvious to her. This is no time for games or foolishness. There's nothing keeping her here once her ankle is better. The clock is ticking. If you want her to stay, you need to play all your cards. Right now."

"I hear you, and I agree. I know what I need to do."

"And you'll let me know first thing tomorrow how it went, right?"

He rolled his eyes. "Maybe not *first* thing."

"First thing or no more free advice, and I have a feeling you're going to need much more advice before you make the close with this woman."

Landon waggled his brows at her. "Once I 'make the close,' your services will no longer be needed. Trust me on that."

"Ew. Don't be gross."

"Nothing gross about it. Got lots of satisfied customers who can attest to that."

"Get out of my house. Right now."

Laughing, Landon stood, rinsed his mug and put it in the sink.

The phone rang, and Hannah took the call. "Hey, Tweedledee. Funny you should call while I've got Tweedledum here with me, and he's extra *dumb* today."

Landon glared at her even as he wanted to laugh. Under no circumstances could he confirm for Hannah that she was funny.

"Lucas says he has news, and I have to put the phone on speaker so we can both hear." She pressed a button. "Are you there?"

"I'm here," Lucas said.

"How you feeling?" Landon asked.

"Good. Dani and I have been sitting on some news for a few days."

"Abbotts don't sit on news."

"I can't believe we actually kept a lid on this one. We're engaged."

Hannah let out a scream that startled Callie. "It's good news, baby girl! Uncle Lucas found someone to take him off our hands."

"Very funny," Lucas said, sounding elated. "We told Mom and Dad when it happened, but we wanted to talk to Dani's parents and take a few days to ourselves before we told everyone else."

"Congratulations to you and Dani," Landon said as an oddly hollow feeling overtook him. His twin brother was getting *married*. "That's big news."

"I couldn't be happier. We want to do it soon so we can get busy having a bunch of kids."

"That's not happening," Dani said into the phone.

"It's on, baby. You promised me seven."

"I did no such thing."

"Don't worry, Dani," Hannah said. "We believe you."

"Hey!" Lucas said.

"Welcome to the family, Dani," Landon added. "We'll be here to support you as you put up with him."

"I'll remember this when your turn comes," Lucas said. "We've gotta go call Gramps to tell him the news, even though Dad probably already told him—and took credit for the whole thing. Talk to you guys later."

"Love you all," Hannah said.

"We love you, too," Lucas said. "Later."

Landon was convinced his "turn" was a long way off, especially in light of the fact that he couldn't seem to move past Go with Amanda.

"That's some big news," Hannah said after she put down the phone.

"For sure."

"Why do you look like you just lost your best friend?"

"Because I kinda did."

"Nah, that's not true. You guys will still be tight."

"It won't be the same."

"I still talk to Hunter every day now that we're both married."

"You do?"

"Every single day. He stops by to see Callie a couple of times a week, or we meet for lunch. We see him and Megan for dinner at least once a week. We make an *effort*, Landon."

"That seems to be the word of the day." He kissed his sister's cheek and the baby's head. "You ladies have a nice day."

"Good luck. Don't mess this up. I don't want to deal with your pouting ass if this doesn't work."

"My ass doesn't pout."

"Get. Out."

"I'm going. Don't get up. I can see myself out. And, Han, thanks."

"Any time, little brother."

On the way to his truck, Landon stopped to give Dexter another scratch on the top of his cute little moose head. Was that where moose liked to be scratched? He would ask Hannah that the next time he saw her. She was a bit of a moose whisperer. Fred, the town moose, was like a poodle when she was around, and now she had Dexter eating out of the palm of her hand, too.

In a family full of odd characters, Hannah fit right in.

Landon got into his big black pickup truck and backed out of his sister's driveway. He needed to get to work at the farm, and after that, he had a date to prepare for.

CHAPTER FIVE

"God has his plans and his reasons. Sometimes we are supposed to go through things so that we learn lessons."
—Dolly Parton

That morning, Amanda participated in a conference call with work, thankful she'd been allowed to decline the face-to-face option since she didn't feel like dealing with hair straighteners or makeup. Thankfully, her boss was also her mother, Joyce, who had started the meeting by welcoming Amanda back and asking how she was doing—even though Amanda had already spoken to her before the meeting. The Q&A was for the rest of their team.

"I'm doing okay," Amanda said. "Still hobbling around on crutches and trying to shake off the near-death experience. But otherwise, I'm hanging in there."

"I know I speak for all of us when I tell you how thankful we are that you're on the mend," Joyce said. "You gave us a heck of a scare."

I gave myself a heck of a scare, she thought. "Thank you for the kind thoughts and the flowers and sending the new computer and phone. I promise to get back to work next week."

"Take your time and come back when you're ready."

Their colleagues had been so wonderful to Amanda since the fire. "I really appreciate the support."

"How close is the Green Mountain Country Store to officially rolling out the product line?" one of the salesmen asked.

"Close," Amanda said. "They were waiting to coordinate with their new catalog, which is in final stages, and next week, I'll finally be training their sales force."

"Excellent. We're all looking forward to seeing how it goes there. It's a great test for markets in smaller towns."

"We think it'll do very well here. We have the full support of the Abbott family, particularly the CEO, Lincoln Abbott, who's backed the line from the get-go."

Amanda was determined to prove he'd been right to go all in with their products.

They moved on to other items on the agenda, including the upcoming trade show season that was a big part of their business. The ten-member sales team took turns attending the shows and doing product demonstrations in the hope that retailers would choose to carry their line.

That's how she'd landed the Green Mountain Country Store account. She'd first met Landon's brother Colton at a trade show in New York after he'd been sent by Lincoln. Later, she'd found out that Lincoln had also been trying to help along Colton's relationship with Lucy by sending him to New York, where Lucy had lived at the time.

From what Amanda had been told, Lincoln had faced an uphill battle in convincing his business-partner children that the line could be successful in their store and in the catalog. Amanda was certain that Linc had been right. She expected their product line to be very popular at the store—and especially in the catalog.

Funny how much had happened since she first met Colton in New York. Now she was staying with his brother after another of his brothers had nearly been killed saving her. Speaking of

Lucas, she was long overdue to thank him in person for saving her life. Maybe she could get Landon to take her to see him later.

She glanced at the clock on the stove.

Landon ought to be home by now.

She immediately dismissed that thought. Was that what it'd come to? Her life revolving around his comings and goings? Well, sort of... There was no need to worry about him driving on mountain roads, as he was an expert at such things, but since the fire, she felt anxiety over the dumbest things. Add Landon being late coming home from a night shift to the list of things that had triggered her lately.

When noon came and went with no sign of him, she figured out he'd probably gone to work at the tree farm for the day.

Hours later, she was standing by the window, watching for him, when the big black truck made the turn into the driveway.

Amanda breathed a sigh of relief. In this cell phone wasteland known as Butler, Vermont, it was stressful not to have a way to check on someone when they were running late. Would she have checked on him if she could have? Well, probably...

How long would this new sense of impending doom last? She had no idea, but as Landon came into the cabin, bringing the scents of pine and woodsmoke with him, she was pouring herself a cup of coffee and trying to act nonchalant. He didn't need to know that she'd worried about him all day. In the seconds she had left before she had to talk to him, she was determined to shake off the freaking doom. Enough already with that nonsense.

"Hi there." He dropped his boots on a mat by the door. "Where're your crutches?"

"I threw them out the back door."

"You did not!"

"I didn't, but I wanted to. I'm fine without them if I walk on my toes." She glanced at him and did a double take when she saw the huge bundle of flowers he'd brought home. "Those are beautiful." The brightly colored blooms were a combination of lilies, roses and some others she couldn't name.

"For you." He handed them to her and then groaned. "I knew I forgot something. I don't own a vase."

"We can improvise. Get one of your beer mugs."

"Wait, *what?*"

"Oh, come on. You have, like, three dozen of them in the cabinet."

"They're *collector's* items."

"You don't want my flowers to die, do you?"

"No."

Could he be any cuter? Nope, not possible. And of course he knew it as he sent her a pathetic look and went to decide which of his precious mugs he could sacrifice for her flowers.

"I guess you can use this one." The mug he handed her had the logo of a bar on it. "I don't go there anymore."

"Reminder that it *can* be washed after use as a vase."

He gave her a withering look. "I know that."

She took the mug from him and went to the sink. The mug was too small for the bouquet, but it would keep the flowers alive. "Why don't you go there anymore?"

"There's a waitress there who got it in her head that we were a thing when we were never a thing." He shrugged. "So I stay away."

Amanda shook from the effort not to laugh in his face, but a gurgle escaped the hand she'd put over her mouth.

"Stop. It's not funny."

"Oh, yes, it really is. You've probably left a million broken hearts in your wake, haven't you?"

"I have not!"

"Yes, you have."

He took a step toward her. "No, I haven't."

"Yes."

Now he was standing right in front of her, looking down at

her with those beautiful golden eyes framed with lavish lashes. "No."

She nodded even as her breath got caught in her throat. That seemed to happen any time he was near.

He shook his head. "Not a million. Not even close."

"Thousands, then."

He smiled, and dear God, her knees went weak. "Are you done?"

"I'm just getting started." *That's the way, Amanda. Grab life by the horns, and don't leave anything on the table.* That needed to be her new motto. And if grabbing life by the horns meant more of Landon Abbott, she was all in. She reached for him, hoping she was reading him right and that he wanted what she did.

His gaze shifted from her eyes to her lips, giving her half a second to prepare before he moved in for the kill. A half second was nowhere near enough time to prepare to be kissed by him. Lord have mercy… The man had the softest, sweetest, sexiest lips, and the weeks of anticipation leading to this moment only made the impact that much more powerful.

Desperate for something to hold on to, she picked him, grasping his flannel shirt as his lips moved over hers and his hands slid down her back to her ass, pulling her in even tighter against him. She'd just managed to catch up to him when his tongue stroked her bottom lip, causing her to gasp.

He took full advantage of the opening to send his tongue to play with hers.

Her knees actually buckled.

Landon tightened his arms around her. That was the only thing that kept her standing as he ruined her with his lips and tongue while his erection throbbed against her belly. Landon Abbott was hard for her, and nothing had ever made her feel more powerful or alive. All thoughts of despair and doom were overshadowed by the wild rush of excitement that came from kissing him.

If he'd dated a million women, then she needed to thank

them all for the practice they'd given him, because she'd never been kissed like this. She actually had cause to wonder if she'd survive their first kiss as it went on for what seemed like hours.

Maybe it was only a few minutes, but it felt like lifetimes had passed before he finally began to slow things down, to come up for air, to reckon with the seismic shift in their relationship that had occurred while they'd been pressed together in his tiny kitchen. He'd turned her entire world upside down, leaving her dizzy and spinning and desperate for more.

"Wow."

His single word summed things up rather well. "Mmm."

"Do you have any idea how long I've wanted to do that?"

That was a question, Amanda. You're expected to answer him. Her scrambled brain didn't want to cooperate. "Um, no. How long?"

"From the first time I ever saw you in our conference room, talking about sex toys the way other people discuss the weather." With his hands on her face, he compelled her to look at him. "I wanted to take you out of there and bring you here, and keep you in my bed for days and days and days, even though that wouldn't be long enough."

Amanda swallowed hard. "For what?"

"All the things I wanted to do with you."

Holy. *Crap.* "I, um, well…"

Landon laughed and then kissed her some more, as if he couldn't get enough now that they'd crossed the invisible line that'd been keeping them apart for weeks. Was it normal for one's brain to go completely blank while being kissed by the sexiest man she'd ever known?

And then he broke the kiss. "Hold on tight."

"Wha…"

He lifted her off her feet as Amanda scrambled to tighten her hold on his shoulders. Then they were falling onto the sofa with him on top of her, and she was once again left breathless by his nearness, the scents of pine and woodsmoke, the soft lips that moved on her neck and the hard press of his erection between her legs.

"Is this okay?" he asked.

"I, um…" *Speak, Amanda. Say words.* "Yes."

"You feel so good, but I knew you would." As he said words she'd never forget, he continued to make her crazy with kisses to her neck, along her jaw and down her throat. "I knew it. I almost went insane that first night we met, knowing you were out with Luc."

"I, un… Ah…"

His soft laughter was nearly as sexy as his kisses. Hell, everything about him was sexy, which was what made him one of the two most popular men in the Northeast Kingdom. And with his partner in crime officially off the market, there'd be a line out Landon's door as soon as the word got out that Lucas was now taken. "I love my brother, but I didn't want you anywhere near him."

Amanda turned her head to avoid his kiss. "We, uh, we should talk about this, no?" *No, Amanda, you fool, this is no time for talking. Remember your list and the item about having an orgasm with a man? This is a man who can make that happen. Why do you want to talk?*

"Probably. In fact, when I came home, my only goal was to get you to go out with me tonight and to somehow make you understand that I wasn't just asking you to go with me to eat somewhere other than home, but asking you on a *date*."

"And you thought you needed to clarify?"

"I wanted you to know…"

"What?" The man could make her breathless with just a few words, not to mention what he could do with his lips, tongue and hands.

"That I really like you, and not just as my platonic roommate. I *like* you. I want the chance to get to know you better and to maybe do this…" He kissed her again, just a light touch of lips, but she felt that kiss everywhere. "I never imagined we'd do

this"—another kiss—"before dinner, but that's fine with me."
More kisses.

"I wasn't sure… I couldn't tell…"

"What couldn't you tell?"

"If you took me in because you felt sorry for me or because you wanted… something else."

"I took you in because I couldn't bear the thought of you leaving before we had a chance to really get to know each other. And because I wanted to take care of you. I wanted something else, too, but I wasn't sure if it was what you wanted."

"I've been such a mess since the fire. I'm sorry if I was confusing you."

"No apologies needed. What happened that night was terrifying for all of us, but you in particular."

"Not just me. You almost lost your brother. Your *twin* brother."

"I almost lost *both* of you. It was a wakeup call about making sure my priorities are in order." As he spoke, he rocked against her suggestively, every press of his hardness against her most sensitive area setting off a wild craving for more of him. "And right now, you're at the very top of my priorities list."

To her great mortification, tears filled her eyes and spilled down her cheeks.

"What's wrong?"

She shook her head and swiped angrily at the tears. "I'm so mad with myself."

"Why?"

"Because it took almost dying in that fire to realize I was living half a life before. Actually, calling it half a life might be generous. It was really an eighth of a life. I've never done *anything*. I… I had some stuff happen when I was younger, some difficult things, and after that, I was just… I was kind of frozen. I never take chances. I never do anything crazy. I never step outside the lines. Since the fire, part of me wants to just go *wild* now."

He listened intently to her, seeming to hang on her every word. "What would going wild entail?"

"I don't even know. I just want to do everything, feel everything, try everything. I want *everything*."

Landon gazed down at her. "We'll do it all. Everything you can think of. We'll do it."

"I can't even walk on both feet," she said, sniffling.

Grinning, he said, "There's lots of wild stuff we can do in the meantime."

She laughed softly at the double meaning behind his statement. "Will you be my partner in crime?"

"I'd love to be. You tell me what you want, and we'll do it. I don't care what it is."

"I don't even know what I want. I just want to stop being so cautious and afraid of everything. That's no way to live."

"Being caught in a fire is a scary thing. You shouldn't beat yourself up for being traumatized after something like that."

"What's my excuse for all the years before the fire? I've been a wimp, Landon. I never take any risks or do anything exciting because I'm so busy worrying about what might go wrong. I'm tired of living like that. I want to be *wild*." She hooked her hand around his neck and brought him for a kiss. "Will you walk on the wild side with me, Landon?"

"Hell, *yes*."

His emphatic reply made her laugh. "No boundaries, no limits, no rules," she said. "Just wild fun."

"Yes, yes and *yes*. Let's start right now."

The words *right now* were a sobering reminder that she had his attention for the moment, but when a man could have any woman he wanted, his eyes would be wandering once again. She could go wild with him, but under no circumstances could she fall for him. Their arrangement would be temporary, and she needed to remember that. As if she'd been hit in the face by a snowball named Reality, she pulled back from him, or as much as she could with him on top of her. "I'm starving. Are we going out?"

"We're definitely going out." He sat back and offered her a hand to help her sit up. His cheeks were rosy, like they got when he'd been out in the cold. Did kissing her have the same effect? "How do you feel about Asian fusion?"

"I've been known to be a fan."

"There's a new place a couple of towns over. I heard it's good."

"Do you like Asian fusion?"

"Uh, I don't even know what it is, to be honest. It sounds fancy."

Amanda tried and failed not to smile. "You're very cute, but I don't need fancy. Where would you go if you were by yourself and just wanted to grab food?"

"Kingdom Pizza, probably."

"That's fine."

"I want something better for you."

"I don't need better. If the point is hanging out and getting to know each other, pizza is fine with me."

"As long as you'll let me do better another time."

"Knock yourself out, champ."

"I will, and you'll never see my wild side coming. You want first dibs on the bathroom?"

"Sure. I'll be quick. I already showered." She got up from the sofa and took a second to find her balance.

"Are you okay?"

"Yep. Hey, I meant to ask if we can see Lucas at some point." Was it her imagination, or did her request annoy him? She quickly added, "I owe him a big thank-you for what he did during the fire."

"Of course. I'll call and ask if they want us to deliver dinner to them after we eat."

"Perfect." She started to hobble away, but stopped and turned back to him, feeling the need to make sure he understood. "I only want to thank him. That's all it is."

"Lucas told me today that he and Dani got engaged."

"Did they? That's great news."

"Sure is." Was that relief she saw in his expression? Was he still worried that she might be interested in Lucas? As she changed into clean jeans and a warm turtleneck sweater, she tried to think about what she could say or do to make sure Landon knew there was only one Abbott brother she wanted to get wild with.

And it wasn't Lucas.

CHAPTER SIX

"You can always amend a big plan, but you can never expand a little one."
—Harry S. Truman

That went well, Landon thought after a shower as he changed in the bedroom into jeans he wore only on special occasions and a red Henley. In deference to the fact that this was a date, he put on the sweater his sister Ella had given him for Christmas. It was white with a red design on it. Not his usual style, but he trusted Ella's judgment. If she liked it, Amanda probably would, too.

Was he actually hoping he was wearing something a woman would like on him? This situation had gone from bad to worse in the course of thirty minutes of sexy kisses that had his blood running so hot, he wondered if he should skip the sweater even though it was still cold outside. Only because he wanted to look nice for her did he leave the sweater on and go in search of "dress-up" boots that qualified as such because they hadn't been dragged through mud and slop and snow.

He so rarely gave a shit about what he wore that he didn't have a lot of nice clothes. Would that put him at a disadvantage in comparison to the men she usually dated? And what kind of men did she date? Probably suit-wearing dudes with cushy jobs in offices. That'd never be him. If that was what she wanted—

"Stop, will you?" He sat on the bed and bent to tie his boots. "She just kissed your freaking face off and asked you to go wild with her. She's here, when she could be anywhere. That has to count for something, right?"

A throat clearing had his head whipping up to find Amanda leaning against the doorframe. Had she heard him muttering to himself? Shit…

"Ready when you are."

"Okay." He stood and really looked at her, and *holy wow*. "You look…" She'd done something to her eyes that made them pop. Her brown hair fell in shiny waves around her shoulders. "Really pretty."

"So do you." She flashed a saucy grin and turned to hobble back into the living room.

Landon watched her go, his gaze fixed to tight jeans hugging a sweet ass. Holy shit. She was so fucking sexy, and she kissed like a dream. He couldn't wait to kiss her again, but first things first. He told his hot blood, his libido and everything else to stand down and shut up. This was not the time for random boners or acting like a dog in heat.

It was funny, really. If you'd told him a few months ago that he'd be panting around after any woman, he would've laughed. Women had always been about harmless fun. He didn't do serious or committed or any of the stuff his siblings had gotten into in the last couple of years. One by one, they'd fallen like felled oaks into relationships destined to last forever.

Before Amanda had come to town and blown him away with her fresh-faced sexiness and blunt talk about sex and sex toys, he would've scoffed at the idea of settling down with one woman when he could have *all* the women. How was it possible that she could've come storming into town and turned his whole world upside down in the span of an hour-long presentation?

That didn't happen unless you allowed it, he reasoned, except reason didn't play into his reaction to her. He thought about his brother Will, who'd met his wife, Cameron, a couple of years ago after she slammed her Mini Cooper into Fred, the town moose. And his brother Colton, who was now married to Cameron's business partner, Lucy. Or Hunter, who'd been in love with Megan for years before he finally did something about it. And when he had, that was it for him. *She* was it for him.

They had fallen one after the other, Ella with Gavin, Charley with Tyler, Hannah with Nolan, Wade with Mia and now Lucas with Dani. Even their cousin Grayson had joined the parade, falling for Lucy's sister, Emma. Not to mention, Cameron's dad, Patrick, was off traveling the world with Mary, their former office manager at the store.

As all this had played out right in front of him, Landon had remained on the sidelines, perplexed, though happy that people he cared about had found true love. But he hadn't had any burning desire to experience happily ever after for himself.

Until that day in the conference room when everything had changed.

He ought to be annoyed with Amanda rather than following her around like a besotted puppy. Everything had been going along just fine for him until she showed up and sent him spinning. The pre-Amanda Landon Abbott didn't go seeking out advice about women from the likes of Hannah, who'd never let him hear the end of it. No, he hadn't needed Hannah's help pre-Amanda, or anyone else's when it came to women.

So it ought to piss him off that he'd become this insecure, uncertain idiot who was worrying about what to wear to freaking Kingdom Pizza, where he ate two or three times a week usually.

He whipped the sweater over his head, tossed it on the bed, took two steps toward the door and then stopped, turning back to grab the sweater and put it back on. "You're such a fucking idiot," he muttered.

"Did you say something?" Amanda asked from the living room.

"I was looking for my keys."

"You left them on the kitchen counter, next to the flowers."

While telling himself to calm down and stop acting like a fool, he went to get the keys. He realized he should call Lucas and Dani to see if they wanted food and ask if it was okay if they came by. He found Dani's number on the notepad he kept by the phone.

She answered the phone. "Hi, Landon."

"How's it going over there?"

"Good. Luc is having a really good day. He was awake for most of it."

"That's great news. Are you guys up for a quick visit? Amanda asked if she could see him."

"Of course. We'd love to see you guys."

"We're going to grab dinner at Kingdom Pizza first. You want anything?"

"Nope, we're good. Your family made sure of that."

"Okay, see you soon."

He returned to Amanda in the living room.

"What'd you do to your hair?" She reached up to smooth the strands. "It's standing on end."

"It's the sweater's fault. I wasn't sure if I wanted to wear it."

"It looks nice on you."

"You think so? It's not really my thing, but my sister gave it to me, and…" Why was he babbling about a stupid sweater that had already gotten way too much of his mental energy?

"I like it. You look very handsome."

That sealed it. He was wearing the sweater, and maybe he'd thank Ella the next time he saw her. "You ready?"

"Whenever you are."

Landon got the coat he'd chosen for her at the store, a black parka that was really more like a blanket than a coat, according to his sister Charley, and held it for Amanda. With his coat on, he offered her his arm to hold as he walked her slowly toward the truck that had red lights on top and fire department license plates. "You want me to grab your crutches?"

"I really don't need them if I can balance on my toes."

When they reached the truck, Landon opened the door and gave her a lift into the high-profile truck.

"Thanks. Not sure I could've pulled that off."

"I gotcha covered."

He drove them into town, watching for Fred, who was often found standing in the middle of the road, oblivious to cars, and everything else, for that matter. Fred followed his own set of rules. The last thing Landon needed was to smash his relatively new truck into the side of an unyielding moose. In cases of vehicle versus moose, the moose almost always won.

Recalling the state of Cameron's poor little car after her altercation with Fred had Landon chuckling softly to himself.

"What's so funny?" Amanda asked.

"I was thinking about how my brother Will met his wife, Cameron, when she crashed her car into the town moose—and how the car came out on the poorer end of the altercation. The moose was fine. The car? Not so much. And when I met Cameron, she had two black eyes from the air bag."

"Damn, that moose is tough."

"I know. That's why we have to really be careful when we drive around here in the dark. You never know where he's going to plant himself."

"That's kind of scary."

"Nah, he's a pussycat. You just don't want to crash your car into him."

"How can a massive moose be a pussycat?"

"You'll have to meet him to fully appreciate him."

"That's fine. I'm good."

Landon laughed at her emphatic statement. "Oh, come on. If you want to truly go wild in Butler, Vermont, you have to meet

Fred. If you stick around here long enough, you'll have a Fred encounter. We think he has a crush on Cameron."

"How can a moose have a crush on someone?"

"He seems to show up wherever she is. Such as when he came strolling into the tent during their wedding."

"Stop it. He did not!"

"He did. We've got photos to prove it. My sister Hannah is the family moose whisperer, though. You haven't lived until you've seen tiny Hannah turn that thousand-pound bull moose to putty in her hands."

"How does she do that?"

"We have no idea. But she marches right up to him and gives him hell, and he does whatever she tells him to while Nolan has a meltdown over her staring down that massive moose."

"I love your family," she said, laughing.

"They're certifiable."

"I bet it was never boring growing up in your house."

"God, no. Never. It was a madhouse."

"I can only imagine."

Landon glanced at her. "Do you have siblings?"

"Two who are much older than me. They were both in college by the time I hit high school."

"Where are they now?"

"My brother lives in Alaska, and my sister is in Oregon. I haven't seen them in years."

"I can't imagine not seeing my siblings for years."

"You're lucky to have them all close by."

"I know, even if sometimes I don't feel lucky when they're all up in my grill about something. It's not easy being one of the younger brothers. Every one of them has an opinion about everything I do."

"You had a lot of parents."

"Yep, and I still do. They drive me crazy."

"I've seen you with them. You also love them like crazy."

"Sometimes."

"All the time."

"If you say so."

"I say so. I've seen it with my own eyes. You're so lucky to have nine siblings you're actually close to. Do you know how rare that is?"

"Yeah, and I appreciate them, as well as my eight cousins, who are also like siblings to us. We grew up in a gaggle."

"Lucky. We didn't have any other family close by when I was growing up, so it was mostly me and my parents. They split when I was in high school, and my dad took a job out of state, so I hardly saw him either."

"That must've been tough."

"It was. I was closer to him than my mom, but he traveled so much for work that I couldn't stay with him. My mom and I went through some tough years before we found our groove. We're close now, but back then, we did nothing but fight. I never imagined for a second I'd end up working with her."

Landon pulled into a parking space at Kingdom Pizza. "You'll have to tell me how that happened. Hang on. I'll come around for you." He got out of the truck and was on his way around the front when a blond woman came out of the restaurant, let out a squeal and launched herself at him before he had a second to prepare or fend her off. He was nearly knocked off his feet by the impact.

"Where have you *been?*" Chrissy and he had been "friends with benefits" over the years. "I haven't seen you in weeks!" She playfully slapped his chest. "I left you a couple of messages."

As he struggled to catch up, she kissed him square on the lips, with Amanda seeing the whole thing play out from the passenger seat of his truck. Landon tried to gently extricate himself, but Chrissy wasn't having it. Somehow he managed to pry her hands off him.

"What're you doing tonight?" She gave him her trademark suggestive smile. "Want to come over?"

"I'm, uh, with a friend."

Chrissy cast a glare at the truck. "Who's that?" She turned up her nose like she'd smelled something rank.

"I, ah, I have to go. See you around?"

"Whatever." After casting another hateful look toward his truck, she stalked off.

This is great. Just what he needed when he was finally on another official date with Amanda. *Ugh.* He opened the passenger door. "Sorry about that."

"Sorry about what? I didn't see a thing."

Was she really going to pretend that hadn't just happened with Chrissy? If so, she really was different from every other woman he'd known. "There's a huge puddle. Let me help you." He slid his arms under her and lifted her out of the truck, using his hip to push the door closed and setting her down on the sidewalk, holding on until she found her balance. "You good?"

"I'm good."

Landon held the door for her, waiting for her to hobble in ahead of him. "Take a seat, and I'll bring you a menu." He helped with her coat and held the chair for her before going to get a menu. All the while, his mind raced as he wondered when she would get pissed about what she'd seen with Chrissy. That had to be coming, right?

Working behind the counter was another woman he'd dated years ago. *Fantastic.* Thankfully, Jessica didn't leap over the counter to kiss him.

"Landon!" She looked a little closer. "You are Landon, right? No beard."

"Yes, it's me."

"How are you? I heard about the fire and that Lucas got hurt. Is he okay?"

"He's doing great. Thanks for asking."

"Tell him I'm thinking of him."

"Will do. Could I please grab a menu?"

Her brows knitted. "Why do you need a menu? You get the

same exact thing every time. A large sausage and pepperoni with green peppers and mushrooms."

"I'm with a friend."

Jessica looked around his shoulder, apparently found Amanda waiting for him and frowned. "Sure." She shoved a menu at him. "Let me know when you're ready to order."

Yikes, Landon thought. It was dangerous to go out in this town with Amanda. The last thing she needed was to be reminded of how many women he'd dated in the past. That had nothing to do with her or them.

He brought her the menu and sat at the table while she decided what she wanted.

"I'll do the house salad with grilled chicken and an iced tea, please."

"Coming right up." He went back to the counter to order her salad and his pizza and got a beer for himself along with her tea.

"Thirty-two eighty-five," Jessica said without looking up at him.

Landon ran his card and dropped a five-dollar bill into the tip jar.

"Please be seated, and I'll bring it out when it's ready."

"Thanks." Landon returned to the table, feeling Jessica's glare burning a hole in him. What the hell was her problem, anyway? They'd been out a couple of times, had some fun… He wondered if he'd ever understand women or what made them tick or what made them mad. Why would Jessica care if he was out with Amanda?

"What's wrong?"

He looked up from his internal diatribe to find Amanda watching him. "Nothing."

"Judging by the way you stomped back to the table, some-thing's up."

Landon figured he might as well come clean with her, because there was no point in trying to hide the fact that he'd enjoyed an active social life in the past. "I dated the woman at the counter for a month or two about five years ago. Apparently, I'm an ass for coming here with you while she's working. Or something like that. Who knows?"

Amanda ran her hand over her mouth as her eyes glittered with amusement.

"You think that's funny?"

"I do."

"I'm glad you do. The next time we go out, it's not going to be in Butler."

"Even in this cell phone-free never-never land, I'm sure word is getting out that Landon Abbott is on a *date* with someone they don't know. Hearts are shattering all over the Northeast Kingdom as we speak."

"Har-har. It's not like that."

"Isn't it?"

He appreciated that she seemed more amused than annoyed. "Not really."

Her raised eyebrow expressed a world of skepticism. "Hmm."

When Jessica brought their food, the plates landed with a clatter on the table. "Can I get you anything else?"

"No, thanks," Landon said.. "I think we're good."

She turned and walked away.

"Chilly," Amanda said as she poured Italian dressing on her salad.

"She has no reason to be. The thing between us was no big deal, and it was over years ago. Why's she acting like that?"

"Is that a rhetorical question, or do you really want to know?"

"I really want to know." Landon took a bite of his pizza, hoping Jessica hadn't laced it with poison, and chased it with a sip of ice-cold beer. Damn, that was good.

"If I had to guess," Amanda said, casting a subtle glance at Jessica, "what you deem to be 'no big deal' might've been a big deal to her."

"No way. It was nothing. We skied together a few times in a

big group, hung out after, partied a little here and there. It was never a thing."

"Did you sleep with her?"

"Well, yeah, but…"

"There you go. It was a big deal *to her*. You probably broke her heart when you moved on."

"I've never picked up that vibe from her, and I see her all the time. I'm in and out of here a couple times a week, and she's never acted like she has tonight."

"Because you're usually by yourself, and she's still hoping you might come back around to her. Let me ask you this… When was the last time you came here with a woman?"

He gave that some consideration. "I don't think I have."

"Aha. Just as I suspected. Tonight, you're with me, which means there's no chance for her. At least not right now."

"Not ever. That's over."

"For you. That's not necessarily the case for her."

Frustration threatened to overwhelm him. He was on a date with her, and here they were discussing his track record with other women. That was the last thing in the world he wanted to talk about with her. She must think he was a complete asshole. Suddenly, he felt a desperate need to fix that—if he still could. "I don't want you to think I'm a man-whore. I swear I'm not."

"Okay," she said with a small smile that indicated she hardly believed him. And, really, why should she with the evidence she'd accumulated to the contrary in the last thirty minutes?

Fucking hell. This date was turning into a full-fledged disaster. Wait until Hannah got ahold of this nonsense. She'd have a freaking field day with it.

Thankfully, they got through dinner without further encounters of the female kind, but he'd utterly failed in using the time to get to know Amanda better. However, she'd certainly learned more about him—all things he didn't want her to know.

CHAPTER SEVEN

*"I think I've lived long enough to understand that plans really
are very overrated."*
—Viola Davis

*L*andon had hoped Amanda would tell him about the to-
do list she'd made for her second chance at life. After
that intense make-out session earlier, he had even more
interest in helping her to check a few of those items off her list.

As if that was going to happen now. She was probably
disgusted by him, and who could blame her? On the way back to
the truck, he again lifted her over the mud puddle and deposited
her into the passenger seat. When he walked around the front of
the truck to the driver's seat, he glanced into the restaurant and
saw Jessica glaring at him as she cleared the plates from their
table.

Ugh.

It had never once occurred to him that she or anyone else
had taken their time together seriously. How could they when
he never made promises or committed to anything other than a
good time in the moment? He'd been all about having fun and
trying to make sure no one got hurt. Apparently, he'd failed

rather miserably at that last part—and now Amanda knew that, too. *Great.*

His stomach was tied up in knots, and for the first time ever, pizza had given him heartburn.

"Where're we going?" Amanda asked as he drove them on dark, winding roads.

"To Dani's place. Luc is staying there."

"Oh cool, but I was hoping to see the farm."

"I'll take you there in the daylight." That was, if she was still interested in hanging with him after tonight's train wreck.

The outside light was on at Dani's when they arrived. Landon parked next to Lucas's truck, the navy blue version of his. Landon had delivered Luc's truck to Dani's when he heard Lucas would be coming there when he got out of the hospital. He realized it would be difficult for Amanda to climb the two flights of stairs to Dani's apartment. "I'll give you a lift up the stairs."

"I can do it."

"No need. I've got you covered."

He scooped her up out of the passenger seat and stepped through squishy mud, taking care not to fall and possibly injure both of them. They went up the stairs to the landing on the third floor, where he put Amanda down and again waited to make sure she was steady before knocking.

Dani came to the door with Savannah in her arms. Petite and curvy, Dani had reddish-brown hair and big, expressive eyes. The baby was blond, rosy-cheeked cuteness. "Come in." She led them into the small apartment, where Lucas was on the sofa, covered by a down comforter that Landon recognized from the store. Luc's broken left arm rested on a pillow.

"Have a seat," Dani said. "Can I get you anything?"

"No, thank you," Amanda said. "We're fine. We just wanted to check on you guys."

"We're doing great." Dani took a seat next to Lucas, who'd made room for her. When Savannah strained toward Lucas,

Dani handed her over to him, careful to avoid his injured arm. "Except for his arm, the patient is doing really well."

"That's a relief," Amanda said. "I just want to tell you... What you did... Thank you, Lucas. Thank you *so* much."

"I was just doing my job."

"You saved my life. I was so scared, and then there you were. I'll never be able to properly thank you."

"I'm glad we both made it out of there." Lucas snuggled the baby with his good arm. "We've got a lot to live for."

Landon watched as Amanda shuddered from reliving the horror of that night, and decided to change the subject. "Did they say when you can come back to work?"

"Another six weeks at least." Lucas scowled at his broken arm. "If the fire didn't kill me, the lying around just might."

Like Landon, his brother hated to be inactive.

"Heard you guys made a hell of a rescue the night of the storm."

"Yeah, we found them. Just in time, too. One of them is still in the hospital but expected to make a full recovery, thankfully."

"Good news all around," Lucas said. "So what're you guys up to?"

"Nothing much," Landon replied. "Just had dinner at the Kingdom."

When Savvy started fussing, Dani stood to pick her up. "Bedtime for my angel. You want to help, Amanda?"

"Sure, I'd love to." She got up and hobbled after Dani.

"You look a lot better," Landon said to his brother when they were alone.

"I feel much better. Go grab us a couple of cold ones."

"Are you allowed to have beer?"

"Yep. I haven't taken anything for the pain today."

Landon got up, went to the kitchen, opened two beers and brought them back, handing one to Lucas.

"Thanks. Before Dani comes back, I need a favor."

"What's that?"

"Can you run to Montpelier and pick up something for me when you get the chance?"

"Sure. What do you need?"

"The engagement ring I ordered for her."

"I still can't believe you're actually engaged."

"I know," Lucas said with a cocky grin. "Just when I thought I'd never find anyone who could stand me, there was Dani and Savvy to change my life forever."

"I'm happy for you." Landon put his beer on the table and sat back in the chair, wishing he had the secret recipe for the kind of happiness his brother had found with Dani.

"What's the matter with you? You're all spun up over something."

Landon would ask how Lucas could tell that, but it was a twin thing. They just knew. "It's just been a very weird night."

"How so?"

"Things with Amanda have been at a bit of a standstill, until tonight, that is. We had a little breakthrough, you might call it, which was totally effed when we went to Kingdom."

"What happened?"

"I ran into Chrissy. She practically jumped me, kissed me, etc. right in front of Amanda. Then there was Jessica…"

"Who wasn't happy to see you there with a date?"

"Yes! And I have no idea what her problem is. We were over a hundred years ago. The last freaking thing I needed was all that happening in front of Amanda when things were starting to move in the right direction—finally."

"Everyone has a past, Landon. I bet she does, too."

"Maybe so, but hers isn't being thrown in my face. After tonight, I'll be afraid to step foot outside the door around here with her."

"Does she know you're into her in a way you haven't been with the others?"

"I think so. I mean, I guess…"

"This is the time for very clear communication. Put it out there. Tell her how you feel so she can have no doubts."

"Look at you giving out relationship advice," Landon said with a grunt of laughter. "Who'd a thunk it?"

"Not me until I met Dani, and everything else ceased to matter. If it's like that for you with Amanda, make sure she knows it. You can't help what other people do, but you can certainly make sure she knows your truth."

"That's a good point."

"I know."

Landon sent him a withering look. "Thanks again for not dying in that fire."

"I had to stick around to make sure you stay out of trouble and don't mess it up with Amanda."

"I don't want to mess it up with her. I really like her. I have this panicky feeling about her leaving and me missing out on this chance with her."

"Then don't let that happen. Don't hold anything back. All the usual bullshit doesn't work here. You gotta dig deeper. I promise you, it's worth the effort. It's so completely worth it."

"Did you kids set a date yet?"

"Probably later in the summer. It doesn't really matter to us when it happens. We already feel married in all the most important ways."

"I'm happy for you guys."

"We're happy for us, too."

"When you were first with Dani, how did you deal with, you know, your track record, I guess you'd call it?"

Lucas thought about that for a second. "It helped that I met her in Stowe, and we spent some time there before we came back here. But I told her I'd dated a lot, that I'd never really done the serious thing before, but I felt ready for that, which mattered to her because of Savvy. After what she went through losing Savvy's father when she was pregnant, Dani wasn't about to bring me into her daughter's life long-term unless I was serious about both of them. I had to man up or run the risk of blowing it. Since losing them wasn't an option I wanted to consider, I manned up."

"What exactly does that entail?" Landon couldn't believe he was actually asking that question of Lucas, of all people, but since he didn't want to fuck it up with Amanda, he asked.

"It means taking it seriously. No bullshit. When Dani asked for time to get her life here established, I gave her time, even if it killed me to put things on hold with her for months. But it was what she needed. With Amanda, don't let her think for a second you want anything—or anyone—other than her. And if you don't honestly feel that way about her, then don't pretend you do."

"I really like her. A lot. Like, more than I've liked anyone since... you know."

Lucas stared at him. "Really?"

"Yeah."

"Maybe you should tell her that."

"I'd have to tell her about... about Naomi..." Saying her name felt like lancing a still-healing wound.

"Would that be so bad?"

Landon shrugged. "I don't talk about her, except when I see her mom."

"Maybe you should. It would give Amanda some perspective."

"I guess." The thought of resurrecting that old hurt made him queasy and sweaty. "Why does this have to be so hard?"

"Because it *matters*."

Landon nodded. That was certainly true. Before he could say anything more, Amanda and Dani returned to the living room.

When Amanda smiled at him, the feeling that went through him was a reminder of why he was in this situation in the first place. It was because she made him feel things that only one other person ever had. Only Lucas had ever known how Landon really felt about Naomi. The rest of his family had thought she was a close friend. They hadn't known he loved her, because he hadn't wanted anyone to know that.

"That little girl is indeed an angel," Amanda declared, but Landon noted that she looked sadder than he'd ever seen her and wondered why.

"You won't hear us say otherwise," Lucas said as he took Dani's hand and encouraged her to snuggle up to him.

Dani moved carefully into Lucas's one-armed embrace, as if she was still afraid of hurting him.

"We should go," Landon said. "Lucas needs to get some rest." And Landon wanted to be alone with Amanda, to talk some more, to try to fix the impression this evening had left her with.

"That's not what Lucas needs," Lucas said suggestively.

Dani put her hand over his mouth. "Be quiet."

"Don't want to be quiet," Lucas said, his words muffled by her hand.

"That's our cue," Landon said to Amanda as he stood, helped her up and held her coat for her to put on.

"How's the ankle?" Lucas asked her.

"Better but still sore. I can walk on my toes, thank goodness. The crutches are worse than the injury."

"I can attest to that the few times I've been on them," Lucas said. "They suck." He pulled himself off the sofa to see them out.

Landon noted how slowly his brother moved. "You're sure you're doing better?"

"Positive. Don't worry."

"Will you be at Mom's on Sunday?" Landon asked.

"That's the plan."

"Okay, see you then. Call me if you need anything."

"We will." Lucas patted Landon on the back. When he had Landon's attention, Lucas tipped his chin toward Amanda, who was hugging Dani. *Man up.* Lucas mouthed the words so the women wouldn't hear them.

Landon nodded. "Take it easy."

"You, too."

"Oh, hey, thanks for taking care of the horses for me," Lucas said.

"No problem. Happy to do it."

"I'll be back at it soon."

"No worries. Take your time."

They stepped out of the apartment, and Landon said, "Hop aboard my magical mystery ride."

Amanda smiled and held on to him as he lifted her into his arms. "Don't drop me."

"Wouldn't dream of it."

"What's this about horses?" she asked.

"We have two of them at the farm that we use for the sleigh rides during the season. Usually, Luc tends to them because he lives there, but I've been doing it since he got hurt."

"That's good of you."

"It's no big deal."

"I'm sure it is to him."

Landon settled her into the passenger seat of his truck.

"Thanks for the lift."

"Any time." He wanted to kiss her, but he wasn't sure he'd still be welcome. There'd be time to revisit that impulse when they got home. Or so he hoped.

CHAPTER EIGHT

*"No valid plans for the future can be made by those who have
no capacity for living now."*
—Alan Watts

"*A*re you ready for bed?" Dani asked Lucas after she shut
off the outside lights and locked up.

"Only if you are."

"I could make myself ready." As he headed for the bedroom,
she said, "Go slow."

"I'm sick of going slow. I want to get back to normal."

"And you will, but it's going to take time. If I have to actually sit on you to keep you from doing too much too soon, I
will."

He raised a brow and gave her his best sultry look. "Is that
supposed to be a threat of some kind? Because having you sit on
me hardly equates to punishment."

She rolled her eyes. "Is everything about sex with you?"

"Not everything, but I'm more than ready to pick up where
we left off before the fire."

"That's not happening any time soon."

He gave her ass a grab. "Yes, it is."

She dodged him. "No, it isn't. Now brush your teeth and take a leak and be a good boy."

"Being good is boring. I want to be very, very bad."

"Brush your teeth."

"I love when you use your stern mom voice on me."

"I'm practicing on you for when I'll need it for Savannah."

When he finished in the bathroom, she took her turn while he painfully got himself situated in bed, closing his eyes to breathe through the pain that riddled his entire body any time he moved. The doctors had told him it would take a while to get back to full steam. Lucas hadn't wanted to hear that. He wanted to hold his fiancée and make love to her and play with his little girl.

Dani got into bed, and even the subtle movement of the mattress had him wincing.

"Sorry," she said.

"Don't be. Get over here and snuggle up to me."

"I don't want to hurt you."

"You'll hurt me if you don't."

She moved very carefully to prop his injured arm on a pillow before resting her head on his chest as he looped his good arm around her, all the while gritting his teeth against the pain.

"God, this fucking sucks."

"It beats the alternative."

Her comment was a stark reminder of how she'd lost the first man she'd been engaged to in an ATV accident when she was three months pregnant with Savvy.

"I'm sorry. I shouldn't have said that. I have no complaints."

"Don't be sorry. It does suck, but I'm so freaking thankful you didn't die that all I can see is the silver lining."

"Thank you for reminding me of the silver lining."

"There is one. You're still here, we're all safe, and we've got so much to look forward to."

"You're one hundred percent right, and I'll try to keep my bitching to a minimum."

"It's okay if you want to bitch. I know that being sidelined is hell for you."

"Only because I can't hold you and kiss you and love you the way I want to or play with my little girl."

"You will soon enough."

"Not soon enough for me."

"It was nice to see Landon and Amanda."

"Yes, it was. It doesn't bug you to have her here, does it?"

"Why would it?"

"Well, I was kinda in a rage over the two of them when we first met."

"A lot's happened since then. She's no threat to me."

He squeezed her shoulder. "No, she isn't, and *everything* has happened since then."

"When we went to tuck in Savannah, she got emotional."

"How so?"

"She asked if she could hold her, and when she gave her back to me, I noticed she was crying."

"Did she say why?"

"She didn't, and I didn't feel like I should ask."

"Could be just emotional overload after the fire. I've found myself in tears a few times thinking about what happened, what could've happened, what I might've missed. The worst part was knowing how tortured you'd be after what you went through after losing Jack. I hated doing that to you."

"Thank you for not dying. I very much appreciate that."

He gave a soft laugh that he instantly regretted. "I'm not going anywhere."

"All kidding aside, I love you. And I can't wait for you to feel better so we can get back to normal in all ways."

"I love you, too, and I can't wait either. We're going to make up for all this lost time, so you'd better rest up."

Dani laughed and kissed his chest. "Get some sleep, tiger."

Lucas gave a low growl and kissed her forehead. He wasn't

sure how he would survive until he could do much more than that.

TONIGHT HAS BEEN INTERESTING, AMANDA THOUGHT ON THE DRIVE home to Landon's on dark winding roads. After he'd told her about Fred hanging out in the middle of roadways, Amanda found herself keeping a lookout for him even if she couldn't see anything beyond the beam of the headlights. The fear that they might smash into a huge moose was better than thinking about the things she'd learned about Landon in the last few hours or the mini meltdown she'd experienced while holding Savannah.

About Landon... Of course she'd understood that a handsome, sexy, charming man like him—and his equally adorable twin brother—would be popular with women, but to see it firsthand... That'd been rather jarring.

She'd be lying if she didn't admit that it had given her pause to see a woman throw herself at him and kiss him right in front of her, or to witness the behavior of the server at the pizza place. Though she'd played it down with him, it had rattled her, especially after the big step forward they'd taken together earlier.

Was spending this time with him going to turn out to be another huge mistake?

She didn't know, and that uncertainty had thrown her off-balance.

"Could I ask you something?" he said as he navigated the winding roads that led to home. His home. Not hers. She had no home to call her own, which was another thing that felt wrong since the fire.

"Sure."

"When you came out of Savannah's room, you looked really sad and maybe like you'd been crying. Were you sad?"

"A little."

"Because of the fire?"

She shook her head.

"Do you want to talk about it?"

"I… Not really, but I will. I'll tell you."

He reached for her hand. "You don't have to."

"I know."

When they got home, he came around to get her again, taking care as he had all evening to make sure she could safely navigate the treacherous terrain with her bad ankle. She held on tightly to the arm he offered and walked slowly toward the front door.

They removed their shoes inside the door. Landon hung their coats and immediately went to tend to the fire.

Amanda sat on the sofa and removed her sock to take a look at her ankle, which was far more swollen than it had been earlier. It was also badly bruised, from her ankle to her toes. Ugh.

"That looks painful," Landon said.

"It doesn't feel good."

"I'll get you some ice." He went into the kitchen, grabbed the ice pack she'd been using from the freezer and returned with that and a chilled glass of the Chardonnay she enjoyed.

"Thank you," she said, taking the wineglass from him.

"Welcome." He positioned a sofa pillow on the table for her foot and placed the ice pack over her ankle. "Does that feel okay?"

"Feels good."

"Need anything else?"

"Nope. I'm good."

He went back to the kitchen, got a beer from the fridge and came to sit next to her on the sofa, turning so he was facing her. "I'm sorry about the shitshow that tonight turned into."

She blinked and gave him a blank look. "What happened?"

Sighing, he said, "You know what I mean. Don't make me say it."

"Okay, I won't."

He reached for her hand and linked his fingers with hers. "I'm sorry you were sad at Dani's."

"It happens sometimes. I, um..." She took a drink of wine and glanced at him, trying to find the courage to tell him something she rarely told anyone. "When I was seventeen, I had a baby."

"Oh. Wow."

"I gave her up for adoption because I was too young to care for her properly. My mom had me when she was almost forty, and after having essentially raised two families, because my siblings were so much older than me. She said she didn't have it in her to do it again."

"What about the father?"

"He was a one-time mistake at a teenage party at a time when all my friends were losing their virginities. I was under the mistaken belief that I wouldn't be 'cool' if I held on to mine. It was the stupidest thing I've ever done, and the result was just... It was devastating."

"I'm so sorry that happened to you."

"Thanks." She wiped away tears that materialized any time she thought about that time in her life. "Holding Savannah was wonderful, but it was also a reminder of that time. I'm just a mixed-up emotional mess since the fire reminded me of all the things I've failed to do because I've been so busy avoiding anything that could ever hurt me like that did."

"That's understandable."

"Maybe," she said, shrugging. "But it's no way to live. Thus my desire to go a little wild and shake things up."

"Do you know anything about her or her life?"

"I get pictures once a year. She's a beautiful twelve-year-old named Stella, with my hair and her father's green eyes. She's into soccer and dance and lost her adoptive father to a heart attack when she was seven. They've moved around a lot, but overall, she seems to have a good life in Albany, New York. It helps me to know she's happy, and at some point, when she's ready, her mother knows I'd welcome hearing from her."

"I'm so glad you're able to know how she is."

"Me, too. Adoption has come a long way from the days when it was locked down and mothers could never know anything about the babies they gave up."

"It's better this way. For everyone."

"I agree."

"I really appreciate you telling me. I know it's probably not something you tell just anyone, and I'm honored you told me."

"I'm glad you know. If you're wondering why I'm such a weirdo, that might give you some insight."

"I don't think you're a weirdo. Not at all."

"I'm well aware of the fact that I can be difficult to get to know. I'm far more cautious than I used to be."

"Believe it or not, I understand that better than you might think. I want to tell you something about me now. Something no one but Lucas knows."

"Before you say anything, Landon, I just want to say… You don't have to. Just because I told you about my daughter doesn't mean you have to bare your soul. You don't owe me anything. The time we've had together has been fun, and I've enjoyed it very much. But it doesn't have to be more than that, if you don't want it to be."

"That's the thing." He looked more serious than she'd ever seen him. "I *do* want it to be. More, that is." Keeping his gaze fixed on their joined hands, he said, "I haven't done serious before, and there's a reason I've kept my distance from stuff like this and worked the surface with other women."

"You only have to tell me if you want to. Please don't feel obligated."

"I don't feel obligated. That's the least of how I feel with you."

"What do you mean?"

"You've got me all wound up and spinning my wheels trying to figure out how to take the next step with you when I've never taken that step before. I talked to Hannah about it, and she said I needed to make an effort, to show you how I feel and what I want, but when I tried to do that, it turned into a complete disaster."

"It wasn't a *complete* disaster," she said, smiling.

"Yes, it was! The last thing in the world I wanted was Chrissy throwing herself at me or Jessica pitching a fit because I had you with me."

"Those things weren't your fault."

"Weren't they? I've dated both of them in the past—and many others—and never promised any of them anything. I swear to God, I never promised them *anything*."

"But that didn't stop them from hoping for more."

"I didn't encourage that. They knew the score with me from the get-go, and if they changed the rules, they did it without my involvement. I've always been respectful toward the women in my life."

"I have no doubt that's true."

"It *is* true. Just because they wanted more and I didn't, that doesn't make me an asshole. I was honest with them always, and not one of them could say otherwise."

"You can't blame them for wanting to be the one who changed Landon Abbott's mind about happily ever after."

He rolled his eyes at her gently teasing comment. "Whatever." After glancing down again, he seemed to force himself to look directly at her. "I never wanted any of that stuff until I met you."

The statement hit her like a punch to the gut, leaving her winded for a second.

"I went out of my way to avoid it because of something that happened to me a long time ago. And that's what I want to tell you about. If you want to hear it."

"I do," she said softly, moved by how hard he was trying to connect with her, to make her understand him better. She squeezed his hand, hoping to encourage him.

"When we were kids, Luc and I had a friend named Naomi.

79

She grew up with us, was in my class or Lucas's every year and was just someone who was in our lives at school and outside of school. In middle school, we ran around with a group of kids, and she was always part of that crowd. What no one other than Lucas knew was that I really, *really* liked her. By the time we were sophomores in high school, my like for her had morphed into love that I had no idea how to handle in light of the fact that we'd always been just friends. With Lucas giving me a hard push, I finally asked her out, and she said she was so happy I'd finally asked. She said she was going to ask me if I didn't ask her soon."

Dear God, he was adorable with the way he smiled at that memory. "That's so sweet."

"It was. That day was, like, seriously, one of the best days of my entire life." He drew in a deep breath and then released it slowly.

Amanda felt like she should brace herself for what was coming next.

"A few days later, before we got a chance to go out, she got sick. She had a terrible headache and a fever, and they thought it was the flu."

"But it wasn't?"

He shook his head. "Turned out to be bacterial meningitis."

"Oh no. Landon..."

"She died after ten days in the hospital. I never saw her again after the day I asked her to go out with me."

"Oh God." Heartbroken for both of them, Amanda blinked back tears. "I'm so, so sorry."

"Ever since then..."

She moved toward him, the ice pack falling to the floor as she wrapped her arms around him. "I get it. You don't have to say any more. I understand completely." She understood better than anyone else probably ever could, having been there herself.

"I'm not an asshole to women, Amanda. I swear to God I'm not."

"I know. I knew that before you told me about Naomi."

"It happened a long time ago, but it changed me."

"Of course it did."

"I've had years to imagine what might've been with her if things had worked out differently."

"You also have a benchmark."

He pulled back to look at her. "What do you mean?"

"That's a term we use in business to measure the success or failure of something. Naomi was your benchmark. You know how that felt, and you were unwilling to settle for less."

"Yes, exactly," he said, sounding relieved that she understood. "For the first time since that happened, I want to try again to go there. Which is a pretty big deal for me."

"I'm very honored that you feel that way about me."

He smoothed a strand of her hair back from her face. "I was so happy when you let me bring you home with me after the fire. But then I didn't know how to get back to where we were heading before that."

"Where were we heading?"

His lips curved into the adorable smile that would be her undoing. "We were inching toward something, and don't pretend otherwise."

"I won't, and I'm sorry if I've been weird since the fire. It was just such a life-altering event. I've been spinning ever since, reevaluating my whole life."

"In what way?"

"I've been making lists of things I've never done, things I want to do."

"Like what?"

She thought about the top two items on her list and had to summon the nerve to share some of the bigger ones with him. "I've never found my Naomi, for one thing."

"What else?"

"I want to learn to play the piano, drive a stick, have a baby that I get to keep—at some point, not immediately. I've never skied or zip-lined or been to Europe. When I look back at my life, there are more things I *haven't* done than things I have done. I want to stop being so concerned about protecting myself from getting hurt that I miss out on things."

"So you've never been in love?"

She shook her head. "Nope."

"Is there other stuff on your list?"

"A few things…"

"You don't want to tell me?"

"Not yet," she said, giving him her best mysterious smile. "Some things are better discovered than discussed."

"Sounds intriguing."

She continued to smile as she shrugged. "I guess we'll see."

"So where does this leave us?"

"I believe it leaves us wanting to give this thing between us a chance. Am I right about that?"

He leaned in closer to her, his intention clear. "You are."

Amanda placed her hand on his face, running her thumb over the stubble on his jaw, and leaned in to meet him halfway. "As long as we understand that I'm looking to shake things up, and I have no idea what that's going to entail."

"I understand, and I fully support your desire to step outside your comfort zone." He surprised her with a sweet, chaste kiss. "A lot happened tonight. You want to sleep on it and see what's what tomorrow?"

His suggestion was actually a relief. A lot *had* happened, and she did need time to process it all, but she hadn't realized that until he said the words.

"Yes, but under one condition."

"What's that?"

"Your bed is huge. There's no need for you to sleep out here when you could be sleeping in your own bed."

"With you?"

She gave him a coy look. "Unless you'd rather not…"

Laughing, he said, "I'd much rather be with you."

"All right, then."

"All right, then."

Neither of them moved for a long time, awareness crackling between them like a live wire. The moment ended when Amanda blinked as she realized she was staring at him. "I, uh, do you want the bathroom?"

"You can go first."

"I'll be quick."

He helped her up and waited until she was steady on her feet to let go of her hand. "Take your time. I'm going out for some more wood."

"Okay." Amanda ducked into the bathroom, closed the door and leaned back against it, taking a deep breath to calm herself after the intense discussion. Her mind whirled as she tried to process everything she'd learned about him over the course of this evening and to reconcile it with what she already knew.

One thing was for certain—the more time she spent with him, the more intrigued and attracted she became.

CHAPTER NINE

"Have patience with all things,
but first of all, with yourself."
— Saint Francis de Sales

*L*andon went outside without a coat, needing to cool off
before he got into a bed with Amanda. When she'd
invited him to join her, his libido had surged from
simmer to boil in a hot second.

He wasn't sure what it was about her that made her so
different from other women he'd known. Maybe it was because
she didn't throw herself at him and hadn't shown her entire
hand at the get-go. She'd maintained an aura of mystery, which
meant he'd had to work at getting to know her. The conversation he'd had with her just now was deeper than anything he'd
ever shared with anyone. They'd both suffered traumas in the
past that had helped to shape them into the people they were
now, and it made Landon feel less alone with the painful memories of Naomi after sharing her with Amanda.

He took a series of deep breaths as he looked up at the clear
sky full of stars and tried to prepare himself to platonically sleep
in a bed with the sexiest woman he'd ever met.

"Yeah, sure, you can do this." He filled his arms with wood he didn't need because he'd gotten some earlier and took it inside. "It's no big deal. It's just sleeping."

After their heated kisses earlier, he'd assumed things between them would move to the next level fairly quickly.

But then Chrissy and Jessica had happened, which had led to the conversation about the child she'd given up and what he'd been through with Naomi, and suddenly, everything had turned serious. He had whiplash from the series of events that'd transpired since he came home with flowers earlier. On the plus side, he'd wanted to move things forward with Amanda, and he'd succeeded in doing that. But nothing had gone according to plan.

Back inside, Landon built up the fire that would keep them warm throughout the night and made sure both doors were locked. He didn't usually worry about locking his doors when it was just him, but the first night she'd stayed with him, Amanda had asked if he'd locked the doors. Since it made her feel safe, he'd done it every night since.

The bathroom door was open and the light on in the bedroom. "Knock, knock. Is it safe to come in?"

"All good. Come on in."

He stepped into his bedroom and found her in his bed, propped up on pillows, her hair down around her shoulders. Landon leaned against the doorframe and feasted his eyes on the sight of her in his bed.

"What?"

"I like how you look in my bed."

"You've seen me in your bed before."

"I liked how you looked then, too."

"Are you going to stand there and stare all night, or are you going to join me?"

"Definitely going to join you, but not until I stare for a little bit longer."

"Landon," she said on a nervous laugh. "Stop."

"You don't like when I stare at you?"

"You're flustering me."

"You're pretty when you're flustered—and when you're not." Landon laughed when she lifted the covers up and over her head. "You can run, but you cannot hide."

"Good to know."

He grabbed pajama bottoms and went into the bathroom to change and brush his teeth. When he returned to the bedroom, she was still in hiding deep under the covers. He got into bed and went looking for her.

She jolted when his cold hand found her warm shoulder.

"Come out, come out, wherever you are," he said in a singsong voice that had her giggling.

"I didn't realize I was inviting the Big Bad Wolf to join me in bed."

"Sure, you did. You knew exactly who you were getting." He tunneled through the covers until he was nose to nose with her. "Hi there."

Smiling, she said, "Hi."

"Thanks for inviting me to your sleepover."

"It is your bed, after all."

He nuzzled her neck, making her shiver as her hands curved tentatively around his shoulders. "My bed is much nicer with you in it."

"I'm not sure if I can handle being in bed with shirtless Landon."

"I'll bet you can handle it just fine."

"I don't know about that."

"How about we give it a try?" He shifted so he was hovering above her, propped up on his arms and fighting to maintain control as she ran her hands all over him.

"So many muscles," she said softly as her touch electrified him. "How do you have so many muscles?"

She expected him to actually talk when he was hardly

breathing? "Ah, rock-climbing, skiing, fire department training, among other things."

"Whatever it is, it's working for you."

"Is it working for you, too?"

"Oh yeah…"

Landon lowered his hips and pressed his hard cock against her. He wanted her so fiercely that he had to keep telling himself it wasn't time for that. Not yet, anyway. But then her hands moved down his back and coasted over his ass, digging into his flesh to bring him in even closer, making his eyes roll back in his head. "Ah, Amanda…"

She wiggled under him, seemingly unaware of what she was doing to him. "Hmm?"

He was on the verge of suggesting they move things along to the next stop on their journey when the house phone rang, startling him out of the lust-filled stupor he'd fallen into. "Shit. I have to get that. I'm always on call."

Amanda released him, and he dove for the phone. "Abbott."

"Got a house fire on Sugar Mill Road, Lieutenant. Are you able to respond?"

"On my way." He put down the phone and drew in a deep breath as he tried to switch gears from turned on to turned out. "I have to go to work."

"So I gathered."

He glanced at her. "I'm sorry."

"I understand. This is your life."

"It is."

She gave him a wary look. "Will you be okay?"

He took one second to kiss her. "I'll be fine." Landon got out of bed and moved quickly to change into thermals, jeans and a long-sleeved T-shirt. "Get some sleep."

"Be careful."

"Don't worry. I'm always careful."

He was out the door two seconds later and on his way into town with lights flashing. The address of the fire wasn't far from his brother Will's home. With the streets deserted, he could drive faster than usual, but as always, he kept an eye out for moose and other obstacles. On the way, he tried to decompress from the episode in his bed so he could focus on work, but with his blood still running hot through his veins, it was damned hard to shift gears.

When he arrived at the scene, Landon found a house fully engulfed in flames and trucks from the Butler Volunteer Fire Department already there. Off to the side, a group of people huddled together, wrapped in blankets.

"Everyone out?" he asked Richard Smith, the department's chief.

"Everyone except the family dog."

"I'll go after him."

"You don't have to."

"I'd like to try."

"Get suited up, then. You got five minutes. In and out."

Landon moved quickly to don the gear he carried in his truck at all times so he'd be ready for calls such as this one. He was on his way inside within a minute, following directions from the family about where the dog might be hiding. With the fire raging in the front half of the house, he entered through the kitchen in the back. He'd been told the golden retriever might be under the dining room table, which was located to the left of the kitchen. Thick smoke filled the entire downstairs as he made his way to the dining room, a flashlight helping to lead the way.

Sure enough, the dog was huddled under the table.

When Landon dropped down to go after him, the dog retreated farther under the table, snapping at him when he extended a hand.

"Come on, buddy. I'm here to help."

The dog wasn't having it.

Landon grabbed his collar and pulled as the dog fought back, biting his wrist hard. Ugh, that hurt, but at least he couldn't break the skin through the thick gloves. "Listen, dude. You don't

want to crush the hearts of your family members, now do you?"
He had no idea if the dog could hear him through the oxygen
mask he wore. One more time, he grabbed the dog's collar and
pulled hard, and when he got the dog close enough, he quickly
wrapped his arms tight around the dog's solid body.

Landon's radio crackled to life. "Hurry up, Abbott." The
chief's order and the tense sound of his voice put Landon on
notice that he was running out of time to get the dog out of
there.

Keeping his tight hold on the heavy animal, he stood and
rushed back toward the door, tripping over something and
nearly falling at one point. He had no idea how he managed to
hang on to the dog and remain standing, but they reached the
doorway in the seconds before a loud crash sounded behind
them as the second floor collapsed.

Well, that'd been rather close.

When they were outside, he put down the dog, who ran off,
hopefully toward the family that loved him.

Landon removed the mask that covered his face, bent at the
waist and took some deep breaths of cold air.

"Good job," the chief said. "You crazy bastard."

Landon laughed. "I like dogs better than most people. I'll
always save the dog."

Over the next several hours, he helped the rest of their team
fight the fire until it was under control. Neighbors had taken in
the family that had lost its home, and there'd be plenty to do at
the site in the coming days as they confirmed their suspicions
that a faulty woodstove had started the fire.

Landon drove toward town exhausted and chilled to the
bone as the sun rose over Butler Mountain, casting a warm glow
over the picturesque town. As he was scheduled to work that
night, he had the day to get some sleep ahead of his regular shift.
In his early twenties, he might've stayed at work rather than
going home to sleep. But as he got older, he'd learned to take
care of himself so he could take care of other people.

He never knew when he'd be needed for search and rescue or fires, so he tried to keep his battery charged rather than running on empty most of the time the way he used to. Besides, with Amanda sleeping in his bed, he had good reason to go home rather than work around the clock. He couldn't wait to see her and hold her and be with her. The rush of emotions tied to her left him feeling a bit lightheaded and off-balance as he drove home, thinking about the convergence of the past and the present.

After he'd lost Naomi, he'd shut down to any feeling that could cause him pain when it came to women. He'd kept things light and fun and muddled through without taking chances on anything below the surface.

That strategy had prevented him from experiencing more of the heartbreak he'd endured after Naomi died. But it had also kept him walled off from anything meaningful. Until he'd met Amanda, he'd never wanted to change the status quo that had worked so well to protect him since his tragic loss.

And now he was on the verge of risking everything for a woman and doing so with his eyes wide open to the potential for disaster. He couldn't deny the possibility of being hurt like he'd been before, and it scared him. For a time after Naomi's shocking death, he'd had reason to wonder if he'd ever be the same again. The family had rallied around him and Lucas in the loss of their friend, but no one other than Lucas had known how much greater the loss had been for Landon.

He'd refused to discuss it with anyone other than his twin, who was the only one who knew that he'd finally worked up the nerve to ask her out days before the illness struck. Landon would never know what might've been with Naomi, but he'd always had the feeling their relationship would've been significant.

Hannah had met her first husband, Caleb, when they were in middle school, and their love had gone the distance until he died in Iraq.

Would it have lasted forever with Naomi? He had no way to know, but it was certainly possible. He hadn't thought about her and what might've been for them in a long time, even if the dull ache of her loss had remained with him over the years. Only since Amanda had come into his life and opened the door to new possibilities had he started thinking again about what might've been with Naomi.

He'd already had more with Amanda than he'd ever had with Naomi. Thinking of what it had been like to hold Amanda made him almost desperate to be with her again, even knowing the risk he was taking with every passing minute he spent with her.

On the way through town, he made a quick stop at the diner, where he knew he'd find his brother Hunter at that hour, helping Megan prepare for the morning rush. "Knock, knock," he said, sticking his head into the diner, which wouldn't be officially open for another fifteen minutes. "Young, impressionable brother coming in, so don't do anything that can't be unseen."

"Shut up and come in." Hunter was seated at the counter with Megan, helping her roll silverware into paper napkins. His eldest brother had dark, wavy hair and brown eyes.

"There's coffee if you want some, Landon." Megan had her blond hair up in a ponytail with a pen pushed through it.

"Thanks." He helped himself to a cup of coffee and stood behind the counter to drink it.

"You get called out last night?" Hunter asked without looking up from his task.

"Yup." Landon held out his arm for them to see. "And bit by a dog for my troubles."

Hunter looked up and winced at the huge bruise on Landon's wrist. "Ouch. That's not very nice."

"The poor guy was scared."

"How's Amanda?" Megan asked.

"She's doing better. The ankle is still giving her some grief, though. Actually, she's the reason I came by. You still have your piano, right?"

"Uh-huh," Hunter said as he rolled another set of silverware and added it to the growing pile on the counter.

"Amanda wants to learn how to play. Do you think you could show her the basics sometime?"

"I could try. I've never actually taught anyone, so I have no idea if I can."

"You could," Megan said. "He plays for me all the time. He's really good."

"I know, which is why I thought of him when she said she wanted to learn. She's on a quest, I guess you could call it, to do things she's put off now that she's got this second chance at life."

"That's cool," Megan said. "And it's sweet of you to want to help her."

Landon shrugged. "I get where she's coming from. Nothing like getting caught in a fire to remind you that there's no time like the present to go after what you want."

"Is that what you're doing, too?" Hunter asked. "Going after what you want with her?"

"Maybe so."

"Told you." Megan nudged Hunter with her shoulder. "When are you going to realize I'm right about most things?"

"Thanks a lot," Hunter said to Landon.

Landon grinned at their good-natured bickering. "Want to catch me up?"

"After your birthday, I told Hunter there was something brewing with you and Amanda, and he said, nah, Landon doesn't do serious. In fact, he said, Lucas doesn't either. He was also wrong about that."

"We love when Hunter is wrong about something," Landon said. "It happens so infrequently that you have to really enjoy the moment."

"I know!" Megan said. "It's maddening how he's almost always right. I have to get mine where I can."

"Um, hello," Hunter said. "I'm right here, and I can hear you."

"Was I or was I not right about Landon and Amanda?" Megan leaned in, cupping her ear as if to hear him better.

"Yes, dear, you were right."

"You're my witness that it does happen once in a while, Landon."

"I'm writing this down for you."

"Thank you. Now, tell me more about what's going on with Amanda."

"We're in the negotiation stage, I guess you might say."

"You're serious about her, then?" Hunter asked.

"I think I could be."

"You don't know for sure?"

"She's in kind of an odd place right now after the fire. She's determined to shake things up. I told her I'd help her, but I'm not really sure how that's going to play out for her long-term or how I fit into her plans."

"That sounds kind of risky for you," Hunter said, frowning.

Hunter's aversion to risk was well known within their family. As the chief financial officer for their many businesses, he avoided risk like the plague.

"I'll be careful. Don't worry." Landon glanced at the clock on the far wall and saw it was almost seven. He needed to get home so he could get some sleep and have time with Amanda before he had to work later.

"I will worry," Hunter said. "I don't want you crushed if she moves on without you."

The thought of that pained Landon. "I don't want that either. Don't worry. It's all good, for now, anyway. I'll tell Amanda to hit you up about the piano?"

"Sure."

Landon put three one-dollar bills on the desk next to the cash register to pay for the coffee. "Thanks again. You guys have a nice day."

"You, too," Megan called after him.

As he drove home, Landon thought about what Hunter had

said about looking out for himself in the midst of Amanda's second chance at life. It was a valid point, but he was determined to make a real effort with her. Perhaps if he took advantage of this opportunity to show her what was possible with him, her journey would lead her to him in the end.

He pulled into his driveway and glanced at the unassuming cabin. It'd been a wreck when he bought it. He'd made it into a home with a lot of time and effort, the same kind of time and effort he'd have to expend to make a go of it with Amanda. Knowing she was in his house made him almost giddy with anticipation as he gathered a fresh bundle of wood and then used his key in the door.

When he stepped inside, he was surprised to find Amanda standing at the stove, wearing one of his flannels over the tank and pajama pants she'd worn to bed.

"Hey," he said. "You're up early."

"I never really went back to sleep after you left."

He kicked off his boots and hung up his coat before crouching to tend to the woodstove. "How come?"

"You were going to fight a fire—my new biggest fear. Triggered some anxiety."

With the fire stoked, Landon stood, crossed the room and hugged her from behind, kissing her neck as he peeked around her to see that she was cooking eggs. "I'm okay."

"You smell like smoke."

"I know. Sorry. I'll go shower."

She covered the hand he'd flattened against her abdomen. "Stay."

He tightened his hold on her. "I'm here, and I'm fine."

"Did you go into the house while it was on fire?"

For a second, he thought about lying to calm her fears, but he didn't want to be dishonest with her. "I went in for the family's dog."

She shuddered. "I can't bear to think of you willingly walking into a fire."

"I do it all the time, sweetheart. I'm very well protected."

"So was Lucas, and he was nearly killed saving me."

"Nothing like that had ever happened to either of us in all the years we've been working for the department."

"Still, don't pretend it *can't* happen."

"I'd never deny that, but I can't have you losing sleep every time I get called out."

"I'm sorry. I don't mean to make it about me when you're the one who was in danger."

"You're still recovering from a very frightening experience. It's only natural that any thought of fire would trigger your fears. But I'm highly trained and very experienced. You really don't need to worry about me."

"And yet I did anyway."

"That's very sweet of you." He held her for a long time as she used a spatula to move the scrambled eggs around in the pan.

"I made extra for you."

"Thank you."

"We also have those chocolate chip muffins your sister Charley made."

"That's great, because I'm starving."

"You have to let go of me."

"Don't want to."

"Don't really want you to."

"Can I hold you some more after breakfast?"

When she nodded, he let her go, but not before the simple contact with her had him right back to where he'd been when he left her last night—dying for more of her, and that, right there, was how he knew she was different from every other woman he'd met since he lost Naomi.

CHAPTER TEN

*"We could never learn to be brave and patient
if there was only joy in the world."*
—Helen Keller

*A*manda had never been happier to see anyone than she
was to see Landon when he came in the door looking
tired and dirty and better than any man had a right to look.
She'd had a rough night since he left, tossing, turning, worrying,
reliving her own near miss until she finally gave up on sleep and
got up to watch TV for a few hours.

After breakfast, she did the dishes while he showered. He'd
declined the coffee she'd offered him, because he said he needed
to sleep at some point.

When he emerged from the bathroom, she was sitting on the
bed waiting for him. Her gaze traveled over his bare torso and
landed on the massive bruise on his wrist that she hadn't noticed
earlier. "What happened to your arm?"

"The dog wasn't interested in being rescued."

"He *bit* you?"

Landon stretched out on the bed next to her, propping his
head on his uninjured arm. "It's okay. He was scared."

Amanda took his other hand and ran her fingertips gently over the nasty bruise. "Does it hurt?"

"Not too bad. I was wearing thick gloves that protected my skin." He gave her hand a gentle tug. "Come here."

Amanda slid closer to him, sighing with relief when he tucked her in close to him. Despite his shower, a hint of smoke still lingered, mixed in with the appealing scents of body wash and shampoo. She tried not to focus overly much on the smoke.

"I don't want you to worry about me when I'm working."

"I'm kind of a hot mess since the fire, no pun intended."

Landon chuckled. "It'll take a while for you to get past that."

"What if I never do? What if I can't bear the thought of what you do for a living in light of what happened to me?"

"You'll be okay. The memories of that night will start to fade as you make new ones."

"Are you going to help me make new ones?" she asked in a teasing tone.

"I'd love to."

His quick, serious reply threw her. "Landon…"

"Shhh, get some sleep. I'm right here, and everything is okay."

Amanda took a deep breath and released it, trying to calm her fears and relax so she could get some badly needed rest. While he slept next to her, she dozed, dreaming of fire. She woke with a start when the phone rang.

Groaning, Landon rolled over to pick up the bedside extension. "Abbott." After a quiet second, he said, "Hey, Charl." He listened for a second. "Yeah, we can do that. Tell Dad we'll be there." Another pause. "Yes, she's here. Hang on." He handed the phone to Amanda. "My sister Charley for you."

Amanda wondered why his sister was asking to talk to her. "Hello?"

"Hi there. How're you feeling?"

"Much better, thanks."

"That's great. I wanted to tell you the girls are all getting together at my house tonight. We'd love to have you join us, if you'd like to come."

"Oh, sure. That'd be fun."

"Great, put Landon back on, and I'll tell him to bring you before his shift. One of the others will take you home after."

"Thanks for the invite."

"Of course. See you soon."

Amanda handed the phone to Landon. "She wants to talk to you."

He took the phone. "Yes, Charley, I'll bring her. Yes! Shut up. I'm hanging up now." The phone beeped when he ended the call. "Such a pain in my ass."

"What did she say?"

"To make sure I get you there, as if I couldn't do it without her saying that."

Amanda turned so she could see him and smiled at the scowl on his face. "I have a feeling you've given your sisters ample reason to be bossy with you."

"Maybe," he conceded, returning her smile.

"What did she say about your dad?"

"He's having an all-hands family meeting tomorrow at three and wanted to know if we can make it."

"What goes on at those meetings?"

"Could be anything, knowing him. We all have a small stake in the business, so he keeps us in the loop."

"It's cool that you're all part of it."

"My grandfather wanted all eighteen of his grandchildren to be part of the business, even if most of us aren't active in the running of it. Hunter, Will, Wade, Charley and Ella have bigger shares as managing partners with my dad, but the rest of us stay involved in a variety of ways. My contribution is the Christmas tree farm."

"Your family and the business fascinate me."

"We're positively fascinating," he said with a grin. "He asked if you could come, too. Hope it's okay that I said you'd be there."

"Of course. I know they're waiting on me to get back to work to train the staff on our product line."

"That ought to be an interesting day in the history of the family business." He glanced at her as he played with her hair. "Did you sleep?"

"I did."

"Do you feel better?"

"Sort of. I had weird dreams."

"What kind of dreams?"

"I was chasing you through a fire, trying to rescue you."

"You won't have to rescue me. I can take care of myself. I promise you don't have to worry about me."

"And yet…"

"It's kinda nice that you worry about me. That means you like me."

"Of course I like you. Why would I be in your house and your bed if I didn't like you?"

"Just checking."

"I can't believe you're still wondering about that."

"So we're on the same page?" he asked.

"I don't know. Are we?"

"If you want this, you and me, then yes, we're on the same page."

"And that's what you really want? When you could have anyone—"

He pounced, kissing the words right off her lips, wiping her brain clear of any thought that wasn't about more of him. "Any questions?" he asked much later.

Amanda emerged from the kiss to realize her arms were around him and he was more or less on top of her. "Um, no. No questions."

"Good."

"No, wait. I do have one question."

"What's that?"

"I told you how I want to shake things up."

"What about it?"

"It's okay if you'd rather put this on pause until I figure things out."

"The fire at the inn taught me something, too." He ran his fingers through her hair. "Right now is all there really is. We can make plans for the future, but my Gramps likes to say that plans have a way of making fools of us."

"I like that. It's so true."

"I understand where you're at and what I'm getting into. I want to help you get what you want, whatever that might turn out to be."

"You're very sweet."

He scoffed at that dreaded word. "Nah."

"Yeah."

"No." He kissed her again, softer this time, giving her tenderness rather than the heated passion of last night's kisses. "All I know is that I've wanted you, desperately, from the first time I ever laid eyes on you."

"Because I blew your mind talking about sex toys the way others talk about Tupperware?"

"No," he said, grinning. "But that didn't hurt anything. It was *you*. All you. You were so sexy and confident and pretty. So very pretty."

"I'm not confident, Landon. It may seem that way, but I'm really not."

"I say you are."

"I like the way I look to you."

"I like the way you look to me, too." He waggled his brows, proving he really was too adorable for words. "I like you. I've never wanted to go all in with anyone before. Not like this. You aren't going to let me down, are you?"

"I'm going to try not to."

"Tell me what you want." He dropped his head to her pillow, his hand on her face. "Tell me what you want so I can help you get it."

"I want adventure and meaningful work that I enjoy and love and good sex and babies and a *real* life." The words were out of her mouth before she took even a second to decide whether she should say such things to this particular man.

"Sweetheart, you've come to the right place for all of that."

"Have I?"

"Absolutely." He smoothed his thumb over her cheek as he seemed to devour her with his eyes. "I have a confession to make."

"What's that?" she asked, automatically wary of the many sins Landon Abbott might potentially confess to her.

"I read your notebook the other night."

Her mind raced as she tried to remember the things she'd written. "Oh, um, well…"

"I saw that one of your goals is to have an orgasm with a man."

Amanda groaned and covered her face with her hands. "You did *not* see that."

"I did." He tugged on her hand. "Come out and face the music."

"Absolutely not."

"Oh, come on. Don't be silly. How can I help you achieve your goal if you won't look at me?"

"I'll be moving out later today so I never have to look at you again."

Landon laughed and threw a heavy arm around her middle to keep her from getting out of the bed.

Mortified, she tried to scoot out from under his arm, but he wasn't having it. Instead, he held her tighter and kissed her cheek and neck. "How do you want it? Fingers? Tongue? Cock? You can have any or all of the above."

"I'm *dying*."

"How can the sex toy girl be embarrassed so easily?"

"This is different. That's work. This is…"

"This is the real life you want so badly, so don't die before we see to your goals." His lips were persistent on her neck while he cupped her breast and teased her nipple.

Another thought occurred to her that made her go tense all over.

"What?"

"This isn't why you suddenly brought me flowers or wanted to go out with me last night, is it? Because you want to be the man who, you know…"

"Makes you come?"

"Landon!"

"No," he said, shaking with silent laughter. "I wanted to go out with you again long before I read your very interesting list of goals. I was trying to give you space to recover after the fire, but the whole time, I was waiting for you to feel better so I could do this." He kissed her neck as he pinched her nipple between his fingers.

She gasped in shock when she suddenly felt his lips on her bare nipple and realized that while she'd been hiding, he'd been lifting her shirt to gain access.

She buried her hands in his hair, and he glanced up at her.

"You're back."

"Don't look at me."

"But I love to look at you." The tricky devil continued to move her T-shirt up until she moved to take it off. "Mmm, so pretty." His heated gaze traveled over her bare breasts.

Her impulse was to cover herself, but he anticipated that, pinning her arms over her head. "Is this okay?" He bent his head to lick and suck her other nipple.

"Yeah," she said on a gasp. She'd done this with other guys. Of course she had. So why was it so different when *he* did it? Why did it feel like every nerve ending in her body was attached to the nipple he was soothing with his tongue and warm, gentle pulls of his lips?

He kept it up, moving from one side to the other and back again, until she was about to come from that alone.

She pressed against him, trying to find relief for the pressure building between her legs.

He glanced up at her as her nipples tingled from the attention he'd given them. "Shall we continue toward your goal?"

Amanda looked at his handsome face and took only a second to think about it before she nodded. She was still embarrassed that he'd seen her list, but what did that matter when Landon Abbott seemed determined to make one of her most pressing goals come true?

"How do you want it?" He kissed a path to her belly button and dipped his tongue into the hollow indent.

She'd had no idea until then that her belly button could be an erogenous zone. "I, uh…"

"Do you need me to review the choices for you again?"

"No." She didn't need to hear that suggestive list again.

"So what's your choice?"

"This must be what it feels like to make a deal with the devil."

His big smile indicated that he took that as a compliment. He would.

"How would you like your devil to serve you, my sweet?"

"Surprise me."

"You really are walking on the wild side, I see. All righty, then. Close your eyes and focus only on what you feel. Nothing else but that." He hooked his fingers in the waistband of her pajama pants and quickly removed them and her panties. "And keep your hands up there and out of my way."

A full-body blast of heat overtook her as he used his broad shoulders to part her legs. As she tried to imagine what she must look like, naked and spread open before him… *No, don't think about that, just…* Oh *God…* Without giving her time to ease into whatever was about to happen here, he sent his tongue on a fact-finding mission that had her gasping and writhing and on the verge of explosive release faster than she'd ever gotten there before.

The man was clearly gifted if he could make that happen in a matter of seconds.

However, with his face buried between her legs, the last thing she wanted to think about was how he'd learned to…

Holy hell.

His fingers slid into her, curving up to find a spot deep inside that rendered her speechless.

"Ung."

"What's that?"

"I, uh…"

He sucked on her clit as he bent his fingers, and Amanda achieved one of her life goals with a screaming, full-body orgasm that made every other one she'd ever had seem like a warmup for him, so she'd be ready when Landon Abbott came along to show her what she'd been missing.

"Check that box." He sounded awfully pleased with himself, and really, why shouldn't he be if he was capable of *that*? "How about another just to prove that one wasn't a fluke?"

Before she could catch up to him, he'd gone back for more.

Holy shit. Be careful what you wish for, she thought as she held on for dear life to his headboard as he took her on an even wilder ride.

"How we doing?" he asked as she panted her way through the aftermath of her second man-made orgasm.

"Uh, well…"

Landon laughed at her babbling incoherence. "I'll take that as a thumbs-up?"

"Uh-huh."

"Hold that thought." While she tried to catch her breath, he went into the bathroom. She heard water running, and when he returned, he was completely naked and holding a foil packet. "More?" he asked, cocking an eyebrow as he stood next to the bed, fully confident and fully erect.

Amanda nodded. Maybe it was too soon and too much and too *everything*, but whatever. In her post-near-death-experience life, she was determined to live to the fullest, and having sex with Landon Abbott would definitely be worth any risk that might be involved.

"How's the ankle?"

"It's okay."

"And the rest of you?"

"Feeling good and hopefully about to be even better."

"You know it," he said with a wolfish grin as he rolled on the condom and rejoined her on the bed. "Is this too much too soon?"

She loved that he was having the same thought. "Absolutely."

Her emphatic reply seemed to take him aback. "We don't have to…"

"I know." She reached for him, and he came to her, wrapping his sexy body around her. "Before the fire, I would've said not yet. Now I know better. I know how fast things can change, and I want to experience everything right now."

"Everything?" he asked, raising a rakish brow.

"*Everything.*"

"That's a rather broad mandate."

The dirty way he said that made her giggle. "I've been such a fool up to now, taking the safe and expected path. I want to color outside the lines, have adventures and take some chances."

"And having sex with me does some of those things?"

"It does all of those things. You're an adventure worth taking a chance on."

"I'm glad you think so."

"Now, are you just going to talk, or are you going to help me color outside the lines?"

"Coloring outside the lines is my middle name, baby."

CHAPTER ELEVEN

"Our plans never turn out as tasty as reality."
—Ram Dass

*L*andon couldn't believe his good luck. Not only did he have sexy, beautiful Amanda naked in his bed, but she was looking for adventure. He loved a good adventure and was happy to oblige, even if a nagging doubt in the back of his mind had him wondering if he was taking advantage of her by indulging this particular request.

"You aren't going to come back to reality at some point and hate me for this, are you?"

"I could never hate you."

He thought about Chrissy and Jessica and other women who'd wanted to be the ones to change him, and the doubts intensified. "Yes, you could, and I'd never want that."

"I don't want to think about the future or the past or anything other than what's happening right in this moment." She ran her hands over his back and down to cup his ass, giving a gentle tug that told him exactly what she wanted from him. "And I like what's happening in this moment."

Was it possible she was maybe taking advantage of him

rather than the other way around? Yes, it was, but he could live with that. He'd wanted her for weeks, and with her offering herself to him, he wasn't about to say no. Maybe the fact that she'd had such a scare was causing her to be less cautious than she would've been before, but it was also a good reminder to him that he needed to seize the moment right along with her.

He had no way to know if he was starting something lasting with Amanda or serving as her second-chance fling. Did it matter?

Well, yeah, kinda... Other women had used him for sex, and he hadn't thought a thing of it. If *this* woman was using him to feed her adrenaline high, that'd be a huge bummer. However, as long as she was living in his house and sleeping in his bed, he had the chance to show her he could be much more than a fling.

Despite his concerns, he kissed her and touched her and lost himself in her.

"Now, Landon," she said, sounding breathless.

He'd done that to her... He'd made her breathless, and he was going to make her scream—again. As he pushed into her, he focused on one thing—lasting long enough to make it as good for her as it could possibly be. But that wasn't easy. He'd been wanting her for weeks, and now that it was finally happening, he struggled to maintain control, to keep it from ending too soon.

So he went slow. Giving her a taste before retreating. Rinse and repeat until she was clinging to him and moving with him and so caught up in the heat they created together that it didn't matter if he lost control during the best sex he'd ever had. As it was happening, he already knew that. And when he reached down to where they were joined to send her over the finish line, he was more than ready to go with her.

He came down on top of her as his heart raced while his body thrummed with satisfaction and pleasure. He'd wondered how his brothers could possibly settle for one woman in their beds for the rest of their lives. If this was what they had with their partners, then it was no wonder why they'd gone all in with the women in their lives. If it was always this way with Amanda, it would be more than enough for him to be happy forever.

But the nagging doubt remained. Did she feel the same way, or was he going to be a passing fling as she sought to fully live out her second chance? He wasn't sure, and the not knowing would surely drive him mad.

MUCH LATER, LANDON DROVE AMANDA UP A WINDING HILL TO Tyler and Charley's mountaintop retreat.

"This place is incredible," she said when the big house came into view.

"Tyler is a day trader. He's loaded, and he built this place before he met Charley, hoping he'd someday have a family to fill it with. Except, Charley has always said she doesn't want to get married or have kids."

"And he doesn't mind?"

"He's crazy about her. From what I've heard, he said he'd rather have her than a dozen kids with someone else."

"That's very sweet."

"He's a nice guy, and we like her a whole lot better since she's been with him. We call him the Charley Tamer."

"Does she know that?"

"Oh God, no. She'd beat the shit out of us if she heard that."

Amanda laughed at the look of pure fright on his face. "And she's capable of beating the shit out of you?"

"She fights *really* dirty."

"I suppose she'd have to with seven brothers."

He scoffed. "She's lucky to have us."

"I'm sure she feels very lucky."

He pulled up to the house and got out to help her, lifting her from the truck and settling her on the blacktop as he eyed the house with trepidation. "Don't let them say or do anything to give you second thoughts about me."

"They wouldn't do that."

He huffed out a laugh. "Yes, they would."

"Don't worry. I'm not easily scared off."

"I hope not." He looked down at her, impossibly handsome and adorably sincere. "Today was fucking awesome."

"Yes, it was."

"I wish I didn't have to work the next few nights."

"How come?"

He gave her a withering look. "You know why. I have much better things to do than work."

"I'll still be there in the morning."

"You promise?"

She smiled up at him as she nodded. "Have a good night at work."

"Have fun with the vipers known as my sisters."

"Be nice. They're not vipers."

"I'll kill them if they do anything to turn you off of me."

"You helped me achieve one of my major life goals today—five times over. It's going to take an awful lot to turn me off you."

His face lit up with the smug, arrogant grin she was growing to love. "Is that right?"

"That's right. Now go to work and don't worry about me." She went up on tiptoes to kiss him. "All is well."

"Landon!" Charley called from the door inside the garage. "Put it on ice, and let her come in!"

Glaring in the direction of his sister's voice, he offered an arm to Amanda to escort her inside. "Make sure someone walks you to the car. I don't want you to fall."

"Yes, dear."

"I mean it."

"I'll be careful. Don't worry. I have no desire to extend my recovery. I've got things I want to do that require a working ankle."

Charley met them at the door and opened it. "Say goodbye, Landon. You're not invited to this party."

"I'll call you later." He kissed Amanda's cheek. "Have fun, and don't make eye contact with Charley. She's feral."

"Haha." Charley extended her arm to Amanda to help her up the small flight of stairs. "Now go away." Once Amanda cleared the doorway, Charley shut the inside door. "What've you done to him? He's like a lovesick puppy."

"Is he?"

"For real. Never seen him like that."

Amanda was secretly pleased to hear that, but mindful of Landon's warnings about his sisters, she just shrugged. "Not sure." She handed over her coat to Charley, who held Amanda's arm while Amanda removed her shoes. "Sorry to come empty-handed."

"Don't worry about it. The others brought enough for an army. Come in." Charley led the way through her spacious, modern kitchen into a family room where a roaring fire had been lit in the massive fireplace.

Amanda eyed the fire warily, but before she could fixate on it, Dani came over to hug her.

"Glad you could come," Dani said. "I've been instructed to drive you home whenever you want to go."

"Instructed by who?"

"Landon called Lucas and asked if I'd bring you home."

"Ah, I see. That must've happened while I was in the shower." She thought it was sweet of him to make sure she had a ride home. "Where's Savannah?"

"With Lucas. He insisted he felt well enough to sit at home with a sleeping baby."

"I'm so thankful he's doing better."

"We're thankful you both are."

Hannah, Ella, Cameron, Lucy and Megan came over to say hello, each of them hugging her and making her feel welcome.

She was helped into a chair and told to put her foot up on the ottoman. "I feel like Cinderella after the ball."

"Only around here, the magic slipper is a boot," Cameron said. Her long blond hair was captured in a messy bun, her hand flat against her pregnant belly. She looked ready to pop at any time.

The women settled around a table laden with snacks and desserts. Charley filled a plate for Amanda and brought it to her.

"Thank you."

"What can I get you to drink?" Charley asked, her eyes warm and friendly, making Amanda think Landon exaggerated about her ferociousness.

"Some white wine if you have it would be great."

"Do we have white wine, ladies?"

"Hell yes," Hannah said. "And there's plenty to go around since most of us are preggo."

"We were wondering when you were going to fess up, Han," Ella said. With dark shiny hair and brown eyes, Ella resembled her older sister, Hannah.

"Guilty as charged and couldn't be happier about it, although Nolan and I wanted to keep it a secret for now until the dreaded first trimester is over."

"We're thrilled for you and Nolan," Ella said as the others extended congratulations to Hannah on news they'd figured out for themselves some time ago. "And we won't say anything. Don't worry."

"Did you guys hear we might get *more* snow this weekend?" Lucy asked as she captured her red hair into a ponytail.

"Ugh," Megan said. "Enough already."

"We start getting stir crazy around this time," Hannah said for Amanda's benefit. "Winter in Vermont goes on *forever* some years."

"Sorry I'm late," Emma said as she came in. "Grayson gave me perfect directions, and I still managed to get lost."

"You haven't missed anything," Charley said. "Amanda just got here, and we haven't even grilled her about Landon yet."

"Oh good. I want to hear that." Emma smiled at Amanda. "We've all had our turn in the hot seat. Looks like it's yours now."

"Lovely," Amanda said, amused by them.

"*Soooo*," Cameron said, batting her eyelashes, "how's Landon?"

"He's fine." Why should she make it easy for them?

Lucy tag-teamed off to Cameron. "And you guys are…" Lucy rolled her hand, hoping Amanda would fill in the blanks for them.

Amanda knitted her eyebrows, hoping she was conveying that she didn't understand the question.

"They want to know if you're doing it or not," Charley said.

Ella pounced. "*Charley!* Don't ask her that!"

"Why not? Everyone was asking me when I was staying with Tyler after I fell off the mountain."

"What was it like to fall off a mountain?" Amanda asked.

"Painful. He challenged me to run during a snowstorm, and I ended up at the bottom of a steep drop. I screwed up my knee, had to have surgery, and since my parents were away at the time, Tyler insisted on nursing me back to health."

"Because he had the only one-story house," Hannah added, rolling her eyes.

"You have to give him credit for overruling the entire Abbott family to get his way," Charley said.

"He was very determined, as I recall," Lucy said.

"He was," Charley said, her smile fading.

"What's wrong, Charl?" Hannah asked.

"I think he's going to ask me to marry him. Like, for real ask me."

"Oh damn," Ella said. "Why do you say that?"

"Just a vibe I'm picking up on."

"You don't want to marry him?" Dani asked.

Charley glanced at Ella, seeming pained.

"Charley has always said she doesn't want to get married or have kids," Ella said. "She was very honest from the beginning about that with Tyler."

Charley moaned. "I love him so much. More than anything. But I still have no desire to be married. Why can't we continue as we are, both of us here by choice, not because a piece of paper says we have to be?"

"You should tell him that," Amanda said, hoping she wasn't overstepping as the new girl. "Remind him again that you still feel the same way you always did and say what you just did to us, about how it's more important for both of you to be there because you want to be, not because you're legally required to be."

"I don't want to hurt him," Charley said softly. "He's the best thing that's ever happened to me."

"Tell him that, too," Dani said. "That'll matter to him."

Charley wiped away a tear. "The new girls are pretty smart." She waved her hand. "Let's go back to grilling Amanda. That was better than me spilling my guts. She never did tell us if they're doing it."

"And she doesn't have to," Ella said with a pointed look for her sister.

"We're... enjoying each other's company." Amanda chose her words carefully out of respect for Landon's privacy in the hornet's nest that was his family.

"Landon doesn't do serious," Charley said tentatively. "You know that, right?"

"He might be changing his mind on that," Hannah said as she dipped a carrot into ranch dip and popped it into her mouth.

Again, Ella pounced. "What do you know?"

"Nothing," Hannah said, her gaze shifting to the left. "I'm just saying—"

"You did that thing you do with your eyes when you're lying," Ella said. "Did you see it, Charl?"

"I did, so spill it, Hannah, and don't leave anything out."

"Ugh, I hate having sisters," Hannah said.

"You love us," Ella said. "Now tell us what you know, because I'd hate to have to beat it out of you."

"As if you could," Hannah said disdainfully.

"Um, do I need to remind you of all the times we beat you up back in the day?" Charley asked.

"You did *not* beat me up."

"Uh, El, want to help me out here?"

"We absolutely did beat you up every time Mom put you in charge of us."

Hannah rolled her eyes. "I let you."

"What*ever*!" Charley howled with laughter. "Now tell us what you know about Landon right now."

Hannah gave a tentative glance in Amanda's direction.

"Speak freely," Amanda said. "I'm dying to know, too."

"I'll only say that I happen to know, for a fact, he's not messing around with you. He really likes you."

"I already knew that," Amanda said, smiling. "What else have you got?"

"That's it."

"So you guys are, like, together?" Megan asked.

"We're taking it a day at a time for now and not putting labels on it."

"He came by the diner and asked if Hunter would give you piano lessons."

That news surprised Amanda and touched her deeply. "He did? He didn't tell me that."

"He said you're all about trying new things now that you've got a second chance at life, and you've always wanted to learn to play the piano."

Amanda was moved nearly to tears by his sweetness "That's true. I did say that. It's very nice of him to arrange that for me."

"Come to our house for dinner one night this week. You can sit with Hunter for a bit."

"Thank you, but Landon is working the next few nights."

"I'll drive you. No worries. Let me talk to Hunter, and I'll let you guys know what night works."

"Thank you."

"What other new things are you looking to do besides learn the piano, Amanda?" Cameron asked.

"I'd like to learn to ski, drive a stick, zip-line, travel to Europe and figure out a real career for myself, among other things."

"You don't have a real career now?" Lucy asked.

"It's more of a job than an actual career. I dropped out of college after two years of majoring in marketing, and when I couldn't find a job, my mom offered me a temporary job working on her sales team. Eight years later, I'm still doing that."

"What do you think you might like to do?" Hannah asked.

"I don't want to dominate the conversation," Amanda said.

"Don't worry about that," Charley said. "We thrive on fresh meat."

"I take it I'm the fresh meat?" Amanda asked, amused.

"We've all been through it." Emma affected a comically grave expression. "It's best to just give the hungry beasts what they want and get it over with."

The others lost it laughing.

"I'd be offended if she wasn't absolutely right," Ella said.

"The Abbotts and Colemans can be a tough crowd, but I've found them to be worth the effort," Megan said.

"Same," Cameron said.

"Yep," Lucy said.

"Agreed," Emma said.

"That's certainly been my experience so far," Dani added.

"I don't really know what I want to do," Amanda said, "but it might be something to do with writing and telling stories. I'm fascinated by people and what makes them tick. For instance, I could write for days about what's gone on in this living room since I arrived." While the others laughed, she continued. "I've met so many interesting people through my work, and I always want to know more about them, but there never seems to be enough time to dig into their stories the way I'd like to. That interests me."

Lucy glanced at Cameron. "Are you thinking what I'm thinking?"

"I'm thinking exactly what you're thinking."

"Can one of you clue in the rest of us?" Hannah asked.

"We've been talking about how we might personalize the catalog with more stories about the people who work for the company, like Mildred Olsen and Elmer, to start with," Cameron said. For Amanda's benefit, she said, "As you know, Elmer's parents started the business, and Mildred is in her nineties and is the company's longest-tenured employee."

"I'd love to write those stories, but I've never really done anything like that before, although I have written catalog copy— tons of it, actually."

"Tell you what," Lucy said. "How about you give it a whirl with those two, and if we don't think they add quality to the catalog, we reserve the right to say so?"

"That'd be amazing!" Amanda said, thrilled and overwhelmed.

"Good, then you're hired," Cameron said.

"Thank you so much!" Amanda couldn't recall the last time a professional challenge interested her as much as this one did.

"Thank you for offering," Lucy said. "Since we had this brilliant idea, we've been trying to figure out how to implement it. We'll get in touch with you tomorrow to coordinate times."

"Now that you guys have concluded this staff meeting," Ella said, "I want to know what else is on Amanda's list of things to do with her second chance."

"And I want to know what would be on *your* list if you were me," Amanda said. "What would going wild look like to you, or what would you do if you could do anything you wanted?"

CHAPTER TWELVE

"If I can create the minimum of my plans and desires,
there shall be no regrets."
—Bessie Coleman

The other women appeared to give Amanda's question some considerable thought.

"If I had everything to do over," Hannah said, "I might've made a run at acting."

"Really?" Ella asked. "I've never heard you say that before."

"I used to love being in school plays and thought for a while I might do something with that, but then Caleb and I got married, and one thing led to another, and here I am at thirty-seven, remarried with a baby, another on the way, and it's not something I think much about anymore. What about you guys? What would you do?"

"I would've had more sex," Cameron said bluntly.

"Do tell," Ella said, smiling.

"I was always somewhat timid in that regard, and I wonder now why I was like that. What would it matter if I'd had safe sex with more guys?"

"It wouldn't have mattered," Megan said. "I agree with you.

More is more in that regard." She glanced at Amanda. "I hope you don't think we're suggesting you run around and do it with every guy you meet."

Amanda laughed. "I know what you mean, and I hear what you're saying. It's all about living life to the fullest, however that may be for you."

"Exactly," Cameron said. "And believe me, I don't sit around pining for the old days when I woulda, coulda, shoulda with guys I used to know. I am more than satisfied in that regard with Will."

"Ew," Charley said. "Stop right there."

"Me, too," Megan said. "With Hunter."

"Same," Emma said. "Grayson."

"I can't with you people," Charley said, making a disgusted face.

"Count me in—with Lucas," Dani said, sticking her tongue out at Charley, who groaned and covered her ears.

"So besides all the sex," Amanda said, smiling, "what else do you guys wish you'd done or still want to do?"

"I have no regrets about anything," Emma said. "I have my daughter, and now we have Gray, and I love our life here. I don't sit around wishing for anything other than exactly what I have right now."

"That's very sweet," Amanda said. "It must be so comforting to feel you're exactly where you belong."

"It is. I went through a lot of years of uncertainty and difficulty to get where I am now, so maybe that helps me to know a good thing when I have it."

"I agree with my sister," Lucy said. "After I met Colton, things just seemed to fall into place for me in all aspects of my life. That's not to say I wasn't fine before him, but I'm so much better *with* him than I was by myself."

Megan nodded in agreement. "I feel the same way, although I wasn't as 'fine' before Hunter as you were before Colton. I was kind of spinning, trying to figure myself out, and Hunter definitely helped me to get to what mattered to me. He encouraged me to pursue my desire to write novels, and I'm working on my first one now."

"I love that," Amanda said. "That's exactly the kind of thing I'm talking about. What is it that I've always wanted to do, and how do I make that happen? The lesson I've learned is that the future is right now. Don't put off the things you want to do, or you might never do them."

"I think it's so cool that you're reevaluating everything after the fire," Ella said. "A lot of people would've curled up into a ball after something like that."

"I did that for the first few days, but since then, I'm trying to stay focused on making some changes."

"I can't help but ask," Hannah said tentatively, "how our brother fits into that."

"He's agreed to be my partner in crime," Amanda replied.

"For now or… Well…" Hannah shook her head. "I'm sorry. I don't mean to pry, but I don't get the feeling from him that he's looking for a temporary adventure. I think he might be ready for more than that."

"We've talked about it, and we've agreed to take it a day at a time and see what happens."

"Fair enough," Hannah said. "He's my baby brother. I guess I'm a little protective."

"I totally understand."

"Where's Mia tonight?" Emma asked.

"In Boston for some wedding stuff," Cameron said. "I can't believe the wedding is already next weekend."

"That's going to be so much fun," Ella said. "I can't wait for all of us to get on that bus Dad rented. Can you even imagine?"

"Nope," Charley said. "I can't."

"What's the plan for that?" Dani asked. "Lucas told me about it before the fire, but I haven't heard the details."

"We leave next Friday around noon," Ella said. "The rehearsal and rehearsal dinner are Friday night, and the wedding is on Saturday afternoon."

"Landon asked me to go, but I have nothing to wear," Amanda said. "I lost everything in the fire."

"I can help with that if you don't get a chance to shop," Hannah said. "We're about the same size. My closet is your closet."

"That's very nice of you. Thanks."

"No problem."

By the time Amanda left with Dani a couple of hours later, she felt like she'd acquired a whole group of new girlfriends— more friends than she'd ever had in her life, a thought she shared with Dani.

"I know what you mean," Dani said. "I feel the same way. I have some good friends at home, but this group is something else altogether. They're all so accomplished and smart and so generous. I love being around them."

"I do, too. That was a lot of fun tonight."

"It was."

"How's Lucas feeling today?"

"A little better every day. My biggest challenge is keeping him from doing too much too soon. He's not taking well to convalescence."

"He's used to being very active."

"Right, but I keep reminding him that this is temporary, and if he doesn't chill, it'll take even longer."

"That's true."

"So things are good with Landon?"

Amanda smiled at the memory of the hours they'd spent in bed earlier. "Things are good. Yes."

"I love that. He's been so great since the fire, checking on us and bringing food and running himself ragged to cover his work and Lucas's. I've become a big fan of my fiancé's twin brother."

"I'm a big fan of his, too. He's done the same for me."

"They're both really good guys."

"Yes." Amanda thought for a second, trying to decide how much she should say to Dani. "Could I ask you something, just between us?"

"Of course."

"Does it bother you that Lucas was super popular with women before he met you?" And then she thought better of it. "I mean, you knew that, right?"

Dani laughed. "I knew, and it doesn't surprise me. I mean, look at the two of them, right?"

"Right."

"But it's more than just how handsome and sexy they are— and I mean that platonically where Landon is concerned."

Amanda laughed. "I gotcha."

"It's how good and kind and sweet they are, too. Those things matter more to me than how Lucas looks. He was so incredible to me and Savannah from the very beginning. When he found us in that ditch, he took such good care of us. That impressed me more than anything. I think I fell a tiny bit in love with him that first night."

"I had the same reaction to Landon the first night we went out."

"But not to Lucas?"

Amanda groaned. "I *love* Lucas. I did even before the fire, but for whatever reason, it's just different with Landon, and I know how bonkers that must sound."

"No, I get it. When I look at Lucas, I see so many things that aren't there when I'm talking to Landon. He's become a very good friend, but that's all it'll ever be."

"I find it fascinating that we can have such opposing reactions to identical twins."

"Well, they are two different people, even if they look exactly the same."

"That's true. Did you think Hannah seemed a little annoyed about me seeing Landon when I'm going through this life shakeup?"

"I'm not sure I'd call it annoyed so much as concerned. From what I've seen, the Abbotts love to bicker and push each other's buttons, but when it comes right down to it, they'd take a bullet for each other."

"What must it be like to be part of a family like that?"

"Yours isn't close?"

Amanda shook her head. "I have two much older siblings. I haven't seen them in years."

"Do you talk to them?"

"An occasional text or email, but we're not close. Not like the Abbotts are. What about you?"

"I'm a one and only, but I have a best friend named Leslie who grew up next door to me who's like a sister."

"It's good that you have her."

"For sure. When I lost Jack, Savannah's father, Les was the one who saved me. Others were there and tried to help, but she was the only one I wanted."

"I'm so sorry you lost him."

"Thanks. I think of him every day, and I see him in Savannah all the time. She smiles like he did."

"I give you credit for surviving that."

"I didn't have any choice. I had a child to think about. I thank God for her all the time. She's the one who truly saved me. Before she arrived, I didn't think I was going to survive it, but she gave me a purpose and a reason to get out of bed in the morning."

With some directional help from Amanda, Dani pulled into Landon's driveway.

"Could I ask you something, Dani? And will you promise not to tell anyone I asked?"

Dani put the car in Park. "Of course. Anything you want."

"Is the assistant manager position at the warehouse still open?"

"It is. We've had a lot of applicants, but no one who's truly qualified yet."

"I might be interested."

"You'd probably be *over*qualified."

"Maybe, but I'm looking to simplify my life, get off the travel bandwagon and put down some roots. I like it here, and I'd love to work for the Abbotts. I don't have warehouse experience, but I know retail, and I think I could be an asset to you."

"I'm sure Linc would go for it. I can ask him if you'd like."

"Hold that thought for a short time, if you would. I need to figure out a few things before I decide for sure."

"No problem. Keep me posted. We're looking to have someone in the job by mid-August."

"That timing would be ideal. Let me get back to you, and keep it between us for now?"

"Will do. You know where to find me when you're ready." Dani got out of the car to help Amanda up the stairs to the porch.

"Like Lucas, I'm looking forward to being back to normal so I won't need help for the simplest things."

"I'll tell you the same thing I say to him—chill out and relax while you can."

"Yes, ma'am. Thanks for the ride and the info about the job."

"My pleasure. Are you guys going to Sunday dinner?"

Landon hadn't mentioned it to her, but he probably would. "I suppose we are."

"Great, see you then." Dani waited until Amanda had slowly made her way inside the house, using the key Landon had given her, before she drove off.

Amanda went straight for the woodstove and used the wood Landon had brought in before he left for work to stoke the fire. She couldn't believe how chilly it still was in the mountains in early June.

She'd changed into pajamas and one of Landon's warm flannel shirts when the phone rang. The caller ID said BUTLER VOL FD, so she took the call. "Hey."

"Hi there. I wondered if you'd be home yet."

"Just got here about fifteen minutes ago. Thank you for arranging my ride with Dani."

"No problem. Did you have fun with the girls?"

"So much fun. My stomach hurts from laughing."

"That sounds about right."

"Megan told me you also arranged for piano lessons for me."

"I meant to tell you that, but I got distracted earlier."

She smiled at how he described their afternoon in bed. "Is that right?"

"Oh yeah. Very distracted. I hope it's okay I asked Hunter about teaching you."

"It's very sweet of you. So far, you're being an awesome partner in crime."

"Glad you think so."

"Megan invited me to dinner one night this week and said Hunter could show me some of the basics while I'm there."

"If it's a night I'm working, I can go with you as long as I have a radio with me."

"Really? That'd be awesome."

"Sure, we can make that happen. I have to tell you… Normally, I like working nights, but not so much this week."

"And why is that?"

"Gee, I wonder. Could it be the smoking-hot woman who's sleeping in my bed?"

"I thought we were exclusive. What's her name?"

"Haha, you know her well, in fact."

"Not really, but I'm working on getting to know her better. You'll never guess what happened tonight."

He groaned. "I'm not sure I want to hear this."

Amanda laughed. "You'll like it. I mentioned how I want to do more writing about people and their stories. Cameron and Lucy hired me to write some profiles for the catalog, starting with Mildred Olsen and your grandfather."

"That's great, Amanda. Good for you."

"I'm super excited about it. I've got experience writing

catalog copy, and for years, I've been trying to talk my mom and the management team into doing more profiles of how people are using our products for our catalog. But they feel that people would be too embarrassed to discuss our products that way. Writing about your family's business and the people who run it will be so much fun."

"Look at you, shaking things up. I'm happy for you."

"Thanks. I'm looking forward to it." After a pause, she added, "Today was a really good day."

"For me, too. I like hearing you sound happy."

"It feels good to be making some changes that get me closer to where I want to be. Also, Hannah offered to loan me a dress for the wedding if you still want me to go with you." He'd asked her before the fire, but they hadn't talked about it again since.

"Of course I want you to go. I have to take a run to Montpelier at some point in the next few days to pick up the ring Lucas bought for Dani. You can come with me and go shopping if you'd rather have something new."

"That sounds fun."

"We'll do that. Tomorrow or the next day. Whenever you want."

"Okay."

An alarm sounded in the background on his end. "We're getting a call. Got to run."

"Be safe."

"I will. Don't worry. I'll see you in the morning."

"I'll be here."

"You'd better be. I want you to do something wild."

"What's that?"

"Sleep naked."

"I can't do that! I'll freeze."

"No, you won't. The down comforter on my bed will keep you nice and toasty. Come on. You want to walk on the wild side, right?"

"I do."

"Then I want to think about you naked in my bed waiting for me to get home in the morning."

"Fine."

"You'll do it?"

"I'll do it."

"That's my wild girl. See you, all of you, in the morning."

When the phone went dead, Amanda smiled and hobbled over to put the portable phone back on the charger. Before she'd come to Vermont, she hadn't seen a phone like that since she was growing up at home in Missouri. It still boggled her mind that people in Butler lived without cell phones because there was no reception in their town. That had been the biggest adjustment to being there for her as a cell-phone-addicted kind of girl.

She realized she hadn't checked her phone in hours. What was the point when you had no reception? She dug it out of her purse and took it with her to bed, logging on to Landon's Wi-Fi so she could get her texts and email. But before she got into bed, she recalled his instructions and tossed her phone on the bed while she removed her clothes and snuggled under the comforter.

With her teeth chattering, she questioned the wisdom of dancing on the wild side when it was still cold in Vermont. She sent an arm outside the cocoon to find the phone and brought it under the covers to check her messages and emails while Landon's soft flannel sheets brushed against her hard nipples.

"The man is a devil," she said, wishing he was there to keep her warm.

She'd received a message from her mother asking her to choose the trade shows she wished to attend that summer so they could set the schedule. Amanda scrolled through the dates and locations—New York City, Los Angeles, Seattle, Chicago, Austin, San Antonio, Phoenix, Charlotte, Baltimore. In a usual summer, she attended up to seven trade shows. As she scrolled through the options, she only felt dread.

The last thing in the world she wanted to do was attend yet another trade show in yet another city where she wouldn't get to see anything other than the inside of a hotel or convention center.

As she closed her email, she realized she was going to have to have a conversation with her mother before too much longer. Because she worked so much and lived out of suitcases, she'd managed to save quite a bit of money over the years, especially since she'd made the decision three years ago to give up the apartment she used to have in Chicago.

She had the ability to take some time to figure out her next move—and to take the trip to Europe she'd been saying for years she was going to take "one of these summers." That was going to happen *this* summer. Before she could chicken out or come up with a thousand different reasons not to do something she'd always wanted to do, she logged on to the travel site they used for work and bought a one-way ticket to Paris for early next month.

When her phone dinged with a confirmation email that contained her itinerary, a feeling of pure joy overcame her as she put down the phone and snuggled in to sleep.

If this was what going wild felt like, she couldn't wait to see what tomorrow would bring.

CHAPTER THIRTEEN

"A journey is a person in itself; no two are alike.
And all plans, safeguards, policing, and coercion are fruitless.
We find after years of struggle
that we do not take a trip; a trip takes us."
—John Steinbeck

*A*fter everyone left, Hannah stuck around to help Charley finish cleaning up.

"You don't have to stay," Charley said. "I can do it."

"I don't mind, and I wanted the chance to talk to you."

"About?"

"What's going on with Tyler." Hannah picked up a towel and began to dry the dishes that Charley was washing.

"Everything is fine with him. I don't want you to think otherwise."

"I don't. I see you guys together. I can tell you're both happy."

"We are."

"So why do you think he's about to upset the applecart?"

"I don't know. It's just a feeling I have."

"Let me ask you something… Would being married to him really be so awful?"

"No! Not at all. I want to spend the rest of my life with him. I have no question in my mind about that. I just don't get why we have to make it official and legal to do that. I love the idea of us being together because we *want* to be, not because we're legally bound to each other. I know that's hard for you to understand after having been married twice."

"Not so hard. I get where you're coming from. It means something to you that both of you are here only because you want to be, not because you have to be."

"Yes, that," Charley said, sighing. "I know it's an unconventional philosophy, especially in a family like ours that's all about marriage and kids. I've just never wanted that for myself, and being in love with Tyler hasn't changed my mind about any of it."

"You need to make sure he understands that."

"I know, but the thought of revisiting that subject makes my stomach hurt. I want him to be happy, too, and part of me thinks if it really means that much to him, I'd go along with it. That's how much I love him."

"You shouldn't sacrifice something that's important to you to make someone else happy. That doesn't work long-term."

"What if I'm all wrong about this, and I end up screwing up the best thing to ever happen to me?"

"It's not wrong to be true to yourself, Charley. You can't lose yourself in the process of making someone else happy."

"How did you get so wise about these things?"

"I'm wise about everything. You should know that by now."

Charley rolled her eyes and laughed. "Jeez, I walked right into that trap."

Hannah laughed and then hugged her sister. "You don't need to worry about screwing things up with Tyler. That man is wild about you."

"Yes, he is," Tyler said from the doorway, startling them.

"Hey." Charley released Hannah and turned to him. "I didn't hear the door." On a quick glance, Charley noticed his dark, wavy hair was messy from the knit hat he'd removed, and his blue eyes looked bluer than usual. He was wearing contacts more often these days, and she was still getting used to him without the glasses he usually wore. What had he heard them say?

"I gathered that," he said. "Did you ladies have a nice time?"

"We did, as always," Hannah said. "But I'm going to head home to see if Nolan succeeded in putting Callie to bed." She kissed Charley and Tyler on her way out. "Talk to you tomorrow."

"Thanks for the cleanup help, Han."

"Any time."

After the door closed behind Hannah, Charley took a tentative look at Tyler. "I'm not sure what you overheard."

"Just your sister saying I'm wild about you, which I am, but I'm wondering why she felt the need to remind you of that." He came to her, placed his hands on her face, compelling her to look up at him. "What's going on inside that head of yours, Charlotte?"

Determined to be honest with him, Charley swallowed her fears. "I, uh, I've been picking up on a vibe."

"What kind of vibe?"

"I might be wrong…"

"You won't know for sure unless you tell me about it."

She swallowed hard. "I've gotten the feeling over the last couple of weeks that you might be thinking about what's next for us, and I'm sort of concerned about that."

"Ah, damn, Char. I'm really sorry you were worried. I've been working on a little surprise for you, but it's not what you think."

"Oh. Really?"

"Yeah." He took her by the hand. "Come on. Let's get comfy, and I'll tell you about it."

As they got ready for bed the same way they always did, side by side in the huge master bathroom, Charley tried to think about what kind of surprise he might have in store for her. She liked to stay one step ahead of the people in her life, but Tyler was the exception to that rule. He could be harder to read than some of the other people she knew, and that, in turn, made him endlessly interesting to her.

There were times, such as this, that she couldn't believe she'd once found him boring. She'd not been bored once since she got to know him better and realized that under his quiet, unassuming exterior was a deeply intelligent, passionate, fascinating man whom she loved with all her heart.

Falling off a cliff had turned out to be the best thing to ever happen to her, because it had given her the chance to really know the man who'd insisted on caring for her after the accident—and every day since then.

He got in bed after her, bringing a small gift bag that he handed to her. "Half that gift is for me, so don't get too excited."

"What's the occasion?"

"Do we need an occasion for me to give you a gift?"

"No, but I don't have anything for you."

"Yes, you do."

"I do?"

"Uh-huh. Open that, and I'll tell you."

Charley fished out a velvet jeweler's box from the tissue paper and glanced at him before she opened it. "Oh, Tyler… What…" Inside were two rings, one bigger than the other. The smaller of the two was all diamonds that glittered in the glow from the bedside lamp.

He took the smaller of the two and held it up for her to get a better look at it. "Do you like it?"

"It's beautiful," she said, fighting a feeling of dread. "But I don't want—"

He touched a finger to her lips to stop her. "I know, sweetheart. I heard you from the beginning when you said you don't want to get married, but I want everyone else in the world to know you're taken." He slid it onto the ring finger of her left hand and then held up her hand to see how it looked.

Charley couldn't contain the tears that filled her eyes. "This might be the sweetest thing you've ever done."

"Now you have to put mine on me."

She took the second ring from the box and slid it onto his left hand. "I love you, Tyler. Thank you for not trying to change me."

"Why would I try to change you when I love you just the way you are?"

Charley leaned in to kiss him. "That, right there, is really the sweetest gift you've ever given me. I never imagined I'd find someone who loves me despite all my rough edges."

"I love your rough edges as much as your smooth curves." His hand landed on her ass and gave a gentle tug to bring her closer to him.

"I thought you were going to propose."

"I'd never do that to you."

She smiled at the mildly offended expression on his adorably handsome face. "I should've known better."

"Yes, you should have. But the rings... They're okay?"

"They're better than okay. They're amazing symbols that we're together by choice."

"Together *forever* by choice."

She nodded as she kissed him. "Could I ask you something?"

"Anything you want."

"Does it ever bother you that we're not going to get married or have kids?"

"Nope."

"Do you mean that? Really?"

"I mean it. It doesn't bother me because you were honest with me about what you wanted—and didn't want—from the beginning. I haven't spent all this time with you hoping I was going to change your mind about something so important to you."

"I'm not sure why I feel the way I do about those things. I only know that it's always been that way for me."

"So you've said from the beginning. I get it. I get you, sweetheart. I love you. Only you. Forever."

"I love you, too. Only you. Forever."

He kissed her and held her close. "How about we consummate this non-marriage of ours?"

"Yes, please."

LANDON LEFT WORK THE SECOND THE CLOCK HIT SEVEN THE NEXT morning, eager to get home to Amanda. Thinking about her warm and naked in his bed had made for a long night at the fire station as he'd tossed and turned and had weird dreams about chasing someone who refused to be caught. Was that a metaphor for his situation with Amanda? He had no idea. All he cared about was getting to her as quickly as possible.

Even as he told himself to slow down, to take it easy and not go all in until she figured out her life plan, he realized on the ride home that it was probably already too late to be warning himself about her.

He was already all in with her and had been for quite some time, if he was being honest. Because of what he'd once felt for Naomi, he recognized the signs. First of all, he was incredibly attracted to her. Second, he wanted to spend as much time with her as he possibly could. Third, he was completely on board with supporting her through this period of change in her life, wherever it might lead. Finally, he might be willing to upend his own existence if it meant having more of her.

That last one was the most interesting of all to him. He loved his life in Butler, enjoyed his work with the fire department and at the tree farm. He liked having his big family all around him and being able to see them whenever he wanted to. Landon wasn't looking to shake up anything. His life was fine the way it was, so going all in with a woman who was looking to shake up everything was a huge risk for him and one he was taking while being fully aware of the many ways it could go wrong for him.

He didn't care if it went wrong. Not when she was naked in his bed, living in his house and wanting him to be her partner in crime. Wild horses couldn't keep him from her, but apparently, Fred could. After spotting the moose standing in the roadway, Landon slammed on his brakes, the truck fishtailing for a second in the mud on the road before coming to a halt about six feet from Fred.

Landon put down the window. "Move along, Fred. I've got somewhere *important* to be. Naked, sexy woman, warm and cozy in my bed! Let's go!"

Fred let out a loud moo but otherwise seemed unaffected by Landon's request.

"Maybe if you had a naked woman in your bed, you might be a little less ornery." Fred had no reply to that. "Why would you want to stand in the middle of the road when you could run through the woods with no fear of getting hit by a car or truck?"

Fred shot him a look that could only be called disdainful.

"I can't believe I'm having an actual conversation with a moose." Landon laid on the horn, which only earned him another perturbed look. "Come on, dude. Be a pal, would you? I've got the most awesome woman sleeping in my bed, and I just want to get home to her. Would you *please* move?"

Fred let out another loud moo and began to move forward, slowly working his way toward the brush. What did the trick? The sexy woman or the word *please*? Landon didn't know and didn't care. "Thank you," Landon called after him.

"Moo."

Annoyed by the delay, Landon hit the gas and headed for home. "Freaking pain-in-the-ass, cock-blocking moose!" He needed to tell Hannah to do something about Fred and his propensity to get in the way of true love.

Landon nearly slammed on the brakes again after having that thought.

True love?

What the actual fuck was he thinking? He liked Amanda a

lot, but he wasn't in love with her. Was he? How would he even know? The only time he'd felt anything like love for someone he wasn't related to had been Naomi, and he'd been a teenager when she died. How the hell was he supposed to know if what he felt for Amanda was *love*?

Way to make things even more complicated. Ugh. "Just chill the fuck out and stop with the crazy thoughts, will you, please? She's got a lot on her mind right now, and the last thing she needs is some horny dude messing with her effort to reinvent herself."

He pulled into his driveway and came to a stop, throwing the truck into Park and taking a second to make sure he was prepared to go in there and be with her without doing something stupid like blurting out words she was in no way ready to hear. "You're in no way ready to say them either, jackass, so keep your mouth *shut*."

How do people survive this shit? he wondered, and not for the first time. There'd been a few months after Naomi died when he'd had reason for concern about his own health. Was it possible for a broken heart to simply stop beating? Even though they hadn't known the full measure of his affection for Naomi, his parents and siblings had surrounded him with love and support during that dark time, and eventually, he'd rebounded.

But he'd never forgotten how badly those months had sucked, nor had he ever stopped mourning the loss of Naomi's young life.

He got out of the truck and went inside, going directly to the bedroom door to look in on Amanda, who was asleep. His heart beat erratically as he got undressed, used the bathroom and got into bed with her, snuggling up to her warm, naked body. The sense of relief at being back with her was overwhelming, which was just another thing to be confused about. He'd never felt that pervasive sense of relief at being with any woman before.

She was turning him all around, and he was along for the ride with her no matter where it might lead.

Amanda stirred, her soft backside brushing against his hard cock. "You're home."

"I'm home. How'd it go sleeping naked?"

"Pretty well, all things considered. It seems to be getting even better, actually."

Landon laughed as he cupped her breast and ran his thumb over her nipple, making her shiver. "How do you feel about morning sex?"

"In theory or practice?"

"Definitely practice."

"Practice does make perfect."

When she would've turned toward him, he stopped her. "Like this." He kissed her neck, stroked her breast and then slid his hand down between her legs to find she was more than ready for him. "Hold that thought."

She grasped his arm. "I'm on birth control. I'm safe if you are."

The thought of sex without a condom only added to the excitement, which was already off the charts. "We get tested quarterly at work. I can show you…"

"That's okay. I believe you."

"So then, we're going to just…" He blew out a deep breath. "Well, okay, then."

Amanda rocked with silent laughter. "You going to be okay, Lieutenant?"

"Uh, can I let you know after?"

"I'll be here waiting to hear how it went."

"Might be quick." He gritted his teeth as he pushed into her from behind, his eyes nearly rolling back in his head from the blissful pleasure that overtook every part of him. He'd already known that nothing else could compare to making love to Amanda, but this… *God…* He moved them so she was on her knees and he was behind her, and the view of her smooth back and sweet ass fed the fire inside him as he moved in her.

"Your ankle…"

"Is fine."

He reached around to ensure that she'd be right there with him when this came to a sudden, cataclysmic finish. And the finish didn't disappoint. He nearly blacked out from the incredible high. They came down on the mattress in a tangle of limbs, his arms wrapped around her, his face buried in the fragrant silk of her hair. "Holy moly."

"Mmm."

"In case you're still wondering, that went really, *really* well."

Again, she shook with silent laughter, making him smile as he wallowed in the happiness that came from being with her. It wasn't something he could explain or understand. Why this woman and not the many others he'd known? He didn't know the answer to that age-old question. All he knew was that with every minute he spent with her, he only wanted more.

CHAPTER FOURTEEN

*"There is something good in all seeming failures. You are not to
see that now. Time will reveal it. Be patient."*
—Swami Sivananda

*L*andon drove them into town that afternoon for the all-
hands meeting his dad had called. Linc had asked her to
attend, most likely to discuss the training on her company's product line, which was set for Monday.

When they reached the bottom of the stairs that led to the
offices upstairs, Landon said, "Hop aboard, my sweet. I'll give
you a lift."

"I can probably do it."

"But I was so looking forward to getting my hands on you
again. Don't disappoint me."

"I'd never do that. Knock yourself out."

"Don't mind if I do." He gave her ass a grab before he lifted
her and headed up the stairs. "I need your ankle to get better so
we can zip-line and teach you to drive a stick and all sorts of
other fun stuff, but I sure will miss carrying you around."

"And I'll miss being carried around by you." She took advantage of the opportunity to fix his messy hair and kiss his cheek.

"Oh, for crying out loud," Hannah said when they reached the landing at the top of the stairs.

"Don't be doing that stuff in front of the children." Hannah shielded Callie's face so she couldn't see her uncle kissing Amanda.

"She sees far worse at home, I'm sure," Landon said.

"That's true," Hannah replied.

Landon groaned as he put Amanda down. "Gross."

"Not even kinda."

"I'm sorry, Callie." He kissed the baby's chubby cheek. "You call Uncle Landon if it ever gets to be too disgusting to stay at your house."

"Oh, whatever. You'd last ten minutes with a baby."

"That's not true!" He glanced at Amanda, seeming concerned she might think he couldn't handle kids. "I'll take her any time for as long as needed."

"That's very nice of you, but I love my child too much to trust her to the likes of you."

"I could do it, Hannah," Landon said. "I mean it."

Before Hannah could respond, Linc called for everyone to get in the conference room.

"This came for you, Amanda," Emma said, handing her a FedEx envelope.

"Thank you. Looks like the monthly mail delivery from my office." Amanda took it with her into the conference room, where most of the family had already gathered.

Molly and Elmer greeted Amanda with hugs and concern about how she was doing.

"I'm much better," she said, touched by their warm greetings. "Landon is taking very good care of me."

"He'd better be," Molly said with a smile and kiss for her son.

Everyone seemed surprised to see Lucas when he came in with Dani and Savannah.

"What're you doing here?" Hunter asked him.

"I heard it was all-hands, and since I have hands, that includes me."

Linc jumped up to find seats for Lucas and Dani. "We could've updated you, son."

"It's fine." Luc lowered himself gingerly into the chair his father got for him. "I'm going nuts from doing nothing. It's good to be out."

"Well, it's good to see you," Linc said. "It's good to see all of you. I called this meeting to go over a few things that're coming up that'll affect us all. First up will be the long-awaited training next week of our sales team for the intimate product line. Wade, can you give us an update on that?"

"My update is this: Amanda, I need you."

While everyone else laughed, she gave him a thumbs-up. "I'll be there for you. I promise."

"Thank God."

"Believe it or not, training the sales force won't be as traumatic as you think," Amanda said.

"It would be for me," Wade said bluntly. "I've known most of those women since I was a little kid. I can't do it. I just can't."

"I got you covered."

"God bless you."

"Can you be at the Grange bright and early on Monday morning?" Linc asked her.

"Sure thing."

"Excellent. Cameron and Lucy, can we get a catalog update?"

"We're down to the final photo shoot, which will take place next Wednesday and Thursday." Lucy got up and handed out a piece of paper that had the schedule on it. "If anyone can't do it at their appointed time, let me know, and we'll move things around."

"What about the cousins?" Will asked. "How come only Gray is on the schedule?"

"Grayson agreed to do it," Lucy said, "but Noah said, and I

quote, 'There's no way in hell I'm doing that.' He said he's completely consumed with rebuilding the inn and has no time for anything else. Izzie is doing the shoot for us, and the rest of the Colemans are in Boston, so we need to be happy with what we've got. Landon, I did the math on your schedule to figure out that your four days off happen next week, so you should be free, right?"

"Sadly, yes," he said to laughter from his siblings.

"Excellent. We need your handsome face in the catalog."

"Why do I have to do underwear?" Colton asked. "I feel objectified."

"Oh, shut up," Lucy said. "You prance around naked half the time. Putting underwear on is civilized for you."

"Note to self," Hunter said, "never visit the mountain without calling first."

"You know it, brother," Colton said with a smug smile. "There's a *lot* of honeymooning going on up there these days."

"Shut your mouth, or the honeymoon is over," Lucy said.

"Yes, dear."

"Has anyone considered what's going to happen when the women receiving this catalog realize the male models live here in Butler?" Megan asked.

Lincoln gave her a blank look. "No. Why?"

Megan covered her mouth with her hand, clearly trying not to laugh.

Amanda picked up her meaning. "I believe Megan is saying we're apt to be overrun with women wanting to meet the men in the catalog."

"That." Megan pointed to Amanda. "Exactly that."

"Being overrun would be a good thing," Linc said. "Isn't that one of the goals of the catalog? To get people to come to the store?"

"Sure," Will said, "as long as that's the *only* reason they're coming."

"It'll be fine," Linc said.

Amanda wasn't so sure about that, but didn't say anything more. They'd find out soon enough.

"One more thing for the catalog," Cameron said. "We had the idea to do some profiles of people who've been associated with the business for a long time. Amanda has offered to do them, and we're going to start with Elmer and Mildred for the first ones. If you're up for it, that is, Elmer."

"I'd be delighted," Elmer said with a wink for Amanda.

Could he be any cuter?

"What a great idea," Linc said. "I can't wait to read them."

Amanda was thrilled that he liked the idea. "I'm looking forward to working on them."

"Last item on the agenda," Linc said, "is a reminder that we're leaving from here at noon on Friday. We need to be in Boston for the rehearsal at five o'clock."

"Mia and I are heading for Boston on Wednesday," Wade said. "She's got a final dress fitting on Thursday, and Cabot has all kinds of plans for us. He's so excited."

"He's adorable," Cameron said. "Imagine spending all that time hoping and praying he'd find his missing daughter."

"I can't," Linc said. "What was done to him was unconscionable."

"Does Mia talk to her mom at all, Wade?" Lucy asked.

"Once in a while. Things aren't great between them, as you might imagine."

Amanda had heard how Mia's mom had taken off with her when she was a baby, hiding from her child's father, and how Mia had uncovered her mother's deceit after Hunter discovered her Social Security number belonged to someone who was dead. Mia had learned that her whole life had been a lie—and she'd found the father who'd never stopped looking for her. Amanda wondered how Mia could ever forgive her mother for such an epic deception.

It boggled the mind.

They were on their way back to Landon's when Amanda

opened the package that Emma had given her and sifted through bills, junk mail and other items forwarded from her office. A plain white envelope caught her attention. Amanda opened it to find three sheets of paper. The first was a cover letter with a logo on it that stopped her heart.

Dear Ms. Pressley,

Enclosed, please find a letter we received from your biological child's adoptive mother and your child. Per your request, we have sent it along to you. After you've had a chance to review the enclosed inquiry, please contact our offices via the toll-free number listed below to discuss next steps. Of course, you are under no obligation to respond, should you choose not to.

"Amanda? What's wrong?"

"I, uh, there's a letter. About my daughter. It's from her and her mother."

Landon looked over at her. "What does it say?"

"I haven't read it yet."

"Do you want to wait until we get home? We can read it together."

"Yeah. I'll wait." It'd be only a couple of minutes, but she absolutely could not do this alone.

"Are you all right?"

"I don't know. I didn't expect this. She's only twelve. They said she couldn't contact me until she was eighteen unless something about her situation changed."

"Oh wow. I wonder what happened." He reached for her hand. "Hold on to me. I'm here."

"Thanks." Amanda's hands were shaking, and suddenly, she was freezing.

Landon drove faster than he usually did and got them home quickly. "Coming for you," he said as he got out. "Hang on." He helped her out and escorted her inside, took her coat and settled her on the sofa. "Let me just throw a log on the fire." After he did that, he tossed his coat aside and joined her. "Look at me."

Amanda forced herself to meet his gaze, which was full of concern and affection.

"Whatever it says, you'll be okay."

"How do you know?"

"Because you're strong and capable, and nothing in that letter will change those things."

She nodded, hoping he was right, and took a deep breath, steeling herself for whatever she was about to find out.

"Do you want me to read it first?"

"Would you?"

"Of course."

Amanda handed the two pages over to him.

He quickly scanned the cover letter before turning his attention to the second page. "Oh wow."

"What does it say?"

"'Dear Amanda, I'm writing to let you know that a situation has arisen that I didn't foresee, and in light of our correspondence over the years, I thought you'd want to know. There's no easy way to say this, but I'm dying.'"

"Oh my God," Amanda said, gasping.

"'I've been diagnosed with stage-four brain cancer and have been advised to get my affairs in order. As you might imagine, my only concern is for Stella.'"

Amanda tried to process what she was hearing, knowing that Stella's adoptive father had died when she was seven, but it was too big, too much, and she almost couldn't hear Landon's voice over the roar in her own ears.

"'When we first adopted Stella, I bristled at the idea of having to share her with you, even through periodic updates and photos. I wanted her to be all mine, especially after her father died, but she's never been all mine. She's yours, too, and as I got to know you through our letters, I realized how lucky I was to have someone else out there who loves her like I do. Which is why, when I received this devastating diagnosis, my second thought was about you.

"'As you know, I don't have a lot of family, and we've moved so much due to my job that there really isn't anyone else I can ask to finish raising my beloved child who would love her and care for her the way I do.'"

By now, Amanda was rocking on the sofa. She'd wanted to shake things up, but she'd never imagined anything like this.

"'It's a big ask. I know that. But there it is. I'm asking, and I thought you might want to hear from Stella, too.'"

Landon shuffled the pages and read from the third one.

"'Hello, it's me, Stella, and as you know, I'm twelve years old.'"

Stella. Tears filled Amanda's eyes as the old familiar ache took up residence in her chest.

"'My mom and I talked about what we should do after we found out why she's been having so many headaches.'"

Tears ran unchecked down Amanda's face. She was filled with disbelief and the strangest feeling of hope that made her feel guilty in light of what they were dealing with.

"'My mom said you gave me up because you were too young to take care of a baby. Because of that, we thought your situation might be different now, and it might be possible for you to take care of a twelve-year-old who is a good student and a good kid. I really am! I do what my mom tells me to do. I work hard in school and get really good grades. I also play soccer and do dance. Before we consider other options, my mom and I decided we should reach out to you. She called the agency, and they agreed to forward our letter to you because of our situation. They said you checked a box on the adoption form allowing contact before I turn eighteen if anything changed for me. I know it's a lot to ask of anyone, but if you are as interested in meeting me as I am in meeting you, maybe we could start there and see what happens? If not, that's okay. I understand this is a very big thing to ask of anyone, especially someone who doesn't even know me! The agency said if you contact them, they'll put us in touch. I hope to hear from you, but if I don't, I'll just say thank you for bringing me into the world. Love, Stella.'"

Oh my God, Amanda thought. *Could she be any sweeter or cuter?* She wiped away tears that continued to fall. "Can I see the letter?"

Landon handed it to her.

She scanned the loopy, middle-school handwriting and read the letter for herself, devouring every word all over again.

"She seems like a very special young lady," Landon said.

"So special."

"How do you feel about what she's asking?"

"I'll do it. Of course I will."

"You don't want to think about it?"

"What's there to think about? She's my child, and she's going to need a home."

"It's so awesome that that's your first impulse, but you're not under any obligation to do this. You know that, right?"

"I do. I know that, but it doesn't matter. I want her. I've yearned for her from the minute I signed those papers. I knew it was the best thing for both of us at the time, but she's right. Everything has changed for me since then."

"For what it's worth, I'd do the same thing in your shoes."

"You would?"

"Absolutely. So I'm only playing devil's advocate when I remind you of the list of things you want to do."

"None of that matters now. The only thing that matters is Stella." Her voice broke as she spoke of her child.

"That's a beautiful name."

Amanda nodded and covered her mouth, trying to contain the sob that came from the deepest part of her.

Landon put his arms around her and held her while she cried, smoothing his hand over her back.

They stayed like that for a long time, until the room had gone dark and her tears had subsided.

"Thank you."

"I didn't do anything."

"You were here, and that helped tremendously."

"I'm happy to be here with you, and I'll do whatever I can to make this easier for you."

"I'm going to get to meet my *daughter*."

"Yes, you are."

Amanda thought of the trip to Paris she'd impulsively booked that would have to be canceled. Or, maybe she could take Stella with her.

Stella.

Her child wanted to meet her and maybe come to live with her. Emotions she'd never experienced before flooded her system in a wild burst of endorphins. "Maybe this is why I survived that fire. So I could be there for her."

"Maybe so."

"Wouldn't that be something?"

Landon smiled and nodded. "It's so sad about her mom, though. She's going through a lot at only twelve."

"I know. I thought that, too. This is so, so, *so* not about me..."

"It's a little bit about you."

"I just, I wonder... How soon do you think I'll get to meet her?"

"Probably pretty soon. If you call the agency in the morning, they'll help you set something up."

Amanda put her hand on her stomach, which was suddenly full of butterflies. "This day turned out much differently than I expected."

"My Gramps always says, 'You never know what's around the next bend.'"

"It's so true. I couldn't have seen this one coming. That's for sure."

"Do you feel like you could eat?"

"I doubt it. I'm buzzing like I've had a dozen cups of coffee."

"How about a movie, then?"

"I thought you had to work?"

"I do, but I have a radio, and I'll get there eventually."

"It's fine if you go. I promise I'll be okay. I'll sit here and stare at the TV while I think about how I'm going to get to meet my *daughter*."

Landon smiled at her. "I'm happy for you."

"I'm happy for me, too, but I have to remember what she's going through and keep telling myself it's not about me."

He took hold of her hand and brushed his lips over her knuckles. "I'm going to keep reminding you it's about you, too. Of course it is."

"I'll understand if this is too much for you."

"Huh? What? It's not too much. Why would you think that?"

"We just started, you know, *something*... And this sort of changes the game."

"It doesn't change anything for me."

"Even if it changes everything for me?"

"Even if. And for what it's worth, Butler, Vermont, is a great place to raise kids."

Amanda smiled and leaned in to kiss him. "Thank you for being so awesome. I'd be losing it if I was alone right now."

He tightened his hold on her and kissed the top of her head. "You're not alone anymore."

CHAPTER FIFTEEN

"Patience is bitter, but its fruit is sweet."
—Jean-Jacques Rousseau

*L*andon went through the motions of heating up some of Ella's lasagna for them and serving the salad his sister had made to go with it. After preparing a plate for Amanda and one for himself, he carried both into the living room where he'd left her sitting, and found her staring off into space. "Dinner is served."

She took the plate from him. "Thank you."

"I called the station, told them something has come up and to call me if they need me to come in. So I'm all yours tonight." He had extra hours on the books from the night he was called in, and there would never be a better time to use them than tonight.

"I didn't even realize you were on the phone."

"You were busy staring at the TV."

"You're the best for doing that. I'm okay, but it's better with you here."

"I didn't want you to be alone tonight." He put his plate on the table and returned to the kitchen for the glass of wine he'd poured for her. When he sat next to her to eat, he discovered his own stomach was roiling as he tried to absorb the events of the last hour. He'd meant it when he told her he was happy for her to have the opportunity to know the child she'd given up for adoption and possibly take her in when her mother passed away.

But he couldn't help but wonder what it would mean for them. They'd just managed to move off the starting line, and now she was thoroughly—and understandably—distracted by this major news about her daughter. How did he fit into this new development? Did he fit into it? Would he be part of it?

Though he normally ate like a horse, he only picked at the tasty lasagna and salad. He did the dishes, cleaned up the kitchen and put on a movie that neither of them watched.

While she used the bathroom before bed, he stoked up the fire and stared at the flames with unseeing eyes. Right when things between them had begun to move in the direction he'd wanted from the beginning, she'd received the letter that had upended everything.

But like she'd said earlier, it was all about what Stella needed, first and foremost. They'd have to figure out the rest as it happened.

He took his turn in the bathroom and slid into bed wearing flannel pajama pants and a Butler Volunteer Fire Department T-shirt. The days of sleeping naked were probably over for now, a thought that filled him with a profound feeling of sadness that he immediately dismissed as selfish.

Amanda snuggled up to him, and he put his arm around her.

"How're you doing?" She'd hardly said a word for hours, and all he wanted was to know what she was thinking and feeling.

"I don't know. Mostly, I'm counting the hours until I can call the agency in the morning. Maybe I'll get to talk to her as soon as tomorrow."

"I hope you don't have to wait long."

"Me, too. I'll go mad." She raised her head from his chest. "I'm apt to be a little distracted for a minute or two."

"I understand. Anyone would be."

"It really helps to be with you while this is happening."

He kissed her. "I'm glad you feel that way."

Landon slept fitfully and was up at daybreak, hoping to get in a full day at the farm before the night shift at the fire department. He moved quietly around the room as he got dressed, trying not to disturb Amanda.

"You're up early," she said.

"I'm working at the farm today."

"What goes on there in the off-season?"

"Today, I'm mowing, which is critical so we don't get overrun with weeds. We also spray fungicide on every tree once a month between April and September, and then we give them all what we refer to as 'haircuts,' which is really about shaping and trimming. This month, we start the herbicide program to keep the weeds from impairing the growth of the trees. It's actually a year-round process."

"I had no idea."

He came to sit on the edge of the bed next to her. "Most people think it's jingle bells and hot chocolate in December and the rest of the year off, but it's not like that at all."

"Do you do all that yourself?"

"Most of it. My brothers Max and Colton help out after their sugaring season ends. They split their time between the mountain and the farm in the summer."

"Maybe I could come see what you do there at some point?"

"Any time you want. What're you up to today?"

"After I call the adoption agency, I'll be making plans for the staff training that starts Monday and checking in with my mom about some other work stuff. I suppose I need to tell her what's going on with Stella."

"How do you think she'll take that?"

"I have no idea. We never talk about that time in our lives. It was traumatic for both of us."

"I'm sure."

"Landon…" She reached for his hand and kept her gaze

pinned on their joined hands. "I don't want this to mess up things between us. I want…"

"What do you want, honey?"

"You." She looked up at him with big eyes and sleep-rumpled hair, and to him, she'd never been more beautiful. "I want you."

Moved by her sweet words, he leaned his forehead against hers. "I want you, too. I want to be there for you during all of this with Stella, and everything else, for that matter."

She raised her free hand to his face, caressing the stubble on his jaw. "That means so much to me."

"No matter what happens, everything will be okay. I believe that. Things work out the way they're meant to."

"Is that another of your grandfather's sayings?"

"One of many. But he's right. You have recent proof of that. All your plans don't matter in the least when you get caught in a fire or hear from the child you gave up for adoption twelve years ago."

"It's true."

"Are you up for going to Hunter and Megan's tonight maybe?"

"I think so. She said she'd call me today to confirm."

"I'll come home early from the farm, we can run to Montpelier to pick up the ring for Luc before he drives me crazy asking me to get it, and you can get a dress for the wedding. I'll have you back in time for dinner."

"Sounds like a plan."

"Do you want me to stick around until you call the agency?"

"You don't need to. I'll be all right."

"I'll call to check on you in a bit."

"I'll look forward to that."

He kissed her, wishing he had nothing to do and could spend the day with her, but the trees didn't take care of themselves, and he'd been slacking off since the fire. It was time to get back to work. On the way through town, he stopped off at the diner to get coffee and a breakfast sandwich to go.

The only ones in the diner that early were Hunter, Megan and Elmer, all of whom were happy to see Landon.

"You want the usual?" Megan asked.

"Please. To go."

"Coming right up." She went in the back to give Butch, the cook, Landon's order.

"How's it going, son?" Elmer asked.

"Good, I think. Were your ears ringing this morning?"

"No more than usual. Why? Should they have been?"

"I was quoting you to Amanda."

"Which one of his masterpieces did you use?" Hunter asked as he rolled silverware.

"Things work out the way they're meant to."

"Ah, yes," Elmer said, smiling. "That's one of my favorites."

"What's the context?" Hunter asked as Megan rejoined them.

"Amanda is dealing with some stuff, some big stuff, and it's going to change her life rather significantly."

"Is that right?" Hunter said. "How so?"

"I'm not sure if I should say anything."

"You can tell us." Hunter glanced at Landon. "It won't go any further."

"Promise," Elmer added.

"I promise, too," Megan said.

Because he desperately needed to tell someone, he decided to take them at their word. "She gave up a child for adoption twelve years ago when she was too young to care for a baby. Yesterday, she heard from her daughter." As he said the words and connected the dots, he felt removed from the situation, as if it were happening to someone else and not him. He told them about Stella's mother's illness and the situation they were in. "Needless to say, I need you to keep those promises. Amanda wouldn't want this all over town before she's had a chance to figure out what's what."

"Wow," Hunter said. "That is a big deal. How does she feel about it?"

"I think she's excited to have her daughter in her life, while being mindful of the circumstances with the mother's devastating diagnosis. The letter she got from her daughter was adorable and sweet. She sounds like an amazing kid."

"What an awful, wonderful, exciting and terrifying thing to have happen," Elmer said.

Landon nodded as he poured himself a coffee to go and stirred in half-and-half. "It's all that for sure."

Elmer eyed him with the shrewd gaze that never missed a trick. "How do you feel about it?"

"I'm happy for her to have this opportunity. She's ached for that girl for twelve long years, and it seems like maybe she'll have the chance to finish raising her and be part of her life."

"I can see that you're happy for her, but how do *you* feel?"

Landon walked around the counter and took a seat next to Hunter. "I'm not really sure, to be honest. Amanda and I have been trying to figure out what's going on between us, and now it's like a bomb has gone off in the middle of our brand-new relationship. It's a lot to take in."

"If you're not interested in being a stepfather, you probably ought to put the brakes on with her," Hunter said.

"I wouldn't mind being a stepfather if it meant I got to keep Amanda in my life."

Elmer smiled warmly at him. "That's the way. Filter out all the crap and take it down to what's important to you."

"She's important to me."

"And she knows that?"

"She does."

Elmer nodded. "That'll matter to her as she figures this out."

"After the fire, she made a list of things she wants to do. I'm worried she won't get to do them now, and she might regret that later."

"A twelve-year-old isn't the same as a baby," Hunter said. "She can work through her list with her daughter."

"I guess," Landon said, still feeling out of sorts.

"This leaves you feeling like you're on the outside looking in, right?" Megan asked.

"Something like that."

"Nothing saying you couldn't be part of it from the start," Hunter said. "If you want Amanda, you get her daughter, too. They'll be a package deal."

"I know, and I'm fine with that. It's just that things between us are still kind of new, and it's a lot to toss into a new relationship."

"Not to mention the first real relationship you've had," Elmer added.

"Not to mention... I'm still figuring out how to make things work with her, and now there's a child, too."

"You should talk to Luc about that," Hunter said. "He went through a similar thing when he met Dani and Savannah."

"I think it's a little different in this case," Elmer said. "Savannah was part of the equation from the beginning for Luc. Landon and Amanda have been circling the wagons, as they say, for weeks now, and this definitely throws a wrench in the wheel."

"How is it that you manage to cut through the crap to sum things up so perfectly?" Landon asked his grandfather.

"My special gift." Elmer's eyes glittered with amusement. "This is a tough one, pal. No way around that. You and your lady have had a somewhat rocky road, and things were finally smoothing out for you when your applecart was upset once again. The best thing I can tell you is to make her aware that you want to be part of this new phase of her life. Your support will mean everything to her."

"I agree," Megan said. "Absolutely."

"Thanks, guys. It helps to air it out with you."

"That's what we're here for," Elmer said. "We're not just about the eggs and coffee at this diner. We deal in free advice, too."

"On many a day, we serve far more free advice than coffee," Megan said.

Elmer laughed. "Ain't that the truth?" To Landon, he said, "You working at the farm today?"

"That's the plan."

"Is tonight still good for Amanda to come for dinner?" Megan asked.

"That's the plan. I'll bring her if you don't mind one more."

"Not at all. I thought you were working."

"I am, but as long as I have a radio, I can do it."

"See you around six thirty?"

"We'll be there."

"Have a good day, son," Elmer said.

Landon squeezed his grandfather's shoulder. "You, too, Gramps. Thanks again."

"Any time."

Landon took his breakfast with him and ate in the truck on the way to the farm, where his first order of business was feeding and watering the horses and cleaning out their stalls. He put them outside to get some exercise while he worked. Next, he gassed up the zero-turn mower with the sixty-inch cut that he used to mow the corridors between the rows of trees. He had a smaller one he used for between the trees.

Landon cut a lot of grass this time of year, which gave him far too much time to think. As he mowed the first five acres, he let the story play out in his mind, from the day he met Amanda all the way through to this morning. For a time, he'd thought it wasn't going to happen between them and had blamed himself for that. He'd had no idea how to play the game when a woman got to him the way she did, so of course he'd played it all wrong.

It'd taken until this week to finally feel like they were getting somewhere, and now she would be indefinitely distracted by the situation with her daughter. And rightfully so.

That's where her attention needed to be.

He felt like a dick for wondering where that left him or how he fit into this new scenario.

At ten, he took a break and went inside to use the phone in the loft where Lucas had lived before he met Dani. Now that they were happily living at Dani's, Landon doubted that his brother would come back to the loft.

Landon dialed the number to his house and waited while it rang.

Amanda picked up on the third ring.

"Hey," he said. "Did you talk to the agency?"

"I did. They said they'll contact Stella's mother to arrange a time for us to talk on the phone. If that goes well, we can FaceTime."

"That's great."

"The lady I talked to at the agency said she was so relieved to hear from me. I guess they were concerned after Stella and her mom pitched this idea to them. The agency had advised them not to get their hopes up because there was no guarantee I'd be willing or able to get involved."

"Stella and her mom will be relieved to have something in place for when the time comes."

"I'm going to have to go to wherever they are, I suppose. I should meet her before she comes to live with me."

Landon's heart sank at the thought of her ending up somewhere far away from him. "Probably."

"Would you go with me?"

And just that quickly, his heart soared again. "Yeah, of course. I'd love to meet her."

"Really? You would?"

"I would, Amanda. She's important to you, so she's important to me. I told you I want to be there for you through all this, and besides, I'm your partner in crime, right?"

"Right." He heard a sniffling sound. "I appreciate that so much."

"Are you crying?"

"Maybe a little."

"How come?"

"Because you're so amazing. A lot of guys would be running for their lives from this situation."

"I'm not going anywhere, except with you to meet your daughter."

"I should have more info by the time I see you."

"Sounds good. I'll be home by two to go to Montpelier, and we're due at Hunter and Megan's at six thirty."

"I'll see you when you get here."

Landon put the phone back on the charger and returned to work, feeling encouraged by the conversation. She wanted him to go with her when she met her daughter. That was a good sign. In this confusing and unpredictable situation, he took the good news where he could find it.

CHAPTER SIXTEEN

*"Great works are performed not by strength
but by perseverance."*
—Samuel Johnson

After the call from Landon, Amanda's next order of business was updating her mother on what was going on. Her nerves were all over the place as she made that call. She and her mother never discussed Stella. Her mother never asked about her or wanted to see pictures. It was like she'd wanted to pretend the baby had never happened, probably because the loss had been so painful for them both.

"Hi," Joyce said when she picked up. "I was just going to call you. How're you feeling?"

"Much better."

"That's good news. Did you get the email about the trade show schedule? As our senior sales associate, you get first dibs on what you want to do."

"Yes, I know."

"Is there a problem?"

"Not a problem so much as a challenge."

Joyce sighed. "What kind of challenge?"

Amanda closed her eyes and forced herself to say the words. "The kind where my daughter gets in touch to tell me she'll soon be orphaned and in need of a home."

For the longest time, Joyce said nothing.

"Mom? Did you hear me?"

"I heard you."

"And?"

"I'm not sure what I'm supposed to say to that."

"You could say, 'It's amazing that she reached out to you and that you're going to have your daughter in your life.'"

"So you're going to do it, then?"

"Of course I am."

"You know you don't have to, right?"

"I do know that, but it never occurred to me not to step up for her. Why wouldn't I when I can certainly provide a loving home for her now?"

"Where're you going to do that? You live out of suitcases on the road two hundred days a year."

"I'm well aware of how my life was."

"Was? Past tense?"

"I think so, Mom."

"Are you giving me notice?"

Amanda hadn't intended to do that today, but what was she waiting for? She already knew she wanted to change her life, and in order to have any kind of meaningful existence for herself, her daughter and Landon, she needed to change jobs. "Yes, I guess I am. I want you to know how much I appreciate the opportunities you gave me with the company. I've appreciated it so much, but I want something different now."

"Because of Stella?"

"Partially, but also because of me. I'm tired of living out of suitcases and not having a real home or a life outside of work. The fire was a huge wake-up call that I need to make some changes. I'd had that epiphany before I heard from Stella. And now that she's in the mix, I have even more incentive to figure out my shit and decide where I'm going to live."

"You'll be coming home, then?"

Amanda took a deep breath and held it for a second. "I don't think so."

"Where will you go?"

"I think I might stay right here in Butler, if Stella doesn't mind moving to Vermont. They live in upstate New York, so I could take her there a few times a year to see her friends."

"What's so exciting about that small town in Vermont that you want to stay there permanently?"

"So many things. It'd be hard to sum it up until you see it." She didn't want to tell her mother about Landon. Not yet. She didn't want her mother to think she was making life decisions based on a man. He was definitely part of the equation, but she was the bigger part of it. This was about her, first and foremost. She wanted to be someone her daughter could be proud of and set the right kind of example. To do that, she needed a job that didn't require her to travel constantly and a home in a place where a child could grow and thrive.

Butler felt like that kind of place.

"What will you do for work?"

"I've inquired about a job with the Abbott family's business. They're launching the catalog and warehouse this fall."

"Won't you find that boring after what you do now?"

"Not at all. They're building the catalog and warehouse from the ground up, so it's an exciting time for their company. This week, they're launching our product line and doing a family photo shoot for the catalog. I haven't been bored one minute since I've been here."

"Well, I'm going to have to get there to check this place out before much longer. Of course, I'll want to meet Stella, too."

"We'll make that happen for sure," Amanda said, surprised but delighted at the genuine interest her mother was showing in meeting Stella. "When the time is right."

"I've been wanting to talk to you about my own situation."

"What about it?"

"I'm thinking about retiring and planned to ask if you were interested in my job, but I guess that's a moot point now."

"Maybe not," Amanda said, thinking fast. "I'm sure the company realizes by now that they'd need two people to replace you since you work sixty hours a week. What if I coordinated the trade show element, and you hired someone else to manage the sales force?"

"Didn't you just say you want to work for the Abbotts?"

"I do, but I think I could handle that part of your job, too. I'm going to have a child to support, college to pay for. The extra income will help."

"That's an interesting idea. I'll pitch it to them and let you know what they say."

"And you'll convey my two weeks' notice?"

"I'll do that. It's going to be odd not to work together anymore," Joyce said, sounding sad about the changes.

"We'll still talk all the time, and I'm going to want you to come visit—and eventually meet your granddaughter."

"I'd like that."

"Well, then, we'll make that happen as soon as possible."

"Keep me posted?"

"I will. Thank you again for everything you've done for me, Mom. The job has really meant the world to me."

"You did a great job for us. Don't be surprised if you hear from Martin," she said of her boss. "He'll want to keep his top sales rep in the family."

"Thanks for the warning," Amanda said with a laugh. "I'll be ready for him."

"Let me know how the training goes with the Abbott sales force."

"Will do. We train on Monday."

"I'll speak to you soon, then. Love you, honey."

"Love you, too, Mom." Amanda put down the phone, feeling

oddly emotional after hearing those words from her mother. Their relationship had become very businesslike and transactional after Amanda went to work for her. She was interested to see how things would evolve between them when they no longer worked together.

The phone rang again, and she grabbed it without checking the caller ID. "Did you forget something?"

"What? Who's this?"

"Amanda. Who's this?"

"Is Landon there?"

"No, he's working."

"Tell him Chrissy called. *Again.*"

The line went dead before she could say anything. "Lovely." Amanda shook that off and went back to thinking about the call with her mom.

"So, that happened. You quit your job." She took a second to let the words register, expecting to feel regret or fear or something other than elation. "I quit my job."

Smiling, she stood, stretched and did a happy little dance that she instantly regretted when her ankle objected. "Buzzkill." She returned to the sofa, put her foot on a pillow and powered up her new laptop for the first time to prepare for the Abbott training and to revisit the work she'd done on the catalog for the intimate line.

For the first time in a while, she actually felt like working, which was a welcome relief and a sign that maybe she was getting back to some semblance of normal. Call it the "new norm," full of exciting challenges and adventures to come. She refused to slip back into old habits of living half a life that focused almost exclusively on work.

That was no way to live, and those days were over.

It was like she'd torn up her life plan and started over with a blank page that she could fill any way she chose. The first two items on her blank page would be Stella and Landon. Everything else that came along would be like frosting on the sweetest cake.

Just knowing she didn't have to travel from city to city all summer was enough to fill her with joy.

After an hour of reviewing the catalog and other work-related emails, she called up a web browser and dove into a deep rabbit hole of real estate options in the Butler area. That's what she was doing when the phone rang with a call from the adoption agency.

Amanda pounced. "Hello?"

"Ms. Pressley, this is Kathleen calling with more information. Do you have a pen handy?"

"I do." With her fingers poised on the keyboard, she was ready.

"Stella and her mother, Kelly, are available for a call tonight at nine p.m. Does that work for you?"

"Yes," Amanda said, blinking back tears. "That works."

"Excellent. Here's the number at which you can reach them."

Amanda typed the number, which was in the 518 area code, and repeated it back to Kathleen to make sure she had it right. "Please let them know I'll call at nine."

"I'll do that, and I wish you all the best. I can only imagine how you must be feeling."

"It's hard to put into words."

"We have counselors available should you need someone to talk to."

"Thank you. I'll keep that in mind. So far, I'm doing okay, but there've been a few tears."

"I'm sure. For what it's worth, Stella seems like a delightful young lady."

"I can't wait to talk to her. Not sure how I'll last until nine."

"Please let me know if there's anything I can do for you. We're here if we can be of assistance."

"Thank you again."

"My pleasure."

Amanda ended the call and immediately figured out how long it would take to get from Butler, Vermont, to Albany. "Ugh, almost four hours. Longer than I thought. Oh well, that's still closer than a lot of other places she might've been."

She was spinning and realized that, but couldn't seem to help the desperate need to know everything about her daughter now that the door had been cracked open to allow her into the child's life in a much more meaningful way. Since she'd received that letter, she'd had to keep reminding herself that what was the most wonderful thing to happen to her was coming at the price of a devastating loss for Stella.

By the time Landon came home at two, Amanda was about to combust from the way time seemed to move backward all day. Every time she looked at the clock, it was only one minute later than the last time.

"I'm very happy to see you," she said to him.

He took off his boots, hung up his coat and came to sit with her on the sofa. "And why is that?"

"Other than all the obvious reasons, my brain is going to implode at some point in the next seven hours."

"What happens in seven hours?"

"I get to talk to Stella. And her mom, Kelly."

"Wow, that's exciting."

"I know! Except time is moving backward today, and I'm about to lose my shit."

"We can't have that." He leaned in to kiss her. "I can think of many good ways to distract you from clock watching."

"Is that right?" He smelled of clean air, pine and freshly cut grass.

"Oh yeah. I'm endlessly creative when it comes to distractions."

Amanda bit her lip as she smiled. She already felt better just having him there, and any distraction he provided was sure to be helpful.

He cupped her cheek and stared at her. "Happy and excited looks good on you."

"Does it?"

"Yeah."

"You're seeing me at my best and my worst lately."

"I like every version of Amanda."

He couldn't have said anything that would mean more to her. Before she could respond, he kissed her, and like always, his kisses required her full attention. They ended up reclined on the sofa with her arms around him as one kiss became two and three, and then she lost count. She strained against him to get closer, wanting to ride the wave of euphoria she'd been on all day and to share that feeling with him.

While he kissed her, she unbuttoned his blue plaid flannel in search of sexy man chest. She was stymied by the T-shirt he wore underneath, which she yanked from the waistband of his jeans.

"This sofa's not big enough for what's happening here," he said against her lips.

"What's happening?" she asked, playing it coy.

"You're trying to rip my clothes off, and I want to fully encourage that." He pushed himself up and off her, extending a hand to help her. "Right this way." Walking slowly so she could keep up, he led her into the bedroom, where he quickly removed her sweatshirt and the tank she wore under it as well as the pajama pants she'd never changed out of.

When he would've started next on his own clothes, Amanda said, "Wait, let me." She pushed the flannel off his shoulders and lifted the T-shirt over his head, revealing a lean, muscular chest and abdomen that was covered with the perfect amount of golden-brown hair. After flattening her hands on his chest, she slid them slowly down over the best six-pack she'd ever seen, stopping at the button to his jeans.

"You know how to torture me."

"What did I do?"

Chuckling, he said, "You know what you're doing."

"What am I doing?" She dropped to her knees in front of him.

"Oh fuck. I wish I could take a picture of you right now so I could never forget how incredibly sexy you look."

"No pictures."

"Let me take a good long look, then."

She smiled up at him as she gently worked the zipper down over the huge bulge.

He helped her with the jeans and kicked them off, leaving him only in boxer briefs that hugged his hard cock.

Amanda kissed him through the underwear, drawing a tortured-sounding groan from him. She ran her hands up the backs of his legs to cup his ass, pulling him even closer to her as she worked her fingers inside the back of his boxers to start removing them. With the waistband halfway down his cock, she stopped and worked the length of him into her mouth, pulling the underwear down as she went.

His fingers tangled into her hair as he trembled from the effort to hold back.

She took as much as she could and then retreated, repeating the process over and over.

"Wait," he said when he apparently couldn't take any more of that. "Let's do this together." He sat on the edge of the bed and reached for her, bringing her onto his lap. "Is this okay?"

Amanda nodded and took him in, moving slowly to come down on him as his head dropped back and his hands gripped her ass.

"God, that's so good," he said on a long exhale. "All I could think about today was what it feels like to be inside you. I can't get enough."

She rolled her hips. "I can't either."

"Yes, like that. Ride me." His eyes flew open, his gaze colliding with hers in a moment of unity that was unlike anything she'd ever experienced with a man.

She felt like he saw inside her as they made love with a kind of reverence that was all new to her.

Landon surprised her when he wrapped his arms tight

around her and stood, bringing her with him without losing their connection.

"Where're you taking me?"

"All the way." He turned them, lowered her to the bed and came down on top of her. "Is it wrong that I've wanted to do nothing but this since the first time I found out how fucking awesome it is with you?"

"Nothing wrong with that."

Without missing a beat with his hips, he drew her nipple into his mouth and ran his tongue over the tip.

Amanda raised her arms over her head, surrendering completely to him and the way he made her feel. Sex with an athletic man was a revelation. His stamina was admirable, which was the last rational thought she had as he picked up the pace and had her screaming from the orgasm that crashed over her suddenly, without the usual slow build. When it happened a second time a few minutes later, she was truly shocked.

The man was a god, in bed and out. That much she knew for certain as he came down on her in the aftermath of his own pleasure, breathing hard and sweating from the effort he'd expended.

"Wow," she said.

"Mmm. So good." He kissed her neck, along her jaw and then her lips. "I knew it would be from the first second I saw you."

"It's because I was holding a dildo. Admit it."

"That didn't hurt anything," he said with a laugh, "but it was you. I had a reaction to *you* that I'd never had to anyone other than Naomi. When I realized my brother did, too, I wanted to cry. I wanted you all to myself."

"Is that why you insisted on bringing me home with you from the hospital?"

"Absolutely. I'm a shameless opportunist, and hey, it worked for Tyler after Charley got hurt. I could only hope it would work out that way for us, too."

"And how's that going so far?"

"It's better than anything has ever been."

She recalled in that inopportune moment that she had forgotten to give him the message from Chrissy. "One of your friends called while you were out."

"Who?"

"Chrissy."

CHAPTER SEVENTEEN

*"Never cut a tree down in the wintertime. Never
make a negative decision in the low time.
Never make your most important decisions when
you are in your worst moods. Wait. Be patient.
The storm will pass. The spring will come."*
—Robert H. Schuller

*L*andon cringed at the mention of Chrissy as he withdrew
from Amanda and landed on the bed next to her. "That
'friendship' is in the past."

"Does she know that?"

"We've never had a conversation about it, if that's what
you're asking, but we also never had any kind of commitment.
We were friends with occasional benefits. That's it—and she
knew it."

"And now that's over?"

"Of course it is. I'm with you now."

"And this is different than that?"

He stared at her, seeming incredulous. *"Yes."*

"How is it different?"

"You want me to, like, describe how it's different?"

"That'd be good." She tried not to laugh as he struggled to understand what she wanted from him.

He pretended to be annoyed. "You're enjoying this, aren't you?"

"Just a little." She propped her head on an upturned hand and waited him out.

"You want to know how it's different…"

"That's what I said."

"For one thing, you're not like anyone I've ever known."

"How so?"

Landon grimaced. "You challenge me."

"Is that what I'm doing right now? Challenging you?"

"Yes, you're challenging me to put words to feelings, and I'm not really sure how to do that."

"You're doing great so far. Tell me more about these feelings."

He turned his head to look at her. "I feel something when I'm with you. Something I only ever felt for Naomi. Like you said, she's my benchmark. I know what that was like, and it's not as if I was running around looking for that again. But when it appeared on that day in the conference room at the store, I recognized it for what it is."

"And what is it?"

He huffed out an exasperated laugh. "Something I want more of."

"Is that rare for you to want more?"

"You already know it's unprecedented since Naomi."

Turning on his side, he ran his fingers through her hair and caressed her cheek. "I want to be with you all the time. I had to force myself to stay on that freaking mower until two, when all I wanted was come home. When you heard about Stella, my first thought was I hope I get to meet her, that I can be part of it with you. When I was working, I kept thinking about her and you and trying to figure out how I can support you as you bring her into your life."

His gaze flipped up to meet hers, earnest, sincere, adorable.

"I've had a lot of fun with women. I won't deny that. But I've never had to nearly tie myself to the mower so I wouldn't skip out on work to get to someone as soon as I possibly could." After a pause, he added, "I'm not sure if that's what you were looking for, but that's how I feel."

"That's pretty great."

"I have no interest in Chrissy or Jessica or anyone but you. I want this, between us, to be officially exclusive. Would that be okay?"

"Well, since I'm living in your house, it'd be kind of complicated to date someone else right now."

His expression went blank with shock.

Amanda laughed as hard as she'd laughed at anything since before the fire upended her world. She laughed so hard, her sides ached. "I'm teasing you, Landon. Joking. *Hello?* You've heard of that, right?"

"My brother and I wrote the book on teasing," he said, scoffing. "I can't believe you actually tried to get one over on me."

"You didn't honestly think I was serious about dating other people while I'm *living* with you, did you?"

"Of course not."

"Liar. I totally got you."

"Did not."

"Did too."

He glared playfully at her. "*Not.*"

She stuck out her tongue at him. "*Too.*"

"I can think of better uses for that tongue."

"Landon…"

"Yes, Amanda?"

"Just for the record… I don't want to date anyone but you."

"That's good to know."

"And it's not just because I'm living in your house. It's because of you. You make me want things I've never had, things I never thought I'd want."

"Like what?"

"A real life. A real relationship. A home. A family." She rested a hand on his chest and felt the rapid beat of his heart under her palm. "I realize it's far too soon to talk about those things—"

"It's not too soon. I want them, too."

"Even if Stella is part of the picture?"

"Especially then."

The rush of emotion caught her by surprise, but that was happening a lot lately. "I have to tell you something."

"What's that?"

"I quit my job today."

"Wow. More big news."

She nodded.

"How'd your mom take it?"

"Better than expected, actually. Turns out she's thinking about retiring, and we talked about me continuing to do part of her job remotely. It's something I could do fairly easily from wherever I am, and it would be a nice source of additional income."

"That sounds good."

"The best part is it gets me off the travel circuit, which will be important for when I have Stella."

"True."

"I also asked Dani if she might consider me for the assistant manager position at the warehouse."

His smile stretched across his face, lighting up his beautiful golden-brown eyes. "Really?"

She nodded. "Would that be okay? I probably should've discussed it with you before I mentioned it to her. It's your family's business, after all."

"It's absolutely fine with me. Why wouldn't it be?"

"I don't know. I'm all over the place lately. I'm still figuring out this new version of myself. I'm apt to be a bit of a mess for a while."

"You're not a mess. You're like a butterfly emerging from your cocoon and spreading your wings."

"That's a lovely metaphor."

"It's true. I'm looking forward to watching you fly."

She cupped his cheek and kissed him. "That's the sweetest thing anyone has ever said to me."

THEY MADE A MAD DASH TO MONTPELIER TO PICK UP THE RING and find a dress for the wedding and were back in Butler by six to drop off the ring to a very thankful Lucas. After they left him, Landon drove Amanda to Hunter's house, feeling as if they'd had an important breakthrough during that momentous day. They'd agreed to be exclusive, and she was making some big changes that would keep her in Butler. That was the best news of all. He was relieved to know she was looking to put down roots in his town, that she wanted to work for his family's company and finish raising her daughter there.

These were all good things, and he'd done something rather impetuous earlier when they were in Montpelier, but he couldn't tell her about that. Not yet, anyway, but he hoped he could show her what he'd bought for her sooner rather than later. It counted as the craziest thing he'd ever done, but she seemed like a gamble worth taking.

With everything moving in the right direction, why did he still have a nagging feeling that despite all their progress, things were still far from settled between them?

He couldn't say, and that uncertainty kept him off-balance long after they arrived at Hunter's and settled in for a delicious dinner and a piano lesson for Amanda.

After dinner, while she went with his brother into the room where the piano was located, Landon helped Megan with the dishes.

"Thanks for dinner," he said. "That pulled pork was amazing."

"Glad you enjoyed it. It's all thanks to the Crock-Pot, which was on all day while we were at work."

"My mom used to call the Crock-Pot a miracle worker when we were all at home. Actually, she had three of them at one point."

"Your mom never ceases to amaze me."

"I know. She's awesome."

Megan finished loading the dishwasher while Landon wiped the table and the countertops.

"Thanks for the help."

"No problem."

"Let's go sit. My ankles are swollen after being on my feet all day."

Landon grabbed his portable fire department radio off the counter and followed her into the living room, taking a seat next to her on the sofa. Their dog, Horace, who was Homer Junior's brother, jumped onto the sofa and settled on her lap.

She put her feet on a pillow that she placed on the coffee table as she stroked the dog's ears. "Ah, that's much better. On days like this, it's hard to believe that pregnancy is supposed to be the most natural thing in the world. I feel like I got hit by a bus."

"Are you working too hard?"

"Maybe, but I'd go crazy stuck at home. I like being at the diner and seeing everyone."

"Still, you ought to take it easy. People can refill their own coffee."

She gave him a curious look. "That's actually not a bad idea. Two strategically placed stations would save me a lot of walking."

"Do it. No one would mind."

"I'll see what Hunter and Elmer think."

"You know they'll be all for anything that makes it easier on you."

"They will. Elmer is on me every day about overdoing it."

175

"That sounds like him. He adores you."

"And I adore him right back." She gave him a curious look and lowered her voice. "Things with Amanda seem good. You two are very cute together."

Landon glanced toward the open door of the room where Hunter and Amanda were talking about scales and registers. "Are we?"

"Very."

"We've had a lot going on, and that's about to become even more so." Amanda had shared her news about Stella with Hunter and Megan over dinner, and they'd pretended to hear it for the first time. Landon felt guilty about that, but he had a feeling she wouldn't mind that he'd shared it with them.

"The news about her daughter is incredible, even if it's coming from a very sad event for Stella and her mom."

"I know. Amanda is elated but trying to keep it in check in light of what they're going through."

"That's got to be a very fine line for her to walk."

"It is. I'm glad we had these plans with you guys so she had something fun to do to get through the hours before her call at nine."

Megan rested a hand on her pregnant belly. "I'm trying to imagine what it would be like to talk to your child for the first time twelve years after you gave birth to them."

"I can't get my head around what she must be feeling. I'm just trying to be as supportive as I can be."

"It's hard for you, because you two are starting something new and possibly important, and this has thrown a curveball into everything."

"Yeah."

"As much as you want to be part of this thing with her and Stella, it's really going to be about the two of them at first. You know that, right?"

He nodded. "I'm trying to figure out how I fit into it."

"It's a big deal that she's making plans to stay here. I think that's in large part because of you."

"I hope so."

"It is, Landon. Of course it is. She could go anywhere, but she's choosing to stay here."

"She also likes the town and is interested in our family's business."

"Mostly, though, she's interested in you."

"I'm glad you think so."

"You don't?"

"I do. It's just that I'm not sure if we're looking at a long-term thing or a fling."

"Has she asked you to be part of what's happening with her daughter?"

"Yes, but—"

Megan held up her hand to stop him. "That's all you need to know."

"How do you mean?"

"If she wasn't looking beyond the temporary with you, there's no way she'd ask you to be part of her relationship with Stella. I'm not a mother yet, but I'm one hundred percent confident about that much."

"Huh. I hadn't thought of it that way."

"I think you need to chill and enjoy the ride. Don't overthink it."

"That's easier said than done."

"Because you legitimately care about her. That's why everything seems so unsettled."

"Is that what happened to you when you were first with Hunter?"

"Totally. I had no idea how he felt about me, and when he clued me in, I felt like I was skiing the black diamonds in the fog with no poles."

"Yikes. How long did that last?"

"Awhile. Until I caught up to him. Love is a funny thing. It's the best feeling in the world, but it also comes with so many secondary emotions."

Her use of the word *love* stunned him. It was one thing for him to think that way, but a whole other thing for someone else to go there.

"Why do you look like you've just seen a ghost?"

"You dropped the L word."

"Isn't that what we were talking about?"

"I, uh, well…"

Megan lost it laughing, covering her mouth in a failed effort to contain it. "You're so stupid."

"Hey! It's bad enough I have to hear that from your husband and our other siblings, but I thought you were a friend."

"I *am* your friend, and that's why I'm telling you you're stupid. The reason why this is so confusing, Landon, is because you're *falling in love* with her. And vice versa. Why do you think she's arranging her new life to include you? It's not just because the sex is good, you fool."

"Now you're just being mean."

"Awww, I'm sorry. You know I love you."

"Too late. You can't take it back now. And PS, I'd already started to come to that conclusion about the L word myself, so I'm not as much of a fool as you think I am." Despite the jabs, he adored her. Mostly, he adored the way she loved Hunter.

"You'll thank me later for giving you the lowdown on what's going on here."

"I think you're spending way too much time with Gramps."

Megan laughed again. "That might be true. I'm starting to quote him without even knowing I'm doing it."

"Who are you quoting, love?" Hunter asked when he and Amanda came into the room.

"Your grandfather."

"He's got her brainwashed," Landon said.

"I can think of worse people to be influenced by." Hunter effortlessly arranged Megan so she and the dog were on his lap with his arms around her, the baby bump and the dog. They made for a cute little family.

Landon extended his hand to Amanda, inviting her to join him.

She cozied up to him, and with her in his arms and the scent of her hair enveloping him in a cloud of sweetness, he felt himself settle ever so slightly into the possibility that he was, in fact, falling in love with her.

That was a rather earth-shattering revelation to a guy who'd gone out of his way to avoid the L word his entire adult life.

But if falling in love meant getting to be with her every day, well, then that was just fine with him.

"How was the lesson?" Landon asked her.

"It was great. Hunter showed me a few things I need to practice. I'm going to order a keyboard online."

"We might be able to get you one through the store," Hunter said. "We have suppliers for just about everything."

"Even better."

"I'll check with Charley tomorrow and let you know."

"Thank you." To Landon, she said, "Are you ready to head home?"

"Whenever you are."

Amanda stood and found her balance while holding on to Landon's shoulder. "Thank you, guys, so much for dinner and the piano lesson. I really appreciate it."

"Our pleasure," Hunter said.

"Don't get up," Landon said. "We can see ourselves out. Thanks again."

"Any time," Megan said.

Landon helped Amanda down the stairs and into his truck. "How're you holding up?" he asked as he drove them home.

"This last hour will be the longest of my whole life."

"Probably, but just think, in an hour, you get to talk to Stella."

"I can't wait." She looked over at him. "I know you have to go to work—"

"I can hang out until you make the call."

"Oh good," she said, sounding relieved. "I was so hoping you might be able to stay."

"Barring a rescue call, I'm all yours." That was true in ways he was only beginning to fully understand.

CHAPTER EIGHTEEN

"Patience is the art of hoping."
—Luc de Clapiers

*A*fter Landon and Amanda left, Hunter and Megan continued to snuggle on the sofa until she was yawning so much, he insisted they turn in early. He let out Horace and locked up for the night.

On the way upstairs, Hunter said, "I think my little boy Landon is falling in love."

"I know. I told him that and freaked him out a little."

"He didn't already realize it?"

"He said he was getting there on his own, but he seemed a little startled to have it spelled out so clearly by someone else."

Hunter put his arms around her, gazing down at her with the love and affection that had become part of her daily life since he made her fall in love with him. "You know what I don't miss?"

"What's that?"

"All the time I spent wishing for everything we have now. I wouldn't go back to that for anything. That uncertainty is the worst."

"It is. Landon is really struggling with trying to figure out how he fits into her life, especially in light of the new wrinkle with her daughter."

"That's really quite a challenge for both of them," Hunter said.

"It is, but I think they're up to it."

"I do, too. It's funny how both he and Lucas could end up taking on kids. They're a couple of kids themselves."

"No, they're not," Megan said. "Despite how it might seem sometimes, they're actually fully grown men."

"They are? Really?"

"They are."

"Huh, I must've missed that memo."

"Guess what? So is Max."

Hunter pulled a shocked expression. "Wow. I might need a minute to process this."

"Face the facts, love. Your baby brothers aren't babies anymore."

"I can't get my head around this development."

Megan yawned again and snuggled into his embrace, practically asleep on her feet.

"Let's get my baby mama tucked into bed."

She was almost asleep when he slid into bed a few minutes after her. "Need my kiss." Even though her eyes were closed, she felt his smile against her lips. "Love you."

"Love you, too. Thanks for marrying me and making me the happiest guy in the world."

She managed a smile with the last of her energy. "You didn't give me much choice." They had this conversation frequently.

"The choice was all yours, my love."

"Best thing I ever did was marry you."

"I'm glad you feel that way." He put his arms around her and settled her head on his chest. "Sleep. I've got you."

. . .

THE FINAL FORTY-FIVE MINUTES WERE, INDEED, THE LONGEST minutes of Amanda's life. "What if she doesn't like me?"

Landon sat next to her on the sofa, holding her hand and doing his best to keep her calm. "She'll love you. How can she not?"

"What if she changes her mind?"

"She won't."

"What if I can't do it? I've never been anyone's mother. What if I screw her up?"

"You won't. After reading her letter to you, it's obvious she's already a great kid. You'll just be taking over what her mother started."

"When are you going to get sick of me and tell me to get out of your house so you can get your life back?"

"Um, never? I love having you here."

"I can't imagine why. All I've done is cry all over you and bring massive amounts of drama to your previously peaceful existence."

"That's not all you've done, and my peaceful existence was boring compared to having you here."

She laughed. "You're crazy."

"In case you haven't noticed, I'm crazy about you. You've got enough going on without worrying about me getting sick of you. That's not going to happen."

"It *could* happen."

He kissed her, probably to shut her up, and really, who could blame him? "Not going to happen."

"I'm lucky to have such a good friend at a time when I need one very badly."

"Everything is going to be fine. I know it. Just keep breathing and take it one minute at a time."

"I'm still figuring out how to do that. I'm used to having plans for my plans, and nothing is going according to plan."

"You're writing a whole new plan, and I've got a good feeling about this one."

At one minute before nine, Landon got up, retrieved the portable phone and handed it to her. "Do you want me to stay?"

"God, yes."

Smiling, he returned to the sofa and put his arm around her. "Keep breathing."

"I'm trying." Her hands trembled as she dialed the number she'd all but memorized and listened to it ring. And when the voice of a young girl answered with a cheerful "Hello," tears flooded her eyes and spilled down her cheeks.

"This is Amanda. Your, um…"

"Biological mother."

"Yes. It's me."

"Thank you so much for responding to our letter and for calling. I wasn't sure if you would."

"Your letter touched me so deeply. How's your mother doing?"

"She's mostly okay right now, but we know that's not going to last."

Stella's matter-of-fact summary impressed Amanda and broke her heart, too. "I'm so, so sorry for both of you."

"Thank you. We're trying to be realistic and make plans. I'm a planner. I always have to know what I'm doing."

Amanda gasped. "I… So am I. I joke that I have plans for my plans."

"Then I get that from you."

"Yes," Amanda said, closing her eyes in a failed attempt to stop another flood of tears.

"That's the weird thing about being adopted. I don't know where any of these things come from. Like my hair color or my eye color or who I look like."

"You look like I did when I was your age, but you have your father's green eyes."

"Wow. It's so cool to finally know that. Do you still talk to him?"

"No, I haven't seen him since before you were born."

184

"Oh. Can you tell me his name?"

"Jimmy."

"Were you guys together for long?"

"No, it was a short-lived thing, and he was away at college by the time I found out I was pregnant with you."

"Did he know about me?"

"He did." Amanda tried to think of how to answer Stella's unspoken question. "We were both really young and not in any way prepared to take care of a baby."

"I understand."

"We wanted to do what was best for you, but you should know that giving you up broke my heart. I was never the same afterward."

Landon squeezed her shoulder.

Amanda leaned into him, closing her eyes to absorb the blow that hit like it had just happened five minutes ago rather than twelve years. That was the downside of feeling everything after being numb for so long.

"Thank you for telling me that," Stella said. "I've had so many questions about where I came from and stuff. It's good to know."

"I'll always tell you anything you want to know, if I can."

"Are you married?"

"Nope."

"Do you have a boyfriend?"

Amanda raised her head off Landon's shoulder and glanced at him.

He nodded.

"I think maybe I do."

Stella laughed. "You're not sure?"

"It's kind of new still. We haven't really put labels on it yet."

"What's his name?"

"Landon."

"That's a nice name."

"He's a nice guy."

"Is he cute?"

Amanda laughed. "I think so, and so does every other woman in the town where he lives."

Landon scowled playfully at her.

"So it's like that, huh?"

"He tells me he's become a one-woman kind of guy lately." Amanda wasn't sure if she was saying too much or if it was appropriate to share such things with a twelve-year-old, but she was determined to be honest with her.

"That's the best kind of boyfriend to have. My mom tells me not to date boys who need all the girls to like them. She said the good ones only like one girl at a time."

"Your mom is very wise."

"What should I call you?"

The sweet, innocent question tugged at Amanda's heart. "How about Amanda?"

"That would be okay with you?"

"Of course."

"Okay."

"Could I ask you something?" Amanda said.

"Sure."

"How would you feel about living in Vermont? When the time comes…"

After a brief pause, she said, "I suppose that would be okay."

"It's only a few hours from where you live now. I could take you there to see your friends any time you wanted."

"That'd be cool. We only moved here last summer, but I have a couple of new friends. What's it like in Vermont? I haven't been there."

"It's so pretty here. There are mountains and trees and beautiful streams that freeze in the winter."

"Are you from there?"

"No, I'm from St. Louis, Missouri, originally. I came to Vermont for work, and I've fallen in love with it."

"Where do you work?"

"I work for a company that sells products to stores, and I

go around training their sales teams on how to sell our products. I also go to a lot of trade shows every year, but I'm changing jobs so I don't have to travel so much." Amanda prayed Stella wouldn't ask about the products she represented.

"Are you changing jobs because of me?"

"No. I'm doing it for me, but it'll be better for you, too."

"What's your new job going to be?"

"I'm still working that out, but I promise I'll provide a stable, comfortable home for you when you need it. And in the meantime, I'll do anything I can to help you through this difficult time."

"It's really nice of you to be so cool about all this. I'm sure it was a surprise to get my letter."

"It was the best kind of surprise to hear from you, but I'm very sorry about the circumstances."

"Yeah, me, too. Well, I guess I ought to go take a shower and finish my homework."

"It was really nice to talk to you. Can we do it again soon?"

"Sure."

"Call me any time you want on this number, and let me give you my cell number. The service isn't great in this town, but I'll call you back as soon as I can if I miss your call."

"Wait, the cell service is bad in your town?"

"It is. Is that a deal-breaker?"

"It may be," Stella said, laughing.

Her laugh was the best thing Amanda had ever heard. "Believe it or not, you do get used to it."

"I'm not sure that's possible."

"You'll have to trust me on that."

"If you say so. My mom was wondering if she could say hello real quick."

"Of course. I'll talk to you soon."

"It was really nice to talk to you, Amanda. Thank you, you know… for what you're doing."

"I'm so, *so* happy to talk to you, too." That had to be the understatement of Amanda's lifetime.

"Here's my mom."

"Hi, Amanda, this is Kelly. Thank you so much. It means the world to both of us."

"I'm very sorry for the reason you need my help."

"I'm trying to make peace with it and do my best to support Stella. She's really a terrific kid." Kelly's voice broke.

"I could tell that from her letter and even more so after speaking to her."

"You should know I have good life insurance, and she's my beneficiary. You won't have to support her entirely on your own, and her college will be covered."

"That's not a concern, but thank you for letting me know."

"It matters to me that you stepped up before you knew any of that."

Amanda used a tissue to mop up her tears. "I've never stopped thinking of her. Not for one minute."

"That matters to me, too. I'd like for you and Stella to meet in person as soon as we can make that happen."

"Would the weekend after next work for you?" Amanda wanted Landon with her, and with his brother's wedding that coming weekend, she couldn't ask him to miss it.

"Yes, that'd be fine."

"Very good. I'll speak to you before then, and we'll make some plans."

"I hope you know that you've provided peace of mind for someone you've never met."

"I wish there was more I could do."

"This is more than enough. Stella will want to call again soon."

"I'll be here. Any time. Maybe we could FaceTime next time."

"I'm sure she'd love that. Thank you again."

They said their goodbyes. Amanda turned off the portable

phone and placed it on the coffee table. After a long moment of silence, she said, "So that was my daughter."

"That was your daughter." He drew her into his arms and held on tight. "She sounds delightful."

"Doesn't she?"

"I can't wait to meet her. I can only imagine how you must feel."

"I feel very lucky I'm getting this second chance with her, but awful about what's happening to Kelly."

"It's a very fine line between elation and devastation."

"Yes," she said, relieved he understood. "And I'm fully aware it's a lot to bring into our relatively new situation."

"I'm not a *situation*. I'm your *boyfriend*. You said so."

"And that's what you want? To be my boyfriend?"

"Hell yes. Only if you'll be my girlfriend."

"Nothing would make me happier." She leaned her head on his chest. "Thank you for being so great about all this."

"I assume you'll be just as great to me whenever we run into my exes around town."

Amanda laughed at the outrageous statement. "Because that's exactly the same thing."

"I'm glad you see it the same way I do." He kissed the top of her head. "Let's go to bed and snuggle."

"Is that code for have sex?"

"How'd you know?"

"A wild guess. Don't you have to go back to the firehouse?"

"I'll get there. Eventually."

Amanda had talked to her daughter and survived the emotional overload, thanks in large part to Landon and his steady, calming presence. Not only was he fun, funny and a god in bed, but he was also one of the best people she'd ever met.

It would be so easy to fall madly in love with a man like that.

189

CHAPTER NINETEEN

*"Patience and perseverance have a magical effect before which
difficulties disappear and obstacles vanish."*
—John Quincy Adams

They spent all day Saturday together until Landon had
to leave for work. On Sunday, they went to dinner at
the barn, and after a fun and funny time with his family, Landon
asked his dad if he could borrow his Range Rover for a short
ride.

"Of course," Linc said. "But is there something wrong with
your truck?"

Landon followed Linc to the mudroom to get the keys.
"Amanda wants to learn to drive a stick, and yours is the only
one in the family."

"Can she do that with her ankle?"

"Her ankle is much better, so I'll let her decide if she wants to
try it yet. I can at least show her how."

"Sounds like a plan." He handed over the keys to Landon. "So
things are good between you two?"

"Very good. Amazing, in fact."

"That's great to hear. Dani mentioned Amanda might be

interested in working at the warehouse, and I heard she's got appointments with Mildred and Elmer this week for the catalog."

"That's right."

"I'm happy for you, son. She's a lovely young lady."

"Yes, she is." Landon looked around his dad's shoulder to make sure they were still alone. "When she was in high school, she gave up a daughter for adoption. The child has recently come back into her life." He explained about what was happening with Stella and Kelly. "Amanda is going to step up for her, and I guess that means I will, too."

"That's a big deal. How do you feel about that?"

"If you had asked me a few months ago if I was ready to be a father figure to anyone, I would've laughed. But now there's nothing funny about it, you know?"

"I do know."

"Right," Landon said, laughing. "Ten kids."

"I've always said it takes a very special man to become a father to someone else's child. I thought that with Gray and Simone, and now Lucas and Savvy. It's a beautiful thing to open your heart to a child because you want to, not because you necessarily have to. Not that I ever felt like I had to with you kids, but I think you get my meaning."

"I do. And from what I've seen and heard so far, Stella is a delightful kid. We're going to Albany to meet her in person the weekend after the wedding."

"It's good that you're going with Amanda for that."

"I'd never want her to do that alone. She's been so emotional since the fire. She says it's because the brush with death surfaced all the crap from after she gave up Stella. She was just starting to deal with it when she got the letter from the adoption agency."

"It's a lot for anyone to cope with, especially when starting a new relationship."

"Yeah, it is."

"I wouldn't be your dad if I didn't tell you to look out for yourself in the midst of her emotional tsunami."

"I am."

Lincoln tipped his head and gave Landon a shrewd look. "You sure about that?"

"I'm trying."

Linc nodded. "Don't take your eye off that ball, son. I understand the desire to be there for her, especially with what she's dealing with. But make sure she's there for you, too."

"I hear you."

"Good, then my work here is finished."

"Is your work ever actually finished?"

"No. Never."

Landon laughed at the emphatic way his dad said that. "It's your own fault for having ten kids."

"Believe me, I tell myself that every day. All kidding aside, though, I'm here if you need me."

Landon gave his dad a quick hug. "Thanks. I always know that."

Amanda came hobbling into the mudroom. "There you are. I wondered where you went."

"Sorry. I was borrowing my dad's keys so I can teach you how to drive a stick. You ready for your first lesson?"

She clapped her hands with delight. "Sure."

"Go easy on my clutch," Linc said over his shoulder as he returned to the kitchen. "She's delicate."

"What's a clutch?" Amanda asked in all seriousness.

Linc spun around, looking stricken. "Oh my God."

Landon laughed at the face his father made. "Relax, Dad. We'll take good care of her. Don't worry." He retrieved their coats off the row of hooks that were labeled with each of their names. His was second to last.

"I know I've said it before, but those hooks are the sweetest thing I've ever seen."

Landon held her coat for her. "Ever?"

Amanda turned her back to him and slid the coat on. "Ever. I love your family."

"They love you, too."

She turned back to face him. "Do you think so?"

He scooped her hair out of the back of her coat and let it slide through his fingers. "I know so. They tease you like you're one of us. That's always a good sign."

"They do make me laugh, that's for sure."

They walked outside to the Range Rover that was his dad's pride and joy. Landon helped her get settled in the passenger seat. When he was seated in the driver's seat, he pointed to the pedals on the floor. "Note the presence of the third pedal."

"What is that?"

"The clutch. Pressing that allows you to change gears. I'll show you." He wiggled the stick shift to take it out gear and fired up the engine. "Watch." He pushed in the clutch and shifted the car into Reverse. "The secret to driving a stick is releasing the clutch slowly as you give it gas." The car began to roll backward. "See?"

"I think so."

At the end of the driveway, he brought the car to a stop. "I'm pressing the clutch again to go from Reverse to first gear."

"How can you tell where the gears are?"

He pointed to the drawing on the shifter nob. "This is a five-speed, so there's a fifth gear for when you're on the highway." With the car in first, he slowly released the clutch as he gave it some gas.

"How do you know when to shift?"

"Listen." As the engine revved, he shifted into second. "You hear how it seems to be asking for the next gear?"

"Um, not really."

"Keep listening. You'll hear it. After a while, it becomes instinctual. You know right when to shift based on how the car is performing."

"This is more complicated than I thought it would be."

"It's really not once you get a feel for it. The hardest thing about driving a stick is when you're stopped on a hill. That's how Hunter taught me, and I was freaking out."

"How come?"

"When you drive an automatic, the car stays in place when you go from braking to accelerating. It wants to roll backward with a stick. That's why going from stop to start on a hill is the hardest part. I'll show you." Landon drove them a couple of miles to the access road that led up to Colton and Lucy's mountaintop home and brought the car to a stop on the hill. "The trick to this is working the fine line between where the clutch releases and the accelerator kicks in. But first, this is what happens if you don't hit that sweet spot." He demonstrated how the car would roll backward. "If you're stopped at a light with a car behind you when that happens, that's a problem."

"There's no way I can do this."

He laughed. "Of course you can. This is how you make it so that doesn't happen. You release the clutch at the same time you push the accelerator."

"What about the brake?"

"You don't need it."

"Oh my God. No way."

Laughing, he said, "It's also critical to never leave a manual transmission out of gear when you park on a hill. You want to put it in gear and make sure the emergency brake is on, or it's apt to roll away."

"That can happen?"

"Yep. Happened to me once, and the car got wrapped around a tree. My father was not happy. I spent an entire weekend banging out the dent in the trunk while he reminded me— repeatedly—that I was lucky the car *only* hit a tree and not a person."

"Yikes."

"My argument was that if it hadn't been in gear, how could I have walked away from it?"

"So wait, it can pop out of gear?"

"Yep, which is why the brake is critical. The emergency brake on that car had been broken for a while when that happened. My dad had to eventually concede that I was right about leaving it in gear. He paid to get the brake fixed."

They arrived at the top of the mountain, where the family's sugaring operation was headquartered. Colton and Lucy lived in a cabin on the property.

Landon turned the vehicle to head back down the hill. "This is where driving a stick is fun."

"What're you doing?"

"Point and shoot." He let the car roll down the hill, gaining speed as it went until Amanda was screaming and laughing as he navigated each curve, bringing the car to a stop at the bottom of the hill. "Fun, right? It's like sledding in a car."

"You're insane."

"I know every bend and hook of that road. You were never in any danger."

"Whatever you say. Please don't get me killed before I have the chance to meet my daughter."

"You're completely safe with me." He glanced over at her. "You want to try it?"

"Uh, not really."

"Oh, come on. Where's my daring, wild badass who wants to try everything?"

"I'm afraid of wrecking your dad's prized Range Rover."

"You won't wreck it."

"Are you sure?"

"Positive. Come on… Be wild."

She blew out a breath. "If you say so."

Landon turned the car around so they were positioned facing the uphill climb, applied the emergency brake and got out of the car. They met in front, and he kissed her. "You got this."

"I sure hope so."

"Your ankle feels okay?"

"Yeah, it's good."

"All right, then, take me for a ride." He waggled his brows for emphasis.

Amanda laughed, got into the driver's seat and adjusted the seat closer to the pedals.

"Release the emergency brake and then get a feel for the clutch. This one releases close to the top."

"Like this?" The car lurched forward and stalled.

Landon bit his lip to keep from laughing. "Not quite."

She glared at him. "I can hear you laughing."

"I'm not laughing."

"Liar."

"Try again." He walked her through the steps needed to get the car moving forward. As they crested the hill, he told her to stop. "Take it out of gear, release the clutch and hit the brake. Good. Now, this is the test."

"I'm scared."

"Don't be. There's nothing behind you to hit, so if the car rolls back a bit, you're fine."

"Gulp."

"Let up on the clutch slowly as you press down on the gas. You feel that? Yes! Like that. Perfect."

"I did it!"

"You did. Excellent job. Now stop again."

"Do I have to?"

"Yep."

"Ugh. Okay." She brought the car to a stop but forgot to employ the clutch. Again, the car lurched forward and stalled. "Damn it."

"If the car is in gear when you're stopping, you need to push in the clutch."

"Now you tell me."

"I said that."

"When?"

"You're cute when you're pissed."

"Your charm isn't going to get you out of this."

"Good to know." He loved being with her. He loved everything about her, even the stubborn set to her jaw as she tried to learn something new. "Let's go through it again." He went over each step required to get the car moving without rolling backward. "Ready to try?"

"No."

"Yes, you are."

"No, I'm not."

He put his hand over hers on the stick shift. "Let's do it together."

"Is that a metaphor?"

Landon laughed. "Slowly let off on the clutch as you press down on the gas. Let's do it."

The car stalled again.

"It hates me."

"Nope. Try again. You'll get it."

"What's that burning smell?"

"My dad's pampered clutch."

"He's going to be able to tell I ruined it."

"You won't ruin it. Just relax and feel the car. It'll guide you."

"Okay, Zen Landon. Whatever you say."

"Less talking. More driving."

After two more false starts, she succeeded in moving the car up the hill, letting out a victory whoop that made him laugh.

"Now we're talking." He let her enjoy the victory for a minute before he told her to stop again.

"No! I don't want to."

"Yes. Do it. And don't forget the clutch."

"Fine." She glided to a smooth stop.

"Excellent. Now get going again." This time, she went from stop to go and smoothly accelerated up the hill. "There you go! You've got it."

"Yahoo! Check me out!"

"Don't mind if I do."

"I did it, Landon!"

"Yes, you did. That's the hardest part of driving a stick. If you can do that, you can do anything."

"Thank you for teaching me."

He put his hand on top of hers on the shifter. "My pleasure. Now, let's go down the hill, and you can take me for a ride."

"Are we still talking about driving?"

"For now."

"Thanks for this." She glanced over at him. "It helps to stay busy."

"We'll keep you very busy this week and next, and soon enough, you'll get to see your girl."

"I can't wait."

CHAPTER TWENTY

*"A tree is known by its fruit; a man by his deeds. A good deed is
never lost; he who sows courtesy reaps friendship, and he who
plants kindness gathers love."*
—Saint Basil

*A*manda officially returned to work Monday morning
with the training for the Abbotts' sales team that was
set to take place at the Grange, a function hall in town. Ella and
Charley had provided a continental breakfast for the salespeo-
ple, who were mostly older women. From what Amanda had
been told, many of them were second-, third- and even fourth-
generation members of their families to work for the company.

She had tailored her presentation accordingly.

After everyone had a chance to get coffee and a Danish,
Charley asked them to take their seats so they could get started.
Ella and Charley were heading back across the street to work
the floor in the store with Cameron and Lucy while the sales
team was in training.

Wade Abbott stepped up to the podium. "Good morning,
everyone. As the director of health and wellness, it's my honor
to welcome you today to this special training event for our new

intimate product line. For the record, this was one hundred percent my father's idea, so any complaints or concerns should be directed to him."

While the others laughed, Wade flashed that unmistakable Abbott grin—a little bit mischievous and a whole lot sexy. Each of the Abbott men had that unmistakable *something* that made them catnip to women, and they got it from their dad and granddad, who were just as charming.

Which was why Amanda couldn't wait to see what happened when the catalog hit and women came from all over in hopes of seeing the male models in person.

"All kidding aside," Wade said, "we're pleased to expand our offerings to include this new line, which is sure to come with tons of questions. Thank goodness Amanda Pressley is here today to answer all your questions, because that saves me from having to do it."

The ladies laughed and clapped as Wade ceded the floor to Amanda. "Thank you, Wade. I'm happy to take one for the team today. Let's talk about sex toys, shall we?"

A titter of laughter went through her captive audience. They'd been given a brochure that detailed each of the items that would be for sale in the store.

Using a PowerPoint slide show, Amanda went through a detailed description of each item, how it worked, what it did for the user and why past customers loved it so much. She was hitting her stride when Landon walked in and headed for the back of the room, where he leaned against a wall. She stumbled, but only for a second. Damn him! The man could flummox her just by walking in the door. "As I was saying…"

Landon grinned, clearly pleased that he'd messed with her groove.

She pressed on but stumbled again when she saw a young woman approach him and kiss his cheek. Would it be professional to stop her presentation to tell that woman to get the hell away from him? Probably not…

"One of the things we've found to be a fun and effective way to market our products in stores such as yours is to make the customers look for them. Make it a bit of a scavenger hunt, if you will. Once the catalog hits and the products are included, people will want to find them in the store, too. If you keep them somewhere that takes a little looking, it'll keep customers in the store longer as they look for them."

Amanda gave her audience a second to wrap their heads around that idea while she tried not to glare at the woman talking to Landon with animated gestures. To his credit, he was paying more attention to Amanda than he was to the other woman. He caught her gaze, smiled and winked.

Damned man would be the death of her.

"Let me take a few questions at this point." She didn't usually do questions yet, but her train of thought had left the station the second she saw that woman kiss Landon.

A woman with white hair and glasses raised her hand. "I'd like to know how people talk about the products with customers without feeling embarrassed."

"That's a great question," Amanda said, and it was one she'd fielded many times before. "We're so preconditioned in our culture to think of anything having to do with sex or pleasure as taboo. Let's agree to leave that thinking out of this conversation. Human beings were given the ability to find physical pleasure within their own bodies. Sex isn't just about procreation, it's also about pleasure, and that doesn't end just because someone has been ill or is widowed or doesn't have a partner. Our product line is all about the notion that pleasure is for everyone, no matter their age or circumstances, with or without a partner. If you can approach it from that mind-set, you'll find that it quickly becomes routine to talk about things that might've embarrassed you a short time ago. I hope that answers your question."

"It does," the woman said.

"Other questions?" Hearing none, Amanda said, "Excellent, now let's get up close and personal with the products."

"Your lady is good at this, son," Linc said when he joined Landon at the back of the room.

"She sure is." Landon looked over at his dad. "She gave notice to her mom."

"We can certainly find a role for her to play in our company, and if it helps you out, too, that's even better."

"Thanks, Dad. I have a vested interest in keeping her in town."

"I see that, and it sure makes me happy for you."

"I'm rather happy for me, too. She's... well..."

"She's the one."

Nodding, he watched Amanda as she interacted with the sales ladies, laughing and talking with her hands. "Is it normal to feel..."

"Everything?"

Landon shifted his gaze to his dad again. "Yeah."

Linc nodded. "It's perfectly normal, but it's a lot to process at first."

"Is that how it was for you when you met Mom?"

"Just like that, and it was immediate. When you've never felt that before, it's shocking when you realize what it is. Although, your mother tells me this isn't the first time for you."

Landon stared at him. "She said that?"

"She reminded me of your affection for young Naomi, and I was ashamed to admit I hadn't noticed it was something extra for you. Of course, your mom knew."

"I... I didn't realize she knew." But Landon did remember his mom going out of her way to be available to him during that difficult time. He remembered that very vividly.

"Not much gets by her."

"I know that from personal experience."

Linc threw his head back and laughed quietly so as not to disturb the training session. "The downside to being the ninth of ten kids. Your mom was fully trained by the time you came along."

"Definite downside."

"But the upside is she made sure you got through the dreadful experience of losing Naomi."

"True." He glanced at his dad. "I've come to realize I've gone out of my way to avoid anything that could ever hurt me the way that did."

"Understandable. But if you do that forever, you run the risk of missing out on one of the best things in life."

"I know that now. Amanda has shown me it's worth the risk to feel the way I do about her."

"I'm so delighted to hear that. She's a terrific gal. We're all quite fond of her."

"I'm quite fond of her, too," Landon said, grinning. "In fact, I'm going to have a word with her while they're on a break, and then I've got to get to the farm."

"Ah, yes. Max said you guys are shearing this week."

"Yep. He's giving the haircuts while I mow. It never ends."

"You do a great job there, Landon. Not sure I say it often enough."

"Thanks for that and the words of wisdom."

"My pleasure. Tell Amanda to come by my office and see me after the training."

"I'll do that."

As Landon walked to the front of the room, saying hello to women he'd known all his life, he knew a moment of complete contentment. Things were falling into place for Amanda and for them as a couple. Was it only a week ago that he'd felt the need to seek out Hannah's advice on how to move things forward with Amanda? They'd traveled light-years since then, and he quite liked the place they were in now.

She lit up with a smile when she saw him coming.

In front of their entire sales team, he kissed her on the lips. "Great job."

"Thanks. Who was that kissing you?"

He had to think about that for a second. "Oh, you mean Becky?"

Amanda frowned adorably. "Is that her name?"

Smiling, Landon said, "We've been friends since kindergarten. You can sheathe your claws, tiger. We never dated."

She gave him a haughty look. "My claws are not out."

"Whatever you say."

"I thought you were working at the farm today."

"I am, but I couldn't miss this."

"I hope you found it entertaining."

"Extremely. I also found it inspiring. You're very good at what you do."

"Thanks. I've enjoyed this job, but I'm ready for the next challenge."

"Speaking of that, Dad said to stop by his office after you're done here. I think he wants to talk to you about a job."

"I'll stop to see him before I go to Mildred's for the interview."

"You've got Gramps tomorrow, right?"

"Yep."

"And you're sure you feel comfortable driving again?" They had picked up her rental car at the inn parking lot the night before.

"Totally fine. My ankle is so much better."

"Okay, then. I'll see you at home later?"

"Yes, you will."

He kissed her again. "I can't wait."

AFTER THE TRAINING ENDED, AMANDA WALKED ALONG THE sidewalk to the diner where she'd cross the street to get to the store. Just as she was about to step off the curb, a gigantic moose came strolling down the center of Elm Street and stopped about five feet from her to take a good, long, measuring look at her.

Amanda held her breath, uncertain of what was happening.

"Fred is sizing you up," a voice next to her said, startling her.

She took her eyes off the moose only long enough to glance at Hannah, who was holding baby Callie.

"Sizing me up?" Amanda said, her voice higher than usual.

"Yep. He's deciding if he likes you for Landon."

"What if he decides he doesn't like me?"

"I'm not sure what'll happen. He may try to run you off."

Amanda whipped her head around to stare at Hannah. "Run me off? What does that entail?"

"It hasn't happened before, so I can't say for certain. Fred tends to approve of the people we choose for ourselves, but we can't take that for granted."

"And of course you know how crazy that sounds?"

Hannah shrugged. "I can't help if I understand him at a different level than everyone else does."

"So what's the secret to getting across the street?"

"You wait until he's ready to move. Or you go around him. Seeing as how you're still nursing that ankle, I'd wait in case he decides to give chase."

"Give chase," Amanda said. "Lovely."

"Usually, he is, but as my husband and family like to remind me, he is a wild animal, so you have to prepare for the unexpected."

"I'll just wait for him to move along, then, I guess."

"Good call."

After a full minute passed in which the gigantic moose didn't blink as he continued to stare at Amanda, Hannah stepped off the curb and approached him.

"Nothing to see here, Fred. Move along."

A male voice came from behind them. "*No, Hannah. Get my daughter away from that moose. Right now.*"

"Daddy is always spoiling our fun," Hannah said to Callie, but she returned to the sidewalk as Nolan joined them.

"Come see Daddy, angel."

Hannah transferred the baby to her father. "Don't get her dirty."

"I'd rather get her dirty than eaten by a moose."

"He is not going to *eat* her. He loves her."

Amanda wondered if they considered this conversation "normal."

"Fred!" Hannah's sharp command shifted the moose's attention to her, which was a relief to Amanda. That stare was intimidating.

"Let Amanda cross the street. We *like* her. It's all good."

Fred let out a loud moo that made Amanda nearly jump out of her skin and took a step forward. And then another.

She let go of the breath she'd been holding as she watched him walk away, slowly, as if he was in no particular rush.

"I think you passed the test," Hannah said.

"Well, that's a relief."

"My wife is stark raving nuts, in case you were wondering," Nolan said.

"But he loves me anyway," Hannah retorted, making a face at him.

"Someone's gotta."

They were too adorable for words, Amanda decided. "Thanks for helping me get his approval. I'm sure it was much more about you than me."

"He does tend to follow my lead," Hannah said in all seriousness. "Were you headed to the store?"

"I was. I'm hoping to find your dad there."

"Callie and I just saw him in his office."

"Thanks. I'll see you later."

Hannah waved Callie's hand for her. "Say bye-bye to Auntie Amanda."

"Bye, Callie," Amanda said, touched to be given auntie

status. Looking both ways for cars—and recalcitrant moose—Amanda crossed the street to the store, taking pains not to look at the blackened hulk of what remained of the inn next door. The place was crawling with workers cleaning up the debris.

She entered through the main doors and immediately felt calmer and more centered. The Green Mountain Country Store was one of the most magical places she'd ever been.

It would be hard to capture the essence of the place in mere words, but she looked forward to the challenge of using the personal experiences of people connected to the store to tell its story. She wandered through the toy department, past the household goods and the apothecary on her way upstairs to the offices, all the while wishing she had time to linger. The store drew her in like nowhere she'd ever been, and the thought of working there excited her.

Emma was eating lunch at her desk when Amanda walked into the reception area. "Hi there. How was the training?"

"It went very well."

"I give you credit," Emma said, flushing. "I'm not sure I could cover that topic with that audience."

"Eh, I'm used to it. If you've seen one sex toy, you've seen them all."

Emma laughed. "If you say so."

"Is Linc available by any chance?"

"Sure. He's in his office."

"Thanks."

"How's the ankle?"

"Much better, thank goodness."

"Glad to hear it."

Amanda had started to walk away when she recalled that Emma had a daughter. "Your daughter…"

"What about her?"

"How old is she?"

"Just turned eleven. Why?"

"I'm not sure if you've heard, but at some point, my twelve-year-old daughter will be coming to live with me."

"I did hear about that, and I'm happy for you even if the circumstances are tragic."

"I know. I've been trying to keep that in mind as I think about having her with me. Maybe when Stella comes, we could get the girls together. She'll need all the friends she can get."

"I'd love that, and Simone would, too."

"Great. Thank you."

"Good luck with it all. If you need someone to talk to who understands girls that age, I'm right here."

"I'll absolutely take you up on that. Thank you."

"Sure."

Hunter came out of his office. "I thought I heard you. I wanted to tell you I found that keyboard we talked about. Would you like me to order it for you?"

"That'd be great. Can I give you my credit card?"

"I'll order it through the store account and get you a good discount. You can pay for it when it arrives, if that works."

"It does. Thank you so much. I can't wait to be able to practice."

"I'll call you at Landon's when it comes in."

"Perfect. Thanks again."

"No problem."

Amanda went to Linc's office and knocked on the door. "Hi there."

"Amanda, hi. Come in." Linc stood and gestured for her to have a seat. "The training seemed to go very well this morning. You did a wonderful job."

"Thank you. I'm glad you were pleased."

"Very much so. You handled their concerns like the pro you are."

"It takes a minute, but once they realize these products aren't that different from other health and wellness items, it does get easier for them to speak about them without getting embarrassed."

"I appreciate your outstanding effort to help them see that. I think the product line will be a huge hit in our store and especially in the catalog."

"I agree. What do you think of the idea of hiding the products in the store to make it a bit of a scavenger hunt to find them?"

"Brilliant. I talked to Wade about that, and he agrees."

"I'll make myself available to the sales team this week to work out any concerns or remaining issues."

"And then what's next for you?"

"I was hoping to discuss that with you."

"I heard from Dani and from Landon that you're interested in a position with our company."

"I am. She mentioned the assistant manager job at the warehouse."

"That's open, but we have another thing coming up that I think might interest you even more."

"What's that?"

"Catalog director. Cameron and Lucy have overseen the first iteration of the catalog, but it's going to be issued quarterly, so we'll need fresh content and art for the cover with every new edition. With the first catalog hitting in September, we're going to need Cam and Lucy focused on the website and e-commerce full time, which leaves us in need of someone to oversee the catalog going forward. Would that interest you?"

Amanda didn't even have to think about it. "One hundred percent yes."

Linc's smile unfolded slowly across his handsome face. "You sure about that?"

They shared a laugh.

"It's perfect. There's nothing I'd rather do. I've been wanting to write more, and the kind of profiles I'll be doing for the first catalog is the sort of thing I'm eager to do. That position would be a perfect fit for me."

"I had a feeling you might say so." He handed her a sheet of paper that detailed the offer, including salary and benefits.

Tears appeared out of nowhere, as they often did these days. "I'm sorry." She accepted the tissue he handed her. "I'm sure Molly told you I've been an emotional disaster area since the fire."

"She certainly didn't put it that way."

"Well, it's true. I'm on emotional overload. Your son has been a saint."

"He's a good boy."

"He's a wonderful man."

Linc nodded. "That he is."

"Have you heard about my daughter?"

"I have."

"At some point, she'll be coming to live with me, and it's important that I'm upfront with you about how she'll be my top priority."

"I wouldn't expect anything different. This is a family-friendly company. I raised ten children while running this place. I never missed a game or a play or a parent-teacher conference, and I don't expect my employees to either. We cover for each other as needed, and we put family first. Always."

The trickle of tears became a torrent. She used the tissue to mop them up. "I'm mortified."

Laughing, Linc got up and came around the desk to sit next to her in the other chair. "Don't be. You've had a lot to deal with all at once. Anyone would be overwhelmed."

"Your company is exactly what I need right now, and I gratefully accept your wonderful offer. I promise to work very hard for you."

"I have no doubt that you will, and we're thrilled to welcome you to the team—and the family."

"Thank you so much. I promise not to be one of those people who cries at work."

His warm smile touched her. "It'll all be fine. I promise. My father-in-law likes to say that we usually figure out our path when we're already on it, and I've found that to be very true."

"That sounds about right. I suppose I need to get busy finding a place to live and buying sheets and towels."

"I know just the place to get everything you need—with an employee discount."

CHAPTER TWENTY-ONE

"I plant a lot of trees. I am a great believer in planting things for future generations."
—Penelope Keith

After leaving the store with her offer letter in hand, Amanda walked back to the Grange, where she'd parked her rental car. It was such a beautiful sunny day, and more than anything, she wanted to see Landon to share the news about her new job. But first, she had her meeting with Mildred. After that, she'd go find Landon.

Mildred lived in a tiny house on the outskirts of Butler and welcomed Amanda into her cozy home with a friendly smile. At a quick glance, you'd never know the woman was in her nineties. She had snow-white hair and lively hazel eyes. "You must be Amanda. Come in."

"Thank you so much for seeing me, Mrs. Olsen. I really appreciate it."

"Please, call me Mildred, and I'm delighted to have the company. Could I offer you a cup of tea or coffee?"

"Tea would be wonderful."

"Right this way." Amanda followed her through the living

room to a galley kitchen. "Have a seat and make yourself at home."

"Thank you."

Mildred prepared the tea with an expert-level attention to detail, brought the delicate china pot to the table to steep and went back for teacups, cream and sugar and shortbread cookies. When everything was set up to her satisfaction, she took the other seat at the small table.

Amanda took her notebook out of her purse and stirred cream into her tea.

"You have to try the cookies," Mildred said. "They're from the store. Some of our most popular."

Amanda took a bite of a cookie, and the lemony, buttery sweetness exploded on her tongue. "Oh wow. That's good."

"Don't tell anyone, but I eat a box of them a week."

"Your secret is safe with me."

She leaned in to add, "The good thing about being ninety-two is you can eat whatever the heck you want, within reason, of course."

"Of course," Amanda said, delighted by her. "So tell me how you got started with the company."

"I was eight when Elmer's daddy hired me to sweep the floor for a dollar a week. That doesn't sound like much these days, but at the time, it made a big difference for my family. I came every day after school to sweep, and every Saturday morning. After I finished school, I joined the bookkeeping department, and I'm still there more than eighty years later."

Amanda took notes as Mildred spoke. "That's an amazing accomplishment."

"It's been a wonderful life, to be sure. I'm the last remaining first-generation employee of the store. I've seen it all, I'll tell you."

"What's the greatest change you've witnessed during your tenure?"

"The sheer volume of customers that come through our

door, and with the catalog coming, I imagine that number is only going to get bigger. Our company is growing in leaps and bounds, thanks in large part to Lincoln's leadership. He's such a nice boy, and so very smart. Elmer will tell you he's injected so much energy and passion into the business."

Amused to hear Linc, who was at least sixty, referred to as a "boy," Amanda said, "How do you feel about the changes?"

"While I've always loved the nostalgic atmosphere in the store and don't think that should ever change, I understand that times change, and we have to do the same to stay relevant."

"That's a very evolved attitude."

"It took me a while to come around, but Linc's an inspirational leader. He's committed to keeping the business moving forward. You didn't hear this from me, but there's even talk of a second store in Stowe."

"Is that right?"

She nodded, her eyes twinkling over her teacup. "The kids don't know yet."

"That's a big scoop."

"Sure is. Linc, Elmer and I talked about it over lunch last week, and it sounds to me like Linc is pretty far down the road with the idea. He's even located a space he's interested in."

"When will he tell the kids?" Amanda asked, intrigued by the family dynamics.

"When he has all his ducks in a row. The kids tend to be more conservative about new things. If it was up to them, there'd be no website, no catalog, no warehouse, no intimate line. They prefer to keep things the way they've always been, whereas Linc sees the bigger picture."

"That's the exact opposite of how you'd expect it to be."

"For sure."

"Tell me more about you. Did you grow up in Butler?"

"I did. We lived three streets over from Elm, right near where Hunter and his Megan live now. I could walk to the store after school. I was twenty when I married my Herman, and we had fifty-two wonderful years together right here in Butler until he passed."

"I'm so sorry for your loss."

"Thank you, honey. It was twenty years ago now. I miss him every day, but I've made a nice life for myself. I'm very thankful to still have my work. Hunter keeps me very busy."

"Can you tell me about your specific role within the company?"

"I oversee all the accounts receivable. In other words, the money coming in."

"I see."

"I also prepare quarterly sales reports for Hunter and give him advice on things he needs to know, such as when one of our vendors is experiencing hardship or if one of our accounts is in arrears. That kind of thing."

"How do you feel about working for someone so much younger than you?"

"Oh, I love working with Hunter. He's so smart and savvy. I've learned so much from him. He's like a beloved grandson to me. I can't wait to meet his little one. I'm going to spoil him or her rotten. I've already crocheted two blankets for the baby."

"That's lovely."

"It's been a lovely life."

"Could I ask you something else?"

"Anything. I'm an open book."

"You grew up in Butler, lived here your whole life. Have you ever wished you lived somewhere else?"

"Not for one second. I have everything I need right here."

"Did you travel?"

"My Herman and I went somewhere every year for ten years straight because we thought we ought to see the world. Without fail, I'd no sooner get there than I couldn't wait to come home. After the tenth year, I confessed to him that I didn't want to travel anymore. You know what he said?"

"What?"

"He said, 'Oh, thank you, Jesus. I don't either.'"

Amanda laughed. "I love that!"

"I was so relieved! For the rest of his life, we were two home-bodies who were perfectly content with our little town, our work, our friends, our home, our church and each other. We never wanted for anything more than that." She paused and tipped her head. "Well, we wanted children, but that didn't happen for us, so we adopted other people's children, like Molly and her sister, Hannah. Those two girls gave me a *lot* of adopted grandchildren. Eighteen between them!" She patted a spiral-bound journal. "I have all their birthdays written down so I won't forget them."

"It sounds as if you're very content."

"I am. My life may sound boring to a sophisticated gal such as yourself."

"Not at all. It sounds delightful."

"It is. Do you know what the secret to a happy life really is?"

"Please tell me."

"It's all about simple pleasures. Love, friendship, satisfying work, faith, a sense of community and a desire to be part of something bigger than yourself. People run all around looking for fulfillment, often missing the simple things that're right under their noses."

"You have no idea how badly I needed to hear that."

"Have you been running around, then?"

Amanda nodded. "Yes, I have."

"And not finding the fulfillment."

"Not until I came here and found a much simpler kind of life."

"Is it working for you?"

"It is."

"Simple doesn't have to be boring. Simple can be very exciting. Just ask my Hunter about how exciting his life is now that he's married to the woman he loves. The boy positively sparkles, he's so happy."

"I've spent time with them. I've seen that."

Mildred nodded. "I knew for a long time that he had his heart set on her, and I hoped and prayed she'd finally look his way."

"He's helping me learn to play the piano."

"Oh, he's a wonderful piano player! You couldn't have a better teacher."

"That's what everyone says."

"I've prattled on and on. Tell me about you and whether it's true you might be sweet on our Landon."

Amanda smiled and put down her pen. "It's true."

"Oh, that's wonderful. Those two boys are just the most delightful young men. I have a real soft spot for them. Landon brings me a Christmas tree every year, sets it up and puts the lights on for me."

Amanda was ridiculously charmed by that. "Does he?"

"That he does, and he stays until it's decorated to my satisfaction. I look forward to it every year."

She couldn't believe that the story brought tears to her eyes, but then, everything did lately. "That's so incredibly sweet."

"It is indeed, and if you want to know who he is, who he *really* is, that ought to tell you everything you need to know."

"It does. For sure. But I already knew he was special."

"Always has been. I've taken particular pride in being one of the few people who can tell those two rascals apart. They've made it their mission in life to try to fool me, but I'm not having it."

"I love that."

"I love them. They're good boys, like their brothers and their father and grandfather. The best people you'd ever want to know."

"I've seen that for myself. I love their family."

"Do you have a lot of family of your own?"

"A brother and sister who're much older and my mom. I... I also have a daughter, Stella, who's twelve."

"That's a lovely name."

"I find myself wanting to spill my entire life story to you."

"Oh, I wish you would. I love hearing about people and their lives."

Amanda told her the story about Stella, Kelly, the request they'd made of Amanda and how excited she was to welcome her daughter into her life, even if her heart was breaking for her and Kelly. "It's such a strange place to be in. Elated in the midst of someone else's tragedy."

"You're not elated that her mother is dying, sweetheart. You're elated that you get to have Stella in your life. Those are two very separate things."

"I hate what they're going through."

"Of course you do."

"It's become clear to me, since the fire at the inn, that I suppressed all the emotions associated with Stella and stuffed them deep inside where they couldn't hurt me every day."

"I can't say I blame you. Whatever it takes to survive something like that."

Amanda nodded, feeling as if she'd known Mildred for years rather than an hour. "The fire shook me up. It made it impossible for me to keep everything buried anymore. Poor Landon has been such a saint, letting me weep all over him for days after the fire."

"A few tears wouldn't put a man like Landon off. He's made of tougher stuff than that."

"I've seen that for sure. He's been the most amazing friend to me."

"That's such a wonderful place for two people to start. My Herman was my very best friend long before we ever became a couple. He was my best friend for the rest of his life. I still talk to him as if he's here, and it always makes me feel better to tell him what's in my heart. How does Landon feel about your daughter coming into your life?"

"He can't wait to meet her."

Mildred smiled. "That sounds like him."

While Amanda took more notes, Mildred shared funny stories about people who'd worked for the store and some of the customers who'd come through their door.

Much later, Amanda glanced at the clock on Mildred's stove, stunned to see the time. "We talked for so long!"

"Time flies when you're having fun."

"This was wonderful. I'm so glad we got to meet, and I can't wait to write about you for the catalog. Did Lucy call about the photo? Isabella Coleman is going to take it this week."

"She did, and I'm looking forward to seeing my Izzie."

"Great. Thank you again for your time and your stories and the wisdom."

Mildred got up to walk Amanda out. "It was my pleasure. I hope you'll come by any time you need wisdom. As Elmer likes to say, that's one thing we've got plenty of."

Amanda hugged her at the door. "I'll be back for more very soon."

"I'll be here. Any time. I wish you all the best with your sweet Stella. And I hope things work out for you and Landon. I like you for him."

"You couldn't pay me a higher compliment." Fred might not yet be certain about her, but it was nice to know that Mildred was. "Could I ask a favor? Could you give me directions to the Christmas tree farm?"

"Of course."

A few minutes later, Amanda was on her way out of town, her mind racing as she thought about Mildred and how she would tell her story for the catalog. Mildred had given her so much to think about—and not just for the story. What she said about making a happy life in a small town like Butler had really resonated with Amanda. Everything she needed was truly right there in Butler, which had begun to feel like home to her in a way that nowhere else ever had.

She took a couple of wrong turns but eventually found the

tree farm and parked next to Landon's black pickup truck. No one was around, but the doors to the barn were open, and in the distance, she heard the faint sound of a machine. She decided to take a short walk to see if she could find him. Under bright sunlight, fields of trees dotted the landscape for as far as she could see. They were various sizes and shapes, and the fragrant scent of evergreen filled the air, making her think of Christmas in June.

Mindful of her recovering ankle, Amanda stayed on the well-worn paths that wound through the farm. About half a mile from the barn, she spotted Landon on a massive mowing machine and made her way toward him. She'd almost reached him when he finally noticed her coming, his face lighting up with a warm, welcoming smile.

He wore a faded blue T-shirt, jeans, work boots, noise-canceling headphones and a ball cap on backward. Work clothes had never looked sexier. He cut the engine to the tractor. "This is a nice surprise."

"I wanted to see this place I've heard so much about."

"And?"

"It's beautiful."

"I don't know about that, but it's a living." He held out his hand to her. "Want to go for a ride?"

She stepped forward to take his hand. "On that thing?"

"Yep."

"Sure. How do we do this?"

He helped her onto his lap and put his arms around her. "Ready?"

"As ready as I'll ever be."

"Put these on," he said, handing her the headphones.

When she had them in place over her ears, he started the engine. Amanda felt the vibration through her entire body. The big machine lurched forward, but Landon tightened his grip on her as he drove them through rows of trees that seemed to go on for miles.

Sitting back against him, she was filled with peace.

CHAPTER TWENTY-TWO

"If you think in terms of a year, plant a seed;
if in terms of ten years, plant trees; if in terms
of one hundred years, teach the people."
—Confucius

*A*manda took in the vast landscape of the farm, realizing what a big job it must be to take care of so many trees. After about twenty minutes, they reached the far end of the property, a scenic overlook with a breathtaking view of Butler below. Landon turned off the engine and removed the headphones.

"What do you think?" he asked.

"It's so much bigger than I thought it would be."

"That's what she said."

Amanda elbowed him in the ribs, making him gasp with laughter. "I'm serious. This place is huge."

"Trust me, I know. I cut grass and shear trees in my dreams."

"I had no idea there was so much work involved in growing Christmas trees."

"Most people have no clue, but I like it. There's a rhythm to it. Every season brings new obligations to the trees, and after all these years, I've got the routine down pretty well."

"It's impressive."

He laughed. "I'm sure it's been your lifelong dream to date a Christmas tree farmer."

"Maybe not, but I've always had a thing for hot firefighters with hidden talents."

He nuzzled her neck and held on tighter to her. "I have a lot of hidden talents that you haven't seen yet."

"That sounds intriguing, but I don't want to interrupt your work."

"Please interrupt my work. I'm so bored."

"I thought Max was working with you today."

"He was here this morning, but he had a doctor's appointment with Caden this afternoon."

"Is the baby okay?"

"He's fine, just some well-baby thing. Whatever that is."

"That's when they check to make sure he's growing and thriving. And he probably has to have some shots."

"Poor guy."

"And poor Max."

"He's seemed really down lately. I've been worried about him."

"How so?"

"Just kind of quiet and withdrawn, which isn't like him."

"He has a lot on his plate for someone so young. I look at him and see what my life would've been like if I hadn't given Stella up for adoption."

"He's quite a bit older than you were when you had her."

"Still, it's like a bomb going off in your life. I know you all think he's handling it well, but maybe he isn't."

"I keep meaning to talk to Colton to see if he's noticed it, too."

"That's a good idea. From what I'm told, the first year with a baby can be grueling. Even with all the support Max has, it's got to be hard on him. It's not like he expected to be doing this alone."

"Yeah, it was a shock to all of us when Chloe decided to surrender her rights. Max never had much to say about that, but it had to have been an even bigger shock to him."

"Had they been together long?"

"Not long at all, which was part of the problem. Anyway, enough about my brother. What brings you to visit my farm today?"

"I had a little time, and since you're working tonight, I was hoping to spend a few minutes with you."

"I'm glad you did. Have you ever made out on a tractor?"

Amanda smiled. "I can't say that I have."

"You want to give it a whirl?"

"How would that work exactly?"

"Stand up, and I'll show you."

Amanda stood, and with his hands on her hips, he turned her to face him, bringing her down on his lap to straddle him. "Oh, well…"

Landon guided her arms around his neck and pulled her in tight against him. "Just like this."

"Why do I feel like maybe you've done this before?"

Smiling, he shook his head and kissed her. "This is a first. Everything about you is a first."

Amanda wanted to hear more about that, but with his lips moving softly over hers, she didn't get the chance to ask. She was too busy enjoying being with him, kissing him, holding him.

The more of him she had, the more she wanted. "I met Mildred today."

"Did you? She's a nice lady."

"She told me how you bring her a Christmas tree every year."

"I do that for quite a few of the seniors in town."

"It's very sweet of you."

He shrugged off the comment. "It's no big deal."

"It is to them."

"It's just what we do for each other around here."

"I like it here."

"I'm glad you do. That means you might be sticking around, huh?"

"That's exactly what it means. In fact, I landed myself a job today."

"Did you now? Is it with a company I might've heard of?"

"Actually, it is."

"Did my dad offer you the warehouse job?"

"Even better. He asked me to head up the catalog going forward. Cameron and Lucy are going to have their hands full with the website and the e-commerce that'll come from the catalog. He needs somebody to oversee the development of future catalogs. I accepted the job without hesitation. And you're the first person I wanted to tell."

"Congratulations. That sounds perfect for you."

"I'm excited. I like this opportunity even better than the warehouse job. And do you know what this means?"

"What?"

"I have to find a place to live in Butler. I have to buy sheets. I have to buy pots and pans. I have to buy *towels*."

"You're in luck. I have all that stuff at my place."

"That's true, and I do love being there. However, there's no room for Stella there."

"Then we'll find something else together."

He said that so casually, as if that sentence didn't change everything. "Is that what you want?"

"I want to be where you are. So, yes, that's what I want."

"It's probably too soon for us to be even talking about this."

"Probably, but I don't want to go backward."

"How do you mean?"

"We're already living together. If you move out, that's a backward move for us. I want to go forward."

"So that means..."

"We'll find a place together. With room for Stella."

For a long time, Amanda stared at him, trying to find any hint of hesitation or second thoughts. But she saw only a man who cared about her as much as she cared about him, a man who'd accepted the probability of her daughter coming to live with them without missing a beat. This man who brought Christmas trees to the seniors in town had the kind of loving heart she wanted in her life—and in her daughter's life.

"Are we really doing this?"

"Oh yeah, baby. We're doing it, all right." He hugged her so tightly, she couldn't breathe. "And I'm so happy about it."

She flashed a suggestive grin. "Why's that?"

"You know exactly why. It's because I'm falling for you, and all I want is to be with you. Things I do every day, like cut grass, shear trees, fight fires… Everything else is suddenly boring compared to being with you."

Ridiculously moved by his sweet words, Amanda said, "So what you're saying is I basically ruined your life?"

"Not at all. I think, perhaps, you might make my life."

As Amanda hugged him, she realized everything was changing, and a few months ago, that would've scared the hell out of her. Now, she couldn't be happier. "Same."

THE NEXT AFTERNOON, AMANDA MET WITH ELMER AT HIS HOME. Before she even pulled into the driveway, she was already charmed by the sign hanging from his mailbox: JUSTICE OF THE PEACE, NOTARY PUBLIC, FREE ADVICE. What more could anyone want from any one man? Amanda knew from previous interactions that Elmer Stillman was sweet, adorable and full of wisdom that he freely shared with his beloved grandchildren.

She couldn't wait to get to know him better.

Elmer greeted her at the door with a warm, welcoming smile and showed her into his cluttered but comfortable home. Landon had told her his grandfather never threw anything away because he loved to be surrounded by things that made him happy. He wore a red flannel shirt rolled up over his forearms and jeans held up by red suspenders. Central casting couldn't have found a more perfect character to play the role of the doting grandfather.

"What can I get you, my dear?"

"Whatever you're having is fine with me. Thank you."

Elmer made cups of hot chocolate and topped them with whipped cream from a can. "I don't know about you, but I need something sweet around this time of day to pick me up."

"I never say no to something sweet. I used to get in trouble for eating the whipped cream right from the can."

"Ah, yes," he said, chuckling, "I think every one of my grandchildren has been in trouble for that particular thing at least once, particularly your friend Landon and his twin."

"Whipped cream is always worth the trouble."

"On that we agree." He brought a tin of chocolate cookies when he joined her at the table. "You may be noticing a theme here."

"We also agree on the magic of chocolate." Amanda took a sip of her drink. "Delicious."

He sipped from his mug and ate a cookie. "I heard you met with Mildred yesterday. How did that go?"

"It was great. She's such a lovely lady."

"That she is. She's worked for my family's business for more than *eighty* years."

"It's quite an accomplishment."

"Indeed it is, but that's what our business is all about. Family first. One of my greatest pleasures in life is that many of my grandchildren are involved with running the business my parents started. They're fourth-generation proprietors, which is a huge source of pride to me. Imagine, the little general store my parents started way back when now employs so many of their descendants."

"How do you think they'd feel about that?"

"They'd be tickled pink. No doubt about it. They used to tell me there's nothing more important than family. We've tried to instill that atmosphere in the company. Do you know that many of our employees are the second, third and even *fourth* generation of their families to work for us?"

"I've heard that."

"What I love the most is how the kids have found their own niches within the business. We've got Hunter doing the books, Colton and Max making the maple syrup, Hannah's jewelry, Wade with the health and wellness, Lucas's woodwork, Landon running the Christmas tree farm, Will with the Vermont Made line, Ella and Charley overseeing the store and the sales force and inventory, and Grayson handling all the legal work. It's truly a family affair with new family members being added to the team all the time."

Amanda took notes as he talked. "How do you think the arrival of the catalog will change the business?"

"I predict it's going to grow in leaps and bounds. Ever since Linc pitched the idea to me, I've been eager to see how it would work out."

"Does Linc still consult you on business decisions?"

"We talk about most of the big stuff, but then again, we talk about most everything. He's like a son to me."

"I've heard rumblings about a side project you two have been involved in having to do with some matchmaking, perhaps?"

"Not sure where you would've heard something like that."

She smiled at him. "I hear you and Linc are determined to see all your grandchildren settled down."

"Nothing but rumors," he said, his eyes twinkling devilishly. "Speaking of that, how are things with Landon?"

Amanda loved the not-so-subtle segue. "Things are good."

"Just good? It's seemed a little better than good to the casual observer."

"Are you fishing for information?"

"Absolutely."

Amanda cracked up. "I'll only tell you that your grandson is a wonderful guy, and things are really good between us."

"That's what I want to hear. I have a confession to make."

"What's that?"

"From the first time I saw you with Landon, I had a feeling about you two."

"Even though Lucas was there, too?"

"Even though. I can't explain why, but the thought popped into my head that you'd be great for our Landon. Maybe because I saw the way he looked at you."

"How did he look at me?"

"Like a man who'd just stared directly into the sun. A little gobsmacked after having seen the light."

"You saw all that in the span of a few minutes?"

"I pay attention, sweetheart. I don't miss much."

"I'm glad Landon has someone like you looking out for him. I never knew any of my grandparents."

"I'm sorry you missed out on that. I love being a grandfather —and a great-grandfather. It's the best job I ever had."

Amanda wrote furiously to capture that quote.

"Linc tells me you're going to be sticking around to oversee the catalog going forward."

"That's the plan."

"I think you'll make a fine addition to our company."

"I'm glad you think so."

"I do. We all do. You fit right in around here."

"That's so nice of you to say. I feel more at home in this little town than I have anywhere I've ever been."

"Butler does that to people. It rolls out the red carpet and makes you feel welcome. Not everyone can handle the long winters and the other hardships of living in the mountains. But those of us who love it wouldn't want to be anywhere else."

"I can understand why. It's a beautiful place to live."

"That it is, and it's a wonderful place to raise a family."

Amanda smiled, because how could she not smile around this

delightful man? "I guess that means you've heard my daughter will be coming to live with me at some point."

"I did hear that. It's an amazing thing you're doing for her and her mother. You're giving them peace of mind at a time when they need it badly."

"That's a nice way of looking at it. I have all these mixed emotions about it. On the one hand, I'm so happy to have Stella in my life. But on the other, I'm heartbroken for her mother and for her."

"Which is totally understandable."

"Having her in my life is a dream come true, but I hate that it's happening this way."

"I'm a big believer in things happening for a reason, sweet-heart. Years from now, when you look back at this time in your life, you're going to see that everything that happened, from your work sending you to us, to the fire, to meeting Landon, to reconnecting with your daughter... It's all part of a bigger plan."

"I do love a good plan," Amanda said, smiling. "For all the good they've done me lately."

"Ah, that's the thing about plans. They'll make a fool out of you every time."

"That's what Landon said, too, and he gave you credit for that pearl of wisdom. I'm certainly finding it to be true lately. Anyway, enough about me. This story is supposed to be about you."

"This story, my story, is about all of us. If you take away nothing else from our meeting, take that."

"I will. Thank you for making me part of your family's story."

"It's a pleasure to have you, honey."

CHAPTER TWENTY-THREE

"A man doesn't plant a tree for himself.
He plants it for posterity."
—Alexander Smith

On Thursday, Amanda and Landon had breakfast at the diner before meeting his cousin Izzy at the Grange for their ten o'clock photo shoot. They'd heard a few stories from his siblings about the shoot but were about to find out for themselves what it was like to be models. By all accounts, modeling was boring and tedious, but Izzy made it fun.

Amanda, who'd been up late working on her profiles of Mildred and Elmer, was looking forward to meeting the renowned photographer who was Landon's cousin. She'd FaceTimed with Stella the night before, which had been amazing. She already felt like they'd known each other much longer than a few days and could only hope her daughter felt the same way. She wanted Stella to be comfortable with her by the time Stella came to live with her.

"I can't believe I have to spend an entire workday doing this," Landon said as they walked down the street, past Nolan's garage, on the way to the Grange.

When he saw them, Nolan and his assistant, Skeeter, came out to say hello.

"Skeeter, this is Amanda," Nolan said. "Do not shake his hand. He's filthy."

Amanda smiled at the smaller man. "Nice to meet you, Skeeter."

"You, too, ma'am."

"Are you two the models of the hour?" Nolan asked.

"Ugh, yes," Landon said. "My dad is out of his mind using us as models."

"I don't think he is," Nolan said.

"My girlfriend, Dude, says the ladies will be coming from all over looking for the Abbott boys," Skeeter said, giggling.

"That's great," Landon said, his tone dripping with sarcasm. "Just what we need."

"Your girlfriend's name is Dude?" Amanda asked.

"It's short for Gertrude, and speaking of my sweet, here she comes now."

Amanda followed his glance and did a double take when she saw that Dude was at least six feet tall and nearly as broad. Wearing denim overalls and a straw hat, she smiled widely when she saw Skeeter. She had to be a foot taller than him.

The two of them embraced like they hadn't seen each other in years.

"It's better if you don't look," Nolan said, forcing Amanda to suppress a desperate need to laugh.

"You're the sex-toy lady," Dude said.

"I suppose I am. I'm Amanda. Nice to meet you."

Dude's handshake nearly crushed Amanda's hand. "Likewise. You ready for a dog yet, Landon?"

"Not quite, Dude. I still work too many crazy hours to have a dog."

"You let me know when you're ready. I'll hook you up."

"Will do." He put his arm around Amanda. "We'd better get going. Izzy is expecting us."

"Have fun," Nolan said, grinning.

"Don't tell me you're getting out of this," Landon said to his brother-in-law.

"Nope. The three of us are up tomorrow. Can hardly wait."

"Don't let him fool ya," Skeeter said. "He's excited to be a model."

"Shut it, Skeeter," Nolan said. "I am not."

"Are too."

"Not."

Landon and Amanda left them to fight it out as they headed for the Grange.

"This town is the most entertaining place I've ever been," Amanda said.

"That can't possibly be true."

"It is! You don't meet people like Skeeter and Dude in the city."

"They're unique. I'll give you that."

"I wonder what it's like when they—"

Using the hand on the arm he had around her, he covered her mouth. "If you finish that thought, I'll never forgive you."

Amanda dissolved into helpless giggles that she'd barely contained by the time they reached the Grange.

"Are you going to be okay?" he asked.

"I think so. Now, about that dog…"

"What about it?"

"If you're living with someone who works mostly from home, you'd be able to have one, right?"

"I suppose so. Why? Do you want a dog?"

"I've always wanted one, but not having a home makes that somewhat difficult."

"Huh, well. We should talk to Dude, then. We call her Snow White because all the animals follow her around."

"Really? We can get a dog?"

"Sure. I'd love to have one, but my hours are so crazy that it didn't seem fair to the dog."

"I suppose I should make sure Stella's not allergic or anything." When he would've opened the main door to the Grange, Amanda stopped him. "I just want you to know that all this, everything that's happened since the fire…"

"What, honey?"

"It's *so* good. It's all so good that I worry it can't possibly be real."

"It's real, and it's your life now, if you want it to be."

"I do. I want it. I want you. I want it all."

Landon dropped his forehead to rest against hers. "I want it all, too. Everything about this with you feels so good."

Amanda looped her hand around his neck and kissed him.

A throat clearing behind them had them pulling apart a few minutes later. Had they really engaged in a full-on make-out session out in the open where anyone might see them? Apparently so.

"Sorry to interrupt." A tall, smiling woman with long, curly blonde hair held a takeout coffee and had a camera bag hanging from her shoulder.

"Hey, Iz." Landon kissed his cousin's cheek. "Good to see you."

"You, too. This must be Amanda."

Amanda shook her hand. "It's so great to meet you. I'm a huge fan of your work."

"Thank you. I've heard great things about your work, too." Izzy punctuated the statement with a wink. "You've got the whole town buzzing."

Amanda laughed. "That'd be me."

Izzy gestured to the door. "Shall we?"

"Let's get this over with," Landon said.

"Oh, come on!" Izzy gave him a push through the door. "This'll be the most fun you've ever had."

"Somehow, I doubt that."

"Have some faith, cousin! When have we ever not had fun together?"

"True."

"Sorry we're late," Cameron said as she came in with Lucy a minute later.

"We just got here, too," Izzy said.

"Right this way, Landon and Amanda," Cameron said. "We've got you all set up in the restrooms."

They showed Landon to the men's room and Amanda to the ladies' room, where clothing had been hung for them. Amanda changed into a denim dress that wasn't something she would've chosen for herself, but she liked the way it looked in the full-length mirror that had been brought in for the occasion.

"I knew that would be perfect on you," Ella said from the doorway.

"Where'd you come from?"

"I was running late thanks to morning sickness. It blows. Literally."

"That's miserable. I had it bad when I was expecting my daughter." It was still new to say the words *my daughter* out loud, after years of pretending like Stella had never happened.

"How long did it last?"

"I'm afraid to tell you."

"Ugh, the whole time, then."

"Just about."

"Gavin will never be able to handle that. Every time I'm sick, he's heartbroken."

"Poor *you*!"

"Poor both of us."

"It'll be worth it when your little one arrives."

"Absolutely. I've got your accessories out here when you're ready."

"I just need to touch up my makeup. I'll be right out." Amanda brushed her teeth, reapplied mascara and lipstick and ran a brush through her hair, deciding she was as ready as she'd ever be to model.

She came out of the ladies' room and nearly collided with

Landon, who was wearing a brown plaid flannel rolled up over his forearms. "That color is perfect on you."

"Glad you like it." He hooked an arm around her waist and drew her into his embrace.

"Don't mess up my lipstick."

"Come on, you two," Ella said. "We're on a tight schedule."

"Don't be a cock-blocker, El," Landon replied.

Amanda had gotten to see his grumpy side as he prepared to do something he had no interest in doing. "You're cute when you're grumpy."

"You're cute all the time."

"I can't take all this cuteness," Ella said as she adorned Amanda with earrings, a necklace and bracelet from Hannah's jewelry line and topped off the ensemble with a brown velvet hat that Amanda wondered if she could keep.

"You look hot, babe," Landon said. "Mountain chic works on you."

"Is that a thing?" Izzy asked. "Mountain chic?"

"If it isn't, it should be." Amanda smiled at Landon. "We can use that in the catalog."

"Where do you want us, Iz?" Landon asked. "I've got grass that ain't gonna cut itself."

"We'll do you first." Izzy positioned him where she wanted him and went through the various poses she wanted him to do.

As Amanda stood off to the side and watched, she experienced a sinking feeling when she realized that once those photos went live, he'd be even more popular with women than he already was. They'd probably come from all over to lay their eyes—and other parts—on him. The thought made her want to claw the eyes out of those imaginary women.

"He's too cute, isn't he?" Ella said.

Amanda glanced at her. "Funny, I was just thinking that and wondering if I'm going to need a stick to beat off the fans who'll come from all over to try to meet him."

"A stick might not be a bad idea."

"They'll be looking for Gavin, too."

"Let them try," Ella said with a shocking amount of venom that was in marked contrast to her usual sweetness.

"They'll make it another kind of scavenger hunt to find all the hot guys in the catalog."

"Maybe we can do something with that from a marketing perspective."

"Sure, let's start with Gavin."

Ella laughed. "Touché."

Izzy put Landon through the various poses before declaring herself satisfied.

"Your next item is hanging in the men's room," Ella said.

"There's *more*?" Landon asked, clearly not pleased to hear that.

"Much more," Ella said. "We're each doing twelve items."

"Oh my God! You've got to be kidding me!"

"Do I look like I'm kidding? If you don't like it, take it up with Dad. This was his bright idea."

Landon scowled at her and took off for the men's room to change.

"You're up, Amanda," Izzy said.

THREE HOURS LATER, THEY EMERGED FROM THE GRANGE INTO bright sunshine.

"That was the most excruciating thing I've ever had to do," Landon said.

"You're not built to be stuck inside all day mugging for the camera."

"You know it."

"I'm going to need a stick to keep the ladies away from you after that catalog drops."

"What? No way."

"Yes way. They're going to come from far and wide to meet the hot models."

"They are not. Don't be silly."

"Not being silly," Amanda said. "It's going to happen. In fact, Ella is thinking about making a scavenger hunt out of it called 'Come to Butler and Find the Hot Guys in Our Catalog.'"

"She is *not* doing that!"

"She won't have to. They'll do it on their own. I hope you guys are ready for what's going to happen when that catalog lands in mailboxes."

"Nothing will happen."

"Okay."

He stopped walking and turned to her. "You aren't actually still worried about other women, are you? Because you have to know there's no one but you. Tell me you know that."

"I do."

"Why don't you sound convinced?"

"I have some concerns."

He took her by the hand and walked silently to the parking lot where he'd parked his truck. Their plan had been for him to drop her back at his place before he left for the farm. They drove to his house in silence as she wondered what he was thinking. She'd find out soon enough.

When he pulled into the driveway, she expected him to leave the truck running, but he shut it off.

"Aren't you going to the farm?"

"I'll go later to feed the horses." He got out of the truck, so she did the same and followed him inside, trying to gauge his mood. He'd been out of sorts all day, and it was revealing to see a whole new side of him. The second the door closed behind her, he turned to her, hands on hips, expression unreadable. "I want to hear about your concerns."

"It's nothing terrible."

"I still want to know."

"I'm concerned," she said, "that you may get tired of being with just me after a while. You're used to more... variety, shall we say, and I—"

"I'll never get tired of being with you. What else are you concerned about?"

"That you think it'll be enough to be with just me—"

"I know it will be. What else?"

"How do you know that, Landon? You've never done an actual relationship in your entire life."

"And you have?"

"No, but—"

"How do you know that I'll be enough for you?"

"You will be—"

"But how do you know that for sure?"

"I just do."

"I just do, too. I love you, Amanda. I'm in love with you. I want to be with you all the time. This isn't a fling or a passing phase or whatever else you want to call it. This is it for me. You're it for me. I don't want anyone else. Do you have any other concerns?"

Her brain raced to catch up to what he'd said as her heart beat double time. "Ah, no. No more concerns."

He took a few steps to close the distance between them and put his hands on her hips. "Are you *sure?*"

She looked up at him and nodded.

"You don't have anything to worry about where I'm concerned. I promise."

Amanda flattened her hands on his chest and looked up at him, wondering what she'd ever done to be so lucky to have a man like him love her. "That might be the best gift anyone has ever given me."

"You're the only one I want, the only one I'll ever want."

"You're so certain of that. How can you know for sure?"

He took a second to think about that. "Remember when you got Kelly's letter and you never hesitated about taking Stella?"

She nodded.

"That's how I feel about you. Yes. Just yes. Hell to the yes. Yes,

yes, *yes* to all things Amanda." With his hands on her face, he kissed her. "Please tell me you believe me."

"I do. That's the most beautiful thing anyone has ever said to me."

"All I want is more of this, more of you, any way I can get it. Don't doubt for one second that I'm all in with you—and with Stella when the time comes."

"Thank you, Landon. That means everything to me. You've been my rock through all of this, and I'll never forget the way you took me in after the fire, let me cry all over you for days and propped me up after I got the letter about Stella."

"Every minute I get to spend with you is the best minute I've ever spent with anyone."

CHAPTER TWENTY-FOUR

"Heaven grant us patience with a man in love."
—Rudyard Kipling

On the way to work a few hours later, Landon told himself it didn't matter that he was the only one who'd said he was in love and all in with their relationship. She'd expressed gratitude for what he'd done for her, but she hadn't told him she loved him, too, even though he was fairly certain she did.

Why hadn't she said it? And what did it mean that he'd said it and she hadn't? He had no idea, and the not knowing was going to kill him during a twelve-hour shift away from her. After this, he would be off work for four days. He hoped the trip to Boston, the wedding and four days together would give her the time she needed to catch up to him.

The thing about being all in, he was finding, was that it became absolutely critical for the person you were all in with to be there with you. What if she wasn't? What if her feelings for him were wrapped up in appreciation for what he'd done for her after the fire and weren't about love or forever at all?

That thought sent him into a tailspin. Wouldn't that be just his luck to finally find a woman he wanted to be with forever and her not want the same thing? He released a laugh tinged with irony. He probably deserved that after his years of dodging anything that smacked of commitment or more than one night at a time.

When he arrived at the firehouse, he was surprised to see Dani's car parked outside. What was she doing there? He headed inside to find Lucas, Dani and Savannah visiting with their fire department coworkers. Savannah was snuggled into Lucas with his uninjured arm wrapped around her. Landon was relieved to see his brother looking much better than he had the last time he saw him. He'd lost that pasty-faced complexion that was so not like him and had color in his cheeks again. Thank goodness.

"What're you guys up to?" Landon asked.

"Your brother was feeling restless, so I agreed to take him for a ride," Dani said. "We ended up here."

"He's looking much better," Landon said.

Lucas grinned. "Feel free to continue talking about me like I'm not here."

"Don't mind if we do." Dani shot him an annoyed look. "He's driving me batty, Landon. I have to practically sit on him to keep him from doing too much."

"Not that I mind when she sits on me," Lucas said to laughter from the other firefighters.

Dani glared at him. "Shut your mouth, Lucas Abbott."

"I like this woman *so much*," their chief, Richard, said. "She keeps you in line, Abbott."

Lucas scoffed. "She can try."

Dani gave him a quelling look.

"Love you, honey."

"Lu, Lu, Lu," Savannah said.

"She always takes his side," Dani said.

Lucas kissed the top of Savannah's head. "Because she's my best girl."

"We need to get her home for dinner and a bath," Dani said.

"Give Abbott a bath while you're at it," Richard said. "He's a little gamey."

While the others laughed, Lucas stroked the beard that had grown in during his convalescence. "It's hard to shave with only one hand."

"I'll do it for you if you want," Landon said.

"Maybe tomorrow before we leave for Boston. It's starting to get itchy."

"Sure, no problem." Landon walked them out, noting that while Lucas looked much better, he was still moving slowly. "I'll be over in the morning."

"Sounds good," Lucas said. "You doing okay? You look a little weird through the eyes."

"I do?"

"Uh-huh."

Landon wasn't surprised that Lucas could tell just by looking at him that something wasn't quite right. While Dani secured Savannah into her car seat, Landon took advantage of a minute alone with his brother. "Things with Amanda are..."

"What?"

"Good. Really good."

"Okay... So why the long face?"

"I'm not sure she's as into it as I am."

"Why do you say that?"

"Because I basically told her how I feel and what I want, and she didn't say it back."

"Huh." Lucas scratched at the scruff on his face.

"What do you suppose that means?"

"I don't think it means all is lost. She might not be ready to say the words yet."

"What if you'd said the words to Dani and she hadn't said them back?"

Lucas grimaced. "Yeah, that would've sucked."

"It did suck. I mean, I'm glad I got it out there and everything, but all she said was how thankful she is for everything I've done for her since the fire."

"Ouch."

Dani came around to where they were standing. "Can I say something?"

"Of course," Landon said.

"She's had a lot to deal with since the fire. A lot, *a lot*. Give her some room to breathe. She's making the kind of changes that lead me to believe she wants what you do."

"I suppose that's true."

"It *is* true, Landon. She could be anywhere in the world, and she's choosing to be here. You don't think that has something to do with you?"

"Partially."

"How do you mean?"

"She loves a lot of things about being here."

"Mostly you, dude," Lucas said. "She's totally into you. I saw that when you guys came to visit. You just gotta be patient and give her time to sort it all out. I think you'll be happy with where she ends up."

"Patience is painful."

Lucas laughed. "It can be, but the rewards are so worth the pain. Just ask my love, Dani, how happy she is that I was patient and waited for her to realize she couldn't live without me."

Dani gave him a playful slap upside his head.

Lucas grabbed her hand and brought it to his lips, kissing along her row of knuckles. "When it's the right thing, you do what you've got to do," Lucas said, keeping his gaze fixed on her. "Whatever it takes."

"Thanks," Landon said. "This actually helped a lot."

"I'm sure it's hard for you to believe I'm actually smarter than you are when it comes to love," Lucas said before Dani's hand covered his mouth to thankfully shut him up.

"You need to learn to quit while you're ahead," Dani said as Lucas's eyes danced with mirth.

"Take him home and muzzle him," Landon said. "I'll be over in the morning to delouse him before the wedding."

"We'll see you then," Dani said. "Have a good night at work and be safe."

"Will do." When they were both in the car, Landon shut the passenger door and waved as they drove off. Leave it to Lucas to make even falling in love into a competition between them. But that didn't surprise Landon. They'd been trying to outdo each other in just about everything since the day they were born. Everything was a competition, so why not love, too?

As much as it pained him to admit, Lucas was right about being patient. Just because Amanda hadn't opened a vein to profess her love for him didn't mean she wasn't feeling the same way he was. Maybe she just wasn't ready to say the words.

Fair enough. He could wait, as long as he had to, for her to catch up to him. Like Lucas had said, when it mattered, you did whatever it took to make it work.

After tonight, he had four whole days—and nights—to show her what it meant to be loved by Landon Abbott.

He couldn't wait for the morning.

FROM THE MINUTE LANDON LEFT FOR WORK, AMANDA HAD BEEN beating herself up for so spectacularly blowing one of the most important moments of her life. He'd basically put his heart in her hands, and what had she done?

Thanked him for helping her after the fire.

Nothing says "I love you" like gratitude.

She cringed recalling his sweet words and how she'd failed to give him even the slightest bit of what he'd so willingly given her. "God, I suck. How could I not tell him how much he means to me?"

Despite her ankle aching after a busy day, she paced the length of the small house, feeling confined and anxious that she'd made a huge mistake by acting like a fool after he poured his heart out to her. What he'd said about feeling the same way she did about Stella—no hesitation—she'd thanked him for all he'd done for her.

"Ugh!" She'd planned to spend tonight finishing her profiles of Mildred and Elmer, but how could she concentrate on anything else while this awful unfinished business with Landon hung over her?

She couldn't. Making a snap decision, she put her shoes on, grabbed her keys and purse and was out the door a minute later, before she could talk herself out of taking care of this right now, rather than letting it fester overnight.

They were all looking forward to the weekend in Boston, and the last thing she wanted was tension with Landon or him thinking he was out on the proverbial limb by himself when that couldn't be further from the truth.

Amanda navigated dark, winding roads, hoping she'd remembered the way to the fire station correctly. She was so caught up in her own thoughts that she didn't see the gigantic moose in the road until it was nearly too late. Screaming, she slammed on the brakes, and the car fishtailed wildly thanks to the mud still on the road. In the flash of a second, she slammed into the guardrail, and the car pitched forward into darkness, teetering precariously.

In the time it took her brain to catch up with what'd happened, she remembered Landon telling her that at least once a year, someone went off the side of the road into the ravine forty feet below that very spot. Even though she couldn't see the drop, she knew it was there and couldn't bring herself to so much as breathe out of fear of the car falling into the abyss. Blinded by tears, all she could think about was dying before she got to meet Stella.

"Please don't let that happen. *Please.*"

She had no idea how long she was there, fighting to stay calm, before another car came along. Afraid to so much as turn her head to see if the car had stopped, Amanda stayed perfectly still and prayed furiously that the other driver saw her.

Then a man was outside her window. "Don't move," he yelled. "I'm going to get help."

She gave the slightest nod to let him know she'd heard him, but even that felt like too much movement as the car inched forward. Amanda stifled the scream that was trying to get out.

"I'll be right back." Out of the corner of her eye, she saw him run back to his car and take off, leaving her alone again in the dark. How long would it take for help to arrive, and would the guardrail hold in the meantime? The thought of plunging into darkness was terrifying.

The tears kept coming, but she was too afraid to move to mop them up. One near-death experience had been more than enough to give her the wake-up call she'd needed to stop sleep-walking through life. She certainly didn't need a second reminder to get the message the universe was trying to send her.

Maybe you do need it, she thought, after letting Landon leave earlier with everything left unsaid.

God, if I die, he'll never know that I was coming to find him, to tell him...

What? What were you going to tell him?

That I love him. That I want him and a life with him and Stella and whatever children we may have together. I want this town and its moose and its quirky people and the big, loving Abbott family and their amazing business. I want it all. Well, maybe not the ravine below. I don't want that at all.

Hysteria threatened, but she fought it back by breathing through it.

"Please, Landon," she whispered. "Please hurry. I need you."

It felt like a year went by before she picked up the tone of sirens in the distance, easily the best sound she'd ever heard. Forcing herself to continue breathing, she clutched her hands together so the shaking and trembling wouldn't jar the car.

Bright headlights and flashing red lights filled the small space in the car seconds before Landon's panicked face appeared on the other side of the window. "Stay still for another minute, honey. We'll get you out."

She gave a subtle nod to indicate she'd heard him.

Then he was gone, and she wanted to beg for him to come back. *Please come back.* Outside the car, she heard frantic voices that only added to her anxiety. Then a loud clanking sound and the roar of an engine as the car inched backward, away from the precipice. The driver door flew open, her seat belt was released, and she was pulled into the arms of the man she loved.

"I've got you, baby."

Amanda finally allowed herself to fall apart as she clung to him. "Don't let go."

"Never. I'll never let go."

Time ceased to exist. All around them, people were talking, barking orders, retrieving the car, calling for a tow in a mishmash of words and images bathed in the red of emergency lights.

"Does anything hurt?" Landon asked.

"No, I'm fine. Now."

"I couldn't believe it when I saw your car. I thought you were staying home to work tonight."

"I was until I realized I forgot to tell you something really important before you left."

He smoothed the hair back from her tear-stained face. "What did you forget to tell me?"

"That I love you, too, and I couldn't bear for you to go all night wondering why I didn't say it back to you."

His handsome face lit up with pleasure. "You could've called me."

"No, I had to tell you in person. I felt so bad after you left. You said such beautiful things, and my brain, it just froze. When it finally defrosted, I was horrified."

"Shhh, it's okay. Everything is okay."

"I can't imagine how scared Dani must've been when she went off the road, in a blizzard, with a baby in the car."

"Thank goodness Lucas saw it happen and rescued her."

Amanda nodded. "Thank you for rescuing me. I just kept asking you to come and to hurry."

"I got here as fast as I could."

"I was so scared I wouldn't get the chance to tell you that I'm all in, too."

"I'm so glad you did."

She rested her head against his chest, filled with relief to be safe in the arms of the man she loved. "Me, too."

CHAPTER TWENTY-FIVE

*"He, who every morning plans the transactions of the day, and
follows that plan, carries a thread that will guide him through a
labyrinth of the most busy life."*
—Victor Hugo

$\mathscr{L}$andon took her home and stayed with her until she fell
asleep. When he'd seen her car teetering between life
and death, he'd nearly suffered a stroke. He should've
gone back to the firehouse to sleep, but he couldn't bring himself
to leave her.

Richard had told him to take care of her but keep his radio
handy because they were still shorthanded.

The poor girl had had way too many things to be upset about
lately. Another near-death experience had been the last thing
she'd needed when she was only just beginning to recover from
the first one.

While she rested in his arms, Landon ran his fingers through
her hair and caressed her back. He had a crick in his neck, and
his left hand was falling asleep, but there was no way he was
leaving her for even a minute.

"Landon?"

"I thought you were asleep."

"Can't sleep. My brain is racing."

"I'm sure, but you're okay. Everything is okay."

"Keep telling me?"

"As long as it takes."

"I'm so sorry to be a mess again. I feel like you've seen more of that than any other part of me."

"I've seen all the best parts of you, and I love them all. I wouldn't want you crying all over anyone but me."

"You want to hear something about me that you don't know?"

"I want to hear it all. Every single thing you want to tell me."

"I've never had a best friend. I had lots of good friends, but never one that was just mine."

"I was lucky to have one born with me."

"You were, for sure." She looked up at him, seeming madly vulnerable. "Is there room for another one?"

"Absolutely."

"That's good, because you're the first best friend I've ever had."

Nothing had ever touched him the way she did, and he was beginning to understand that nothing else—and no one else— ever would. "I'm honored to be your first best friend." He kissed her forehead and shifted to get more comfortable. "Try to get some rest. We have a fun weekend ahead and so many good things to look forward to."

Landon was relieved to feel her body relax and her breathing even out. His anxiety was still through the roof after seeing her car teetering on the edge of disaster. He tried to calm himself by counting his blessings. Someone had seen her and called for help. They'd gotten to her in time, and she was safe. But it would be a while before he'd get the image of her car on the edge of disaster out of his mind.

Nolan had towed the car into town and promised to fix it so she wouldn't have to deal with the rental car company. He said he'd put Skeeter on it while they were in Boston, and it would be good as new by the time they returned.

He wasn't sure he'd be able to sleep, so he was surprised to wake up to sun streaming through the windows. Remembering that today was the day they were heading to Boston and he had four days off to enjoy with Amanda put him in a good mood to start the day. He got up to make coffee and brought hers back to bed. "Rise and shine, sleepyhead."

Her eyes fluttered open and connected with his, the impact like a punch to the gut. For the rest of his life, he would marvel at how he felt when she looked at him like he personally hung the moon just for her. She made him feel like Superman, Batman and Spider-Man all rolled into one potent superhero who was born to love her and only her.

She sat up and accepted the coffee mug from him. "Thank you."

"You slept good?"

"Really good. You?"

"Surprisingly well, all things considered."

"You mean after having to rescue your girlfriend, or whatever I am, from the edge of disaster?"

"Yes, and you're most definitely my girlfriend." He leaned in to kiss her, and she turned away.

"Not when I have morning coffee breath!"

"I don't care."

"I do!" She put down the mug, got out of bed and went into the bathroom, where she made a big production out of brushing her teeth. When she returned to the bed, she crawled toward him on her hands and knees and kissed him.

Landon pounced, rolling her under him and making her scream with laughter as he kissed her neck and all her ticklish spots.

"I surrender," she said, gasping for air.

"Morning."

She looked up at him, her expression open and approachable and trusting, all things that had taken time for her to give him. "Morning."

"I like making you laugh."

"I'm not sure anyone else could make me laugh after what happened last night." She shuddered.

"Don't think about it. It's over and done with. Everything is fine."

"I was so afraid I'd die before I got to see Stella and to tell you how I feel about you."

"Tell me again. I'm not sure I remember."

She smiled. "You do, too."

He shook his head. "I can't recall."

"I love you, Landon Abbott."

"I love you, too, Amanda Pressley."

"I don't know your middle name."

"Matthew. What's yours?"

"Elizabeth."

"I like that."

"I like you." She cupped his face and brought him down for another kiss. "Make love to me, Landon."

"I can't think of anything I'd rather do."

THEY WERE THE LAST ONES TO ARRIVE AT THE STORE TO MEET THE bus that would take them to Boston. Amanda was greeted by hugs from every member of the Abbott family, or so it seemed, each of them expressing concern and gratitude that she was all right after the accident.

"Now we have something else in common, besides dating identical twins," Dani said when she took her turn to hug Amanda.

"I'd rather not have that in common," Amanda said as she held out a finger to Savannah.

The baby grabbed hold and squeezed. It amazed and delighted her to realize that she'd get to see Savannah and Caden and Callie grow up.

"I know, right? Scary business. We're so glad you're okay."

"Thank you. I guess we both have a lot to learn about driving in Vermont."

"For sure."

Elmer stepped up to hug her.

"I'm fine," she told him. "I promise. I was just a little shaken up."

"Mud can be as slippery as ice sometimes," Elmer said.

"I found that out."

He kissed her cheek. "We're just glad you're all right, sweetheart."

"Thanks for all the concern."

"All right, everyone," Lincoln said, clapping his hands to get their attention. "All aboard for Boston!"

Suitcases were stashed in the luggage compartment as the family lined up to get on the bus, amid laughter, joking, jostling, line cutting and other shenanigans as they made their way onto the bus.

"Welcome to the ultimate Abbott family shitshow," Landon said, speaking so only Amanda could hear him.

She glanced over her shoulder at him. "It's the most fun I've ever had in my entire life."

He hugged her from behind. "I'm seeing it in a new light through your eyes."

"You can't possibly know how lucky you are, because you've never been without the shitshow."

"Whatever you're about to witness at the hands of the rolling shitshow, promise you won't hold it against me or change your mind about me."

"I promise," she said, smiling back at him. "Nothing could change my mind about you."

"Don't be so sure. Three hours on a bus with my entire family is apt to have you running for your life."

"No way."

They ended up sitting across from Will and Cameron, who'd blossomed into nearly full-term pregnancy in the last few days, or so it seemed.

"How're you feeling?" Landon asked her.

"Like a whale."

"Most beautiful whale I've ever seen," Will said.

"He has to say that. He did this to me."

Izzy sat in front of them with a blond man Amanda hadn't met.

"Amanda, this is my cousin Noah," Landon said. "He's the one rebuilding the inn."

"Oh, nice to meet you," she said.

"You, too."

He didn't seem too thrilled to be on the bus.

Landon leaned in and whispered in her ear. "Long story. Will tell you later." He pointed to the older couple getting on the bus. "That's my aunt Hannah and her..."

"Boyfriend," Izzy said of the man with her mother.

"Okay, then," Landon said. "Ray Mulvaney. He's Lucy and Emma's dad."

"Oh, so they met through your family, then?"

"Yep. So it went like this... Cameron came from New York City to Butler to build the website."

"And crashed into Fred," Cameron said. "I like to get that out there, because if I don't say it, someone else will."

"She's known in Butler as the girl who hit Fred," Will added.

"Got it," Amanda said, amused.

"Then Lucy came to Butler to help me," Cameron said, "and met Colton. Emma and Simone came for Christmas and Hunter and Megan's wedding and met Grayson. With Lucy, Emma and Simone moving to Vermont, Ray, who was widowed, decided to come, too, and now he's dating Aunt Hannah."

"Who'd been alone for twenty years," Landon added. "See what happens when people come to Butler?"

"I'm seeing it," Amanda said.

"And then there's my dad," Cameron added, "who met Mary when he came for my wedding."

"Are they coming this weekend?" Landon asked.

"Absolutely. They said they wouldn't miss it for anything. They're flying to Boston from Paris."

"I'm going to Paris."

Landon stared at her. "You are?"

"Yes, in July."

"When did that happen?"

"During the meltdown after the fire when it occurred to me that I've never been to Europe."

"Can I come?"

"You want to?"

"Hell yes."

Amanda smiled. "Then I guess we're going to Paris."

"You're sure you don't mind?"

"Of course not. I'd love it."

"Holy crap," Landon said, grinning. "I'm going to Paris."

"Listen up, everyone," Linc said from the front of the bus. "We're in for a treat on our ride to Boston. Izzy has put together a slide show from the catalog shoot this week. I don't know about you, but I can't wait to see all our models at work."

Lots of groans and "no, thanks" comments followed his announcement.

"Izzy assures me the shoot went great, and you're all going to be stars."

"That's what I'm afraid of," Amanda said.

"Awesome," Will said.

"If everyone would close the shades on the windows, we'll be able to see the slide show better."

"What if we don't want to see it?" Hunter asked.

"You'll love it," Izzy said.

"Without further ado, let's get this bus rolling," Linc said.

Ella and Charley had brought snacks, Hannah had drinks, Colton provided maple candy, and Izzy had supplied the entertainment. The minute the bus was out of the store parking lot and on the road to Boston, the screen at the front was lowered, and the slide show began with baby Callie.

"Ohhhhh," Hannah said. "Look at my sweet girl!"

Next came Caden, and then the two babies together.

"She's easing us in," Colton said. "Her strategy is to soften us with the babies."

"You found me out, cousin," Izzy said.

Elmer's smiling face came on the screen as he sported a red flannel shirt and matching down vest.

"Sexy!" Lucas said.

"You know it, boy," Elmer said.

"You're going to have every widow lady in New England flocking to Butler looking for the guy in red flannel, Dad," Hannah Coleman said.

"Aw, shucks. I don't know about that."

Molly was next, wearing an oatmeal-colored sweater. Izzy had captured her so perfectly as she looked over her shoulder, an impish expression on her face and her hair down around her shoulders.

"Look at that hot mama," Linc said to groans from his children. "Sexiest model I've ever seen."

He was next, sporting a tweed sport coat.

"Speaking of sexy," Molly said with a growl. "*Meow.*"

"Ew," Hunter said. "Gross."

"Nothing gross about it," Molly said to her oldest son.

"I think I'd rather walk to Boston," Hunter said.

"Take me with you, brother," Will said.

"How did we raise such prudes, Linc?" Molly asked.

"Been asking myself that a lot since Amanda and the toys came to town."

Cameron leaned across the aisle. "I may be the girl who hit

Fred, but you're *always* gonna be the girl who brought the sex toys."

"Oh joy," Amanda said, laughing.

Photos of Hunter, Megan, Will, Cameron, Colton, Lucy, Max, Wade, Mia, Grayson and Emma followed in rapid succession, all of them wearing clothes that would be for sale in the catalog. Izzy had gotten beautiful pictures of each couple in addition to their individual shots.

"I want a copy of that," Hannah said of the photo of her, Nolan and Callie.

"I can hook you up," Izzy said.

Even Simone had been included, to her delight. "Check me out!"

"Cutest model of them all," Grayson said.

"We couldn't have paid for better-looking models," Elmer said.

The group went crazy with laughter, hoots and whistles when Colton appeared wearing long underwear.

"Now *that's* sexy," Lucy said to more laughter.

Izzy had included some hilarious outtakes, including Colton flashing his rear end through the trap door in a union suit, Max vamping for the camera and Wade looking exquisitely uncomfortable as a model.

Dani and Savannah came next, wearing matching flannel nightgowns.

"Aw, look at my girls," Lucas said. "Aren't they beautiful?"

"They sure are, son," Elmer said. "And don't think you escaped the modeling. Izzy's got you on the schedule after we get back from Boston."

"Fabulous," Lucas said with a decided lack of enthusiasm.

"No one gets out of this one, bro," Landon said in the second before his picture appeared on the screen, making him groan.

"Now that right there is the sexiest thing I've seen yet," Lucas said.

"Me, too," Amanda said, drawing more groans and laughter.

Landon flashed her a dopey grin. "Thanks, babe."

She was next, and Landon whistled. "The winner for sexiest model goes to my girl!"

She buried her face in his chest. "Stop."

He put his arm around her. "I'll never stop."

CHAPTER TWENTY-SIX

"Love is patient, love is kind."
—1 Corinthians 13:4

*M*ia's dad, Cabot Lodge, had put them up at the Four Seasons, just down the street from Fenway Park, where the Abbotts hosted a rehearsal dinner in Cabot's skybox.

Amanda had never laughed so much that her sides ached until she spent a full day with the Abbott family as well as their Coleman cousins, their wonderful grandfather, extended family and friends. At the game, she met Landon's cousins Vanessa, Jackson, Henry, Sarah and Ally Coleman, all of whom lived in Boston.

Also in attendance was Mia's father's family, including his sister, two brothers and their children, some of whom Mia was meeting for the first time.

Before the Red Sox took the field against the Yankees, the eighteen Abbott and Coleman cousins surrounded their beaming grandfather and posed for a photo that Cameron took using Izzy's camera. Seeing them all together gave Amanda an up-close look at what Landon's childhood had been like surrounded by siblings and cousins.

"They're a good-looking group, if I do say so myself," Molly said as she slipped an arm around Amanda to watch the photo shenanigans unfold.

"They certainly are."

"My father loves having them all together like this."

"Is it okay to admit that not only have I fallen for your son, but I've also fallen madly in love with your father, too?"

Molly smiled. "Totally okay and completely understandable. I hit the daddy jackpot with that man, and I know it."

"He's the best."

"Yes, he is." After a pause, Molly said, "So you've fallen for my son, have you?"

"Completely." Amanda found him in the crowd, the handsomest one in a group of stunningly good-looking men.

"That's the best news I've heard all day."

"I'm glad you think so."

"We all do, honey. Everyone is talking about how happy he is with you. We've never seen him like this."

Molly's approval meant so much to her. "You heard about my daughter?"

"I did, and I'm so happy for you to have her in your life, although the circumstances are heartbreaking."

"They are, and it's hard to temper my excitement about being with her while keeping in mind what she and her mother are going through."

"Of course it is, but it's okay to be excited about your part of it."

"Is it really?"

"It is. Anyone would be. Think of what Cabot withstood for more than twenty years of searching for his daughter."

Amanda shifted her gaze to Mia's dad, who beamed with unbridled happiness as he interacted with his daughter and her guests.

"He could be so bitter, but he's just pure love and gratitude. I admire that so much."

"I do, too. I can't imagine the ordeal he went through."

"I can't either. I give him so much credit for focusing on the joy and not the bitterness."

"Agreed. What's her relationship like with her mother?"

"From what I've heard from Wade, it's been strained since she found out what her mother did, but she does talk to her. Occasionally."

"That's a very difficult thing to forgive."

"Yes, it is, but back to your situation. I give you permission to be excited about Stella, because I know you'll do everything you can to help her through the loss of her mother."

"I will. For sure."

"And we'll help you while you help her."

Amanda leaned her head on Molly's shoulder. "Thank you for making me part of this extraordinary family."

"We couldn't be happier to have you."

ALL HIS LIFE, MAX HAD HEARD THE STORY OF WHEN HIS PARENTS met, how his dad had taken one look at his mom and somehow known she was going to change everything. How could that happen, he'd wondered, always a little skeptical of such things even as his parents presented a master class on love and marriage for their children to admire and even envy.

And then he went to Boston for his brother's wedding and was introduced to Mia's cousin Caroline, a tall dark-haired woman with gorgeous brown eyes, an infectious smile and cutting wit. She went crazy over Caden, asking to hold him and entertaining him for half an hour before she reluctantly—or so it seemed to Max—returned the baby to his father.

"That is one super cute little man," she declared.

"Thank you," Max said, tongue-tied around a woman for the first time. "I quite like him."

"I can see why. Which one is his mom?"

The innocent question knocked him sideways. Even seven months after Chloe had departed their lives, he sometimes still couldn't believe it had actually happened and had trouble explaining her absence. "Ah, she's not here."

"Oh."

"She's actually not in the picture."

"*Oh.*"

"Yeah." Cue mad awkwardness. "It's okay. We're doing great."

"That must've been rough, though," Caroline said, her pretty eyes brimming with compassion.

"It was, but I'm lucky to have a lot of help and support. My family is great. My parents have been incredible. I have no complaints."

"It's okay if you do," she said in a low, conspiratorial whisper. "You'd have a right to a few complaints."

She'd known him all of an hour, and she got it. "All I care about is him, that he's healthy and happy and has everything he needs. The rest is noise."

"Yes, it certainly is."

"What's your story?"

"I finished college last December and have been looking for a job ever since with no luck."

"What kind of job?"

"I'm a kindergarten teacher. Or at least I want to be."

"Where are you looking?"

"All over."

"You should check out Vermont."

"Really?" she asked with a flirtatious smile. "What goes on up there?"

"Lots of stuff—snow and ice and mud and maple syrup and moose. It's awesome."

"Sounds like it. How much snow are we talking?"

"Uh, like you want a number of feet?"

Her dark brows furrowed adorably. "The fact that you measure it in feet is a concern."

Max laughed. "There's a lot of it."

"What do you do up there?"

"I work for my family's business, dividing my time between the sugaring facility and the Christmas tree farm."

"What goes on at the sugaring facility?"

"That's where we make maple syrup. I work with my brother Colton there and my brother Landon at the farm."

"Do you like working with your family?"

"I love it. I get along great with all my siblings."

"You're lucky to have them."

"As the youngest of ten, there've been times when I would've disagreed with you, but those days are long over now. Do you have siblings?"

"Nope, just cousins I was close to when we were young, but we drifted apart as we got older."

"You'll find your way back to each other when you get more settled."

"Maybe." Ringing laughter had her glancing across the room to where her uncle Cabot had his arm around Mia as they talked with Wade, Molly and Linc. "My uncle is so happy. He's like a whole new man since he found his daughter."

"I can't imagine what he's been through."

"It was so awful. My whole life, I heard about my missing cousin. The day he found her was one of the best days of all our lives. He's such a good guy. What was done to him..." She shook her head.

"Shouldn't happen to anyone. I have a whole new perspective having a child of my own. I'd kill to protect him."

"That's kind of hot," she said with a wink and a smile that rendered him speechless.

"Is it?"

"Hell yes."

He discovered that laughing involved her whole body.

"Like you didn't know the protective-single-dad thing is hot."

"Uh, I didn't. I've been all about diapers and bottles and pacifiers for the last seven months. If being a single dad is hot, that's totally news to me."

"Well, I'm glad I got to be the one to break it to you."

LANDON THOUGHT THE BALL GAME WOULD NEVER END. TODAY had been a blast, but he was ready for some time alone with Amanda, which meant, of course, the game had to go into extra innings before the Sox won with a thrilling walk-off home run. Then everyone had wanted to go out for drinks, but since Landon had technically "worked" the night before, he begged off. While the others sought out after-hours fun, Landon and Amanda walked back to the hotel with Lucas, Dani, Savannah, Max, Caden, Will and Cameron, who was exhausted from being, as she called it, "extra pregnant."

Caden was sacked out on Max's shoulder, his little hand grasping Max's shirt.

"You seemed to have a good time tonight," Landon said quietly to his brother while Amanda chatted with Dani as she pushed Savannah in a stroller.

"I did."

"Call me crazy, but Caroline seemed to be digging my little boy."

"Everyone digs him."

"I meant *you*," Landon said with a laugh. "Idiot."

"Oh. Maybe. We had a nice time hanging out."

"Are you so far removed from the game that you can't tell when a girl is into you?"

"Possibly."

Landon laughed again. "Well, I'm not, and I know what I saw. She likes you."

"I like her, too. It was nice to meet someone who never knew me without Caden, you know?"

"What do you mean?"

"People I knew before expect me to be the same, but I'm not. Everything is different now."

"Huh, I hadn't really thought of that."

"My friends give me a lot of shit because they never see me anymore. I've stopped responding to their comments about how I've turned into a priest since I had a kid."

"They did not say that."

"They did! I know they're just joking. Kind of."

"Max, come on. Don't let that shit get you down. Of course everything has changed for you. Someday it will for them, too, and they'll get it."

"Yeah, but for now, they just think I'm a priest."

"Eh, fuck 'em. What do you care what they think?"

"I don't, it's just that sometimes…"

"What?"

"I don't want you to think I'm complaining about having Caden. I love him more than anything in the world."

"I know that. Everyone knows that."

"I'm only twenty-three, but sometimes I feel like I'm forty or even older. Like tonight… I really like Caroline, but what's the point? She lives here. I'm hours away in Vermont. Even if I wanted to come here and see her, I can't."

"Whoa, Maxi-Pad, take a breath."

Max's thunderous expression was no surprise—it happened every time he and Lucas trotted out the nickname they'd come up with for Max after middle school health class. "I can still punch you in the face with a baby in my arms."

"Easy, killer."

"You and your brother are still assholes."

"My brother and I are offended."

"Whatever."

"About Caroline," Landon said. "If you like her, don't go straight to hopeless. Anything is possible if you want it badly enough."

"Are you talking about me or yourself?"

"Both, I guess. For a long time, it seemed like nothing was going to happen for me and Amanda, and once I found the courage to be truthful with her about what I wanted, it's been... incredible."

"I'm glad for you. She seems like a really nice girl."

"She's the best."

"So this is it for you?"

"I think so."

"Wow. I'm going to be the only single one standing."

"You won't be single for long. Despite what we think, people of the female persuasion seem to find you less revolting than we do."

"Gee, thanks," Max said, laughing. "That's one hell of an endorsement."

"You're a hell of a guy, Max Abbott. Don't let what one woman did make you give up on all of them. That'd just compound the tragedy."

"I hear you. Look at you becoming wise in your old age."

"Shocking, right?"

"I always knew you had it in you."

"I'm glad you did, because I had no clue."

He followed Max into the hotel lobby and caught up to Amanda. As they walked to the elevator, he put his arm around her and kept her close for the ride to the fifth floor, where most of the rooms were occupied by family members. They said good night to Will and Cam and then waited for Max to fish his keycard out of his pocket while balancing Caden.

"You need any help, Max?" Landon asked.

"Nope, we're good. See you guys in the morning."

"Night."

Landon and Amanda were next door and Lucas, Dani and Savannah on the other side of them.

"Night," Lucas said as he walked by with Dani.

"Don't let me hear any noises coming from over there," Landon said.

"Ditto," Lucas said, smirking.

"Might be a good night for ear plugs," Landon said.

Amanda smacked his shoulder. "Shut up."

"He's all yours," Lucas said, rolling his eyes.

Landon opened the door, ushered Amanda in ahead of him and let the door close behind them. "Wait."

She turned to him, and he could tell he took her by surprise when he wrapped his arms around her and kissed her with hours' worth of pent-up desire pouring forth in a kiss that went on for what felt like forever.

"*Whoa*," she said. "What brought that on?"

"Hours and hours and *hours* surrounded by my family. That's what."

"Aw, did you have to be on your best behavior?"

He cupped her ass and tugged her in tight against his erection. "I did, and it was painful."

"How painful?"

"Excruciating. I had to keep my hands and lips and every other part of me to myself."

"I thought I took care of all that this morning."

"That was a hundred years ago, and besides, it's your own fault for being so damned sexy in that dress." When he'd seen her in the red dress she'd worn in deference to the Sox, he'd nearly drooled all over himself. He helped her remove the cute little denim jacket she'd paired with the dress and then ran his hands over her luscious curves. "I can't help myself. You just do it for me."

"Likewise."

"Nice how that works out, huh?"

"Nicest thing ever."

"Is it? Really?"

"Of course it is, Landon. Between everything that's happened with you and having Stella back in my life, not to mention your amazing family, who I already love so much… Sometimes I just want to pinch myself that it's all real."

"It's so real." He kissed her some more and then wrapped his arms around her, needing to have her close to him. "I saw you on your phone earlier. Were you still talking to Stella?"

She nodded. "We were texting all night—because it's easier now that I'm out of the mountains. She was having a rough night."

"Because of her mom?"

Amanda nodded. "Kelly has been feeling really lousy since yesterday, so Stella stayed home from a slumber party she was looking forward to because she didn't want her mom to be home alone."

"Ah, the poor kid. That's a lot for her to deal with. Isn't there anyone else who can help them?"

"They moved to the town where they live now a few months before Kelly was diagnosed. She was transferred with her job, and they didn't get the chance to meet very many people before she got sick. Kelly's friends live mostly out of state."

"The thought of Stella and Kelly dealing with an illness of that magnitude alone is a bit overwhelming."

"I agree. I was thinking I might go there at some point. They need help, and I can do that for them. Maybe I could work on the catalog remotely for a while."

Landon's heart sank at the thought of her being hours away from him, possibly for months or even longer. But he knew it was the right thing to do. "I'm sure you could."

"Would you visit me on your days off?"

"Of course I would."

She looked up at him, her expression madly vulnerable. "It's a lot to ask of you."

"It's not a lot. It's what you do for the people you love. You show up and support them no matter what they're going through. You're there for good times and bad times."

She clung to him. "I feel so very lucky to be loved by you."

"I feel just as lucky to be loved by you. And I want you to do whatever you have to do for Stella and Kelly and not worry about me."

"Thank you for understanding." She drew him into another kiss, and after that, there were no more words, only desperate kisses and soft moans and searing pleasure. They pulled at clothes and fell onto the bed in a tangle of arms and legs, her softness welcoming him as he landed on top of her, being mindful of her injured ankle.

"I can't get enough of you," he said.

"Same. Being with you this way has become my favorite thing ever."

"This day seemed to crawl. I was having fun and enjoying my family and the game, but all I could think about was how much longer until I could be alone with you."

"That's very sweet."

He scowled. "It's not sweet. It's depraved."

"I like you that way."

"Oh yeah?"

"Uh-huh."

"Then you won't care if we skip the preliminaries and race straight to the main event?"

"I won't care at all."

He pushed into her, muffling her loud gasp with a kiss. "Shhhh. We're surrounded on all sides."

She bit her lip and gave him a wide-eyed look that made him laugh.

"You can do it."

"Not sure I can."

Landon took hold of her hands, lifted them over her head and kissed her to keep her quiet as he moved in her. If there was anything that felt better than being with her this way, he hadn't found it yet, and he was done looking. This was all he needed to be happy. She was all he needed.

CHAPTER TWENTY-SEVEN

*"I was made and meant to look for you and wait
for you and become yours forever."*
—Robert Browning

Mia was awake an hour before her alarm was set to go off. She turned on her side to watch her gorgeous husband sleep, which was one of her favorite things to do. For so long, she'd dreamed about him and the life they had now. When she'd been trapped in hell with her ex, thoughts of Wade Abbott had kept her sane.

And when the shit with Brody had hit the fan, she'd run to Wade. It had been a huge risk because she hadn't seen him in more than a year by then and had no idea whether the feelings she'd had for him had ever been reciprocated.

They'd been platonic friends. Nothing more. But she'd wanted so much more with him, and when she'd asked him to marry her so Brody couldn't force her to marry him to keep her from testifying against him, Wade hadn't hesitated.

He'd shown her his heart that first day and every day since then. Back in the days when she'd been locked in a nightmare, it had never occurred to her that the kind of happiness she'd found with Wade even existed. Now she knew better.

They'd been married for months already, but after she found her long-lost father, he'd insisted on throwing them the big wedding that would take place today. Mia would've said they didn't need the over-the-top wedding, but she'd loved every minute of planning it with her dad, who was so thrilled to have her back in his life.

Wade opened his eyes and caught her staring at him, which happened at least once a day. He smiled as he reached for her.

Mia cuddled up to him and closed her eyes against the rush of emotion that surprised her. She would've thought she had things under control, but apparently, that wasn't the case.

"What're you thinking about?" he asked.

"You and us and today and everything that led us to this day."

"If I hadn't lived through it, I might not believe it actually happened."

"I didn't think I'd be excited for today, but I am. Does that make me a typical girl wanting to play dress-up?"

"I'm excited, too, and I didn't think I would be either. At first, it was like we were doing this for your dad, and now..."

"Now, it's for us."

"Yeah. I'll always love the way we got married the first time, in my grandfather's living room with the rings he and my grandmother gave each other and only Ella and Gavin there to witness it."

"That was perfect."

"It was the best day of my entire life."

"Mine, too."

"But it's okay for this one to be just as good."

"Is it?"

"Absolutely," he said. "This time, we get to do it up big, with everyone we love there to see it."

"Not everyone." Mia's feelings toward her mother had been complicated since she found out her mom had basically stolen her from her father when she was a child and had gone to elaborate lengths to keep her hidden from him. "She called the other day."

"You didn't say anything."

"What's there to say? I'm getting married—again—and she's not invited or welcome to attend. I never thought I'd be estranged from her, and I don't want to be. It's just hard to reconcile what she did with the man I've come to know."

"It's impossible to fathom why she felt the need to take you from him."

"And I've yet to hear an explanation from her that makes sense."

"You may never hear one."

"I'm starting to realize that."

"I know how it pains you to have tension with her, but you ought to just let things ride for a while and see how you feel in a few months. She's lucky you still talk to her at all."

"We shouldn't talk about that stuff today. This is our day, and none of that crap has any business being part of our celebration."

"You're right. None of that matters today."

"I can't wait for you to see my dress."

"I can't wait either—for that and everything else I get to have with you, Mrs. Abbott."

"I love you so much, Wade. From the first time I ever saw you, you've had my heart."

"I love you, too, my sweet Mia, undisputed love of my life."

She smiled up at him. "How about we get married all over again?"

"Let's do it."

THE WEDDING CABOT THREW FOR HIS DAUGHTER AND SON-IN-LAW would go down as one of the most spectacular things Amanda had ever witnessed. Someone compared it to a royal wedding, and Amanda found that description fitting. Every detail had been seen to with loving care by a man making up for more than twenty years without his child in his life.

Possibly more than anyone else in attendance, Amanda understood how he must feel about having Mia back. Amanda had always known where her child was, but living without her had been brutal. She couldn't imagine what he'd gone through not knowing where Mia was or if she was safe for all that time.

But none of that drama was present in the celebration that day as their two families came together to celebrate Wade and Mia. The entire day was magical, from the astounded expression on Wade's face when Mia first appeared at the back of the cathedral in her stunning dress, to the tears streaming down Cabot's face as he escorted his daughter down the aisle, to the hug Cabot and Mia shared at the end of a very long road that had led to them finding each other.

Amanda barely knew these people, and yet, like everyone else, she was in tears by the time Cabot finally gave his daughter's hand to Wade. On his way to join his family in the front row on the bride's side of the church, Cabot hugged Molly, Lincoln and Elmer in the front row of the groom's side.

Dani handed Amanda a tissue that she happily accepted. They were sitting together while Landon, Lucas and the other Abbott brothers stood up with Wade. Dressed in black tuxedos, the brothers made for quite a sight. Mia's bridesmaids included Ella, Charley and Hannah, each of them wearing navy blue silk gowns.

The bride and groom were married by a female Episcopal bishop, who was a close friend of Cabot's. She walked the couple through traditional vows before they exchanged vows they'd written for each other.

Wade's voice was full of emotion and love as he gazed at his bride and spoke from his heart. "From the first time I ever saw you at a yoga retreat years ago, I wanted you to be mine. I would've done anything to be able to take you home with me, to build a life and a family with you, but that wouldn't happen for a long, *long* time. And when it finally did, it was the best thing to ever happen to me. *You* are the best thing to ever happen to me. I love you more than you could ever know. I have since that first day, and I always will."

Mia took a tissue from the bishop and dabbed carefully at her eyes. When she had recovered her composure, she looked up at her husband. "I fell in love that first day, too. I thought of you every single day that we were apart, wishing for all the things I have now, things I never could've dreamed of back when it seemed the universe was conspiring to keep us apart. I took a huge chance when I came to find you in the middle of a blizzard. I had no idea if you would even remember me."

"I remembered you," Wade said, smiling through tears.

"Thank God for that and everything that's come since then. I'm so thankful for your family and their support of us even when you told them you were marrying someone they'd never met. I'm thankful for my new family, my dad and all the people who've loved us through this amazing season in our lives. But most of all, I'm thankful for you, Wade, and your love and the life we're building together. You're my dream come true, and I'll love you forever."

The bishop sounded tearful when she said, "It's my great honor, under the laws of the Commonwealth of Massachusetts, to once again declare Wade and Mia to be husband and wife. Wade, you may kiss your bride."

Wade raised his hands to Mia's face and kissed her so sweetly that Amanda was again dabbing at tears.

She joined in the applause that rang through the huge church. The wedding party followed Wade and Mia out of the church and walked the short distance to the Boston Public Garden for photos.

They'd scored a perfect bright, clear, sunny June day. The only thing marring this otherwise fantastic day for Amanda was that Stella hadn't responded to her text that morning asking how her mom was doing.

Amanda walked with Dani and Savannah as well as Lucy, Emma, Simone and Cameron, who was moving very slowly.

"Are you okay?" Amanda asked her.

"I hope so."

"What does that mean?" Lucy asked.

"Don't make a thing of it, but I think I might be in labor."

"*What?*" Lucy's high-pitched shriek probably woke up all the dogs in the neighborhood.

"Hush, Luce. I'm fine. The contractions are twelve minutes apart."

Lucy stopped walking to stare at Cameron. "You're having actual contractions, and you didn't think you should mention that to anyone?"

"I refuse to ruin another wedding. Will is a groomsman, and he didn't need to be worried about me. It's all good. By the time the contractions get closer, he'll be done with his wedding party stuff, and we can find a hospital."

Lucy glanced at her sister, Emma. "She's insane, right? Tell me she's insane."

"She's insane," Emma said.

"I need two more hours, tops," Cameron said. "Go about your business, and don't mind me."

"We're skipping the gardens," Lucy said.

"*No,*" Cameron said. "We can't. Molly wants pictures with the whole family. We have to be there."

"Right after that, we're getting a car back to the hotel," Lucy said. "I'll give you exactly one hour, and then you're telling your husband you're in freaking labor."

"Fine," Cameron said. "If you're going to be that away about it."

"I'm going to be that way about it."

Lucy and Emma linked arms with Cameron, supporting her as they walked two blocks to the gardens.

"Holy crap," Amanda whispered to Dani. "When I was in labor, I couldn't think, let alone participate in a wedding."

"No shit," Dani whispered back. "Lucas told me her mother and grandmother died in labor, and that before she got pregnant, they visited Mass General so she could have a full workup. Everything was fine, but Will is going to flip out when he finds out she's in labor and didn't tell him."

"Yikes. That's scary."

"Which is why Lucy is freaking out."

Amanda was full of anxiety over Cameron being in labor but wanting to pretend otherwise for the time being. As a first-time mother, Cameron was about to find out that babies came into the world on their own schedules, not their mother's. "When is she due?"

"Not for two more weeks, which is why they felt it was okay for her to come on the trip."

"Holy moly."

When they arrived at the gardens, which were in full, glorious bloom, the wedding party was arranged into a group photo. After that, photos were taken of Wade and the brides-maids and Mia and the groomsmen. The Lodge family surrounded Mia and Wade, and then the Abbotts had their turn.

"Amanda." Molly waved her over. "Join us, honey. You're part of the family."

She was determined not to tear up as she took Molly's direction to stand in front of Landon, who wrapped his arm around her waist and pulled her in close to him.

"That's it," he whispered. "It's official. You're in the family."

"Stop, I'm trying not to cry."

"All right, Abbotts." Izzy was positioned on a ladder with her camera directed at them. "Everyone say 'wedding.'"

While the Colemans lined up for a family picture that Lucy took for Izzy, Amanda checked her phone to find no word from Stella. She'd give her another hour and then call to make sure she was okay.

"Walk with me," Landon said, taking her hand.

"Wait." Amanda glanced at Cameron, who was now with Will, Lucy, Colton, Emma and Grayson.

"What's up?"

"Don't make any sudden moves, and don't ever let on that I told you."

"Told me what?"

"Cameron is in labor, but she doesn't want anyone else to know yet."

Landon's gaze shifted to his sister-in-law, who seemed fine until she visibly grimaced. Because Will was talking to Hunter, he missed it. "I don't like it, especially in light of her family history."

"She said she's hours from delivering and doesn't want to disrupt the wedding."

"I'll keep an eye on her."

"That's why I told you."

"Will is going to lose his shit when he finds out she's in labor and didn't tell him."

"She said she feels totally fine, and it's all good."

"I guess we'll see."

They watched as Lucy flagged down a cab and loaded Cameron and Will into the car for the short ride to the Four Seasons, where the reception would be held.

"At least he's with her now," Landon said as they strolled to the hotel, holding hands. "If you're ever in labor, you'd better not hide it from me. I don't care what we're doing."

His words, coupled with Molly's insistence that she was part of their family now, were almost too much for Amanda to process.

He looked over at her. "You do want more kids, right?"

"I do. That's right up there at the top of the list I made after the fire—having a baby I get to keep."

"We'll have cute kids, don't you think?"

"Of course we will. How many do you want?"

"As many as you want to have."

"So ten would be good?"

"Oh, um, well... Not sure I want ten, but more than two would be good."

She looked over at him. "Are we really talking about our future kids?" She kept waiting for it all to go wrong, because that's what she'd come to expect.

"That's what I'm talking about. Whose kids are you talking about?"

"Ours."

"Then we're talking about the same thing," he said.

"And that's what you want?"

"Hell yes, that's what I want."

"How long have you wanted that?"

"Since I met you and realized I'd found someone I could picture forever with."

"I can't believe we're really talking about our kids."

"Believe it. That'll be us before too long." He gestured to Wade and Mia, who were being delivered to the front of the hotel in a chauffeured Rolls-Royce. "Minus the Rolls."

Amanda laughed. "I don't need the Rolls. Just you. That's all."

"We'll get there, sweetheart. I promise."

CHAPTER TWENTY-EIGHT

"Don't rush into love. You'll find the person
meant for you when you least expect it."
— Franzie Gubatina

Cabot Lodge threw one hell of a party, Landon thought as he watched Wade and Mia dance to "Always on My Mind," which was the perfect song for two people who'd spent years yearning for each other before they finally got the chance to be together.

Wade was the "quiet" Abbott, which made it all the more incredible to see him so obviously head over heels in love and not afraid to let everyone know it.

"They make a beautiful couple," Amanda said.

Landon put his arm around her. "They sure do."

Three-quarters of the way through the song, Cabot tapped Wade on the shoulder, asking to cut in.

Wade turned his wife over to her father and stepped back to give them a moment together.

"The song works for Cabot and Mia, too," Amanda said.

"For sure."

You'd have to be dead and buried not to be moved by the sight of Cabot dancing with his daughter, his joy unmistakable.

While Cabot danced with Mia, Molly came out to the dance floor to claim her son.

"My heart can't take this," Amanda said.

Landon put his other arm around her, too, and held her while they watched the others on the dance floor. His emotions were all over the place, which was funny because he didn't get emotional at weddings. But since he'd fallen for Amanda, he got it now. Things made sense to him that never had before.

There was nothing like finding the other half of yourself and knowing she felt the same way. He'd loved Naomi, but sadly, he'd never gotten the chance to see what might've become of that. For the first time, he had the chance for everything with someone, and he was so excited for what the future might hold.

When the dance ended, Wade, Mia and their parents took seats at the head table. The wedding planner handed a microphone to Hunter, who was seated at a table with Megan, Grayson, Emma, Will, Cameron, Lucy and Colton. "As the oldest and wisest of the Abbott siblings, I was chosen by Wade to be his best man today, an honor I don't take lightly."

His opening line was met with loud boos from his siblings and laughter from everyone else.

Smiling at the predictable response, Hunter continued. "On behalf of the Abbotts, Colemans and our grandfather, Elmer Stillman, I want to thank Cabot for his hospitality this weekend and for the fabulous wedding he put together for my brother Wade and his beautiful wife, Mia. For those of you who don't know Wade like we do, I want to tell you a little about him."

"Oh dear God," Wade said loudly enough for everyone to hear.

"Relax, little brother. I'm not going to embarrass you *too* badly."

"Awesome," Wade said as Mia giggled at his distress.

"Wade is our lone wolf, which isn't an easy thing to be in a family of ten kids. Nonetheless, Wade has always been an entity unto himself. As you may have heard, the Abbott kids were raised—fittingly—in a restored barn. Wade found a way to get his own room in the barn by converting a large closet into a bedroom. He would tell you the ability to escape from the madness that surrounded him saved his sanity."

Wade nodded emphatically.

"Despite his need for solitude, Wade is still very much one of us. He's our health and fitness nut, our vegan, our yoga master and one of the very best people I've ever had the privilege to know. If I was ever in any kind of trouble, Wade would be the first person I'd call. Not that I ever get in trouble, mind you."

More boos from his siblings that had the wedding guests laughing.

Hunter carried on despite them. "So knowing this about Wade, you can imagine our shock when he came home with a wife none of us had ever met. Well played, brother. Very well played."

"Thank you," Wade said as he smiled at Mia.

"In the last few months, we've had the chance to get to know Mia and to understand why Wade loves her so much. Your story, Wade and Mia, and your devotion to each other during the years you spent wishing for what you have now, has touched us all. Thank you for including us in your celebration today, and all our best wishes for a long and happy life together." Hunter raised his champagne glass in a toast to the happy couple. "To Wade and Mia."

Echoes of "hear, hear" and "to Wade and Mia" filled the huge ballroom.

The wedding coordinator handed the microphone to Cabot next. "Thank you, Hunter, for those kind words about my daughter and her wonderful husband. I still can't believe I'm able to say the words 'my daughter' and feel only joy and not the heartache that was part of my life for so many years. I certainly don't want to dwell on the past today, and I promised myself I wouldn't cry all day. We know how that's gone so far."

While the others laughed, he took a second to collect himself. "Having you back in my life, Mia, is the best thing to ever happen to me and my family. And to get Wade and his wonderful family as part of the package is a very sweet bonus indeed. I've learned that life is full of ups and downs, love and joy, pain and heartache. You never know what's going to happen, but the one thing I know for sure is that love is all there is. It's all that matters, and knowing my daughter is well and truly loved by such a wonderful man is a special gift. Wade and Mia, I love you both and can't wait for all that's to come."

When Amanda trembled in his arms, Landon realized she was having an emotional reaction to Cabot's speech. "Let's go get some air, sweetheart."

With a minimum of fuss, Landon got her out of the ballroom and found a patio off the hallway that was currently vacant.

She closed her eyes and tipped her face into the warm sunshine.

"Are you okay?"

"Yeah. His speech got to me."

"Of course it did. You understand better than anyone what he's been through."

"It was different for me. I always knew where she was."

"But she wasn't with *you*, so you get how it was for him." He kept an arm around her, needing her close to him. "Still nothing from Stella?"

She looked at the phone she'd had clutched in her hand for hours now. "No, and I'm starting to really worry."

"Why don't you call her again?"

Amanda put through the call on speaker. It rang and rang until Stella's voicemail message answered.

"Hey, it's Stella. Please leave a message, and I'll call you back."

"Hi, it's Amanda calling again. I haven't heard from you, so

I'm worried. Give me a call as soon as you can." She ended the call and exhaled a deep breath. "I don't know what to do."

"You tried Kelly, too?"

"A couple of times."

"Do you want to go there?"

"Right now? We're at a wedding."

"I know where we are, love, but I'm worried, too. Something has to be up for her to not reply to your texts or calls. She was texting you nonstop yesterday from the second we got out of the mountains and found reception."

"Let's give it another hour and then figure out what to do. They could be at a soccer game or something, and we're over here freaking out."

"Take a minute. We don't need to go rushing back to the party."

"I was looking forward to dancing with you."

"We can do that right here." He wrapped his arms around her and swayed to imaginary music.

"As perfect as this is, we need a real song to mark the first time we dance together."

Into her ear, he hummed the refrain from "All My Loving," a song he'd heard a million times growing up with a Beatles fanatic for a father. Landon slowed the tempo a bit to make it suit his purposes.

"That's a good one."

"One of my favorites."

They stayed that way, swaying to the tune he hummed, for quite some time, enjoying the moment to themselves.

"We should go back so they don't think we snuck off to have sex," Amanda said.

"Now that you mention it…"

"We're not doing that."

"It's mean of you to bring it up and then take it away."

She took his hand and led the way back to the reception. "It wasn't an offer. It was an observation."

"Don't say the word 'sex' to me unless you're planning to have it."

Amanda giggled helplessly. "You're such a child sometimes."

"No way, baby. I'm *all* man, and certain words lead to certain things. Proceed with caution."

She rolled her eyes at him. "Whatever you say." Crooking her finger, she got him to tip his head close enough for her to whisper in his ear. "Sex, sex, *sex*."

"I never knew you were so mean."

"Yes, you did."

"No, I didn't."

Their conversation came to a halt when they realized something was going on in the ballroom. The music had stopped, and everyone was gathered around the table where Cameron and Will had been sitting with the others.

"Landon!" His mother's cry sent a chill down his spine as he released Amanda and ran toward her.

"She might be bleeding," Lucas said of Cameron, who was on the floor, "but I can't assess her with this fucking cast on my arm."

Cameron's dad, Patrick, had her head on his leg as he tried to calm her. His girlfriend, Mary, was sitting next to Cam, holding her hand, and Will was on the other side, clearly trying not to lose his shit.

Landon went directly into EMT mode, checking his sister-in-law's pulse, which was steady. "Did you call for EMS?"

"On the way," Cabot said.

"Someone go meet them and get them up here ASAP," Lucas said.

"Landon," Will said, the single word full of panic.

"Amniotic fluid can be bloody." To Cam, Landon said, "Did you feel your water break?"

She nodded. "I stood to use the restroom, and there was a sensation like a cork popping."

"How far apart are the contractions?"

"Nine minutes."

"You're having *contractions?*" Will roared. "And how does my *brother* know that?"

Tears filled Cameron's eyes, which stood out in stark contrast to her pale face. "They were twelve minutes apart, and I didn't want to ruin another wedding." She'd fainted during Hunter and Megan's wedding, which was how they'd found out she was pregnant.

"Oh my God," Will said. "You've got to be kidding me."

"Don't be mad at me on the day our baby is coming!"

Will looked around frantically. "*Where are those paramedics?*"

"Holy shit," a voice behind Max whispered.

Max turned to find Caroline. He hadn't gotten to talk to her yet due to his duties as a groomsman. He'd wondered if the attraction he'd felt for her last night would be present again today. When he'd spotted her in the front row of the church, wearing a sexy, clingy dress with purple flowers on it, he'd confirmed the breathless, edgy feeling was every bit the same as it had been the first time he saw her.

"Is she okay?"

"I think so, but her husband isn't too happy that she didn't tell him she was having labor pains. She's not due for another couple of weeks."

"Yikes. Where's your little guy?"

"Cabot hired nannies to take care of him and the other kids during the reception."

"That sounds like Cabot. He's all about the details."

"You can plan everything except for someone going into labor during the wedding."

"Right? That's why I'm never having kids."

Max stared at her. "*Ever?*"

"Ever. My mom says I'm too young for such pronouncements, but I'm her only hope of grandchildren, so she has to say that."

Led by Colton, the paramedics came into the ballroom, moving quickly to get to Cameron—and not a moment too soon. Will seemed to be on the verge of a thermonuclear meltdown.

"Why don't you want kids?" Max asked Caroline, while keeping an eye on the situation with Cam.

"I never have. I just think I'd be a terrible mother."

"I would've thought that about myself being a father before Caden arrived, but it's funny how you find what you need inside you when necessary."

"So you never looked at him and thought no? Just no?"

"Not for a second," he said, smiling. "I loved him from the first second I ever saw him, and I love him ten million times more than that now."

"Huh."

"You were really great with him last night. You'd probably be better at it than you think."

"But what if I wasn't? What if I was a disaster? It's not like you can give back the kid and say, 'Nope, not for me.'"

Before he could reply, the paramedics loaded Cameron onto the gurney for transport. Will ran after them, promising to keep the family informed of what was going on.

"Why do you look so worried?" Caroline asked.

"Her mother and grandmother died in childbirth."

"Shut up. No way. And you wonder why I don't want kids?"

"She had a full workup before she got pregnant, and the doctors said there should be no reason for her not to have a perfectly normal pregnancy and delivery."

"But you're worried anyway."

"I think we all will be until the baby has safely arrived. And I'm worried about my brother having a stroke or something equally awful in the meantime."

"That's a lot of worry."

"Folks," Cabot said, "we've sent Cameron and Will off to Mass General to have their baby, and while we wait for news from them, they asked that we continue to enjoy the party." He signaled to the band to pick up the music once again.

"Do you want to dance?" Max asked her.

"Sure."

As he walked with her to the dance floor, he tried to reconcile the attraction with the fact that she didn't want kids. He definitely wanted more than just one, and he hoped to one day meet someone who could be a mother to Caden. They were a package deal, and any woman he brought into his life would know that from the get-go.

So while he was well and truly dazzled by beautiful Caroline, they apparently had different ideas about what the future might look like. For now, they could enjoy the party together, and that would be that.

STELLA FINALLY RETURNED AMANDA'S CALL AN HOUR LATER.

"Are you okay?" Amanda asked her.

"My mom had a seizure. She's in the hospital. Sorry I didn't call you back before now."

"Please don't worry about that. Is anyone else with you?"

"No, but I'm okay. The doctor was just here, and the nurses said I can stay."

"What did they say about your mom's condition?"

"I haven't heard anything yet."

"Would it be okay if I come there to stay with you while she's in the hospital?"

"You would do that?"

Amanda closed her eyes against a wild rush of emotion. "Of course I would." She didn't add that the hospital might have to contact child services if Stella didn't have anyone to care for her while her mother was in the hospital. "Text me the name of the hospital. I'll be there in a few hours."

"I... um, thank you, Amanda."

"If anyone asks who's taking care of you, let them know I'm on my way and that Kelly has made me your legal guardian if needed." They'd taken care of that detail shortly after they first made contact.

"Okay."

"I'll see you very soon."

"Text me when you get here."

"I will."

Amanda ended the call and looked around for Landon, finding him talking to Lucas, Dani, Hunter, Megan, Hannah and Nolan. She walked over to join them. "Stella called."

"Excuse me," Landon said to the others as he took her aside. "What's up?"

Amanda filled him in. "I need to go to her."

"Yes, you do. Let me tell my family we're leaving, and I'll see about getting a car."

"You don't have to come, Landon. This is a big day for your family, between the wedding and the baby coming. I'd understand if you wanted to stay."

"Is it okay if I want to go with you?"

"Yes, but—"

"No buts. We're in this together. I'll be right back." He went over to have a word with his parents, and when he returned, Molly came with him.

She hugged Amanda. "I'll be thinking of you."

"Thank you, Molly."

"Keep us posted on how you are and how they are."

"We will. I'm sorry to steal Landon from a family event."

"It's fine. You need him more than we do right now."

Landon hugged his mother. "You'll tell Wade and Mia where we went?"

"I will."

"I'll check in later."

"Drive carefully."

Before they could get waylaid by the entire family, Landon and Amanda left the ballroom and took the elevator to their room to pack.

She went through the motions of putting belongings in the suitcase she'd borrowed from Landon after hers had been lost in the fire. While she changed and packed, she tried to compartmentalize the day's events.

Focus on packing, checking out of the hotel, getting a car, driving to New York.

Don't think about how you're going to meet your daughter for the first time ever in a few short hours, or you might lose your shit.

I'm going to meet my daughter. Today.

Like a tidal wave coming over her, the realization bent her in half, hands flat against the marble vanity in the bathroom.

And then Landon was there, gathering her into his arms and holding on tight. "I've got you, honey. I've got you."

Thank God for him, she thought, and not for the first time. At some point in the last few weeks, he'd become her rock as well as her best friend. "I can't believe I'm going to meet her today."

"I know. You have to be reeling."

She pulled back from him and took tissues from the box on the counter. "I don't have time to reel right now. She needs me, and I've got to get to her before someone thinks they should call child services or something."

"I called down to the concierge. The hotel is arranging for a car for us. It'll be here in fifteen minutes."

"How'd you do that so fast?"

"I told them it was an emergency."

"Thank you."

He kissed her forehead. "Anything for you. What else can I do?"

"How do you feel about driving to New York? I'd be afraid of driving off the road again because I'm a hot mess."

"I'll drive, and you're not a hot mess. You're a beautiful mom about to be reunited with her beloved child under less-than-ideal circumstances."

Amanda's chin quivered as she tried desperately to hang on to her composure.

"You're doing the right thing stepping up for her, and it'll matter to her that you came running when she needed you."

"Keep telling me that, okay?"

"As many times as you need to hear it."

Over the next few hours, she repeatedly needed to hear it as they faced traffic delays and a monsoon-like rainstorm that turned a drive of two hours and forty-five minutes into nearly four hours of hell. They received frequent text updates on Amanda's phone from Lucy about Cameron's condition. The last report had been that she was hoping to be able to push soon.

Amanda's nerves were shredded by the time they reached the hospital and parked. It was nearly eight o'clock by then, and even though she'd been in constant contact with Stella during the ride, she was still as stressed out as she'd ever been.

"Are you ready for this?" Landon asked.

"No," she said, sounding slightly hysterical, even to her own ears. "Not even kinda."

CHAPTER TWENTY-NINE

"Where you used to be, there is a hole in the world, which I find myself constantly walking around in the daytime, and falling in at night. I miss you like hell."
—Edna St. Vincent Millay

$\mathcal{L}$ andon covered her cold hand with his warm one, infusing her with heat and confidence she badly needed. "It's going to be fine, Amanda. You've already met by FaceTime. This is just a formality."

She nodded. "Thank you again for being here. I'm not sure I could've done this by myself."

"Yes, you could have if you had to. No question. Nothing could've kept you from her when she needed you. But I'm glad I could be here."

Amanda glanced at the hospital entrance, steeling herself to give Stella the support she needed. This was about Stella, not her. *Sure, keep telling yourself that.* She sent Stella a text to let her know they'd arrived and were on the way in. "Let's go."

They got out of the car, went in through the main entrance and followed the signs to the elevators. The doors opened on the sixth floor, and there she was, waiting for them. Like they'd known each other forever, Stella stepped into Amanda's outstretched arms and held on for dear life.

Despite the circumstances and the location, it would go down as one of the best moments of Amanda's life. Stella fit snuggly in her arms, her head tucked under Amanda's chin. Her hair smelled of strawberries and cookies and sweetness. Amanda breathed her in, feeling the agitation she'd lived with for twelve long years finally settle.

"Thank you so much for coming."

"There's nowhere else I'd rather be."

"Somehow I doubt that, but I'm thankful anyway."

Amanda reluctantly released her. "This is Landon." She watched as he hugged Stella, too.

"It's so good to see you in person," he said.

"You, too."

"How's your mom?" Amanda asked, even though she already knew from Stella's updates that her condition was grave.

"Not so great." Stella looked up at her, green eyes swimming with tears. "Do you know what hospice is?"

"I do," she said, her heart sinking. "Are they recommending that for her?"

Stella nodded. "They said she doesn't have a lot of time left."

"I'm so sorry, honey."

"We knew this was coming, but still…" Stella shrugged. "It sucks."

"Yes, it does." Amanda hugged her again because she could, and because Stella needed all the love she could get right then.

"She'd like to see you if you're up for that."

"Of course." Amanda was scared and unnerved but determined to step up for Stella—and for Kelly. Whatever they needed, she'd do her best to get it for them.

With her arm linked through Amanda's, as if she was afraid Amanda might somehow escape, Stella led them into Kelly's darkened room.

"Mom," she whispered. "Amanda and Landon are here."

Kelly opened her eyes and looked up at them, relief etched into her expression. "Thank you so much for coming," she whispered.

Amanda took her hand and gave it a gentle squeeze. "I'm here for as long as you guys need me. Just rest and don't worry about anything."

When Kelly closed her eyes, tears leaked out the sides.

Stella grabbed a tissue and wiped them away. "She was really worried about what would happen to me," she said softly.

Amanda put her hands on Stella's shoulders. "I'm here now, and I'm not going anywhere."

WAITING WAS HELL, WILL DECIDED AS HIS WIFE WRITHED IN PAIN with each new contraction. She'd be getting an epidural shortly, and he couldn't wait for her to get some relief. It was absolutely terrifying to watch her go through this, knowing how childbirth had ended for her mother and grandmother. The assurances they'd gotten from top doctors before her pregnancy didn't matter much now that she was in the throes of labor.

He wished for a magic wand to make it over, with mom and baby healthy and fine. That was all he cared about.

They'd been at the hospital for only a short time when Patrick and Mary had arrived, followed an hour later by his own parents and grandfather. They were in the waiting room now, close by if needed, which Will appreciated.

"Will, honey, stop pacing."

He hadn't realized he'd been pacing.

Cameron held out her hand to him. "Come here."

Will went to her and took her hand.

"Will you hold me?"

"Nothing I'd rather do." He crawled onto the bed and gathered her into his arms. "Are you comfortable?"

"I am for the next four minutes."

"Is it worse than you thought it would be?"

"Little bit."

"You're a trouper. I can't wait for this to be over for you."

"I can't wait for it to be over for *you*."

"Huh? It's not about me."

"Sure, it is. My family history has us both spooked right now, and that has to be extra awful for you."

"What's awful for me is that you were in labor for hours and didn't tell me. We're going to have a great big fight about that later."

"Thanks for the warning," she said on a chuckle that turned to a grimace when another contraction started.

"Breathe through it. That's it. Nice and easy."

Her fingers dug into his arm as she rode the wave of the contraction, panting and gasping from the pain. By the time it was over, her face was red and tears were flowing.

Will used tissues to dry her face. "You want me to ask the nurse about the epidural?"

"Would you?"

"Absolutely."

"Come right back?"

"I will. Try to rest before the next one." He got up and went to the nurses' station, looking for their nurse, Dana.

"How's she doing?" Dana asked.

"She's in a lot of pain. Is the epidural coming?"

"I just checked, and she's on the way. Any minute now."

"Okay, thanks." While he was out of the room, Will took one second to check in with the parents.

"How's she doing?" Molly asked.

His dad and Elmer were dozing, but perked up when Will came into the room.

Mary was asleep on Patrick's shoulder, but he was wide awake and looked as stressed as Will felt.

"She's doing great. The epidural is happening soon, and we're both ready for that. Her more than me, of course."

Molly stood to hug Will. "Hang in there, honey. He or she will be here very soon, and this will become a distant memory."

"I'll have to take your word on that. I'm going back in with her. I'll be out as soon as we have news."

"We love you both."

"Love you, too." Will went back to the room and found Cameron asleep, so he stood by the bed and let his head hang down to roll out the tension in his neck.

She came to with a gasp, and he moved quickly to return to his post on the bed to coach her through another contraction. In the birthing classes they'd taken, the dads had been told to expect their wives to want nothing to do with them during labor. Will was glad that Cameron not only wanted him, she wanted him to hold her through the worst of the pain.

The anesthesiologist came in a few minutes after the contraction ended and moved quickly to administer the epidural. She positioned Will in front of Cameron to hold her hands while she worked on her back.

"A quick pinch and then all kinds of relief," the doctor said in a cheerful tone that buoyed Will's spirits.

As long as everyone was upbeat, he had nothing to worry about. Living through this momentous event with Cameron gave new meaning to what Patrick had gone through losing Cameron's mother, Ali, shortly after their daughter's birth. It was unimaginable. The very thought of it was enough to bring Will to his knees.

Cameron stared into his eyes. "What're you thinking about?"

Because he couldn't very well tell her the truth, he said, "I'm thinking of the night we met and how even when you had two black eyes, a fat lip and a smashed-up car, I thought you were the most beautiful woman I'd ever seen."

"That's so sweet," the doctor said.

"He's the sweetest," Cameron said, smiling at him.

She already seemed better than she'd been for hours. Thank God for modern medicine.

"You're all set," the doctor said.

She and Will helped Cameron get settled back into bed.

"You should start to feel much better now."

"I already do. Thank you."

The young doctor smiled. "Then my work here is finished. I'll be by to check on you later."

"Thanks, Doc," Will said.

"You got it."

"Phew," Cameron said on a long exhale when they were alone again. "Thank God for drugs."

"I was just thinking the same thing."

After the epidural, Cameron was able to get some much-needed rest before her labor reached the next stage two hours later. Suddenly, everything seemed to happen much more quickly.

"Would you mind asking your mom to come in?" Cameron asked, looking at Will with eyes gone wild now that the big moment had arrived.

"I'll get her." Will fetched his mother from the waiting room. In the one minute he'd been gone, Cameron's legs had been hoisted onto some contraption, and the energy in the room had changed considerably. Suddenly, he couldn't move or breathe or cope with the wave of fear that threatened to drag him under.

If anything happened to her, he would die. It was that simple.

"Will."

His mother's voice reached him through the panic.

She took hold of his arm and looked up at him. "Breathe."

He forced air past the panic. Cameron needed him. This was no time for a meltdown. The doctors had told them it was perfectly safe for her to have a baby. He needed to have faith in their expertise.

"Will." Cameron reached out to him again as if she knew what he was thinking. She probably did. Her family history had weighed heavily on both their minds throughout her pregnancy.

Will went to her. "How can I help?"

"Get behind her and support her back and shoulders," the doctor said.

He was a stranger to them, which was another source of stress. All their careful planning was for naught, because she was about to give birth hours from the hospital they'd chosen and the doctor who'd followed her pregnancy. However, this doctor had consulted with that doctor, was up to speed on Cam's family history and was going to deliver their baby whether that had been the plan or not.

Over the next hour, he tried to stay calm while Cameron fought an epic battle to deliver their baby.

"Talk to me," she said on a break from pushing.

"I'm here, love, and you're doing so great. Does it hurt?"

"No, just a lot of pressure."

"You're getting so close, Cam," Molly said as she ran a cool cloth over Cameron's face.

"Thanks for coming in," Cameron said. "You're the closest thing to a mother I've ever had."

Visibly moved by Cameron's statement, Molly said, "I wouldn't want to be anywhere else."

"How'd you do this ten times?" Cameron asked.

"*Ten times?*" the doctors and nurses said as a chorus.

Even Will laughed at their reactions. "I'm number three of ten, including two sets of twins."

"Wow," Dana said. "That's amazing."

"The last five fell out," Molly said, making them laugh again. "It's the first five that were a real bitch."

Soon it was time to push again, and Will lost track of time as he stayed completely focused on Cameron. Like fathers everywhere, he felt like an incompetent wimp in the midst of her heroic effort.

At three forty-six in the morning, a lusty wail alerted them to the arrival of their baby.

"You have a son," the doctor said. "And he's beautiful." The doctor wrapped his red little body in a blanket and handed him over to his sobbing parents and grandmother.

"Oh, look at him," Molly said. "He's *perfect*."

Will couldn't stop staring at his scrunched-up little face, the smattering of dark hair on his head, the little pink lips and the tiny tongue that quivered when he cried. He was the most miraculous thing Will had ever seen.

"Hi, little man," Cameron cooed to him.

He immediately stopped crying.

"He knows your voice," Dana said. "Keep talking to him."

"This is your daddy. Say hi, Daddy."

Will wiped tears from his face. "Hey, buddy. It sure is nice to meet you." He reached around Cameron to free the baby's arms so he could shake hands with his son. *He had a son!*

"Do you guys mind if I get the grandfathers?" Molly asked. "Patrick must be beside himself by now."

"Please do get them," Cam said.

"Before I go, does he have a name?"

Cameron looked back at Will, and he nodded.

"His name," Cameron said, "is Chase Murphy Abbott. Chase was my mother's maiden name."

"Oh, I like that. It's a beautiful tribute to your mother, and you've made it so all our baby grandchildren have C names."

"We thought of that," Will said, "and we didn't want to break the streak."

"And Will said he had to chase me, so the name is fitting."

"She led me on a merry chase from the second she crashed into Fred." It was starting to register with him that Cameron had given birth to their baby, and only something wonderful had happened. They had a son, and she was just fine. *Thank you, Jesus.*

"Let me get the grandfathers and Mary," Molly said, heading for the door.

"He's perfect, isn't he?" Cam asked.

"He's the most beautiful thing I've ever seen other than his mother."

"We have a son named Chase."

"Yes, we do. Thank you so much for our son. You were incredible, Cam."

"Couldn't have done it without you."

"That's not true. Except for the *very* beginning, you did all the work."

Cameron laughed, and it was the best sound ever because she'd given birth and survived it. Only now could Will admit to himself that he'd been sure, for all this time, that something would happen to take her from him. He'd been preparing himself for disaster, and the realization that it wasn't going to happen freed him from the crushing anxiety he'd been trying to cope with for months.

Molly returned with Linc, Elmer, Patrick and Mary in tow. As they circled Cam's bed, Will noticed how undone Patrick seemed. He couldn't blame the guy for being terrified of history repeating itself.

"Come in closer, Dad," Molly said to Elmer. "Get a good look at your newest great-grandbaby."

"He's a fine-looking fellow," Elmer said. "Just like his daddy—and his mama."

"You want to hold him?" Cameron asked Elmer.

"Let your dad go first," Elmer said, deferring to Patrick. "He's the rookie among us."

Cameron handed the baby over to her dad, who was standing on the right side of the bed with Mary.

"Hey there," Patrick said, gazing down at the baby with tears in his eyes. "I'm your Grandpa Patrick. Welcome to the family."

"What's his name?" Mary asked.

"Your turn," Cam said, smiling up at Will.

"Meet Chase Murphy Abbott."

"I love that," Mary said. "It's perfect."

"Your mom would be thrilled," Patrick said to Cameron.

"Chase was Ali's maiden name," he said for Mary, Linc and Elmer's benefit.

"I love that," Linc said.

"And it makes for three baby grandchildren with C names," Molly added. "And two with S names—Savannah and Stella."

Will was touched that his mother included the children Lucas and Landon had acquired when they fell in love with Dani and Amanda, but Molly's mantra had always been "the more the merrier."

"This family is growing by leaps and bounds," Elmer said.

"We need to tell the others," Cam said. "If you get me my phone, we can send a text and picture."

Mary fetched Cameron's phone from her purse and took the picture of the new family that they sent to Will's siblings and cousins as well as their closest friends.

"And now," Molly said, "we need to leave this new family to get some rest."

Will had never been more exhausted. He could only imagine how Cameron must feel.

The others left with promises to be back to visit in the morning. Will helped Cameron use the bathroom and then get settled in bed so she could attempt to breastfeed the baby. He sat on the edge of the bed, watching over them, his heart so full of love, he feared it might explode.

"Thank you for him, for us, for everything," he said, his voice gruff with emotion.

Cameron's smile lit up her face. "Thank you for rescuing me in the mud and forgiving me for hitting your precious Fred."

He leaned in to kiss her. "Nothing has ever been more precious to me than you and Chase are."

CHAPTER THIRTY

"Obstacles do not block the path, they are the path."
—Anonymous

*L*andon and Amanda learned the news about baby Chase when she received a text from Cameron announcing his arrival. They were in the guest room at Kelly's house after bringing Stella home to get some sleep.

"Aw, look at him," Amanda said. "He's adorable. Congrats, Uncle Landon."

"Thank you. Will must be so relieved. They both have to be."

"I'm sure everyone is."

"I can't wait to meet him," Landon said.

"I'm sorry you missed being there when he arrived."

He kissed her. "I'm right where I need to be."

They spent the next two days rotating between Kelly and Stella's townhouse and the hospital. In consultation with doctors and social workers, it was decided that Kelly should be transferred to a hospice facility rather than going home. That would happen as soon as she was stable enough to be released from the hospital.

They ate three meals a day with Stella and developed an easy, natural rapport with her. Landon noted the almost incandescent joy in Amanda's eyes every time she looked at her daughter, which was often. However, the joy was tempered by the horrific reality of Kelly's unrelenting illness.

Landon woke on the third day in New York with a feeling of dread. He had to go back to Vermont because he was due to work the next day at the firehouse. With Lucas still out on medical leave, he had to go, but he didn't want to.

Because Amanda could use Kelly's car, the plan was for him to take the rental back to Vermont and turn it in there. All the arrangements had been made. Now he just had to work up the wherewithal to actually leave.

He held Amanda close to him in bed in the guest room at Kelly and Stella's cozy home, wishing he could stay for as long as they needed him.

"You're awake early," Amanda said, yawning.

"I hate that I have to leave today."

"I do, too, but I understand you have to work."

"I'll be back on my next four-day break."

"You have the farm to think about."

"I can get help there. It's fine. If there's one benefit to having a big family, that's it. My grandfather would tell you he can still cut grass. Don't worry. We'll make it work."

"It's a lot to ask."

"No, it's not. I just hope you'll be okay during all this. I worry about you being so focused on Kelly and Stella that you won't take care of yourself."

"I will. I promise. I have to so I can be there for them."

"I'm going to make sure you do, but I sure wish I could be here to take care of you while you take care of them."

"I wish you could, too."

"I love you, and I'm so proud of you for stepping up for them the way you have."

"I love you, too, and that means so much to me. Thank you for all your support. You've been my rock. I know it's a lot…"

"Don't spend one second worrying about me or us. We're solid, and we still will be after this. You've got much bigger things to focus on right now."

She made a slight move that put her ass snug against his erection.

"Sorry," he muttered. "That tends to happen when you're close by." They hadn't had sex since the hotel in Boston.

"Don't be sorry." She turned to face him and snuggled into his embrace, moving against him in a suggestive way that made him groan. "Before you go…"

"We don't have to."

"What if I want to?"

"In that case…"

She laughed as her hands worked their way under his T-shirt, her touch setting him on fire like always.

Then her cell phone rang, and her hands were gone as she turned toward her side of the bed to retrieve her phone. "Hey," she said, listening. "No, that's fine. I'm up. Just give me a few minutes to get dressed. Are you okay?" She listened some more. "I know, sweetheart. I'll see you in two minutes."

"What's up?"

"Kelly had another seizure. The hospital called Stella."

"She shouldn't be getting those calls."

"She insisted on being their point of contact."

"It's too much."

"She says it isn't."

"It would be for me, and I'm more than twice her age," Landon said. "She's an awesome kid."

"I'm glad you think so, and I'm sorry about leaving you high and dry," she said, kissing him before she got out of bed.

"Don't apologize to me. Please don't. What you're dealing with is just…"

She turned toward the bed as she pulled on jeans. "It's life, Landon. Isn't that what your grandfather would say?"

"Yeah," he said, smiling. "That sounds like him."

"It's life—and it's beautiful and messy and painful and dreadful and joyful and everything else," she said as she finished getting dressed. "That's one thing I've figured out since the twelve-year numbness wore off and I started to feel things again. You have to take the bad with the good. That's just how it goes. And if you're really lucky, there's more good than bad."

"There will be far more good, if I have anything to say about it."

"That gives me something to look forward to."

Landon got up, brushed his teeth and pulled on clothes so he could see them off.

Stella was waiting for them downstairs. "Are you still going home today?" she asked Landon.

"I have to, unfortunately. I'd much rather be here with you ladies."

"Thanks for all the support. It really helped."

"I'll be back as soon as I can." The days apart would feel like forever to him, he thought as he hugged her. "You barely know me, but you should know I'm super proud of you for how you're handling this."

"Thanks. My mom has always been there for me. I want to do the same for her for as long as I have her."

"She's raised a wonderful daughter." He hugged her again before releasing her and then hugging Amanda. "I'll check on you guys later."

"Drive carefully."

"I will. Don't worry about me."

"Love you," Amanda said, giving him a wistful look.

Landon understood how she felt, because he was afraid of what was ahead, and he wasn't even going to be there for most of it. "Love you, too."

He stood in the doorway and watched them leave in Kelly's sedan, waving as they drove away, taking his heart with them. For a long time after they left, he stared out the window at the empty street, wishing he didn't have somewhere to be when he was needed there.

Before he left Kelly's, he called the store and asked if someone could meet him at the rental car drop-off in St. Johnsbury. His dad said he'd be there at the appointed time.

On the three-and-a-half-hour ride north to Vermont, Landon had never felt more torn between what he had to do and what he wanted to do. The farther away from Amanda he got, the more wrong it felt. He wanted to be there with her and Stella to support them through this difficult time, but there was no way he could blow off work when Luc was out, too.

By the time he reached the rental car lot, he'd given himself a headache from grinding his teeth the whole way home.

When he came out of the office after dropping off the keys, his dad was waiting for him in the Range Rover. Feeling as if he'd traveled a million miles since they left for the wedding on Friday, Landon tossed his bag into the back and got into the passenger seat, shutting the door a little harder than necessary.

"Take it easy," Linc said, always protective of his prized Range Rover.

"Sorry."

"I can tell you're loaded for bear just by looking at you."

"What the hell does that even mean?"

"Primed for a fight, and if I had to guess, you're in an uproar over leaving your lady to deal with a heartbreaking situation without you."

Leave it to his father to get straight to the heart of the matter. "Yeah."

"It sucks."

"It does."

"But you have to come home to work because your brother is still on medical leave and you can't leave the department any more short-handed than it already is. How'd I do?"

"Bull's-eye."

"For what it's worth, I admire your work ethic."

"For all the good that's doing me when I want to be somewhere else."

"I know it's hard right now, but keep reminding yourself that this situation is temporary."

"I hate that someone has to die for us to get back to some semblance of normalcy."

"That's a terrible reality to have to confront. But if I may make a suggestion…"

"Can I stop you?" Landon asked, grinning at his dad.

"I suggest you start making preparations to become a family of three. You don't have room for a soon-to-be teenager at your place, which means you're going to need to move. Why not take care of that while Amanda takes care of Stella and her mom?"

"That's not an awful idea."

"Gee, thanks, son."

His father's suggestions started the wheels turning in his mind. They needed to find a bigger house to rent or buy, and he absolutely could take care of that so they'd be ready to bring Stella home to Butler when the time came. "I appreciate the idea. It's a good one."

"Since you're new to this relationship business, I'll toss you one more pearl of wisdom, completely free of charge."

Landon laughed. "Can't wait to hear this one."

"Make sure you consult Amanda throughout the process of finding a new place to live. A house she has no input on isn't the kind of surprise a woman tends to appreciate."

"Are you speaking from personal experience perhaps?"

"Possibly." Legend had it that Linc had bought the Abbott family barn sight unseen and "surprised" his bride with her ramshackle new home.

Landon laughed hard.

"My goal in life is to save my children from making the same mistakes I did."

"Your 'mistakes' worked out okay."

"In the end, yes. At the beginning? Not so much."

"Thanks for the laugh. I needed that."

"I'm proud of you, son."

Surprised, Landon looked over at him. "For what?"

"For the way you've stepped up for Amanda after the fire and fought for what you wanted with her, despite the rocky beginning with Lucas and all that business. For doing Luc's share of the work at the fire department and the farm while he's laid up. For not even blinking about the fact that you're going to become a father figure to a teenage girl. For all of it."

"Thanks, Dad. Means a lot to me that you're proud."

"I've always been proud of you, even when you were acting a fool and making us all howl with laughter."

"That's good to know. How're Will and Cam and baby Chase?"

"Doing great and hoping to come home in the next couple of days. Cabot put them up at his home until Cameron feels ready to travel."

"He seems like a good guy."

"He is. We all like him very much. And that wedding was something else, wasn't it?"

"It was for sure. What else is going on at home?"

"I didn't want to tell you when you were off with Amanda, but baby Dexter the moose escaped from his pen while we were away."

"What? How'd that happen?"

"Hannah thinks Fred had something to do with it."

"Hannah would think that."

"Apparently, Dude showed up to feed Dex, and he was gone. There's been no sign of him—or Fred—for days."

"Oh damn. Hannah must be beside herself."

"She is."

"Have people been out looking for them?"

"Hunter, Max, Nolan, Gavin and Tyler were out looking for hours yesterday, but there was no sign of them."

"Jeez. Is it weird that I feel almost as sad about that as I would if an actual kid went missing?"

"Nope," Linc said. "I've been feeling the same way since I heard he was missing."

"It's because Hannah's had enough heartbreak, and none of us want her to have any more."

"That's exactly what your mother said. I've got one more piece of news for you."

"What's that?"

"We think Max spent the night with Caroline after the wedding."

"Shut up! Go, Maxi-Pad!"

"Honestly, Landon. How many times do I have to tell you and your idiot twin brother not to call him that?"

"It's our pet name for him. He loves it."

"Sure, he does," Linc said, chuckling. "Seventh-grade health class for you and your fellow buffoon was one of the worst things to ever happen to poor Max."

"On behalf of my buffoon twin and myself, thank you. We were rather proud of our work when it came to him."

"All kidding aside, your mom and I were happy to see him having a good time with Caroline. He's had a rough few months."

"Yeah, he has. So how'd he get a night all to himself?"

"Mom and I saw that he was having fun, so we suggested to Hannah that she offer to keep Caden with them for the night."

"In case we've never told you, we hit the parent jackpot with you guys."

"Thank you, son," Linc said softly. "I'm glad you feel that way."

"We *all* feel that way."

CHAPTER THIRTY-ONE

"Obstacles don't have to stop you. If you run into a wall, don't turn around and give up. Figure out how to climb it, go through it, or work around it."
—Michael Jordan

Max tried to stay focused on work at the sugaring facility, but his mind was still locked in a Boston hotel room with Caroline. What a night that had been. After he'd danced with her for hours, his sister Hannah had offered to keep Caden for the night, and Max had willingly agreed. He so rarely took any time for himself anymore that he hadn't hesitated to jump on the offer, knowing his son would be with an aunt and uncle who adored him.

Apparently, it had been his parents' idea, which meant they'd probably tuned in to the deep funk he'd been in lately and were hoping a night off from fatherhood would do him good.

They'd been right about that. One night with the supremely sexy Caroline Lodge Fullerton had definitely fixed what ailed him.

She was fun, funny, smart, athletic, sexy and up for anything in bed.

Fuck, he could not be thinking about that unless he wanted to sport wood in the forest. That thought made him laugh.

"What's so funny over there?" Colton asked.

Max hadn't realized his brother was so close by. "Just thinking about something funny that happened this weekend."

"Oh yeah? What's that?"

Think of something, Max… "You know how Caden slept over with Hannah, Nolan and Callie after the wedding?"

"I heard that."

"The kids slept between them, and they woke up to a hair-pulling fight at six a.m."

"That is funny." Colton gave him a curious look. "So what'd you do with your one free night?"

"As you well know, I went out after the wedding with you and your wife and our siblings and cousins."

"And after that? When you walked Caroline back to the hotel. What happened then?"

"None of your business."

"Aha. So it's like that, is it? I hope you used protection."

"Shut up, Colton."

"I'm only busting you. Don't get pissy. I'm glad you had some fun. You needed that. You've been a barrel of laughs lately."

"It's been harder than I thought it would be, to be on my own with Caden. Not that I'm completely on my own with Mom and Dad and everyone else around, but still…"

"The responsibility is all yours. I feel that, and for what it's worth, I've admired the hell out of how you've stepped up for your son."

"What choice did I have?"

"You didn't even see it as a choice. You just saw *him* and that he needed you, and you were there for him. That's cool, bro."

"Caroline said she doesn't want kids."

"Like, ever?"

"That's what she said."

"Huh. Well, that's something to consider."

"Doesn't matter anyway. She lives three hours from Vermont. I don't even have reliable cell service unless I'm up here on the mountain. It was a fun weekend, but that's all it's gonna be."

"Who you trying to convince? Me or yourself?"

"I don't want to talk about it."

"Okay."

They went back to work replacing lines of plastic hose that brought sap from the trees to the sugarhouse, but Max continued to think about Caroline and the night they'd spent together while wondering if he'd ever see her again.

HANNAH HADN'T SLEPT IN DAYS. COMING HOME FROM BOSTON TO learn that Dexter had gotten out of his pen and disappeared had left her devastated. She was barely functioning as she waited and hoped that someone would spot him or Fred or both of them. But days later, there was no sign of either of them, and she was a sleep-deprived zombie as she worried about whether Dex had eaten anything or if he was cold or if he missed her and his home.

She stood at the door and stared out at the dark yard, wishing with all her heart that he was safely tucked into his pen for the night.

Maybe she'd been crazy to think she could provide a good home for a baby moose, but she'd certainly tried to make him happy.

Nolan came up behind her and put his hands on her shoulders. "You need to get some sleep, Han."

"I can't sleep."

"You have to." He gently guided her back from the storm door, shutting and locking the inside door.

"Leave the light on. Just in case."

Nolan left the outside light on. Taking her by the hand, he led her into their room where he undressed her and helped her into the flannel pajamas she wore year-round. "Come on, let's brush your teeth."

"I can do it."

When she emerged from the bathroom, he was sitting on the bed waiting for her and held out his arms to her.

Hannah went to him, sat on his lap and let him surround her with his love. "This reminds me too much of when Homer died." Losing her late husband's beloved dog had been like losing Caleb all over again.

"I know you love Dex, and I'm sorry this has happened."

"Even though you think I'm insane for wanting to keep a baby moose as a pet?"

"I never used the word 'insane.'"

"You thought it."

"I love you, Hannah. Whatever makes you happy makes me happy."

"Even Dexter?"

"Even Dexter. I have to admit the little guy has grown on me."

"Can we bring him inside when he comes home?"

"Absolutely not."

Her shoulders slumped again.

"Maybe for a quick visit," Nolan said.

"Really?"

"Like, ten minutes."

For the first time in days, she smiled.

"There's my girl. I hate to see you so sad."

"I miss him, and I'm so worried about him. He doesn't know how to feed himself or how to stay warm without his blankets."

Homer Junior brushed up against her leg.

Hannah leaned down to pick him up. "You miss your brother, too, don't you?" she asked the dog.

Always mindful of the sleeping baby, he gave a soft yip. He was the best-behaved dog she'd ever known, even more so than his namesake.

"Our family won't be complete until Dex comes home."

"We'll keep looking for him," Nolan said. "He's got to be around here somewhere."

"What if…" Hannah shook her head. It didn't bear considering.

"What?"

"What if he doesn't want to live here anymore and was waiting for his chance to get away?"

"Why in the world would he not want to live here anymore when you've basically turned him into a glorified poodle with three hots and a cot, toys and blankets and a cushy bed? Of course he still wants to live here. Any guy would want to be loved by you."

"He's not a glorified poodle," Hannah said on a huff.

"Is that all you heard?"

"I heard the rest, too, and it's sweet of you to say that."

"He knows he's got a good thing going here, Han. He'll be back. And when he gets here, it won't do him any good if you've made yourself sick worrying about him." With his arms under her, he lifted her and walked around to her side of the bed, put her down and tucked her in with Homer Junior in her arms. "I want you to sleep for Dex and for Callie and the baby. And for me and Homer. We all need you."

"I'll try," she said, her chin quivering.

Nolan got into bed, shut the light off and snuggled up to her and the dog. "I'm sorry you're sad. I'd give anything to be able to fix this for you."

"You've done everything you could, and I appreciate the hours you've spent looking for him."

"Anything for you."

Hannah forced herself to relax and turn off her thoughts to try to get some rest. She was so tired, she could barely keep her eyes open anyway. With Nolan's arms around her, she eased into sleep while forcing herself not to think about where Dex might be, for a little while, anyway.

She had no idea what was happening when a crash woke her from a sound sleep.

"What the hell?" Nolan muttered as he rolled out of bed to go see what'd happened. A minute later, he called to her. "Uh, Han, you're going to want to come here."

She got out of bed, nearly tripping over her own feet and Homer Junior as she went to find Nolan. He was standing in front of the storm door and made room for her to join him so she could see Dexter frolicking in the yard like he'd been there all along.

Hannah let out a cry and rushed into the yard to greet him with a hug. "Where have you been?"

Dexter was so happy to see her, he peed himself.

"Good Lord," Nolan muttered from the stairs to the porch.

"Where were you? I was so worried about you!"

Dexter nuzzled her neck and kissed her face like an overgrown dog.

A loud moo from the brush next to the driveway alerted them to Fred's presence. He mooed again.

"Did you take him, Fred?" Hannah stood with her hands on her hips and glared up at him. "He's not a toy for you to play with."

"Moo."

"I hope you boys had a good time, because he's not allowed to play with you anymore."

"*Moo.*"

"No, I don't want to hear it."

Fred let out a sound that resembled a whimper.

"Aw, Han, you're breaking his heart," Nolan said. "And no, I can't believe I just said those words. Tell him you forgive him."

"I'm mad at him! He *took* Dexter."

"And he brought him back. Look how sad he is."

Hannah whirled around to look at Nolan. "What's happened to you?"

"I feel for the guy. He's in love with you. I know what that's like and how much it hurts to disappoint you."

"You've never disappointed me."

"Not yet, and if I ever do, I hope you'll forgive me, just like you need to forgive poor Fred. They were just a couple of guys out sowing their wild oats."

Another pathetic-sounding "moo" came from Fred.

"Fine. I forgive you, Fred, but don't take him again. I mean it."

"Moo!" Fred went running off into the vegetation.

"Honestly," Hannah said. "I can't believe he thought he'd get away with that. Dex, let's get you to bed. Tomorrow, you can come in the house for a visit. Daddy said it was okay."

"I'm going to regret that weak moment," Nolan said as he opened the door to the pen that he'd repaired after the breakout.

"You can't take it back now." Hannah hugged and kissed Dexter and settled him into his pen, closing and latching the gate so he couldn't get out.

Dex went right to the bowl of food that Nolan had filled for him and ate it all.

"The poor guy is starving. Fred knows nothing about caring for children."

Nolan nudged her toward the stairs and into the house. "Our little family is back together. All is well in the kingdom."

"Do you sometimes think you married a complete lunatic? It's okay, you can tell me the truth."

"*Sometimes?*"

"Haha, very funny."

"You're a complete lunatic, but you're my lunatic, and I love you."

"I know I'm not easy to live with—"

Nolan put his arms around her and silenced her with a kiss. "You're the most entertaining, wonderful, exasperating, delightful, beautiful, animal-loving lunatic I've ever met, and I wouldn't change a single thing about you." He paused for a second, seeming to reconsider his words. "Except how you treat full-grown moose like they're puppies. That I would change."

"Oh stop. It's *Fred*. He's not going to hurt me."

"I want you to suspend your moose-whispering while you're pregnant. That's nonnegotiable."

Hannah gave him a calculating look. "And you'll let Dexter come inside for a visit?"

"A *short* visit."

"Fine."

"Fine."

"When are we going to tell all the people about the baby?" she asked him.

"In a few months, so he can be all ours for a while."

"*He?*"

"God, I hope so. I could use some help around here."

Hannah laughed all the way back to bed.

TIME BECAME LANDON'S GREATEST ENEMY. SECONDS, MINUTES, hours, days passed in a blur of work and endless obligations that kept him separated from Amanda. They talked every day, sometimes more than once a day, but their conversations were always rushed with one or the other being needed for something.

Kelly's condition had deteriorated rapidly. Amanda and Stella spent most of every day with her at the hospice facility.

When he talked to her, Amanda sounded drained from trying to support Stella through the difficult ordeal.

On the fifteenth day they'd spent apart, the night before Landon was due to go to New York for a two-day visit, Amanda told him not to come.

"I won't get to spend any time with you," she said.

Landon wanted to argue with her, to tell her he'd been living for that visit, but he didn't say anything.

"I'm so sorry," she said, sounding tearful. "This is the hardest thing I've ever been through, and I just need to give Stella everything I've got right now. Please tell me you understand."

"I do."

"Are you mad?"

"No, I'm disappointed. I was looking forward to seeing you."

"You'll see me soon. Unfortunately, Kelly doesn't have much time left."

Landon felt like hell for making this about himself. "I wish there was more I could do for you and Stella."

"Hearing your voice every day is what's getting me through."

"Did you get a chance to look at the email with the list of rentals I sent you?"

"Not yet, but I'll do it tonight."

"I'd like to have something ready for you and Stella when you come home."

"That'd be great. I'll let you know."

"There's one I really like that I don't think will be available for long. It's a farmhouse on two acres. That'd give us room for some chickens and maybe a goat or two. They said there might even be an option to buy in a couple of years if we're interested."

"Stella would love to have chickens and goats. She's crazy about animals."

"Did you tell her about Dexter and his big adventure?"

"I did. She can't wait to meet him and Fred. She can't believe your sister actually talks to moose. She wanted to know if she can, too."

"I hope you told her she can do whatever she wants."

"I told her no such thing, Landon!"

"You sound like a mom, babe."

"Do I?" she asked softly.

"You do."

"I love her so much. It's killing me to see her going through this."

"I know. She's very lucky to have you there with her."

"Some of Kelly's college friends came to see her yesterday,

which was nice, but Stella barely knows them. From what I can tell, Kelly focused all her energy on her daughter and her job and didn't have a lot of close friends."

"Stella will have a much bigger life here with us."

"I feel so guilty," she said in the soft whisper she used when she didn't want Stella to overhear her. "Yearning for that life."

"You shouldn't feel guilty, sweetheart. You're giving Kelly incredible peace of mind at the end of her life."

"Yeah. But still… I miss you so much."

"I miss you, too. More than I can say."

"Will you still love me when this is over?"

"I'll love you forever."

"Thank you for that, for everything. I should go. Stella's having a rough day. I need to check on her."

"Call me tomorrow, and check that email."

"I'll do it tonight. I promise."

Landon didn't want to hang up. "Stay strong."

"I'm trying. Love you."

"Love you, too."

He waited until he heard the click on her end before he put down the phone, rather than give in to the urge to throw it across the room. His gaze landed on the box containing the keyboard Hunter had ordered for her. Landon had planned to take it to her tomorrow, but now he wasn't going.

Without taking the time to think about it, he picked up the phone again and called Lucas. His brother answered on the third ring, sounding out of breath.

"What're you doing?"

"None of your business. Why?"

"Never mind." He'd been about to ask if he could come over, but he wasn't going near there if they were getting busy.

"What's up, Landon?"

"Amanda said it would be better if I didn't go to New York tomorrow."

"Oh damn."

"Yeah."

"You want to come over?"

"Not if you're in bed with Dani."

Lucas laughed. "I'm not. I was lifting weights."

"Should you be doing that?"

"Shut up, Mom. I'm fine, and if I don't do something physical, I'm going to lose my shit."

"You mind if I come by?" Landon asked, wincing at the needy tone of his voice.

"Course not. We're not doing anything."

"You want me to bring pizza?"

"I'd never say no to that."

"Cool. I'll see you soon." Landon called in the pizza order to Kingdom Pizza, adding the house salad that Dani liked, and picked it up twenty minutes later. He arrived at Dani's thirty minutes after he hung up with Lucas.

"That was fast," Luc said when he came to the door looking more like his old self than he had since the fire.

"Helps to have something to do. Where's Dani?"

"Giving Savvy a bath." Luc took the pizza and led Landon to the kitchen. He got out plates and silverware. "Thanks for bringing dinner."

"You're helping me more than I'm helping you."

"What's going on?"

"I'm in this strange hell of hoping for someone I barely know to die already so I can have my girlfriend back, which makes me feel like a total asshole, because of course I don't want Kelly to die."

"But she's going to regardless."

"Yeah, it's a very weird spot to be in."

"It is, for everyone involved."

"It's heartbreaking." Landon rubbed the spot in his chest that had begun to ache the minute he left Amanda in New York and hadn't let up since. "I just have this horrible feeling that everything with Amanda is going to get fucked up somehow."

"That's not going to happen."

"How can you be so sure?"

"For some reason that no one can fathom, she seems to actually love you."

"Nice. That's just what I need right now."

Lucas cracked up laughing. "I'm just busting your balls, and you know it. Listen, I've been where you are. I was flat on my ass in love with Dani, and she was saying she needed time to be on her own before we moved forward. So I gave her time, but it was torturous to keep my distance from her when all I wanted was to keep her close."

"I remember."

"It's going to work out with Amanda. You just have to be patient and give her space to breathe during the tragedy she's helping her daughter through. There's no quick fix on something like that. Dani would tell you that."

"What would I tell him?" Dani asked when she joined them with Savvy wrapped in a frog towel.

The baby let out a squeak and reached for Lucas while giving Landon a freaked-out look.

Lucas laughed at the face she made. "She still can't understand why there's someone else who looks just like her Lu."

Savannah hid her face in Lucas's shoulder.

"That's so funny," Dani said, laughing. "You need to grow your hair long for her, Landon. Anything to make you look different from Lucas."

"I'll get right on that."

"So what were you talking about?" Dani asked as she helped herself to salad and pizza and joined them at the table. "And thanks for the salad, Landon."

"Welcome."

Lucas filled her in on the latest with Amanda while Landon forced a few bites past the lump in his throat.

"Lucas is right."

Lucas leaned in, cupping his ear. "Could you say that again, louder this time so the people in the back can hear you?"

Dani rolled her eyes at him and then shifted her attention to Landon. "You and Amanda both are dealing with a very difficult situation, and you should expect that it'll take a while for things to go back to 'normal' after. Normal may look much different, in fact. I learned that after Jack died. And you have the added challenge of bringing Stella into your very new relationship. It's a lot, and you're totally justified in feeling a bit panicky about it all."

"I am?" Landon asked.

"You are. For sure."

"I like her," Landon said to his brother.

"You and me both, brother," Luc said with a warm smile for Dani.

"I like you, too, and I like you with Amanda." Dani put her hand on Landon's arm. "Be patient, follow her lead, be what she needs. That'll matter to her more than anything else you could do right now."

"That's good advice," Lucas said. "And it worked for me, I might add."

"You be quiet."

Landon laughed at the way she put him in his place even as Lucas grinned like a loon. "It's excellent advice, and it's what I'll do even if I'm crushed that I don't get to see her and Stella tomorrow."

"You'll survive," Dani assured him. "And she'll appreciate you even more for giving her the space she needs right now."

Landon nodded, feeling more settled now that he'd aired it out with them and figured out a path forward. "In the meantime, I need to get serious about finding us a bigger place to live so we'll be ready to bring Stella home to Butler."

"We can help with that," Dani said.

CHAPTER THIRTY-TWO

"There is nothing like staying at home for real comfort."
—Jane Austen

*A*fter Amanda gave two thumbs-up to the farmhouse, Landon threw himself into making it a home for them over the next three weeks. He moved out of his place and into the much bigger house and spent every minute he had off painting and cleaning and arranging furniture. On one day off, he drove to Rutland and bought a dining room table and a new sectional sofa for the family room, along with some end tables.

He used his family discount to buy one of the woven table-cloths the store sold in a light celery-green color and relied on his sisters to help him choose linens for Stella's room that he hoped she would like. If she didn't, he'd get her something different.

Amanda had decided to postpone the trip to Paris until next summer because she wanted Stella to have some time in Butler to get acclimated before school started in the fall.

It occurred to Landon late one night as he painted the trim in the family room that both of them were thinking like parents, putting Stella's needs ahead of their own.

They talked by FaceTime just about every night, and he saw the strain Amanda was under in the pinched expression on her face. Similarly, Stella had lost her sparkle, and all he wanted was to hug them both.

Landon was cutting grass at the farm a week later when Lucas came to find him. He couldn't bear to sit at home and wait for the phone to ring, so he'd told Amanda to call Luc if she couldn't reach him. When he saw Lucas walking toward him, he knew why he'd come before he said the words.

Landon killed the engine on the mower and removed his ear covers.

"Kelly died an hour ago," Lucas said.

Even though he'd been expecting it for days, the news hit hard as he nodded to let Lucas know he'd heard him. "What do I do now?"

"Call her to see what she needs."

"Yeah, okay." Thankful for his brother's presence, he walked with Luc back to the barn and went up the stairs to the loft to use the phone. He stood for a second looking at the phone before he picked it up and dialed Amanda's cell number from memory.

She answered on the second ring. "Hi."

"Hey. Luc told me. How're you guys doing?"

"We're okay. Stella said she's glad her mom isn't suffering anymore."

Landon closed his eyes against a flood of tears, amazed by the twelve-year-old's courage and maturity. "What can I do?"

"We need a couple of days, and then maybe you could come pick us up?"

"I can do that. Tell Stella... Tell her I'm so sorry, and I love her."

"I will. Call me later?"

"Yes, for sure."

"Love you, Landon."

"Love you, too."

He ended the call and put down the phone, propping his hands on the counter and letting his head drop forward. "So fucking sad."

"It sure is." Lucas gave Landon's shoulder a squeeze. "What's the plan?"

"I'm going to get them in a couple of days."

"We'll do everything we can to make them feel welcome here."

Landon nodded, relieved to know he'd have the support of his family as he started a new one with Amanda. "Thank you."

AMANDA FOCUSED ON HER TO-DO LIST: PACKING UP THE townhouse, helping Stella make piles of things to keep and things to donate and packing Stella's belongings for the move to Vermont. She tried to take her cues from Stella, staying quiet when she was and talking when she wanted to. Late on their last night in New York, after Stella had chosen the things she wanted to keep, Amanda boxed up the rest of Kelly's clothes to be donated. Earlier that day, she'd turned in Kelly's car to the dealership she'd leased it from.

Her emotions were all over the place, running the gamut from devastation to elation and everything in between. She was, she realized, grieving the loss of Kelly, who'd become a friend in the short time they'd known each other in person and over all the years they'd communicated about the girl they both loved. The sheer unfairness of her early death had hit Amanda hard, and it would take a while to work through the myriad reactions she was having to the loss.

More than anything, though, she grieved for Stella, who'd lost the most important person in her life, after having lost her father only five years earlier. It was possible, Amanda had found over the last few weeks, to feel someone else's grief almost as intensely as they were, especially when you loved them as much as she loved Stella.

The love was bigger than anything she'd ever experienced. It filled every part of her. She loved her so much, she ached with it. Amanda had walked a fine line in keeping her own emotions in check so Stella could feel free to fully express hers. She'd talked lovingly of both her adoptive parents over the last few difficult days, as it seemed her mother's death had resurfaced feelings from when Stella had lost her father.

Amanda couldn't wait to see Landon, to hold him and be held by him. She'd missed him so much over the last month and a half, and it seemed like forever since she'd last slept next to him. Even from afar, he'd been her rock through the most difficult days of her life, and she would never forget that.

In between her time with Kelly and Stella, she'd finished the profiles of Mildred and Elmer, which everyone had loved, much to her relief. She'd drafted more catalog copy for Lucy, who was overseeing the final stages since Cameron had gone on early maternity leave, and had participated in meetings with Linc and the others remotely when she could. Her former boss Martin had called to beg her to stay on to coordinate their trade show presence, and Amanda had happily agreed. The only other person she'd spoken to with any regularity was her mother, who'd called to check in every day or two.

She never did sleep that last night in New York as she finished everything that needed to be done. Landon planned to leave Vermont at six in the morning and would be there by nine or nine thirty, depending on traffic.

At eight, she took a shower and made an effort with her appearance for the first time in ages. As she applied mascara, she realized she was nervous. What if everything had changed between them in the time she'd been gone? What if she'd asked too much of him by asking him to stay away during this difficult time? *What if, what if.* The questions ran through her mind, torturing her with the many ways this day could go bad.

She woke Stella at eight thirty so she'd be ready by the time Landon arrived. "You want breakfast?"

Stella shook her head. "Not yet."

"Is there anything I can do for you?"

"No, thanks."

"If there is, just let me know."

"I will."

Amanda headed for the door, intending to go downstairs to give Stella privacy to get dressed and pack the last of her things.

"Amanda?"

She turned back.

"I just want to say thank you, you know, for everything. I don't know what I would've done without you these last few weeks."

Amanda went to sit next to her on the bed and hugged her. "It was the greatest honor of my life to spend this time with you and your mom."

Stella clung to her for a long time, seeming reluctant to let go. "You really think I'll like Butler?"

"I really do. It's the most special place I've ever lived. And Landon's family is so wonderful. You'll love them. And Simone can't wait to meet you." She made caressing circles on Stella's back. "I know it's super scary to go somewhere new where you don't know anyone, but Landon and I will do everything we can to help you get used to your new home."

"I know people there. You and Landon."

"That's right, and we've got your back. Always."

"Thanks."

"Sure thing. I'll let you get dressed. Landon will be here soon." As she said those words, Amanda's heart skipped a happy beat. She couldn't wait to see him.

The last thirty minutes before he was due to arrive seemed to pass more slowly than all the weeks since she'd seen him. By the time he knocked on the door, her heart was about to explode from the excitement. She opened the door, and there he was, looking better than any man had a right to.

Amanda threw herself into his arms, and as he caught her,

she realized nothing between them had changed. If anything, it had become even *more*. The feelings she had for him were bigger, stronger, deeper than they'd been before he gave her the space she'd needed to tend to Stella and Kelly.

She breathed in the familiar scent of pine and fresh air that she'd always associate with her love. "So happy to see you."

"You have no idea how happy I am to see you."

"I think I know." She smiled up at him as he seemed to stare at her, drinking her in. And then he kissed her, and the feeling of homecoming was so profound that Amanda realized for the first time that "home" wasn't a place. Her home was with him.

"Is it safe to come out?" Stella asked from the hallway.

Laughing, Amanda released him and turned. "The coast is clear."

Stella came into the kitchen with the last box from her room. "Hi, Landon."

"Hey, Stella." He walked over to take the box from her, placing it by the door with the others they were taking to Butler. And then he turned to hug her. "I'm so sorry about your mom."

"Thank you."

"Is this everything that's going?" he asked of the boxes.

"That and a few other bags," Amanda said.

"I'll load up the truck."

Within fifteen minutes, Landon had everything packed into the truck. "I'll give you guys a minute," he said, stepping outside. "Take your time."

Amanda appreciated that he understood the gravity of Stella leaving the home she'd shared with her mother for the last time. "Do you want me to go with him?"

"No, that's okay. I just want to walk through one more time." The leasing company had agreed to handle donating the furniture and clothing to a local organization that helped families in need.

While Stella walked through the two-story townhouse, Amanda waited for her in the kitchen. When she returned with tears in her eyes, Amanda held out her arms, and Stella walked into her embrace as if she'd been doing it all her life.

Amanda marveled at and gave thanks for the easy, natural bond she'd formed with her daughter. They hugged for a long time, until Stella pulled back and wiped her eyes.

"I think I'm ready."

"Okay, honey."

Amanda followed her out of the house and held the back door to Landon's truck for her, waiting for her to get settled before she shut the door. She got into the passenger seat and glanced at Landon, nodding to let him know they were as ready as they were ever going to be.

He reached for her hand and held on to her for the entire ride to Butler.

Amanda watched the scenery go by as she thought of the last few months and the many changes she'd experienced. Her entire perspective had shifted since the fire, along with her priorities. She knew now, without a shadow of a doubt, what really mattered. Love was what mattered, and she planned to love Stella and Landon and the children they'd have together with all her heart for the rest of her life.

She would get to the other things on her to-do list. She would learn to play piano and conquer the stick shift and give zip-lining and skiing a try.

They'd do it all, including the trip to Paris—together.

She began to get excited when the first signs for Butler appeared on the highway, and even more so when they drove through town.

"That's the store Landon's family owns," she told Stella.

"Is that the inn where the fire was?" She'd told Stella about that awful night a few weeks ago.

"Yes, right next door to the store."

Landon took a left turn off Elm Street and drove down a long, winding country road.

"Where are the moose?" Stella asked.

"They're all over the place, but sometimes they like to hide," Landon said. "You'll see them eventually, and my sister Hannah has a pet baby moose named Dexter." He told her how Dexter had finally managed to worm his way into Hannah's house.

It was nice to hear her laugh, Amanda thought.

"Close your eyes, ladies," Landon said as he took a right turn onto a dirt road.

Amanda was vibrating with excitement as the truck bounced along the bumpy road.

They took a final right turn, and Landon killed the engine. "Okay, you can look."

Amanda opened her eyes and let out a gasp at the sight of the farmhouse that'd been painted white since she saw the pictures. The wide front porch had planters with flowers and a swing, as well as balloons and a sign attached to the rail that said, "Welcome Home, Amanda and Stella!"

"Looks like my family has been here," Landon said, smiling. "The sign and balloons weren't there when I left." He got out of the truck and waited for them to join him before leading them inside. "If there's anything you guys don't like, it can be changed."

Amanda was already battling tears before she walked into the beautiful home he'd created for them. "Oh, Landon... Oh my God!"

"Are those good tears?"

Nodding, she hugged him. "It's so beautiful! How do we live here?"

He smiled and kissed away her tears. "Let me give you the grand tour." He took her hand and waited for Stella before leading them to a small sunroom off the main living area, where he'd set up an office for Amanda. "You can work and write and read and practice the piano in here." Against one wall, he'd set up the keyboard that Hunter had helped her get.

"I don't even know what to say. It's perfect. Thank you. You've thought of everything."

"With help from my mom and sisters and Dani and everyone else." He showed them the kitchen, dining room, family room and the downstairs bathroom and then led them upstairs. "I didn't buy dishes or pots and pans, because I know you were looking forward to doing that."

"I can't wait to do that!"

"That's your room there, Stella. Like I said, you can change anything about it."

Stella went into the room and let out a happy cry at the sight of a beautiful new bed and matching dresser and desk.

"My brother Lucas made the furniture."

"It's beautiful, Landon," Amanda said.

"Look, Amanda! There's a window seat!"

"I see it." She squeezed Landon's arm as she noticed that the pad on the window seat matched the quilt on the bed. "What a special room this is."

"Your bathroom is across the hall. I figured you might want to pick out your own shower curtain and towels."

"Thank you, Landon. I really love it."

"I'm so glad you do. Come see our room, Amanda." He was like a little boy on Christmas as he showed them how he'd passed the time while they were apart.

Their room was down the hall from Stella's and included an adjoining bathroom with a sliding barn door. The huge room had a king-size sleigh bed and matching double dresser. "Also compliments of Lucas," he said of the furniture. Their room also had a window seat, as well as a sitting area and a fireplace.

"Is this real?" Amanda asked him, dazzled by everything he'd done. "Are you real? Is this my life now?"

"It's the realest thing ever."

She hugged him hard. "I can't believe everything you did!"

"This project kept me from going insane from missing you."

"It's all so perfect. I've never had a matching bed and dresser before!"

"I'm glad you like it."

"Like it? I *love* it!"

When the phone rang, he went to grab the extension next to the bed while Amanda inspected the bathroom, gasping at the black-and-white tile floor, tiled shower, double vanity and huge soaking tub. It was like something straight out of a dream.

Landon came to the bathroom door. "Mom and Dad are asking if they can bring over dinner to welcome you ladies home."

"That'd be nice."

"You think Stella would be up for meeting the family?"

"Let's ask her."

"Hang on a second, Mom."

They went to Stella's room and found her curled up on the window seat looking out at the yard.

"Honey, Landon's family is asking if they can bring dinner over to welcome us home. There're a lot of them, and we don't want you to be overwhelmed, so you tell us if you're up for that."

"Will Simone be here?"

"I'll make sure of it," Landon said.

"Sure, they can come." She offered a small smile. "I suppose I need to get used to having a big family, right?"

"That's right," Landon said. "They're so excited to meet you."

"I'm excited to meet them, too," Stella said.

Landon spoke into the phone. "Stella says she'd love to meet you all, and she'd especially like to meet Simone." He paused to listen to his mother. "Okay, we'll see you soon."

CHAPTER THIRTY-THREE

"Give the ones you love wings to fly, roots to come back and reasons to stay."
—Dalai Lama

After Landon carried the boxes in from the truck, Amanda helped Stella unpack her things and put everything away.

"This room is so great," Stella said. "I can't believe Landon did this just for me."

"He loves you."

"He barely knows me."

"And he loves you. We both do. If there's anything we can do to make this easier on you, I hope you'll ask us."

"You know… When we first found out how sick my mom was, I felt selfish because my very first thought wasn't for her. It was for me. I was so scared of what would happen to me after she died since my dad was already gone."

"That's not selfish, honey. Of course you were worried about that—and her, too."

"I loved her so much. I loved them both."

"I know you did, and they loved you, too. Your parents would tell you that it's okay for you to love us as well. That it won't take away from what you felt for them."

"My mom did tell me that. She said you and Landon would be good parents to me and that it was okay to be happy with you guys."

"That's a lovely gift for her to give you."

"I might be saying thank you to you and Landon for a while."

"You don't have to thank us. I'm so happy to have you with me. You have no idea."

"Was it hard for you to give me up when I was born?"

Amanda made an effort to keep her emotions in check. They'd talked about a lot of things in recent weeks, but that hadn't been one of them. "It was the hardest thing I've ever done. My heart was broken over it for twelve long years. I never could've given you what your parents did when you were born. Even though I knew it was the right thing for you, not one day went by that I didn't think of you, or wish I could see you and know you."

"It helps to know that."

"It's the truth. Remember when I told you about the fire at the inn?"

Stella nodded. "So scary."

"It was, and afterward, I was more emotional than I'd been in years. I realized that I'd boxed up all my emotions after I gave you up, and it was like they were all trying to get out at the same time. Poor Landon. I cried all over him for weeks, and he was so good about it."

"He's really nice. To do all this for us…"

"I know. Wait until you meet the rest of them. Did I mention he has an identical twin brother?"

"No way!"

"Yep, and when I say identical, I mean *identical*."

"I can't wait."

After the last few dreadful weeks, the Abbotts were just what Amanda needed. They came in with food and laughter and so much love for her and Stella.

Molly put her arms around Stella and told her to call her Grammy.

Stella's eyes had bugged predictably when she met Lucas, who'd laughed at the reaction he and Landon had gotten their entire lives.

They got to meet baby Chase, and Stella had adored meeting Savannah, Caden and Callie, too.

Simone had welcomed Stella to Butler and promised to introduce her to all her friends so Stella would know lots of people before they started school again in the fall.

When Dude and Skeeter came by to welcome Amanda and Stella home, Dude brought another surprise Landon had arranged in advance—a yellow Lab puppy that Dude handed to Stella.

"She's *mine?*" Stella asked, her eyes big with wonder.

"All yours," Dude said, "but only if you're willing to be responsible for taking care of her."

Stella hugged the puppy to her chest. "I am! I'll take such good care of her."

"I heard you were a very responsible young lady who would provide a good home for her."

"I already love her so much. Thank you."

"You're welcome, sweetheart." To Landon and Amanda, Dude said, "I brought a crate and all the stuff you'll need to get started."

Amanda startled the older woman by hugging her. "Thank you so much, Dude. I can't tell you what this means to us."

Dude patted Amanda's back awkwardly. "I'm happy to see her go to a loving home."

They managed to have a combination Sunday dinner, house-warming and memorial for Kelly all in one afternoon. The official memorial for Kelly would be held later in the summer in the Iowa town where she'd attended college.

When everyone had left and Stella and the still-unnamed puppy had gone upstairs to bed, Amanda sat with Landon on the porch swing, holding hands and listening to the crickets as they swayed gently back and forth. "This was one of the best days of my life, and it was all thanks to you."

"It was one of the best days of my life, too, and it was all because you and Stella came home. It's so good to finally have you guys here."

"I'll never, ever, *ever* have the words to tell you how much it means to me that you created this home for us."

"I loved every minute of it. I'm just glad you like it."

"I *love* it." She leaned her head on his shoulder. "After the fire, when I took stock of everything, I thought I needed to take really big risks to feel fully alive. But running around isn't risky. The biggest risk I never took was committing to someone else. Falling in love with you, making a home with you and Stella, that's the greatest risk."

"How so?"

"If something goes wrong, I can't just up and move."

"Nothing will go wrong."

"Of course there's no way to know that, but if it does, I'm not going anywhere."

"Me neither. See? It's rather risk-free. I love you. You love me. It's all good."

"It's so good, and being here in Butler, getting to know your family and spending time with people like Mildred and Elmer, it's shown me that everything I could ever want and need is right here."

"You have no idea how happy it makes me to hear you say that. And the puppy? That was okay?"

"That was awesome. Did you see Stella's face when Dude said the puppy was for her?"

"I did. I loved how happy it made her."

"So now we have a child *and* a puppy."

"Gramps always says, 'Go big or go home.'"

She smiled at him. "I'm so glad to go big with you in our new home."

"Right back atcha."

"You know what would make this perfect day even more so?"

"What's that?"

"Sleeping with you in our new bed."

The words were barely out of her mouth when he'd scooped her up to carry her inside.

"Get the door."

Laughing, Amanda pulled open the screen door, and he kicked the inside door closed behind them. She thought he'd put her down, but he carried her straight upstairs and put her down only when they were standing next to the bed.

"I have one more surprise for you."

"How can there be more?"

"It's under your pillow."

She reached under the pillow and found a velvet box. Gasping, she turned to find him down on one knee. "*Landon!*"

"Remember the day we went to Montpelier so I could pick up Dani's ring while you shopped for a dress?"

Nodding, she blinked back tears as she gazed down at him.

"I got one for you, too."

"That was weeks ago!"

"I already knew then that there'd never be anyone else but you for me. Will you marry me? Will you let me adopt Stella? Will you have more babies with me and make this our home?"

"Yes," she whispered. "One million percent *yes*."

He stood, wrapped his arms around her and kissed her. "Check out the ring. Like everything else, it can be changed if you'd rather have something different."

Her hands trembled as she opened the velvet box to find a

simple, perfect solitaire diamond in a platinum setting. "I love it."

"Are you sure?"

"One billion percent."

He slid the ring on her finger and kissed her again. "Welcome home, Amanda."

EPILOGUE

"And then there was one," Linc said to Elmer over coffee two mornings after Landon and Amanda got engaged. With nine of his children settled into happily ever after with partners he would've hand-chosen for them, Linc was feeling rather pleased with himself.

"We've done some good work," Elmer said.

"Yes, we have." He and Elmer believed they were the reason all the kids had found their perfect mates, and they weren't going to let anyone tell them otherwise. "I adore Amanda, and she's absolutely perfect for Landon."

"I agree. But I have to be honest, he and Lucas definitely surprised me."

"They surprised everyone, but I think they were ready to settle down."

"Call me crazy," Elmer said, "but I could've sworn there were some sparks flying between our Max and Cabot's niece Caroline."

"Indeed there were." Linc leaned in so he wouldn't be over-heard. "Rumor has it they spent the night of the wedding togeth-er." Linc knew Elmer wouldn't be shocked by that news. Having eighteen grandchildren had taught him to go with the flow.

"Is that right? Well, good for him to be getting back in the game. I've worried about him."

"Molly and I have, too. He's a wonderful father to Caden, but he hasn't been the same since Chloe made him a single parent."

"How could he be? That's an awful lot of responsibility, no matter how old you are. What do you think of him with Caroline?"

"She seems like a lovely girl, but there's some significant geography between them."

"True. It's not insurmountable, but it's a challenge, for sure." Elmer stirred cream into the cup of fresh coffee Megan had poured for him. "On another note, did you notice that after she finished taking pictures at the wedding, Izzy danced the night away with Cabot?"

"I did notice that."

"What do we think of that pairing?"

"He's quite a bit older than her."

"Only ten years or so. That's no big deal these days."

"No, it isn't."

"And I think I actually saw our Noah crack a grin or two while we were in Boston. Oh, how I've worried about that boy."

"I know. Me, too."

"There may be hope for him yet."

"We've still got a lot of work to do around here."

"That we do. This is no time to rest on our laurels."

Linc raised his coffee mug to Elmer. "Here's to true love."

Elmer touched his mug to Linc's. "To true love."

$\sim$

Thank you for reading *All My Loving*! I hope you enjoyed it. The Abbotts return on Christmas Eve 2020 with a very special look back at Lincoln and Molly's beginning.

LET IT BE
Butler, Vermont Series Book 6

The heart wants what the heart wants...

Fresh out of college with a psychology degree, Molly Stillman was searching for the meaning of life by taking a summer volunteer gig building houses. The meaning in Molly's life became apparent when her path crossed Lincoln Abbott's. With his brand-new Yale MBA in hand, Linc was bound for Mississippi, ready to spend the summer building houses for Habitat for Humanity. He had a plan, lots of them, actually. But after meeting Molly, he realized plans have a way of showing you who's boss.

One look from the intelligent beauty working by his side on the Habitat house, and Linc knew everything had changed. His longtime goal of studying at Oxford before joining his family's finance business was abandoned in favor of helping to grow Molly's charming family business in Vermont. Too bad Linc's father had other ideas about how his future should unfold, and when forced to make a choice, Linc chose Molly. He chose Vermont and the Green Mountain Country Store, and he never looked back.

Until a phone call from the past forces him to confront the choices he made decades ago and the consequences of saying goodbye, including telling his ten grown children why they've never met his family—a subject that's always been off-limits until now. When Linc decides to go to Philadelphia to clear his conscience and see his father one last time, his wife and children insist on going along. "Let them see what came of this choice you made," his eldest son, Hunter, says.

As they wander down memory lane, Linc and Molly revisit the unforgettable summer that changed both their lives and look back on forty years of happily ever after.

Preorder NOW where you buy print titles or at
marieforce.com/store **to read on Christmas Eve 2020!**

∽

And check out HOW MUCH I FEEL, book 1 in Marie's brand-new Miami Nights Series, debuting Aug. 11.

Read the first chapter of How Much I Feel here
marieforce.com/howmuchifeel

∽

Thank you for reading *All My Loving*! I hope you enjoyed Landon and Amanda's story as well as the chance to catch up with the rest of the family (and the moose)! I'm super excited to write Linc and Molly's story next, and then it'll be Max Abbott's turn to find true love.

Many thanks to the wonderful team that supports me behind the scenes every day: Julie Cupp, Lisa Cafferty, Tia Kelly, Nikki Haley and Ashley Lopez. Thank you to Dan, Emily and Jake for always supporting my crazy career (and doing Facebook Live chats with me during quarantine), and thanks to my fantastic editorial team of Linda Ingmanson and Joyce Lamb, my beta readers Anne Woodall, Kara Conrad and Tracey Suppo, and to my author friend Grace Burrowes, for her help with the adoption laws and procedures. And a big thank you to my Vermont beta readers for all their help: Mona, Isabel, Betty, Juliane, Kasey, Katy, Deb, Jennifer, Nancy, Alice, Jessica and Marchia.

Join the All My Loving Reader Group at *www.facebook.-com/groups/AllMyLoving11/* to discuss Landon and Amanda's story with spoilers allowed and encouraged. Also make sure you're in the Green Mountain Reader Group at facebook.-com/groups/GreenMountainSeries/ and LIKE the Green

Mountain/Butler, VT page at *www.facebook.com/VermontSeries/* to never miss any news about the series.

We'll be back in Vermont on Christmas Eve, and I can't wait for *Let It Be*, Linc and Molly's story. Make sure you preorder it now to read it the minute it goes live. Thanks for your support of this series and all my books. I appreciate my readers more than you'll ever know!

Much love,

Marie

ALSO BY MARIE FORCE

Contemporary Romances Available from Marie Force

The Green Mountain Series

Book 1: All You Need Is Love *(Will & Cameron)*

Book 2: I Want to Hold Your Hand *(Nolan & Hannah)*

Book 3: I Saw Her Standing There *(Colton & Lucy)*

Book 4: And I Love Her *(Hunter & Megan)*

Novella: You'll Be Mine *(Will & Cam's Wedding)*

Book 5: It's Only Love *(Gavin & Ella)*

Book 6: Ain't She Sweet *(Tyler & Charlotte)*

The Butler, Vermont Series

(Continuation of Green Mountain)

Book 1: Every Little Thing *(Grayson & Emma)*

Book 2: Can't Buy Me Love *(Mary & Patrick)*

Book 3: Here Comes the Sun *(Wade & Mia)*

Book 4: Till There Was You *(Lucas & Dani)*

Book 5: All My Loving *(Landon & Amanda)*

Book 6: Let It Be *(Lincoln & Molly)*

The Gansett Island Series

Book 1: Maid for Love *(Mac & Maddie)*

Book 2: Fool for Love *(Joe & Janey)*

Book 3: Ready for Love *(Luke & Sydney)*

Book 4: Falling for Love *(Grant & Stephanie)*

Book 5: Hoping for Love *(Evan & Grace)*

Book 6: Season for Love *(Owen & Laura)*

Book 7: Longing for Love (*Blaine & Tiffany*)

Book 8: Waiting for Love (*Adam & Abby*)

Book 9: Time for Love (*David & Daisy*)

Book 10: Meant for Love (*Jenny & Alex*)

Book 10.5: Chance for Love, *A Gansett Island Novella* (*Jared & Lizzie*)

Book 11: Gansett After Dark (*Owen & Laura*)

Book 12: Kisses After Dark (*Shane & Katie*)

Book 13: Love After Dark (*Paul & Hope*)

Book 14: Celebration After Dark (*Big Mac & Linda*)

Book 15: Desire After Dark (*Slim & Erin*)

Book 16: Light After Dark (*Mallory & Quinn*)

Book 17: Victoria & Shannon (Episode 1)

Book 18: Kevin & Chelsea (Episode 2)

A Gansett Island Christmas Novella

Book 19: Mine After Dark (*Riley & Nikki*)

Book 20: Yours After Dark (*Finn & Chloe*)

Book 21: Trouble After Dark (*Deacon & Julia*)

Book 22: Rescue After Dark (*Mason & Jordan*)

Book 23: Blackout After Dark

The Treading Water Series

Book 1: Treading Water

Book 2: Marking Time

Book 3: Starting Over

Book 4: Coming Home

Book 5: Finding Forever

Single Titles

How Much I Feel

How Much I Care

Five Years Gone

One Year Home

Sex Machine

Sex God

Georgia on My Mind

True North

The Fall

The Wreck

Love at First Flight

Everyone Loves a Hero

Line of Scrimmage

The Quantum Series

Book 1: Virtuous *(Flynn & Natalie)*

Book 2: Valorous *(Flynn & Natalie)*

Book 3: Victorious *(Flynn & Natalie)*

Book 4: Rapturous *(Addie & Hayden)*

Book 5: Ravenous *(Jasper & Ellie)*

Book 6: Delirious *(Kristian & Aileen)*

Book 7: Outrageous *(Emmett & Leah)*

Book 8: Famous *(Marlowe & Sebastian)*

Romantic Suspense Novels Available from Marie Force

The Fatal Series

One Night With You, *A Fatal Series Prequel Novella*

Book 1: Fatal Affair

Book 2: Fatal Justice

Book 3: Fatal Consequences

Book 3.5: Fatal Destiny, *the Wedding Novella*

Book 4: Fatal Flaw

Book 5: Fatal Deception

Historical Romance Available from Marie Force

The Gilded Series

ABOUT THE AUTHOR

Marie Force is the *New York Times* best-selling author of contemporary romance, romantic suspense and erotic romance. Her series include Gansett Island, Fatal, Treading Water, Butler Vermont and Quantum.

Her books have sold nearly 10 million copies worldwide, have been translated into more than a dozen languages and have appeared on the *New York Times* bestseller more than 30 times. She is also a *USA Today* and *Wall Street Journal* bestseller, as well as a Speigel bestseller in Germany.

Her goals in life are simple—to finish raising two happy, healthy, productive young adults, to keep writing books for as long as she possibly can and to never be on a flight that makes the news.

Join Marie's mailing list on her website at *marieforce.com* for news about new books and upcoming appearances in your area. Follow her on Facebook at *www.Facebook.com/MarieForceAuthor* and on Instagram at *www.instagram.com/marieforceauthor/*. Contact Marie at *marie@marieforce.com*.

CPSIA information can be obtained
at www.ICGtesting.com
Printed in the USA
LVHW051609200820
663741LV00011B/885